Sheryl Mallory-Johnson

The Hand
She Played

BooKs

CALIFORNIA

The Hand She Played

PUBLISHED BY WANASOMA BOOKS

First printing WanaSoma Books trade paperback edition: March, 2016
ISBN # 978-0-98222085-4-0

PRINTED IN THE UNITED STATES OF AMERICA

Cover by Maurice Scriber

All WanaSoma titles are available at special discounts for bulk purchases for sales promotion, premiums, fund-raising, educational, or institutional use. For more information contact WanaSomabooks@cox.net or visit www.sherylmallory-johnson.com.

ALSO BY SHERYL MALLORY-JOHNSON

Sense of Love

Love & Regrets

Young Adult Series Books

L.A. Summer: Friends Til' The Blood End

"It's the most breathtakingly ironic thing about living: the fact that we are all—identical twins included—alone. Singular. And yet what we seek-what saves us-is our connection to others."

–Wally Lamb

Part One

&

One

Walking with synchronized strides, we passed the lot littered with debris, the vacant church bathed in graffiti, the houses that had weathered hard times, and those with boarded up windows and brown grass that hadn't withstood the test; we side-stepped broken trees left behind by a mean winter, crunched through dead spring leaves, and stepped over cracked concrete. All the while, Vangie walked with her back straight and chin high, as if repulsed by the ruins of our neighborhood. I ambled alongside her, unaffected by it, and feeling clumsy and awkward.

In many ways, we were one person, with many unspoken secrets. In more ways, Vangie was everything I wasn't but wished to be. Still people insisted that we were identical, even though I didn't have dark, mysterious eyes, golden satin skin, or perfect proportions. My legs were too long and skinny, my torso too short, and my teeth weren't as straight and white as Vangie's.

Vangie said I was "delusional" and blamed our mother for this. Because she didn't know who she'd slept with to conceive us, our mother decided that we had different fathers to solve the mystery. The *V* in Vangie came from her alleged father and the *A* in Angie from my alleged father and our mother, Annette Cooper. That was the extent to which she had shared about the men who had supposedly fathered us. "Name: Unknown. Color or race: Unknown.

State of birth: Unknown. Age: Unknown," our birth certificates read.

In reality, Vangie couldn't accept that I was night and she was day, that she shot for the stars and I was happy watching her fly to the moon, as long as she took me along for the ride. While she had spent the summer preparing for college, I had spent it worried my mother would fall back into one of her spells, but I went along with Vangie's plan for our life since I had no future plans of my own, now that graduation had already come and gone. Joining our classmates to toss our caps to freedom hadn't been important to us. Vangie was happy high school was over and I was happy my mother seemed happy again. After the last man had run off, she hadn't brought home any more unwelcomed houseguests, especially after Vangie had threatened to break a vodka bottle over his head for looking at us wrong.

"My momma's dead and I ain't looking for a new one," my mother had retorted, becoming the rebellious teenager as Vangie became the well-meaning mother. Day after day, the animosity between the two of them had grown until it seemed the walls in our hot, stuffy apartment would crack from all the tension.

With school out, the days were long, the nights an oven cooling off after a daylong bake. I monitored the sun's downward spiral, worried we wouldn't get home before dusk moved in and the streets of Detroit's Lower Eastside took over.

As we passed the drug house dominated by drug dealers, one dude shouted, "Fine ass, Vangie," using his hands like a bullhorn.

Another one yelled out his fantasy about Vangie that was too disgusting to be repeated.

Vangie shot them an intolerant glare, never breaking her poised stride; her golden skin radiated like the setting sun and her coal-black hair swung like a pendulum across her back.

They never noticed me or called out my name. I couldn't blame them. My hair didn't hang or swing, and I'd never cared to dress like Vangie in nice, expensive clothes or too-high heels. I'd rather have an apartment full of food, toilet paper, and soap than a closet full of clothes and shoes some people in our neighborhood would literally kill to have.

We made it safely to Cambridge Apartments, the red brick, low-income housing that should've been condemned or abandoned, along with many other buildings on Detroit's Lower Eastside.

On the third floor, we arrived home, where we had lived longer than anywhere else so far. When the heavy door snapped shut behind us, we stared at the newest, strange man inside our apartment. He couldn't pass for anything but another creep to me. Tall with bony legs and a bony face, he wore checkered Bermuda shorts with a matching shirt, the kind I often saw blowing in the wind at a sidewalk sale, except this one could use a good bleaching.

"Here are my girls," my mother said, leaning to one side like the earth had tilted. Her lips painted maroon, her beloved black minidress and tired white pumps showing off her copper-tone legs told me my mother was in one of her "happy" moods and had brought home her "good time." Sometimes, her good time was an apartment full of people who drank and partied until dawn. Other times, it was a strange man who quickly wore out his welcome.

"And this is Mr. Delford, y'all." She smiled as if we were meeting our new stepfather.

"Y'all call me Dell. Shit. I ain't old." He swiped the sweat, which was leaking from his wet and wavy hair down to his yellow face, with the back of his hand. Right off, I didn't trust his bloodshot eyes and crooked smile.

"That one to the left won't call you nothing. She don't talk for nobody but her sister. Ain't nothing wrong her, though. She's just shy. That's Angie, my angel child. The other one, Vangie, is the devil's." I knew my mother was only joking, hoping for a reaction from Vangie. All she got out of Vangie was a chilling stare.

My mother laughed at the ceiling, swishing her curvy hips to the kitchen. Seconds later she returned to the living room with two cans of beer, one each for herself and her guest.

"What's up? How y'all doing!" Mr. Dell shouted.

Like most people, he seemed to misinterpret my silence as a hearing problem. I could hear and talk just fine; I just refused to talk to anyone but Vangie.

When Mr. Dell extended his hand to Vangie, she swatted it away, looking like she might lash out at him with teeth and nails if he took a step closer.

"Didn't I tell you! Don't mess with Vangie. That girl don't play!"

Mr. Dell backed up two steps and sat his bony butt on our couch, which oozed with foam and rocked from left to right when he sat. The base was missing a leg. A phonebook kept it partially balanced. Our apartment was missing everything. Soon, there wouldn't be water or electricity if Vangie didn't find a way to pay the bills again.

Most of our furniture was handed down and collected here and there over the years. At one time Vangie seriously tried to pretty up our tiny place, but our frequent houseguests couldn't appreciate the finer things in life. If they hadn't broken it, they had stolen it. So, Vangie gave up trying.

Our mother sat on the couch next to Mr. Dell, lit up a cigarette, and took a swig of beer. "Can you believe they mine?" She blew a perfect halo of smoke in the air. "Like to tear me in two coming through."

"They look identical."

"Hump," my mother said. "I'll tell you like I tell everybody, fire ain't ice, snow ain't rain, white ain't black, sweet ain't sour, dumb ain't smart, and good sho' ain't evil. Nothing on this earth is identical. My girls ain't, either!"

"They sho' are fine, I know that. Y'all could be triplets," said Mr. Dell.

My mother ran her fingers through her long, coal black hair, looking off dreamily. "I might be fine, but I wasn't no teenage bride when I had 'em, and that's all I'm gonna say!"

"I know fine when I see fine, baby, and I ain't seen fine like you in a long time." Mr. Dell put his grimy hand on my mother's thigh and caressed it.

I wondered how long we would stand around watching the same story play out. When Vangie finally left the room, I followed, slamming our bedroom door behind us.

I did nothing with myself but fall back onto our bed, cradling my stomach and complaining of starvation. Vangie changed out of her heeled sandals, white miniskirt, and crop-top and into a short satin robe. From her locked hope chest of secret things, she pulled out a white hotel towel and a roll of toilet paper, and then slid her pedicured feet into flip-flops and left our room. Coming or going Vangie showered, as if to wash the scum of this place from her body and mind.

I threw off my grubby high-tops and frayed jean shorts, and climbed between clean white sheets in a T-shirt and underwear. Tired, hungry and thirsty after shopping with Vangie all day for fancy clothes she ultimately did not buy, I wouldn't leave our room tonight, not even for a drink of water, as long as Mr. Dell was in the way.

Vangie returned to the room smelling like a field of exotic flowers and lay next to me in her silk pajamas. While she read a book, I stared at the ceiling. I could tell by her scrunched up forehead that she wasn't in the mood to talk, so I listened to the soulful voice of

Aretha Franklin taking over our apartment. My mother played and replayed "I Ain't Never Loved a Man (The Way I Love You)" until I smothered my ears between two pillows.

A loud crash in the next room startled us both. Vangie hopped out of bed and motioned for me to stay back. I followed her anyway. Through the cracked door, we watched our mother, who was bent over a dustpan, sweeping up a broken glass. Mr. Dell stood behind her, grinding his bony hips against her upturned behind as she swayed to the beat, the two of them laughing and singing and having a good old time.

We returned to the bed we shared, but neither of us could close our eyes. While Vangie locked her eyes on the ceiling, I locked my eyes on her, fearing she would do something to destroy our mother's good time—again.

"What're you going to do, Van?" My voice shook.

Two

T he party's over," Vangie said, sticking a knife to Mr. Dell's throat. His eyes flew open and his head rammed against the headboard as if a snake had bitten him. Had she not withdrawn the knife in time, he would have slit his own throat.

"What the...!"

"Get out!" Vangie said.

"I'm out. I'm out." He raised his hands in surrender.

Vangie's glare told him, if he didn't leave, she would follow through with her threat. He had hung around the apartment for two days too long and had worn out his welcome.

Bloodshot eyes showing shame and guilt, Mr. Dell eased out of bed and couldn't scramble into his cheap clothes fast enough for Vangie. She kicked his run-over alligator shoes, prodding him to pick up his pace.

"Crazy little bitch." Shoes in hand, Mr. Dell dashed for the door on bare feet, stirring her mother out of her stupor.

"Noooo!" Annette cried, lunging for the knife in Vangie's hand. Missing her mark, Annette stumbled, hands first, at Vangie's feet, tangling herself in the sheet.

Vangie sighed heavily. "Mom. Get up."

Annette sobbed, beating the floor with her fists. "I'll never be happy. Never be... Never!"

When Angie came running into the room in silent confusion, Vangie faced a replica of herself: the same dark, round eyes defining exaggerated cheekbones and the same curvy, full lips.

What'd you do? Angie's frightened look cried.

Don't just stand there, help me, Vangie's narrowed eyes said back.

Angie rushed across the room. If they didn't pick their mother up from the floor, hours could pass before she picked herself back up. They tucked Annette in bed, covering up her nakedness.

Leaving her mother in Angie's care, Vangie proceeded to her private sanctuary, never bothering to mention last night. She'd seen Mr. Dell standing at the foot of their bed, lurking in the dark. The cover had slid off during the night, subjecting them to his shameless gawking. He'd thought she was sleeping. She knew better than to sleep soundly with a man in the house. She stayed alert.

Sitting back on the queen-sized bed she shared with Angie, Vangie flipped fervently through the glossy pages of her fashion magazine while listening to the soothing strings of Bach through amplified earphones. The classical music and fashion magazines filled with designer clothes, glimmering jewels, and luxury cars kept Vangie's mind in the world where she believed she belonged.

An hour later, Angie told her that their mother was asleep. The question was whether she would wake up. Angie was terrified that Annette had fallen back into a "spell" and would sleep for days. She stood over Vangie, wringing her hands.

"I'm not apologizing, so don't ask," Vangie said before Angie could speak the words that she had already read on her twin's mind.

"If you don't say you're sorry, she may never wake up."

"Let her sleep, Angie."

"She can't help her spells, Van."

"Stop calling them spells. They aren't *spells.*"

"They look like spells. Besides, if you hadn't tried to kill Mr. Dell she wouldn't be asleep!" Angie's mousy voice came close to shouting.

Vangie gave Angie a long, hard look that only her twin could decode. "If I was trying to kill him, he'd be dead, Ang."

On that note, Angie slinked off without another word.

By noon, Vangie had packed a small travel bag. After putting on a simple minidress and gilded Roman sandals, she stood in front of their fractured dresser mirror, gazing far off while lengthening her lashes with mascara. She then tinted her lips in red gloss and briskly combed through her hair that fell lavishly over her shoulders.

Angie followed Vangie to the front door after she hung up the phone.

"What'll I eat while you're gone?" Angie said.

Vangie slapped two twenty-dollar bills into Angie's waiting hand. "That's all I have, Ang," she lied. She gave Angie a hug and left home worried Angie couldn't survive for three days without her.

"Where's the poor little rich girl sneaking off to this time?" Mr. Reese said as Vangie descended the front steps of Cambridge Apartments. Giving his cigarette a rest, he stood on the bottom stoop. When Vangie attempted to brush by Mr. Reese, he swung his leg up a step, blocking her path.

"Is there anything I can help you with today?"

"I don't need your help," Vangie said coldly.

"I thought you might, seeing as I haven't gotten my rent. I'd sho' hate to see something so young and pretty put out in the street when there are other ways for us to work things out."

Vangie's smirk mocked Mr. Reese's calculating grin. She saw his desire for her in his bulgy, yellow-tinged eyes sunk into ashy brown skin and knew he hoped to persuade her to take a trip to the basement where he stored more than his tools. He likely assumed that she had no choice but to sleep with him in exchange for free rent.

Mr. Reese's eyes darted toward his apartment window and back. "You know I don't mind helping your momma out when she needs it," he whispered.

Vangie could've laughed. Instead, she walked on.

On East Warren Avenue, she caught the Metro to her first destination. Staring out of the window, she marveled at how the city, outside the gloom and doom of her neighborhood, cleaned up, as if someone cared enough to sweep the streets, water the grass, and revitalize the age-old red brick buildings. Historic landmarks whizzed by, reminding Vangie of Detroit's culture, beauty and history, the city where would-be musical icons had once flocked to Motown for fame and fortune; the automotive capital of the world, where big auto companies had once employed thousands of blue collar workers like her mother—poor, single, black, female, and with only a high school education, *yada, yada, yada.*

She had heard the stories and had grown sick of them. If the auto plants hadn't shut down, one after another, she wondered if her mother would've kept a job. It didn't matter, Vangie reminded herself. Those days were history, and she saw no fame, no fortune, and no future in Detroit for her.

On Kercheval Street in downtown Gross Pointe, Vangie found a private bathroom in a coffee cafe where she changed out of her simple dress into a spicy orange bandage one with a crisscross neckline and V back, fastened on her diamond earrings, and slipped her feet out of flat sandals and into stiletto platform ones.

She thought it best on these impromptu trips to relocate to a nice neighborhood, one with lush grass, quaint cottage-style houses, lakefront mansions and upper-class families. Not that these men cared where she lived or who had raised her, she had found.

Catching a breeze beneath the shade of a lush tree, Vangie sat on a bench outside, disregarding passersby who stared curiously at her.

The suit-clad driver of a gleaming Lincoln Town Car pulled up moments later and opened the door for her.

"You must be Vangie."

She offered the driver a small smile and sank into plush leather.

"Is it hot enough for you?" the driver said conversationally as he pulled off.

Vangie only nodded. She didn't know this driver. He was new and younger than the regular driver, whose interaction with her was always purposeful—his job was simply to pick her up and drop her off at a specified location. Most times, he arrived in the Lincoln Town Car, other times in a limousine. During the rides, the driver didn't typically talk. Vangie preferred it that way. This driver's persistent staring into the rearview mirror had her on guard.

"Mr. Stein like his ladies hot, and you are one hot chick, if you don't mind me saying," he continued.

Vangie glared at him, not appreciating his breach of etiquette. He probably thought she was a *real ho* who couldn't spell the word etiquette. She didn't care what he thought, honestly. What choice did she have? Somebody had to make money and pay the bills in their household. Her mother had given up on employment and Angie couldn't work, so the burden was hers to bear. At least when she returned, she would be able to pay the rent, catch up on the overdue bills, and buy other necessities.

Besides, she didn't consider her relationship with men "ho'ing," nor did she consider herself a high-priced call girl. She was too smart to do either. She was also much too smart to turn over a percentage of her pay to someone who hadn't lifted a finger to earn it, only to be slapped around and brought down. And she was definitely too smart to give herself to any man who wanted her, a battle she had fought from a very young age, depending on what kind of houseguest Annette had brought home.

But the battle alone had sharpened her knowledge of men. Men, Vangie discovered, fell into three categories: those without the power or money to satisfy their desires; those with power but no money who satisfied their desires aggressively and manipulatively, like Mr. Reese; and those with power and wealth who paid for their desires outright. Vangie knew which category Jacob Stein fell into.

Before Jacob, there had been others.

First came "Gun," as he was known around the east side. Always in search of new customers, Gun had glided through the neighborhood in his smoky-windowed Mercedes as a show of authority, and garnered respect. Gun could not so easily impress her with his false fame. Drug money, in her view, was for the poor and desperate, not the rich and famous. After enjoying the many luxuries that Gun's money had afforded her, she had moved on to high-caliber guys. She was sixteen years old by this time and had acquired a profound taste for the best that money could buy. Never again would she be caught shopping at stale smelling thrift stores and wearing hand-me-down clothes.

Next came Douglas Phillips, a biotech engineer she had met at a college fair during her junior year of high school. Not even Douglas's high-paid position measured up to her ideals. Mediocre dining, movie dates, and occasional lightweight shopping sprees bored her.

In the summer of her senior year, Vangie had stepped outside her comfort zone, discovering a life of glamour she had only dreamed of through the pages of magazines and movies. She wasn't looking for a job when she walked into Angelica's Boutique in the township of Bloomfield Hills. She had ventured away from home alone to surround herself with beautiful mansions, rolling hills, and peaceful lakes, daydreaming about the life she would one day live.

"If you're here for the job, my wife is at lunch. But I'm in charge while she's gone and I say you're hired." The man had stepped from behind the service counter to shake her hand. "Antonio Moretti. Has anyone told you you're one gorgeous dame?"

She rolled her eyes. "No."

Antonio laughed. "Your confidence will be good for business—lure in the men and persuade them to buy for their mistresses, eh."

She had liked Antonio immediately. He was Italian and in his thirties, with olive skin, dark hair, and naughty emerald eyes. It hadn't taken much dialogue before he placed a "temporarily away" sign on the door, whisked her off in his red-hot Ferrari to an elegant Italian restaurant, one of many that he owned, and interviewed her for a job she hadn't applied for.

It was the beginning of a profitable relationship. With Antonio, Vangie enjoyed shopping sprees at Angelica's Boutique, exclusive dining at Moretti's Italian Cuisine, the finest vintage wines on earth, and impromptu trips to Moretti's Fine Jewelry store, believing all the while that Antonio was her ticket out of Detroit.

Then along came Jacob Stein and the sky was her limit.

At her next destination, the driver chivalrously opened her door. Emulating a scene from a movie, Vangie placed one silky leg out of the car before making her appearance. She was escorted through security of DTW, and into Jacob's Learjet. The fawn leather seats, polished mahogany trim, and flat-screen TVs set her a world apart from anything she had ever known the moment she stepped aboard the sleek aircraft.

Ingrid, the sole flight attendant, welcomed her with a tray of her favorite hors d'oeuvres and a glass of chilled wine from Jacob's private collection. Ingrid was blonde with Carolina blue eyes who had breasts disproportionate to her slender figure.

"Mr. Stein will be right with you."

"Thanks." Vangie scooped beluga caviar onto a toasted cracker and bit into it with sheer delight. One gulp of the delicious wine helped her to forget her life.

After waiting ten minutes too long for Jacob to emerge, Vangie strutted to the back of the aircraft.

"Mr. Stein is tied up! You shouldn't disturb him!" Ingrid called after her.

Ignoring Ingrid's warning, Vangie entered Jacob's hideaway. The low-ceiling bedroom, done up in mahogany walls and silk bedding, had a musky aroma from the premium cigars that Jacob puffed religiously. Wearing a dark suit and open-collar white shirt, Jacob sat on the bed looking like typical Jacob: his legs crossed coolly, his black hair slicked back conservatively accenting his hooded gray eyes, pronounced nose, and wide chin. Something about the combination of power and money made Jacob irresistible to Vangie. His wise investments had elevated him to Fortune 500's list of the richest and most powerful men in America at the age of forty. As Vangie saw it, her time spent with Jacob was a wise investment. Jacob got what he wanted from her and she would get what she needed from him, in due time.

Vangie sauntered up to Jacob boasting a seductive smile.

Ending his business call briskly, Jacob wrapped his arms around her waist and rested his chin in the crevice of her breasts. "I've missed you," he said in his smooth, smoky voice as he gazed up at her with twinkling eyes.

"How much?"

"That question is going to cost me."

Vangie dropped onto Jacob's lap and wrapped her arms around his neck. "I'm worth it."

"Some things in life are priceless, doll." Jacob leaned back onto the bed, pulling her down with him. Beneath them, jet engines roared, preparing for a speedy flight to Atlantic City.

Three

I did nothing with myself other than keeping watch over our mother, and staring at her in silent wonder. A thousand questions crossed my mind, questions that would never solve the mystery of my mother's mind. I shook her shoulder, hoping to break the spell. She didn't stir, nor did her eyelids flutter.

I left my mother's room and walked to the kitchen to find whatever morsel of food I could. There wasn't much of anything to satisfy my appetite: the hard ends of white bread without peanut butter, jelly, or cheese to fill them; white flour and a variety of seasonings, but no chicken to bake or fry. To think, we'd had more than enough food before greedy Mr. Dell showed up. Before Mr. Dell and Mr. Rick, it had been Mr. James, Mr. Dontrell, and many others I would never forget, but no man could pack his belly like that greedy Mr. Dell.

The first of August, when the EBT card replenished, we could replace the food Mr. Dell had gobbled up in two short days. When that day came, I planned to cook a four-course meal and bake a scrumptious chocolate cake stacked four layers high.

In the meantime, I dressed, brushed my tangled hair back into a ponytail, and then walked to the store. The nearest grocery store around advertised beer, wine, check cashing, Lotto, EBT, WIC and fresh produce on a meager sign. There, I bought packaged ham, butter, cheddar cheese, a quart of milk, eggs, a green pepper, one onion, two mushrooms, and a loaf of plain white bread. Two blocks away, I dragged myself inside The Liquor Store and seized a can of beer from the refrigerator.

At the checkout stand, I gestured a smoke, tapping two fingers against my lips, and then pointed to a pack of Red and Whites.

Jimmy, a gruff black man who talked to his customers from behind bulletproof glass, owned the store. "You got ID?" he said.

I shook my head.

He handed me the cigarettes. "Next time don't leave home without it." He wagged his thick, hairy finger at me like he meant business. I nodded as if I believed him. Next time would be just like this time.

When I got home I found my mother sitting on the couch in the living room, dressed in a thin robe. I dumped the grocery bags on the kitchen counter, grabbed the Red and Whites, and rushed to her side.

"Hand me that lighter on the table," she told me.

I was quick to obey her command.

"We got anything left to drink?"

I was back in a flash with a can of cold beer.

"Thanks, baby." She lit up a cigarette and popped the can.

My mother had many personalities when she came alive, sometimes childlike, dripping with apologies, sometimes demanding and barking orders, or sometimes burning up nervous energy that kept the house up nights, before the sadness came back.

I saw her as two people—the old Annette and the new Annette. The old Annette danced through life as if on water, awakening with an intoxicating smile, painting on maroon lipstick and wearing makeup, clothing, and hairstyles that emphasized her beauty, never letting life get her down. After our stepfather, Russell, had disappeared, the old Annette had vanished, leaving behind the new

Annette, whose moods turned bluer and bluer and her happy days fewer and fewer. I sometimes secretly wished Russell would somehow reappear, if only to hear my mother's desperate laugh that painted an illusion of happy times in her mind. No other medicine or sunny day could cure her of her unhappiness like Russell could.

"Where'd your sister go?" she asked me.

Work. I spelled out across the table with my index finger.

"I'll believe it when I see it," she said and inhaled smoke.

I didn't try to convince her that Vangie had a real job, and I had stopped questioning Vangie altogether about the money she had to buy things we couldn't afford, but people talked, even when I tried not to listen. My mother talked the most, accusing Vangie of things I wouldn't dare repeat.

Back in the kitchen, I created a gourmet omelet in my favorite old skillet and prepared golden-brown French toast, flavoring it with a heavy helping of butter and syrup.

I stood over my mother, rubbing my belly.

Eat something, Mom. Please.

She frowned, shook her head, pushed the plate away from her face and walked back to her room.

After cleaning my own plate, I hadn't anything better to do for the rest of the day than to go next door to Miss Coffee's place. The piles of old newspapers, cats, and crowds of furniture that her grandson, West, dragged in from the street comforted me.

Moving comfortably around the small kitchen, I heated a can of chicken noodle soup in a charred pot, poured it into a chipped bowl, and found Miss Coffee in her bedroom buried in clutter, the covers thrown back to reveal her heavy-breasted figure, swelled feet, and veiny legs showing beneath her thin nightgown. Her hair was covered with an old scarf, the bags around her small brown eyes puffy.

A series of wet coughs attacked her, bringing tears to her eyes and agony to her face. Miss Coffee's bronchitis and rheumatism were acting up again.

I handed her the bowl of soup.

"I don't know what I'd do without you and my West. Where's he at, anyway?"

I shrugged. I wouldn't know since I seldom hung out with West anymore. Even when he was lugging in new treasures or moving pieces out to pawn or sell, he was escorted and directed by his girlfriend, Deja. My low opinion of Deja had little to do with her peasant looks and everything to do with her conniving ways. If people were rugs to wipe your feet on, she would wipe her feet and step right over them. Me, she treated like one of West's useless pieces of furniture.

When the front door slammed in the next room, I sprang to my feet.

"On your way out, close my door," Miss Coffee told me.

I closed her door and shuffled into the living room.

"Check out this belly bar," West said. "I think I can get twenty-five for it. Whatcha' think, Angie?"

West seemed to respect my opinion, but mostly, he got a kick out of the expressions I had invented to communicate my perspective. I stared at a small, circular table with one leg that extended too high for an average-sized chair. With my mouth twisted and my eyes rolled up, I told him he wasn't likely to get anything for it. Who would buy a funny-looking table with a too-short chair?

"Twenty, then?"

I scrunched my face even more and pointed my thumb down.

"What about five bucks down at old man Brown's?"

I nodded with thoughtful consideration.

West laughed. "You drive a harder bargain than the Browns, Ang." He stretched out on the couch covered in cat hair and placed his feet on the coffee table.

I did the same. Nibbles and Clover leaped to West's lap; Sir Duke, the playful Chartreux cat, snuggled against me, awaiting a scratch behind his ears.

West was tall and wiry, wore clothes that hung from his shoulders like a crumpled suit on a hanger, had an oddly shaped Afro and contradicting brown eyes—gentle yet disturbed, the second adjective seemingly reflecting his outlook on life.

We were alike in that way, square pegs in a round world. We loved the same TV shows, movies, books, and music, regardless of our seven year age difference. Sometimes I joined West on his daily explorations, probing alleys and dumpsters and raiding abandoned buildings for discarded treasures. To me it was an adventure. Vangie, however, found the idea disgusting.

I hung out with West for hours. This was my home away from home, a place of refuge during my mother's party nights, sleepy days and Vangie's weekend desertions.

This morning I stood at my mother's bedroom door like a block of ice, my feet nailed to the hardwood floor, adrenaline caught in my chest until it felt as if my heart would explode. Blood had splattered across the walls and had dripped onto the floor like bold splotches of paint. The knife my mother had used to slit her wrists tumbled from the tips of her fingers and thudded against the floor, jerking me out of my paralysis.

Do something!

My feet were in motion before my mind caught up. I gathered my mother's limp body into my weak arms, intending to carry her next door to Miss Coffee's apartment. Her dead weight pulled me to my knees and pinned me against the bedrail. Silently, I screamed for help, my eyes a stream of tears.

My mother is dying and I can't help her. I can't do anything on my own. I'm worthless!

As if Vangie had heard my silent cries, she charged into the room. "Oh my God! What the hell happened?"

My mouth opened, but what came out was garbled.

"Scarves! Where are they?" Her words sloshed through my ears like water. "Mom's scarves, Angie!"

I pointed to the dresser, my heavy arm fighting gravity.

Vangie rushed across the room. Throwing clothes aside, she found an old scarf of our mother's, ripped it apart with her teeth, and bound it tightly around our mother's wrists to keep the blood from streaming, something I hadn't thought of. She then called 911, something I couldn't do.

We dressed our mother before the ambulance arrived. Her skin was damp, her eyes were vacant, and her breathing was shallow, all the signs of eminent death. Our mother would die before the ambulance got around to our neighborhood. I was sure of it.

"What do we do now?" My voice matched the tremble in my hands.

"We wait, Angie." Even in the most critical of situations, Vangie could be calm and poised.

My anxiety, on the other hand, was unmanageable, my tears out of control.

I'll never eat again if my mother dies. Never!

"I'm going next door. West will know what to do." I leapt to my feet with a sudden burst of energy.

"No you're not!" Vangie snapped. "It's nobody's business what goes on in here."

I had heard that warning from our mother my whole life and didn't argue with Vangie. Feeling useless, I dropped onto the bed and wrung my sweaty hands, waves of fear washing over me.

Minutes later, a siren screamed down our street. I sprinted out the door and hopped down the stairs two at a time, praying it wasn't too late to save our mother.

Four

Annette was transferred from Wayne County Psychiatric Unit to Walter Ruggers Mental Health Center in Ann Arbor. Despite its neat rows of begonias running the length of the walkway, lush grass, and elm tree archway, Walter Ruggers was a depressing sight to Vangie. After checking in at the visitor's desk, an orderly led her and Angie to an activity room filled with couches, chairs, tables, and crazy people. Patients worked on art projects while others played Ping-Pong, board games or watched TV, those that weren't walking around talking to the imagined, that is. Sunlight pouring through the windows did nothing to cheer up the place.

They found their mother sitting in a folding chair, Annette's thoughts seemingly locked inside her mind, her sad eyes preoccupied with the dust mites swimming in a stream of sunlight. It took Vangie's wind away to see her mother looking more like the living dead than ever before. She moved across the room with stiff steps.

When they walked up, Annette looked past Angie, staring intently at Vangie as if she were condemning her for being born. Agitated, Vangie moved away, standing near the windows and tapping the toe of her shoe. A staff member stood by doing nothing. Vangie was seconds away from ordering her to fetch the doctor when a short man wearing a dress shirt rolled up at the sleeves, khaki trousers, and penny loafers strode into the room. Stopping abruptly, he scanned the room until he spotted his target, and then strode toward Annette.

"How're you feeling today, Annette?"

"I'm...doin'...okay, Doc," Annette said, each syllable dragging lethargically behind the next.

"Good!" Dr. Adler looked from Vangie to Angie. "Twins, I take it?"

"Can I talk to you in private about my mother?" Vangie's tone was clipped.

The doctor gave a quick nod. "Follow me."

Angie stayed behind with Annette, brushing and combing her hair as if she were a life-sized doll.

Vangie followed Dr. Adler to the elevator. They rode down to the basement where she found a plush, contemporary getaway for the doctor and his administrative staff.

In Dr. Adler's office, decorated with exotic artifacts, Vangie cut right to the point. "About my mother. When can she come home?"

The doctor looked as though she couldn't be serious. "Has your mother's condition been previously treated?"

Vangie shook her head slowly.

"Can you explain Annette's..." The doctor put on eyeglasses, glanced down at the open file on his desk, and then regarded her curiously. "*Spells.* What do they look like, contextually?"

"They're hard to explain."

"I gather..." The doctor waited for further explanation.

Vangie cleared her throat to push past the lump in it. "Contextually speaking, she plays dead."

She knew they certainly weren't *spells,* but she wouldn't put it past her mother to play dead just to punish her. Whatever they were, it tortured her to watch her mother kill herself slowly and come back to life as a walking, talking version of her old self only to die off again. Nowadays, she anticipated her mother's "spells," which usually followed a crying fit. When the spells finally gave way, Annette was up again, lighting up cigarette after cigarette, and drinking beer after beer.

Sometimes, their mother wandered around the apartment, starting things she would never finish, like seasoning meat she never cooked or running dishwater for dishes she had placed in the cabinet dirty, thrashing out big dreams that never came true. Happy to have their mother alive and well again, Angie would act as if nothing was out of the ordinary. Vangie, on the other hand, ignored their mother, punishing her for her bizarre behavior that she believed Annette could control.

"Catatonia, possibly," the doctor said, musing.

Vangie blinked. "Cat…what?"

"It's a neuropsychiatric syndrome that has been linked to a number of pathologies… PTSD, severe depression, etcetera, etcetera. Is there a family history of mental health issues?"

Vangie stared despondently and shook her head. There wasn't much of a family history to report. Her mother was an only child, so to speak, born to Della May Watson from Eight Mile, who had died years ago. Her grandfather was serving a life sentence in prison. All ten of his children were conceived in various locations and by various women. Her mother was among his clan.

"Is my mother in good hands, doctor?" Vangie said.

Absently clicking and clacking the button of his pin, Dr. Adler looked thoughtful. "Our patients receive the best of care. I don't have the authority to keep Annette with us against her will, not unless she's a danger to herself or anyone else, but the less stable your mother's aftercare, the higher the risk of repeat suicide attempts. The longer she's with us, I do believe she'll have a good chance for long-term stability."

"Thank you." Vangie strapped on her handbag and scooted to the edge of her seat.

"Do you mind if I ask your age?" Dr. Adler said.

Vangie sighed silently. She had dressed modestly in a beige-laced linen dress that cut off only an inch above her knees and worn wedged heeled sandals to create an impression of chic maturity, but conservatism didn't ward off most men, she had found. The moment Dr. Adler had laid his eyes on her, she had noticed the twinkle in them. She swore she reeked of sex and she didn't know how to cleanse herself of the odor.

"I'm old enough." Vangie left the office before the doctor could ask another question. Her heart dropped to the pit of her stomach as the elevator ascended. She was about to say good-bye to her mother, possibly for good. She had dreamed of this day—wished for it. Now her emotions dueled. She was mournful, resentful, nervous and unsure all at once. She filled her lungs with a determined breath, lifted her chin, and reentered the activity room where she found Angie concentrating on polishing Annette's nails.

"I'm leaving, Mom." There was no need to say where she was going or when she would return. She gave her mother a kiss on the cheek. "I love you."

"Humph," said Annette.

"I'll be outside, Angie." Vangie hurried off without looking back. Tears tried to choke her. She suppressed them with a heart of steel.

Vangie needed a getaway. Once she sealed the deal with Jacob, she would shower, take a dive in the Grand Cayman Island Hotel's oasis pool, explore the palatial grounds, go shopping, or just chill out. Whatever her desires, Jacob would fulfill them.

Summoning her alter ego—her bold and ambitious side that gave her a sense of power and control over her own body—Vangie put on the contraption Jacob had laid out for her: a red lace half-bra attached to red string panties by way of black leather straps, which fit her body like a harness. After attaching the garter belt to her stockings, she pushed her feet into red platform pumps and fixed her hair so that it covered her left eye.

Stealthily, Vangie descended the spiral staircase that led to the suite's posh living space. At the base of the stairs, she took a determined breath and sauntered over to Jacob. He sat on the camelback sofa reading the news on a handheld computer device, waiting low-key for her to sneak up on him. It was a game he liked to play—*the wifey game*, Vangie called it. He had other sex games that kept her confined in the presidential suite longer than she wanted to be confined.

Vangie found the light switch and dimmed the lights. She preferred the dark. Darkness hid everything, including her emotions, or rather the lack thereof. Rays of sun stole through the drawn drapery, reminding her of the time. Last she checked it was time for lunch.

She accosted Jacob, rammed her leg between his, leaned in and went about her task, untying his tie languidly and popping off the buttons of his expensive dress shirt, one by one.

Jacob played it cool, though his battle to maintain self-control affected his sweat glands and his breathing. Lust pooled in his smoky gray eyes. When she unzipped his pants, he lost his composure and conduct.

"Bend over," he said huskily. She did. Jacob commenced to pounding.

For Vangie, sex was mechanical, much like walking. She didn't put much thought into it, concentrating on her ultimate goal and not the task at hand.

Her endurance paid off by the close of their trip; a generous endowment was set up in her name with the untraceable funds wired directly into her new savings account from Jacob's offshore bank. The initial funds would cover her tuition for the first two years of college, half of which would go to Angie. Jacob promised to cover her full college tuition and more, as long as she made herself available at his beck and call.

Five

Five days now and Vangie still hadn't come back home. Food was low and Mr. Reese had come knocking for the overdue rent. How could I pay him without money? How could I visit my mother without a bus pass? How could I do anything without Vangie?

Today, I returned home to find Mr. Reese in our apartment, which sent a chill up my spine when I met his menacing eyes. I'd seen eyes like his before; they couldn't be trusted. To keep the heavy door from caging me in with him, I held it open with a nervous foot.

"I'm here to collect my rent."

I said my usual nothing in response, hoping my puzzled expression would tell him he had no right to be in our apartment without notice, as my mother had told him enough times.

"You're nothing like your twin. Looks to me like you've got sense enough to keep a roof over your head when somebody offers you a hand."

Disliking the feel of his eyes, I prepared to run.

"What's up, Ang?" West stopped at the door and moved past me to eyeball Mr. Reese head on. "Everything good, Mr. Reese?"

"Just fixing this stove. Long overdue."

West followed Mr. Reese into the kitchen. "While your at it, can you call roach busters. Their coming out of my shoes, man."

"Is your name on the lease?" Mr. Reese said, bug-eyed.

West scratched his Afro.

"I didn't think so. When your name's on the lease, come talk to me." Mr. Reese glanced at me as he pulled tools from his tool belt.

West shook his head. "You up for a run, Ang?"

I nodded. Running was all I wanted to do—away from Mr. Reese and his scary eyes.

West and I rode the Metro to a historic building downtown. Walking through the building's lobby, we drew curious stares. Uncomfortable in my skin, faded red tank top, grimy shorts and grubby tennis shoes, I kept my head bowed. West's sagging jeans and grayish-white T-shirt didn't fit in with the fancy suits and dresses, either.

Happy the elevator door had closed and we were alone, I watched the numbers climb as we zoomed smoothly to the twelfth floor. We walked down a long, quiet hallway with nice doors.

"Habib?" West said, peeking his head inside one of the offices as we entered.

"I've been waiting for you!" A man with redish-black skin and straight black-hair said. He threw up his hands.

"Sorry, man."

"You must take it!"

West scratched his Afro. "All of it?"

"It must go!"

"I'll take it off your hands in the morning, man, if I can catch a ride, but today ain't gonna work."

"Today or I get someone else. It's my gift to you. I have no use for it."

West's eyes panned the office wildly as if he saw dollar signs floating through the air.

My mind quickly caught on. The office was loaded with expensive furniture and Mr. Habib wanted West to take all of it for free!

Thirty minutes later, a muddied white moving truck driven by young Mr. Brown, pulled up to the side door of the building where West and I were waiting. West didn't need my help or my brains. I felt useless while he and Mr. Brown's son carefully maneuvered large objects down the elevator until they dripped rivers of sweat. They packed the cab of the truck so tightly there was little room left for me.

Since West didn't trust young Mr. Brown alone with his treasures and didn't want to leave me behind until he returned, I sat on West's lap the whole ride home. Our journey ended outside Brown's Bargain Furniture and Pawn Shop on Second Street.

"I'll give you four hundred for the truckload," old Mr. Brown said, inspecting the two desks and knocking the mahogany wood as if checking for authenticity.

"Don't try to punk me, old man. That's Grade A hardwood and premium leather. You can s-s-sell it new and g-g-get four times more for it." When West got excited, his tongue stalled and his eyes danced.

"Nobody 'round here will pay market price for it. It cost me more in gas to haul it. Who else 'round here will haul it and buy it?"

West looked to me for advice. I gave him a thumbs-up, advising him to boost the price.

"Give me a thousand!" West said, standing taller.

Mr. Brown and his son laughed. "We'll give you four hundred and that's all you gonna get," the son said.

As I saw it, Mr. Brown and his son were one and the same person except one was older and fatter than the other. They both had oily dark skin, wide-set beady eyes, and swine like noses, and they were both scandalous.

I shook my head, telling West no go. We could take our business elsewhere.

"Unload it!" West yelled. In one leap, he landed on the back of the truck and started unloading furniture, one piece after another. I gave him a hand. We beautified the sidewalk with mahogany and leather pieces, giving Brown's Bargain Furniture an instant facelift.

While the Browns threatened to call the police on West for junking up their sidewalk, a pickup truck stopped curbside. The man inside offered to pay one hundred dollars for each desk and twenty-five for each chair. Another car stopped. And another! By the time the traffic cleared, old Mr. Brown was ready to renegotiate.

West walked away from Brown's with a dance in his step. For my help, he handed me twenty dollars from the wad of cash tucked safely in his pants pocket and treated me to dinner at a neighborhood Greek restaurant.

Throughout lunch, West talked of building the finest furniture anyone had ever seen and opening up a furniture store in midtown.

"I'm gonna need your help, Angie," West said.

I smiled, glad to be of use to someone.

"Hey Ang. How's Mom?" Vangie said to me, gliding through the front door in Hollywood sunglasses, and wearing vividly colored jumper shorts with high-heeled sandals that laced up to her knees.

Even though I badly wanted to share every detail of our mother's progress and setbacks, to tell her about Mr. Reese and the past-due rent and how much I'd missed her, my throat was clogged with dust from lack of use. I left her in the silence I'd been left in for too long.

"I said how's Mom?" She stood over me and tapped her toe.

Pushing a loose coil of hair from my face, I gave her a blank stare. "You don't care how she's doing. You're too selfish! And evil!" Talking liberated my lungs and I could breathe easily again.

Vangie sighed. "I should've stayed in the Cayman's for another day." She wheeled her luggage to the bedroom.

I followed. "The Caymans? As in the Caribbean? You went there?"

"I went there."

"But how?"

"How do you think, Angie?"

I pressed my lips together and shrugged.

While Vangie unpacked, I stood by, wishing she had taken me with her.

But who would want to take me anywhere?

"I brought back something for you." She pulled out a pretty bottle of perfume that I would never spray and held up a beautiful peach chiffon dress perfect for a model, not for me. I refused both gifts, crossing my arms and shaking my head.

"Did you bring something back for Mom?" I said, committed to my anger.

"*Passer le sel, veuillez.* Do you know what that means in French?"

"I don't care what it means."

"I think I'll major in French as a second language. You should too, Ang. Spanish is so cliché."

"What about Mom?"

"It means 'pass the salt, please' or something like that."

I stomped my foot. "Did you hear me!"

"I *heard* you. You're standing in my face, Angie."

"Then answer me!"

"You know, for somebody who won't talk, you can be hella bossy. Mom is where she needs to be and she should've been a long time ago."

"She needs to be at home!"

"In your opinion or the doctor's?"

Ignoring her sarcasm, I said, "Can you talk to him or do something?"

"Who else is going to talk to him?" Vangie pinched her lips together.

I dropped my eyes.

"I can't go back to that depressing place. I just can't."

I balled my fists and dug my nails into the palms of my hand, building up the courage to say what was on my mind. "Then I'm not going with you to college! I'm not going anywhere with you!" I had finally said it, my voice louder and stronger than ever before.

"*Ne sois pas stupide*. Do you know what that means?"

"I don't care what it means."

"It means don't be stupid!"

"I'm staying here with Mom until she gets better."

"Then you'll die in this dump!" Vangie screamed after me as I hurried out of the room.

Six

V angie left home early the next day, walking the beautified streets of Midtown, a redistricted area of Cass Corridor that ran from Cass Park to the south and Wayne State University to the north, an area that set itself apart from the corridor's south end. In recent years, coffee shops, condos, and cafes had sprouted up; and Wayne State University students could be seen walking the streets safely or dining at a sidewalk cafe.

Wearing a mint-colored suit jacket with a matching A-line skirt and her flats, she entered a refaced brick building and passed through the glass doors of an old Midtown bank. She hoped anyone seeing her would assume she worked a nine-to-five and was conducting her lunch-hour banking. At her safe deposit box, she inserted her key and opened the small metal door to find the last of the money she had secretly stockpiled, money reserved for her and Angie alone, their only means of escaping the pitiful life they were born into.

Her adrenaline raced, though she did her best to appear poised and steady as she buried her savings deep into her oversize leather handbag.

"Never stash your cash in one spot," Gun had once told her. He'd kept large sums of drug money stashed around his apartment—behind the toilet, under the sink, and inside books. What Gun didn't stash at home, he stockpiled in small amounts in various safe deposit boxes around the city, conducting withdrawals like a legitimate businessman. Vangie had watched and learned.

After closing out her safe deposit box, she left the Midtown S and L and took the Metro, relieved to find a vacant seat where she happily sat alone. Each time the Metro came to a stop, so did her heart. This was Detroit and there was no shortage of violent crimes flooding the news. Basic instinct and hard-earned knowledge had taught her to watch her back at all times. So far, she had managed to avoid attacks, rapes, killings, shootings, robberies, and beat-downs by keeping to herself.

Today Vangie felt her luck was about to run out. She clung tighter to her bag, the palms of her hands moistening the fine leather strap as she glanced around inconspicuously for watching eyes. When the Metro came to her stop, she vaulted out of her seat and hurried toward the exit. Walking briskly down Congress Street, she reached the swanky international bank where she had opened a new account months earlier, slowly consolidating the money she had accumulated since age fifteen.

Once inside the bank, she glanced at the hidden cameras overhead, worried they had recorded her visits. She had been careful, making her visits few and far between and randomly depositing small amounts of cash to reduce suspicion.

"Making another deposit today?" the teller said. His friendly smile always helped to settle her nerves, and so she always made a point to choose his window.

"Into my savings account, please." Steady handed, Vangie removed the crumbled envelope from her handbag and casually handed it to the teller. He sorted out thirty-eight hundred dollars. If his brown eyes held any suspicion, she could not detect it. He handed her a deposit receipt and said he hoped to see her again soon.

With her life savings stockpiled in one central location, she was now ready to do legitimate business.

Wearing a small smile, Vangie left the bank and took a stroll along Jefferson Avenue, finding shade from the hot sun under bridges and in the shadows of skyscrapers. She passed the monstrous General Motors Renaissance Center that had dominated Downtown Detroit for the years her mother had been alive. In a cluster of skyscrapers with rows of beveled-mirrored windows reflecting the Riverfront, the center included one of the tallest luxury hotels in the world. She knew because she had dined there with Antonio, and she recalled staring down from the rooftop in awe of the city of ants below and feeling on top of the world. But her luxury retreats always came to an end, and she would descend from heaven to her depressing reality.

A block or so past the center, Vangie stopped before a high-rise building with similar beveled-mirrored windows. Passing through the revolving doors, she entered a sleek lobby with high-gloss flooring where she found Thomas Jones Investment Services on the directory. She rode the elevator to the ninth floor. The small, upscale office had no receptionist, only a burly black man sitting behind a large executive type desk. His low-cut Afro and mustache were completely gray and his dark suit and silk tie looked tailored. Vangie got the sense that Thomas Jones Investment Services, despite being a one-man show, was a thriving investment company.

The man raised his eyes over the rim of his wired-framed eyeglasses. "Can I help you?"

"I'm here to invest in the stock market," Vangie said confidently.

Thomas Jones lips curled upward, suggesting he didn't take her request seriously. "Have a seat, young lady." He gestured toward a nearby leather chair.

Vangie sat stiffly, primed for questioning.

"How old are you?"

She'd expected the question and had a ready answer. "I didn't know there was an age requirement for investing in the stock market." She arched her brows.

"Well, not necessarily. I'm just curious."

"I'm old enough."

He removed his eyeglasses from his fleshy nose, leaned back in his chair, and clasped his burly hands over his double-breasted suit. "So you want to play the stock market?"

"I'm not here to play, Mr. Jones."

He chuckled. "What's your name, young lady?"

"Vangie Cooper," she said, close to spelling it out for him.

"All right, Miss Cooper. How much capital do you have to invest?"

"Twenty thousand." Her chin rose.

Thomas Jones hesitated before responding. "This twenty thousand... It isn't drug money, is it?"

"Do you ask all of your clients that question?"

"How'd you come into twenty thousand dollars, young lady?"

"From my father's life insurance policy." Her lie was swift.

"My condolences. When did your father die?"

Vangie adjusted herself in her seat, thinking before answering. "I was young."

"How, if you don't mind me asking?"

"In an accident."

"Is your mother alive?"

Her throat snagged. Vangie pushed Annette to the far corner of her mind.

"She's alive."

"Is the insurance money in your possession?" His voice had softened. Maybe he'd noticed the cloud of tears in her eyes.

"Yes."

"At a bank, I hope."

"Yes."

"Will this be a joint account or are you the account holder?"

"The account holder," Vangie said, quickly weighing the options.

"Okay, young lady…" He slid out a desk drawer. "I don't usually take walk-ins…" He glanced at his gold wristwatch. "And I have a ten o'clock on the way, but I'll see what I can do to help you invest your money intelligently. Have you seen one of these?" He handed her a new account form, a legal-sized application with a long list of confusing questions.

"Yes," Vangie lied.

Thomas Jones regarded her. "Whatever you don't understand, leave it blank and I'll walk you through it. Okay?" He took her to a closet-sized room behind his office and left.

Vangie sat at a round table, her nerves prickling as she stared at the mindboggling form. The clock on the wall ticked in the background like a dripping faucet, as did her heart. Maybe it wasn't smart to entrust her future to a man she'd found on the Internet.

Ten minutes crept by before she made up her mind to move forward—win or lose. She filled in the basics—name, address, Social Security number, and driver's license number—and answered the remaining questions to the best of her ability. She reread and reviewed the form as if it were a final exam.

At 11:00, she sat before Thomas Jones's desk again. While he looked over the account form, Vangie's eyes wandered around the room. There were various awards, plaques, degrees, and photos on the wall, including a chummy picture of Thomas Jones with Detroit's mayor, which put her mind at ease.

"Do you know the difference between a cash account and a margin account?"

Vangie shook her head.

"With a cash account, all securities—including your assets, stocks, bonds and such, which includes my commission—are paid in cash, meaning traceable funds, young lady. It doesn't mean a sack full of unmarked bills from who knows where. A personal check will suffice, signed by you, not your mother, brother, aunt, or uncle. You're also free to give me a cashier's check... Or better yet, you can transfer the funds directly from your account to mine, granted you have the sufficient funds above and beyond your initial investment." He paused for confirmation, tilting his eyeglasses downward.

"My funds are sufficient." Vangie smiled to herself.

"Then we're in business. Moving on to margin accounts... Think of a margin account as a line of credit. I, the broker, will lend you, the investor—"

"I'll stick with a cash account," Vangie interjected.

"Hold on, young lady. I want to be certain you understand your options."

"I understand, Mr. Jones."

"A cash account it is." He sighed.

For the next hour, he walked her through each question until she understood both her investment options and what he called her "regulatory obligations."

From there, Vangie took charge. Acting on an investment tip she'd overheard Jacob Stein tell a business associate, she instructed Thomas Jones to invest as many shares as she could buy with her twenty thousand dollars in one particular company.

His grandfatherly eyes broadened. "I know the company." He shook his head. "The worst investment you could make. The price per share just dropped from forty-five dollars to fifty cents. The company is on its way out. I can't, in good conscience, let you throw away your daddy's life insurance policy. I have a fiduciary duty."

"You can't get rich if you're afraid to lose your shirt," Jacob had once told her.

"It's my money, Mr. Jones." Vangie's tone was unwavering.

He sighed again. "It is your money and your investment."

Vangie strutted out of Thomas Jones investment group with a smile. Now, all she had to do was convince Angie to give up her decision to remain poor and stupid, when she had set them up for life.

That Saturday, Vangie caught the bus to Douglas Phillip's house. He lived in Royal Oak, a metropolitan suburb of Detroit with a small-town feel. His newly-built brick house had three bedrooms, two baths, and the standard brick fireplace, providing a quick escape from the Eastside and a cool, comfortable retreat from a hot, stuffy apartment when Vangie needed it.

The door swung open the minute she rang the bell. At five-foot-eleven, Douglas was a teddy bear of a guy with honey-brown skin and wide-set eyes harmonious with his wide smile. He wore jeans and a polo shirt with gym socks. Weekdays, he wore a lab coat over his clothes, working as a biotech engineer for the government.

"Long time no see," he said.

"It hasn't been that long, Douglas." Vangie waltzed into the house.

"That means I've thought about you more than you've thought about me. Make yourself comfortable."

While Douglas carried her travel bag to his guest bedroom, where she would sleep tonight, Vangie kicked off her heeled sandals and got comfortable on the cool leather couch.

Even if Douglas wanted more than a peep show from her, he would never allow himself the satisfaction. If left up to him, they would marry the day she turned twenty-one and live a comfortable life together. Comfortable was beneath Vangie's aspirations, and marrying Douglas wasn't a remote possibility.

Douglas returned to the living room and stood over her. "I picked these up for you." He handed her two fashion magazines and one architectural digest. "Your muse." He grinned. "Have you eaten? I've got lunch — sandwiches, chips, whatever you want." He looked ready to run off and prepare her a plate and pour her a glass of wine.

His patronizing tone rubbed Vangie the wrong way at times. Unlike the other men, Douglas knew the truth about her upbringing. Knowing this seemed to give him a sense of purpose in life. In his eyes, he was her only chance for success. Behind Douglas's sense of purpose lay shame and guilt. What would his family, co-workers, the church congregation think of him lusting over a girl her age, with him being close to thirty.

"I'm not a refugee, Douglas."

"I'm just making sure you're taken care of."

"Thanks. I'm good."

"I can take a hint." He sat next to her on the sofa, positioning himself so he could watch both her and the sports on TV.

The house was quiet, cozy and cool, and Vangie couldn't keep her eyes open. When she opened her eyes, she found herself curled in Douglas's arms with him stroking her hair.

"It's getting late. Are you hungry?" Douglas asked.

"I'm starving."

He laughed. "I thought so."

They drove to downtown Royal Oaks in Douglas's conservative sedan and ate juicy ribs and mashed sweet potatoes at his favorite barbeque spot amongst galleries, boutiques, and bustling nightlife.

"What's up with your aid?" Douglas said, pressing Vangie for a conversation. "Have you taken the initiative to look into it like I said?"

Vangie raked her fork through her half-eaten sweet potatoes, purposely ignoring Douglas.

"What about the scholarships I laid out for you? Did you ever follow up on those?"

No comment.

"Listen to me, Vangie. Those scholarships will offset your total cost for college. You have the grades and the qualifications. Do you know how many students in your situation would kill for a free ride. This is what I do, mentor college-bound students. I know what I'm talking about."

Vangie raised her eyes and gave Douglas a dark stare. "I'm not declaring poverty status." Her tone was sharp and clipped.

"It's not about declaring that you're disadvantaged."

"What's this conversation about then?"

Douglas rubbed his right eye as if to gather patience. "All I'm saying is the money is available. Take advantage of it." Douglas cleaned his hands with a napkin. "You should've gotten your acceptance letter to Michigan State by now…" He seemed sure the call he had made to his alma mater on her and Angie's behalf had increased their chances for admission. They hadn't needed Douglas's help. Having made a pact to rise above the expectations of their neighborhood, they had both graduated in the top tier of their class and had been presented with a list of Ivy League schools to choose from.

"We're not going to Michigan State," Vangie said quietly.

He stopped chewing. "Where then?"

Feeling a sense of obligation to Douglas, Vangie answered honestly. "Stanford."

Douglas laughed. "I'm sorry for laughing, but you have Champagne tastes on a beer budget, Vangie. You and I both know you can't pay the out-of-state fees. Where're you going to get sixty grand a year?"

Vangie smirked. If it was left up to Douglas, she would stay in Michigan and close to him. Well, he was in for a rude awakening.

"I can take care of myself. I always have."

"I hate to see you get disappointed."

"I'm used to disappointments."

"I guess I should congratulate you."

Vangie stared at him expectantly.

"Congratulations."

"Thank you." A small smile curved the corners of Vangie's lips. As much as she tried to suppress her emotions, she couldn't help but feel excited about the prospect of going away to college and leaving home.

"Riddle me this. How're you getting to California?" Douglas said.

"By private jet," she shot back.

Douglas chuckled. "Do you need anything?"

She had been anticipating his question all day. It was Douglas's way of ensuring that she needed him for something.

"Yes. A big favor," Vangie said.

Seven

Midnight.

Cambridge was oddly peaceful amidst the turbulent air between Vangie and Angie—no pulsating beats, shouting neighbors, crying babies, slamming doors, gunshots, or screaming sirens around the neighborhood.

"What kind of house do you want, Van?" Angie asked, initiating the game they had played back when they'd seen no end to going hungry and being poor. Now, Angie used the game to distract their minds on nights when neither of them could sleep.

This time Vangie ignored her twin.

"I changed my mind again," Angie went on, staring dreamily at the ceiling with her arms winged behind her head. "I don't want a country house. I want a cottage with ivy growing wild and a backyard filled with fruit trees for my pies."

Vangie glanced at Angie from the corners of her eyes and went back to reading. It occurred to her that this was merely a game for her twin, who confined herself to a life of mediocrity. The life Vangie envisioned for them exceeded Angie's wildest imagination.

"You can't ignore me forever," Angie said.

Silence.

"I know you think I don't want to go."

Silence.

"I do, Van."

"Have you started your summer reading?" Vangie's eyes never left her book.

Angie sat up. "You heard what the doctor said. Mom needs us!"

More silence.

Angie laid back down. "I'm scared," she murmured.

Vangie faced her twin. "Of what now? You're always scared of something."

"I'm scared Mom will die. No one should have to die alone." Angie's voice was small and spiked with fear.

"Mom's not going to die." Vangie was emphatic.

"What if she does, Van?"

"She won't." Vangie closed *The Unvanquished* by William Faulkner, placed the book back inside the nightstand drawer, and turned to Angie, casting a cynical glare. "What're you really scared of, Ang? And don't lie."

Angie lowered her eyes and twisted her mouth, a clear indicator that her twin had cold feet.

"I can't be your spokesperson forever, Ang."

"I know."

"We'll be together, just the two of us. There's nothing for you to be scared of."

"But we can't afford college, can we?" Angie sounded hopeful.

"We can't afford anything. When has that stopped me?"

"When're we coming home?"

"Soon."

"Soon" was the only timeframe Vangie was willing to commit to. She didn't have the heart to tell Angie she had forged their mother's name and committed Annette to a six-month stay in a mental institution, for her mother's own good. Douglas was her backup. It would give Angie peace of mind to know somebody was watching over their mother while they were gone.

"If I stay, will you leave without me?"

Angie's question stopped Vangie's heart. Leaving her twin behind was choosing life over death for her. Staying, though, would pose a greater threat to her life. She might lose her mind like her mother.

"I can't take this place another day. I can't. I might kill somebody." Against her will, her lip quivered and her tears fell.

"Don't say that, Van."

"I swear to God I will!"

"I don't know what to do," Angie cried.

Drawing close to her twin, Vangie laid a hand on Angie's cheek.

"No stretch of the sea or the circumference of the earth will ever come between us," Vangie said, reciting their childhood oath.

Angie's sniffles grew louder, her tears more rapid. "No stretch of the sea or the circumference of the earth will ever come between us," she repeated

"This is our dream, Ang. Don't ruin it for us."

"I won't."

"You promise?"

"I promise."

Everything scared me. Life scared me, death scared me, loneliness scared me, silence scared me, and talking scared me, but the thought of losing Vangie terrified me the most. To hold on to her, I was willing to do anything and Vangie took full advantage of my weakness.

The tattoo artist, a woman who could pass for a pretty man, talked me through it, distracting my mind from the smell of burning flesh. The shop was on Beauben Street, at the same place where

Vangie had gotten the black butterfly staining her lower back. I expected to pass out from pain. So far, I couldn't stop giggling as the drill etched into my lower abdomen.

When I finished, Vangie took my place in the chair.

And when it was all said and done, we stood side-by-side, examining our body art in the wall mirror. Vangie's design was to the right of her stomach, just above her hipbone. My design was on the left. Vangie had chosen the Chinese symbol for twins, and I went along with it, mostly because it was a simple design—two black figures shaped like a fancy letter X and the number seven. It was symbolic of our eternal love for one another.

"Now we're inseparable," Vangie said.

"I like that," the tattoo artist said, dusting over her work. "Twins forever!"

Part Two

Eight

In the heart of Silicon Valley, Stanford University gleamed like a beacon of hope. Vangie loved the city's rich air, rich people, clean streets, and abundant palm trees that greeted her coming and going. No dead grass, trash-ridden lots, drug houses, or abandoned buildings, only sculptured gardens, cathedrals, and Spanish-style buildings as far as her eyes could see.

By mishap, she was assigned to a coed sophomore dorm with two-room suites. Posters of glorious vacation spots and a bookcase filled with framed photos of family and friends decorated one side of the suite. On Vangie's side, the bare walls and bare shelves gave no hint of her history.

A pretty, spunky girl with doll cheeks, doll eyes, perfectly arched brows, and a coffee complexion walked into the room as Vangie unpacked.

"Hi, roomie! Clarissa." She shoved her hand at Vangie.

Vangie shook Clarissa's hand tentatively. "Vangie."

"I know who you are." Obviously catching her appraising eye, Clarissa said. "We take those roommate surveys literally here at *the farm*. I like your fashion IQ too."

Clarissa, who wore a vintage baby doll dress with flats, was one of the few underclassmen Vangie had come across not wearing flip-flops, shorts, a tank top, jeans, sweats, or tennis shoes. Vangie, like Clarissa, was dressed to make an impression, wearing an embroidered white minidress, and platform sandals.

Another ten minutes and Vangie knew more about Clarissa's life than Clarissa would ever know about hers. Clarissa was a political science major and a native Californian, born and raised in Encino. "Where the Jacksons lived," Clarissa proudly pointed out. "My dad is the CEO and president of his own global media and entertainment firm. Once, back in high school, I told a friend the name of his firm and her big mouth had everyone expecting freebee concert tickets. So, what line of business is your dad in?" Clarissa pressed.

"Not entertainment," was all Vangie offered.

Clarissa laughed. "Smart. Keep it to yourself. Anyway, class recognizes class. You're from Michigan, right?"

Vangie nodded.

"That's one place I've never been. I'll have to visit you, now that we're roomies."

That will never happen, Vangie thought.

Weeks after unpacking, Vangie was repacking, unable to adjust to sharing the small space with someone other than her twin. Most nights she found it hard to sleep without Angie, tossing and turning on the uncomfortable twin-sized mattress. Leaving Angie behind had robbed her of the joy she would otherwise have felt leaving the place that had chained her to poverty since birth, but nothing she said or did would've pulled Angie away from home or their mother.

Clarissa stood in her doorway. "We can't request a change without proving irreconcilable differences. I'm a sophomore. You're a *frosh*. That's grounds for incompatibility in a court of law! I mean, who'd you have to sleep with to get placed in Toyon Hall?"

Vangie continued her meticulous packing, ignoring Clarissa. "I've gone out of my way to be friends with you."

"I don't need friends," Vangie said pointedly.

Clarissa crossed the threshold, waltzing toward Vangie with a conspiratorial grin. "I know someone you'd love to befriend. You know... Biology major, swimming champ, and the only guy you noticed since you've been here."

Fortunately, Vangie was looking away from Clarissa or Clarissa would've caught the shock on her face. Had Clarissa been there that day in the bookstore when she couldn't take her eyes off him? Or maybe it was when she passed him in the main quad? Those were the only times she had encountered him. Both times, his closeness had made her feel hot and clammy inside, like a mid-summer storm had struck. Among the thousands of guys she had come across on campus, of every race, color, and age, *he* was the only one who stood out in the crowd.

"His name is Wade Fitzgerald the Fourth and he's my cousin." Clarissa paused as if for effect. "He asked me about you, by the way. I told him we're roomies."

Clarissa had just given Vangie reason to reconsider her move. She faced Clarissa. "I'm not used to sharing a room."

Not with anyone but my twin.

Clarissa invited herself to sit on Vangie's bed. "I know what you mean. My last roommate was a real bitch!" Clarissa smiled sheepishly. "I'm willing to make it work, if you are." She extended a friendly hand.

Smiling authentically for the first time since arriving at Stanford, Vangie gave Clarissa's hand an amiable shake. If it meant meeting Wade Fitzgerald IV, she could tolerate cohabiting with someone other than Angie.

Without solicitation, Clarissa told Vangie everything there was to know about the Fitzgerald family. Per Clarissa's report, their great-great-great grandmother, Betty Fitzgerald, a freed slave, had been the mistress of Henry Fitzgerald, the master of the plantation. When Henry died, he'd bequeathed his land to his beloved Betty. Somehow, Betty had managed to hold on to her land during the Reconstruction Era and passed one-third of it to each of their sons—Benjamin, Frederick, and Dermot Fitzgerald. Of the three, Dermot had prospered the most.

Dermot had sold a portion of his land to give his only son, Wade Dermot Fitzgerald Sr., the best education money could buy. After being one of the few blacks Harvard allowed on campus during those times, Wade Senior established the Fitzgerald Foundation in 1929, a government-funded medical research conglomerate for colored people. In 1943, the Ku Klux Klan incinerated the building, which the Fitzgerald family later rebuilt in Watts, California as a community center.

It was Wade Fitzgerald II, Clarissa grandfather, who established the long-standing Fitzgerald name as part of America's black elite. Choosing to defy his father's wishes, Wade II attended Harvard Law School instead of medical school and bought his first piece of real estate at age twenty-one. The small duplex bloomed into a portfolio, which included apartment complexes, shopping centers, hotels, and office spaces around the country, yielding millions. And this was not to mention the Fitzgerald family's stock and bond holdings.

"That's family business I don't tell everyone," Clarissa said.

Back in high school, Vangie and Angie had moved from class to class in their own world. During lunch breaks, they preferred to eat alone, and they had never attended a football game or a school dance to appease Angie's discomfort.

Now that Vangie and Clarissa were friends, Vangie experienced college life in ways she had avoided in high school, attending football games, parties, and roaming the campus without a destination. She felt out of place, while Clarissa fit the scene like a well-worn glove. She hung out with Clarissa for one specific purpose: a chance to meet Wade.

Wade, however, had entered his senior year at Stanford and, evidently, didn't waste his time hanging out, either.

According to Clarissa, the longer she kept Wade waiting, the better. "You don't make it easy for someone of Wade's caliber unless you want to cheapen yourself. You keep him curious, let him know you're from equivalent stock."

Vangie went along with Clarissa's childish matchmaking scheme so she didn't ruin any chance she had with Wade.

Tonight, she would finally meet Wade, face-to-face.

"Wade's a real time master," Clarissa said, driving her new BMW 3 series at top speed, racing toward downtown Palo Alto. "Don't be surprised if he and Todd are already eating when we get there." The car hit a pothole in the road, jarring them both.

Vangie stared curiously at Clarissa. "Who's Todd?"

"I told you, didn't I? He's Wade's best friend, the narcissistic ass I'm stuck with tonight because that's what friends do for friends." Clarissa flashed a cheeky smile.

"What do I owe you?"

"I'm starting to believe you really didn't have friends in high school. You don't owe me. If anything, Wade owes me for..." Clarissa's eyes whipped back to the road.

Vangie got the sense there was more to this prearranged blind date with Wade Fitzgerald than Clarissa had let on.

"Wade owes you for what?"

"Hold up. I think I'm lost..." Clarissa stopped at the corner of North First Street and West Santa Clara before proceeding cautiously, looking left and right past the crowds of pedestrians who roamed the street on this clear, warm night. They had passed boutiques, specialty shops, and a dozen restaurants, ranging from sushi bars to Mexican cuisine when Clarissa called out, "Here it is!"

As Clarissa jetted her car into the valet parking for Cappellini's, Vangie reminded her of the question she had conveniently circumvented.

"You don't give up easily, do you, Vangie Cooper?"

You have no idea, Vangie thought.

To hold off the impatient valet attendant, Clarissa raised a finger and turned back to Vangie. "Okay. True confession. Wade never asked about you. He's never even seen you. I know, right? Who hasn't seen you on campus? You're *perf*."

Vangie didn't bother responding to Clarissa's rhetorical question.

"Okay. I'm sorry. I just wanted to be friends." Clarissa placed her hand on Vangie's shoulder, her doll eyes dripping with apology. "You can't be mad at me, Van. I set you up with Wade, didn't I? It took damn good lawyering to talk him into this date. Luckily, I'm his cousin."

Vangie, if anything, was more nervous than angry. Learning that Wade had only agreed to this blind date out of a family obligation sent her emotions on a rocky ride.

"How did you know..." Vangie wondered, aloud.

"That you liked Wade?" Clarissa shrugged. "A lawyer's hunch. Wade has every frosh bowing down to his five-hundred-dollar Ferragamos like he's God."

Great!

When the impatient valet rapped on the window again, Vangie stepped out of the car and filled her lungs with needed air as they walked through the heavy glass door of Cappellini's.

To be alluring to Wade, Vangie had worn a very little lavender dress and her sexiest platform pumps. Her hair draped her shoulder in a graceful curve while a diamond choker and three-karat studs enhanced her look with gleaming elegance. "Always wear diamonds as beautiful as you," Antonio had once told her. It was Antonio who had taught her to recognize the color and cut of a diamond to determine its beauty. If she had never caught Wade's eye before, she hoped she would tonight.

"We're with the Fitzgerald party," Clarissa said haughtily to the strawberry blonde hostess who could pass for one of the local college students.

"Wade is expecting you." Her knowing smile made Vangie wonder if she was one of the chicks bowing at Wade's feet. If the night went her way, Wade would be bowing at hers, she hoped.

She followed Clarissa, who wore a black spandex minidress with stilettos that allowed her to stand five inches taller than five-three; her neck-length hair was tucked neatly behind one ear in a classic vogue look. Clarissa power-walked behind the hostess as if she knew precisely which section of the restaurant and at which table Wade would be sitting.

Vangie took her eyes off Clarissa and took in the posh setting. The dark walls and red tables glowing with candles gave it a romantic appeal and some insight into Wade's status and tastes. She liked him even more, and they hadn't yet met.

The hostess stopped at a corner booth set for four where Wade and, presumably, Todd were seated. Wade wore jeans and an argyle vest over a collared shirt and had an air about him that made Vangie's heart do something unusual—skip a beat and stop momentarily. She was so strongly drawn to him, she couldn't take her eyes off of him. She would blame it on Wade's good looks, but his chiseled features set in smooth, mocha skin, half-moon-shaped brown eyes, and Cupid's bow lips were neither extremely attractive nor unattractive, yet he was beautiful.

Clarissa scurried to the table ahead of her, grabbed a water glass, and chimed a fork against it. "I present to you my gorgeous roomie, Vangie!"

Todd stood first, cupped the lapel of his colorful blazer worn with jeans, a crisp white T-shirt, and an unclipped necktie, and bowed as if she were royalty. Lean as a tennis player with jade green eyes and the keen features of a model, he was clearly stuck on himself.

"A vision of superlative beauty," Todd said before kissing the back of Vangie's hand.

"Vangie, this is my cousin Wade, and this is Todd." Clarissa rolled her eyes at the mention of Todd.

"Nice meeting you," Wade said in marked contrast to Todd. He stood too, but only to let Clarissa slide into her seat. If he looked at Vangie, it was only a glance before he returned to the menu he was perusing.

Heat besieged Vangie's face, turning her red and hot. She couldn't place her emotions—somewhere between humiliation and desire. Before she could feel her legs, Todd spoke up.

"Sit next to me."

She slid into the seat across from Clarissa and catty-corner from Wade.

"You don't mind, do you, my friend?" Todd said to Wade.

"I mind." Clarissa's voice held an irritated edge.

So do I, Vangie wanted to say.

Wade ignored the question. With an impatient grunt, he flagged down the waiter. "I'd like to order"

"My friend can eat a horse," Todd said. "I say, ladies first."

"What drink can I start you off with?" The Italian-looking waiter was looking directly at her.

"Can I see the reserved wine list?" Antonio had taught her that the reserved wine list, offered by an exclusive restaurant to its best customers, included the oldest bottles from the owner's personal cellar. She needed to make an impression at this point.

The waiter smiled and winked as he handed her the leather-encased list.

Confidently, Vangie ran her finger down the pages, searching for the best selection.

"Aren't you a frosh?"

Vangie looked up to find Wade's piercing eyes set squarely on her.

"He means the restaurant's rules comply with the legal drinking age," Todd whispered behind his hand.

"I wouldn't want a lawsuit for aiding and abetting a minor." Wade's eyes bored into her.

"He's bound by propriety," Todd said. "I'm not. Order whatever you'd like. I'll drive you home, personally, if you get faded."

Hot vapors swirled through Vangie's insides, turning her face red again. Her natural inclination was to put Wade in his place by whipping out her driver's license, but she didn't need Clarissa asking how and where she'd obtained a fake Michigan ID, which included her home address.

"Just water, thanks," Vangie decided.

The waiter nodded and turned to Clarissa, who ordered lemonade.

"Water is a more judicious choice, don't you think?" Vangie sensed a slight playfulness in Wade's tone but couldn't be sure.

"He's in training. Off-season he's a lush," Todd said to her.

The waiter promptly returned with their drinks and took their dinner orders.

Throughout the night, Wade remained frustratingly silent. If he wasn't enjoying his exquisitely prepared grilled lamb, he appeared wrapped in thought, not caring whether Vangie or anyone else was at the table. There were no flirtatious stares or seductive glances. His eyes swept over her face as if her looks were less interesting to him than the comings and goings of Cappellini's customers.

Todd, on the other hand, was the epitome of rich and proud, advertising his family's wealth like a talking billboard between bites of filet mignon.

"Here's a pop quiz for you, Todd," Clarissa said. "Can you talk about anyone beside yourself? God! No one cares that *the Bryants* made some unofficial wealthiest black families list. So did the Fitzgeralds, who are listed as number one, while your family barely made the cut off."

Todd chuckled. "Tell us where your family is listed, Clarissa." His words hung in the air while Clarissa's face flushed.

"Clarissa won't say. Want to know why?" Todd whispered loudly behind his hand in Vangie's ear. "Her dad made another list: the wealthiest bachelors. Between you and me, he looked like he'd struck oil."

"You're a punk bitch, Todd! Get your facts straight!" Clarissa looked on the verge of tears.

Todd laughed.

"You're studying to become an attorney, Clarissa, and that's your defense? I'd call that a poor argument," Wade said, weighing in on the conversation.

Clarissa lowered her tearful eyes, her face sheathed in red.

Vangie picked at her linguine with whole clams and mussels, listening quietly. For someone bred around money and status, Clarissa didn't know how to conduct herself in a five-star restaurant, Vangie thought. And Todd, whose jade-colored eyes worked to hypnotize hers, was clearly out to sabotage her plans with Wade before she could put them into action. Todd might have stood a chance if looks were important to her, but she'd set her sights on Wade for more reasons than one.

"So tell me, Vangie," Todd said in the perfectly modulated voice of a newscaster. "Where's your family listed?"

"Good luck getting info out of Vangie. She doesn't publicize her family business, unlike some of us." Clarissa scowled at Todd.

"I'd like to know." For the first time that night, Wade gave Vangie his undivided attention.

"My father is one of Fortune 500's wealthiest men," Vangie blurted out and dived back into her dish to avoid Wade's deliberate gaze.

Todd brought a finger to his temple. "What's his name?"

"You wouldn't know him if I told you," Vangie shot back.

"You'd be surprised who I know. Wealthiest in the nation or the world?" Todd pressed.

"In Canada." Her lie was swift.

"Let me guess. Your dad's white."

This wasn't the first time she had been mistaken for other than just black. Annette Cooper had never dated a white man that she knew of, unless he hung out at Chucky's EastSide Lounge. But the likelihood of Todd knowing much about a wealthy white man from Canada was slim and seemed to be the perfect answer. Vangie let Todd's presumption stand.

"I'd love to meet him someday," Todd persisted.

"If anyone meets Vangie's dad, it won't be you, Todd."

"I don't know if you know this about your roommate, but she's a hater. Haters are gonna hate," Todd countered.

Wade appeared to have lost interest in the table topic.

"So, Canadian, are you?" Todd went on. "Hardcore hockey fan, perchance?"

No comment.

"Sorry to kill the fun, but I have a chem exam that needs my attention," Wade interjected.

Clarissa's eyes doubled in size. "You're leaving? Already!"

"You were thirty minutes late, Clarissa. My leaving early is warranted." Wade pulled his wallet from his jeans pocket and placed two one hundred dollar bills on the table. "Keep the change."

"The pleasure was all mine." Todd kissed the back of Vangie's hand again and slid from the seat.

"It was nice meeting you. Maybe I'll see you around." Wade's tone was more of a "good riddance." He walked away without looking back.

Clarissa picked up Todd's bottle of beer, gulped and belched. "Sorry, Vangie. Wade can be as big a punk as Todd. I swear!"

Vangie could feel the tiny beads of sweat on her upper lip. Her fingers were tingling and her eyes burned with unshed tears. No man or boy had gotten under her skin like Wade Fitzgerald. She didn't know whether she was more upset with Clarissa for making them late, with Wade for being a supercilious asshole, or with herself for not making a better impression.

Nine

Each night, I listened to the quiet. It hovered in our apartment and haunted my sleep. Even when I slept, my mind was alert, the squeaks and creaks in the wood floor and walls startling me awake.

Each morning, I awakened with the same hole in my heart, which deepened as the last days of summer rolled by. I was so lonely, I thought about slitting my wrists and joining my mother at the mental hospital.

I'd survived on the money Vangie had left me—enough to cover rent, food, and bus passes for months to come. I didn't need money for much else. There wasn't much else for me to do besides watch TV or read.

I showered and dressed in shorts and a T-shirt, bypassing the clothes Vangie had left for me to wear. I didn't have a reason to dress in nice, expensive things. Just going next door to sit wasn't a good enough reason.

When I showed up at Miss Coffee's apartment, West opened the door before I could use my key, as if my clunky footsteps had alerted him to my arrival.

"I have business to take care of today. I can use your brains," West said.

Glad to be of use, I happily tagged along.

That night, we watched scary movies until West eventually went to bed. I slept on the couch until Miss Coffee's hacking cough woke me up the next morning.

When I walked into our apartment, my stomach dropped and pressed on my bladder. This wasn't the first time our mail had mysteriously appeared in our apartment. It sat on our coffee table in plain sight. The ghost could only be Mr. Reese.

I peeked behind doors, looked under beds, and checked the closets to be certain I was alone. Before the quiet took over, I turned on the TV, the newest appliance in our old apartment that Vangie had bought for me. This one didn't fade or fuzz, and had a remote control. I stared at the images on the flat-screen, seeing nothing and hearing only my thoughts.

Years ago, when my mother was trying to be the best mother she knew how to be, she left Vangie and me alone. In her mind, we were old enough to take care of ourselves. Thinking back, we were much too young. We lived in a one-room house behind a bigger house. Back then, I talked to anyone and trusted everyone. Vangie watched quietly and listened closely, trusting no one. One night, we heard a knock on the door. I was too small to unlock the deadbolt and had to drag a chair over to the door to reach it.

"Don't open it," Vangie had warned me.

"How come?"

Vangie couldn't tell me why because our mother hadn't given us a reason. It was too late, anyway. The man shoved his way inside.

"I'll kill that bitch!" he shouted in an accent I now know was Jamaican. Tossed from the chair, I lay on the floor, too afraid to move or talk.

Vangie walked right up to the scary-looking man. "She's not here. What do you want?"

The man stopped his hunt for our mother and stared down at Vangie like he couldn't believe something so small could speak so well. "If she ain't here, where she at?"

Vangie shrugged her shoulders as little girls did. "She told me to give you something." Vangie then walked to our mother's room, found the little money our mother had stashed inside her mattress, and gave it to the man. He stared at it like he didn't know why our mother would give him a bag of money, and then laughed.

"You're a smart one. You kept me from killing that woman." On his way out, he helped me up from the floor. "Be smarter next time." It was a warning that had stuck.

We never found out why the Jamaican man was out to kill our mother, and she never figured out how her money had disappeared, but since that day, Vangie had always reminded me to "be smarter."

I wondered if I'd ever be smart enough to leave this place.

Ten

Vangie hadn't seen Wade around or heard from him since their dinner at Cappellini's last week, which unnerved her. Even Clarissa had detected her angst. "Lighten up. Wade likes you. If he didn't, I'd be the first to know," Clarissa had said.

Vangie didn't have the luxury to lighten up, play games or live off her parents' money like most students at Stanford. Every move she made was a game of chess, strategically carried out to achieve her dream.

In the Bender Room, a beautiful and peaceful study lounge on the fifth floor of the Green Library's Bing Wing, Vangie sat near a large sweeping window, her mindless gaze skimming the red rooftops across campus as she contemplated her weekend plans. The call she had received from Jacob Stein two nights ago couldn't have come at a more perfect time. Her plan to snare Wade Fitzgerald was in motion.

Tearing her eyes from the window, she attacked the keys of her laptop computer, whizzing through the final draft of a fifteen-page essay on ethics for her political philosophy class and due first thing Monday morning. She needed the weekend homework free.

Back at the dorm, she found Clarissa sitting on the couch, her head buried in a textbook. Clarissa looked up, her eyes red with fatigue. She pulled her hair back into a tight ponytail, making her doll eyes protrude even more. "I just remembered. There's a pre-law society workshop tonight. Are we going?"

"My father called," Vangie said casually.

"Is everything okay?"

"He wants me to come home for the weekend."

"You're lucky. I haven't heard from my dad in months." Hurt resounded in Clarissa's voice and Vangie didn't know what to say.

When she returned from showering, Clarissa trailed her to the bedroom, where Vangie pulled her empty garment bag from beneath the bed and put on a slinky black Chanel tube-top dress and six inch black platform pumps.

"Looks like somebody's going to a party and I'm not invited." Clarissa sat on the bed and inspected every garment she packed, from skimpy swimsuits, sarongs, and rompers, down to her Victoria's Secret lingerie.

"I need a big favor," Vangie said casually. "Can you take me to the airport?"

"San Jose or San Francisco?"

"Dow." Pride tinged her voice. Walking to the sink, she gathered her toiletries, anticipating Clarissa's next question.

"Where's Dow?"

"Where the private jets take off and land."

"Oh. Sure. I don't mind. Who wants to go to a boring ass workshop anyway?" A new look came over Clarissa's face, one of curiosity. "You dress like that just to go home?" she said.

Vangie shrugged. No explanation was necessary.

The Dow International Airport was a twenty minute drive northwest of campus. Clarissa seemed more than eager to escort Vangie through the nine-gate miniature airport whose steel frame structure and skylights gave it an open, airy feel. Vangie strutted across the terrazzo floors as if she belonged there.

Clarissa lingered behind like her bag girl, gawking at the rows of leather seats peppered with white men dressed for business or for play. She acted like she had never seen an airport before.

"I see why you're dressed up. Girl, you're rolling first class," Clarissa whispered, falling into step with Vangie, who, despite her luggage, was walking swiftly to be on time for her flight.

They arrived at the security checkpoint where Vangie stopped. "Thanks for the ride, Clarissa."

"Hug." Clarissa held her arms open.

Vangie almost shrunk back. No other girl except Angie had wrapped her in their arms and made her feel loved or even liked. After standing stiffly in Clarissa's embrace, Vangie followed the male airport attendant through the portal.

"Tell your dad your roomie says hi!" Clarissa called after her.

Like a magnificent white bird with its wings spread proudly, Jacob's jet sat just outside the terminal window, the low lights glowing inside, making it all the more majestic. Vangie imagined Clarissa's big eyes watching in awe as the bird took flight.

That should put any questions of my status out of Wade Fitzgerald's mind.

"Mr. Stein isn't aboard. You'll be traveling with this gentleman," Ingrid said, directing Vangie's attention to the back of the plane when she walked aboard.

The "gentleman" Ingrid referred to had unruly ash-blonde curly hair combed in no particular direction. He glanced up with melancholy blue eyes and gave her a brief once-over before returning to the handheld computer he was playing with, his ears covered with earphones.

Ingrid's cynical smile gave Vangie pause. Even the atmosphere inside the jet felt uncanny on this flight—cold and empty—without Jacob aboard.

The jet engines rumbled.

"You should buckle up," Ingrid said.

Vangie buckled up and watched the city below shrink as the jet sliced effortlessly through the clouds and leveled to cruising altitude in calm skies.

Two hours into the flight, Ingrid resurfaced, waking Vangie and the male passenger for dinner—steak with asparagus and baked potatoes with sour cream and chives. Vangie caught the guy staring at her on more than one occasion, his blue eyes peeking at her over the seat.

The weather in Florida contrasted markedly with the weather in California. Whereas San Jose's nights were crisp and cool, West Palm Beach was warm and humid.

Vangie strode toward the Lincoln Town Car waiting for her at the curb. The guy from the plane followed. He stood about five seven, which would have put them eye to eye if she wasn't wearing platform stilettos. When they stopped at the same black SUV with tinted windows and shiny chrome rims, each stared at the other to see who would make the first move. Obviously, he had the wrong car.

"I've been instructed by Mr. Stein to retrieve the both of you." The driver assisted Vangie with her carry-on first and then the "gentleman" with his backpack before swinging the door open.

"You first," he said.

Vangie watched him closely before sliding into the backseat. He slid in after her.

"Ronnie." He held out his hand for her to shake. It was sweaty and slow to release.

"Vangie. And please don't ask if it's with a V."

"So, not with an A?" Ronnie's eyes smiled.

Vangie flashed a polite smile and turned her gaze to the entrancing city. She hoped Ronnie would keep to his half of the seat while she kept to hers.

They made their way toward West Palm Beach, a neighborhood of palm-tree-lined streets and estates owned by some of the wealthiest Americans. One day, she would own a sprawling estate like Jacob's, an elegant manor with a heated indoor pool and a panoramic lake view. Jacob called this home his Colonial Lady by the Bay. He had others—in other states and countries—as would she.

When the Town Car passed under the tropical trees lining Jacob's long driveway, the pool called to Vangie. She loved hanging out in Jacob's pool. Tiled in beautiful sapphire, it had a sparkling waterfall, a Jacuzzi, and a lakefront backdrop. Whether she was watching hot rain pour from a sunny sky or admiring a full moon reflecting off the still lake at midnight, the experience was exhilarating.

After placing their luggage at the foot of the entrance, the driver pivoted like a soldier and bade them a good evening. Both Vangie and Ronnie stared at the heavy mahogany and etched glass double door, avoiding eye contact. Vangie could hear music inside the house, a jazzy melody, above muffled voices.

The door flew open. "Join the party!" The man had dark hair, dark eyes, and bushy facial hair. "I believe Jacob is expecting you two." He reached for Vangie's luggage.

"I've got it." Ronnie said.

"It's okay. I'll take it."

Leaving the two men tugging over her luggage, Vangie moved tentatively through Jacob's spectacular mansion. It never ceased to mesmerize her. The layered ceilings and track lighting made it an architectural masterpiece. Jacob's collection of artwork hung on the stately walls. She wasn't allowed to touch the priceless pieces without wearing cotton gloves, and the designer Italian furniture she was surrounded by seemed made for admiring more than sitting.

In the entertainment room, a small crowd mingled around a box-shaped black and gray sectional that could seat twenty or more. Other guests had done what Vangie had in mind, changed into immodest swimsuits to lounge around the indoor pool or bask in the Jacuzzi.

When she entered the room, an Asian girl of about twenty-one approached her holding a mirror inches from her nose. Her skin was a creamy yellow and her hair was cut in an asymmetrical style, curving glamorously around her high cheekbones.

"Have some. It'll get you ready to party." She snorted a thin white line from the ornate mirror. "Fuck yeah!" Her eyes turned glassy and a euphoric smile crossed her lips. Her fingers rose languidly to Vangie's hair, twirling the coal black strands as if feeling fine cloth from another world. "I'm Lisa. Are you here for Jacob?"

Vangie looked at Lisa as if she had two heads.

"Where is he?"

Lisa pointed to the pool.

On the other side of a glass wall, Vangie found Jacob.

He leaped out of the pool at the sight of her. "This is Vangie, everyone! Isn't she a living doll?"

The men saluted her with their drinks and rousing helloes while the women howled as if the party had finally gotten started. There were more blondes than brunettes, and not one had skin as dark as hers.

Dripping wet from his salt-and-pepper hair down to his deeply tanned skin, Jacob grabbed a towel from one of the carts around the pool and haphazardly dried himself. "How was the flight? You've met Ronnie, right? Where is that guy?"

Not knowing or caring where Ronnie had gone, Vangie didn't answer.

Jacob wrapped the towel about his waist and led her back by the hand through the entertainment room and down the wide, marbled hallway to Jacob's NASCAR room. Plaques and model cars decorated the walls and the polished oak floor sported a full-scale stencil of a racecar.

Ronnie sat alone, sipping a beer and watching a wall-mounted TV from a barstool. The buzz of high-speed cars whipping around a track blared through small, but powerful, speakers.

"Ronnie, my boy! Welcome to the Sunshine State for a little R and R and ass!" Jacob laughed. "You've meet Vangie?"

Ronnie stood and stared at Vangie. "We've met."

Jacob turned to her. "Ronnie will be your guest of honor for the weekend. This guy doesn't know the meaning of a good time. Show him a good time, will you, doll?"

Vangie looked from Ronnie's melancholy blue eyes back to Jacob's dilated gray ones, breathing deeply to level off her temper.

"You want me to show *him* a good time?" She arched her brows.

Jacob must have caught the flames in her eyes because he pinched her cheeks with both hands and said. "It's all in fun, doll." He turned his attention to Ronnie. "She's worth a million."

"More than a million," Vangie snapped.

Jacob's plastered-on smile bypassed his eyes. "You do know I was speaking figuratively." He turned back to Ronnie. "You're gonna love her. She's fantastic!"

"You couldn't afford me if I were for sale," Vangie spat at Ronnie. Struggling to maintain whatever dignity she had left, she left the room, located her luggage, and hit the door. The humidity had thickened, dampening her heated skin the moment she stepped into the warm Florida air.

Before she could figure out how to get the hell out of the gated estate on foot, Jacob caught up with her.

"Vangie…this isn't like you. I thought we understood each other." Jacob's voice was butter smooth.

"I owe you, you mean?"

"I can assure you that's not what I meant. You're an adept negotiator. Think of it as a business transaction. Your words, not mine."

For the first time in her life, Vangie felt like *a real ho.*

"If I'd known I was hiring a pimp, I would've negotiated for more," she spat.

Jacob turned pinkish-red. "Is that what you think of me? I've always had a higher regard for you, Vangie. Very high." Condescension dripped from his words. "It's going to be a great weekend, and Ronnie is a nice guy, very nice. He's someone you should acquaint yourself with. Trust me, doll. He's smitten with you."

I did trust you!

Meeting his eyes with cold fury, Vangie's teary glare told Jacob where he could go and what he could do to himself.

"Have it your way. I'll have my driver take you wherever you'd like to go." Jacob walked away, leaving Vangie with something to think about. She had nowhere to go and no ticket back to San Jose. Above all, she couldn't return to campus so soon or her plan to ensnare Wade would be ruined.

Jacob's driver slowly wound around the flagstone driveway and opened the SUV door for her.

Eleven

After a ride around the city without a destination in mind, Vangie's brief flirtation with morality had dissipated and self-preservation had taken over. She returned to Jacobs's mansion. Her future depended on it.

The music had gone from soft jazz to acid rock. Vangie moved deeper into the house in search of Ronnie. Standing on the lush lawn amid stucco cabanas and palm trees, she caught sight of him at the outdoor bar, his blue eyes luminous under the lamp posts.

Vangie sauntered up next to him, dripping with seduction. "Looking for company?"

In his apparent excitement to see her, Ronnie knocked over his beer but caught the bottle before the drink stained her dress.

His cheeks flushed. "You're just in time for the climax."

Vangie frowned. "Is that a pun I should get?"

He turned redder. "I'm not that clever, believe me. Is this your first play party?"

She blinked. "What's a play party?"

"The abridged version: play parties are a way for old rich dudes to chill out." He went on tell her that these parties were bi-annual, hosted by various wealthy men, and fashioned after a Roman Emperor known for his salacious appetite.

Losing interest, Vangie stared off, half listening to Ronnie and feeling naïve for the first time in her life. She came out of her reverie to find Ronnie staring boldly at her.

"Sorry for staring, but you remind me of someone."

"Should I be worried?"

"I probably should be," he mumbled before flagging down the bartender for another beer, which he gulped back practically in one swallow. "I'm full of fuck-ups tonight. Would you like a drink?"

"Yes. Anything."

"You're old enough to drink, right?"

"Would you like to see some ID?"

Red had become Ronnie's primary color. "I'm a believer." After ordering her a drink, he said, "Have you seen the program?" He handed Vangie a five-by-eight black placard engraved with red script. "Reads like a gentleman's convention."

Vangie looked over the weekend agenda with a critical eye: Night Swim, Brunch, Golf, Spa Day. Dinner Party. It looked respectable enough, but she knew better.

"I think I'll forego tee time tomorrow," he said. "My golf swing sucks. How about you? Going to spa day?"

"No."

"Want to go somewhere?"

"Somewhere like where?"

"I know of a great club. Cheap drinks. Nice beats. " He cleared his throat. "I'd be cool to have a dance partner tonight," he said offhandedly.

"Cooler than a play party?" Vangie asked in jest.

Ronnie put on a slow grin. It was the first time Vangie took notice of his good looks. "Right." he said.

On their way out, they ran into Jacob.

"Thought we'd take in the Sunshine State. Got a ride I can borrow?" Ronnie said.

Jacob handed Ronnie the keys to his classic Baltic blue Porsche Speedster. "Have fun, kiddos." He patted Vangie on her butt. "Smart girl."

Smarter than you think!

They hit the highway, roaring down the Ronald Reagan Turnpike at one hundred miles an hour. A bass beat blasted through the speakers. Ronnie shifted gears, accelerating to a deadlier speed, and oblivious to the slick pavement and intermittent rain. Vangie gripped the seat and braced for a crash.

At 2:00 A.M., Ronnie and Vangie stumbled out of the club. A few too many drinks and partying to techno music with Ronnie under a ray of pink and blue laser lights had Vangie's head spinning.

Standing in the drizzle, Ronnie fumbled with the keys to the Porsche, his bloodshot eyes zeroing in on the lock as if he couldn't see past his nose.

"I'll drive," Vangie said, holding out her hand for the keys. She was in much better shape than Ronnie.

"It takes more than a few watered-down drinks to absorb into this liver," Ronnie said, putting on a slow but convincing smile.

They arrived at Jacob's place in one piece despite Ronnie's reckless driving. On their way upstairs, squealing pigs distracted them, at least, it sounded like pigs to Vangie.

Ronnie pressed his finger to his lips. They tiptoed to the entertainment room where they found a litter of half-naked bodies slumbering in what now looked like the inside of a crack house. The source of the squealing was coming from the pool area where a ménage-a-trois of women were doing the inconceivable.

Sobered by the sight, Vangie left Ronnie gawking and headed for their "assigned" room upstairs, wondering what other salacious acts were taking place throughout Jacob's ten-room, thirteen-bath mansion. She could just imagine.

The contemporary white and gray suite had French doors that opened onto a balcony and looked down on Jacob's double tennis court. Vangie hadn't gotten over the pool scene before Ronnie walked into the room, closing the door tentatively as if he wasn't sure he was welcome.

He wasn't.

Avoiding the bed altogether, Ronnie sat in the overstuffed armchair near the French doors. "You don't have to do this," he said.

Vangie knew perfectly well that she didn't have to do anything she didn't want to do, but something else was driving her: desperation. Without another word, she carried her travel bag into the adjoining luxury bathroom and shut the door. Leaning on the bronze sink, she zoomed in on her bloodshot eyes in the framed mirror. Gulping down two cosmopolitans hadn't emboldened her. As she scowled at her own condemning eyes, the purpose of her visit to Florida came back to mind.

The hell with Wade Fitzgerald!

She changed out of her dress and into a sexy white lace bustier with matching string panties. For an added touch, she wore her platform stilettos and unpinned her messy updo. Hair tousled over her shoulders, Vangie drew back the door with gusto.

Time to play…

Ronnie blinked. "You're a knockout."

Her walk measured and provocative, Vangie crossed the room and stood over Ronnie with her hands on her hips. "No licking or sucking. Those are my rules."

I may as well play the role.

"I'm not very complicated." With nimble hands, Ronnie quickly shed his white collarless dress shirt, jeans, his Converse tennis shoes and gym socks. Then he scooted backward onto the bed, crab like. Arms winged behind his head, he stared down his nose at her, his boxer shorts straining to contain his excitement.

"You have a condom?" she asked brusquely.

If not, the party is over.

Ronnie leaned over the bed, fumbled for his pants, and came up with a red latex condom. "Will this do?"

Vangie wanted to roll her eyes. She turned off the lights, instead. Wearing her stilettos, she straddled Ronnie's lap. If he got any more excited, she wouldn't have to go all the way, hopefully.

"Wait…" He squeezed her wrist with a clammy hand. "This might break one of your *rules*, but can I kiss you?"

One kiss can't hurt, and he is paying me good money.

Vangie leaned forward and brought her mouth to Ronnie's. He cupped his hands behind her neck, pulled her closer and wrapped his lips around hers, manipulating her tongue with all the finesse of a snake. Finding herself lost in his baby blues, Vangie shut her eyes

Ronnie unsnapped her bustier with his nimble fingers, and then slid the spaghetti straps off her shoulders. Her breasts became his personal playground for his mouth to frolic, her butt new territory for his hands to explore.

Vangie unexpectedly heated to Ronnie and couldn't ignore the fire kindling in the base of her belly as he kissed her body further south. To regain control of her body and mind, she resisted her desire not to stop him, squeezing his head between her thighs.

"I said no licking."

Ronnie raised his head. "Right." In the gray haze she could make out his frustrated eyes, all traces of lust and fire gone from them. His breath rose sharply as he inhaled and dropped heavily on a slow exhale. He slivered back up her body until his face hovered directly over hers.

"You're not into this, are you?"

"Does it matter?" She went along with his assumption.

"This may sound incredible, but I've never paid ten grand to bone a chick."

"Ten? You must mean twenty?"

"I'm not that guy."

"And I'm not any chick. And it does sound incredible. You're at an orgy."

"A play party."

"Whatever." Vangie pushed Ronnie aside and sat up.

He sat up too and roughed his curls. "Have you tried saying no to Jacob? He's an uncompromising son-of-a-bitch, plucked from the same nut tree as my dad, Zeke the great." From behind his ear, Ronnie pulled out a thickly rolled joint, pressed it between his lips, grabbed a Bic off the nightstand and flicked it. His eyes closed as smoke curled around his smiling mouth. He offered her a hit.

Vangie shook her head. She needed to keep a level head.

"What's your excuse for being here?"

"That's a good question." Disgusted with herself, Vangie went to stand but Ronnie caught her by the hand. "

"Don't go..." His melancholy eyes begged her to stay.

Against her better judgment, Vangie threw off her shoes, swiped up Ronnie's shirt from the floor, covered up, and then climbed back into bed. They sat with their backs resting against feathery pillows, staring through the French doors into the Florida night.

The pungent fruity aroma took over the room and the air she breathed. Hugging her knees, Vangie gazed at the crescent moon while listening to Ronnie postulate about the benefits of smoking pure ganja, which he purchased directly from a guerilla grower out of Mexico.

A few too many tokes and Ronnie completely lost his inhibitions, answering questions she didn't care to ask. Livingston was his last name. He called himself a "Hollywood kid," born the third child of Zeke Livingston, a well-known television and film producer. At the ripe age of twenty-six, Ronnie owned a small share of a major movie studio, his own video game company, along with various unspecified investments in tech companies. Vangie stored Ronnie's portfolio in the back of her mind and kept her life to herself.

He gaped at her, his eyes mere slits. "I'm going to regret tonight."

She gaped back. "Why?"

"You're incredibly beautiful and opportunity doesn't always knock twice."

"Isn't three a charm?" She smiled softly.

Ronnie took another hit of weed. "Let's hope four is magic," he choked out along with a cloud of smoke.

The bedroom door creaked open and Lisa walked in. Vangie made out her asymmetrical haircut in the partial darkness.

"I smell candy," Lisa sang, ambling toward the bed in skimpy panties. Her meager breasts came at Vangie like a stoplight.

It's time to go...

The thought resounded in Vangie's mind but didn't reach her extremities. For some inexplicable reason, she didn't move.

"Lisa!" Ronnie sounded much too excited to see this chick.

Smiling like she was hiding a secret, Lisa climbed aboard and sat between Vangie and Ronnie. "Are you sharing?"

"I'm a generous guy." Ronnie lit another joint and passed it to Lisa, who inhaled deeply, and then exhaled directly into Ronnie's mouth. He received her shotgun without protest, then kissed her sloppily, as though he had dreamed of it. What man wouldn't dream about Lisa? She was gorgeous, and Vangie suspected, cranked up on ecstasy given her ghoul-like eyes and gaping mouth, as though she craved a gallon of water to quench her raging thirst and something to suck on.

"You're a great kisser." Lisa passed the joint back to Ronnie.

"Am I?"

"Fuck yeah!"

"Vangie thinks I suck." Ronnie looked over at Vangie and grinned.

Vangie rolled hers.

Now Lisa's dilated pupils had turned on her. When Lisa nuzzled her nose in her hair, Vangie drew back, hoping Lisa got the message by the "fall back" look on her face.

"You're so soft and fluffy," Lisa purred. "What're you into for fun? Girls, guys, bi, straight...?"

Ronnie laughed. "She's a real fuckin' bow and arrow." He wrapped his arm around Lisa's shoulder and pulled her close. "I'm wide open. What'd you have in mind?" He brought the joint to Lisa's lips, which she generously inhaled.

Feeling trapped in this world of freaks and geeks, Vangie decided it was definitely time to leave before Lisa and Ronnie lured her into a threesome. The thought hadn't fully emerged when she found herself fighting for air and choking back smoke. The dizzying vapors Lisa had shot directly into her mouth, along with her darting tongue, clouded Vangie's mind and her judgment. Coming out of a fog, she shoved Lisa off of her forcefully and came close to giving her an Eastside beat down.

In the back of her spinning mind, she heard Ronnie's riotous laughter. Hurting him too came to her mind without any emotion attached to it. Her main thought was to get the hell out of Florida and get back to school. She slid to the floor and somehow landed flat on her butt. The room spun when she stood.

"Vangie. It's cool," Ronnie said, mid-hysterics.

"Yeah, stay and play," Lisa sang.

Vangie saluted Ronnie with her middle finger and left the room.

On the first level of Jacob's mansion, she found a small corner where she could curl up on a cushioned seat before a bay window.

The next day, Vangie left Florida with her last shred of dignity and no way to pay for her college education.

Twelve

I leaped out of bed and dashed to the kitchen where I pulled out my shiny new baking pans, my new hand mixer, and my new mixing bowls, the ones I had bought with the money Vangie had left me. I remembered baking our first birthday cake like it was yesterday—the same year after our stepfather had disappeared and I'd felt free to do as I pleased around the house. I'd even tried my hand at my first Thanksgiving dinner that year and had come close to burning the free turkey we had stood in line for hours to get. I had it in my mind to talk that year too, but then my mother had brought home Mr. Bill, the first man to replace Russell. My fear of him had forced my words back down my throat every time I tried to speak. So, I kept them safe with Vangie.

While my German chocolate cake baked, I showered and threw on the first clean clothes I found. The clacking of high heels in the hallway sent me sprinting for the front door. Our birthday had fallen on a Saturday this year, and Vangie had promised me she'd try to come home.

It was only Bonifa. She lived across the hall and had once been a welcome guest in our home. My mother never liked being judged on how she lived and whom she loved, and Bonifa had judged her one too many times.

I slammed the door shut.

If not for West, I would have spent the day alone. It wasn't the same as seeing Vangie, but it was nice seeing someone. West wheeled my birthday gift inside.

"Some fool left it over there off Grand, behind the old church," West said.

Though West couldn't hide the scorch marks inflicted from a fire, he had done a nice job restoring the writing desk to its natural beauty. It was dainty, with a pull-down desktop, and it had three little drawers up top.

I threw my arms around his neck, thanking him for my birthday surprise, and then served him a slice of German chocolate cake smothered with flakes of coconut.

West licked his fingers clean over it. "You're not a baby no more, Ang; I remember you at nine. Now, you've grown up on a brotha'." He shook his head disbelievingly. "How does it feel being nineteen?"

I shrugged, feeling alone, frightened and abandoned more than anything. I'd like to believe that West understood my turmoil. He had been abandoned too, by both his parents. At age fourteen, Miss Coffee found him outside Cambridge just sitting and waiting, she had told me. He didn't know his own grandmother from the lamppost, she said, but she couldn't miss him from the devil—he was the mirror image of her son, who didn't know what to do with his life either, except dream and wander.

My age, however, wasn't what had West's eyes on the disturbed side today. I stared curiously at him, tilting my head until he finally came out with what had him so disturbed.

"You know Gram is sick. Real sick. She has a sister in Ohio…" He dropped his head. When he looked up with wet eyes, I knew Miss Coffee was leaving and never coming back.

Eyes wet, I grabbed a pen. "The cats?" I wrote on the palm of his hand.

"I gotta get rid of'em, man. Deja's got allergies."

Deja! Deja! Deja!

I bet Deja had plotted this all along, to get rid of Miss Coffee and the cats so she could have West and the apartment to herself.

"You know I'd kick it with you all day, but Deja's waiting for me. That desk is worth some money, Ang. Hold on to it." He gave me a bear hug and left me alone.

Panic settled into my bones like the worst case of the flu. Since Vangie had left me, I'd grown accustomed to the quiet. Some days, I could even go without the TV or music to fill the silence and sleep without waking to every sound, but I would never get used to the loneliness. It followed me like a dark shadow and terrified me the same.

I was ready to cry myself to sleep when I heard another knock on the door. I didn't hope, wish, or pray it was Vangie. I didn't care anymore.

I cracked open the door and peeked an eye out.

It's that man. What's his name?

"Douglas Phillips. Remember me?" he said, smiling wide.

I remembered him. He had driven us to visit our mother at the hospital.

"You mind if I come in?"

Reluctantly, I widened the door for him to step inside. His sweet and spicy cologne dizzied me as he passed by. He was dressed nicely too, in a brown suit and hard leather dress shoes. In his hand were a dozen red roses.

"I heard it's someone's birthday." He handed me the bouquet of roses. I stared at the velvety petals, speechless, of course. No boy or man, besides West, had ever given me anything so beautiful—or anything at all. Before I'd turned nineteen, I didn't care. Today, it meant the world to me.

"I'd put those in water if I were you."

I hurried off. In the broom closet, used for everything, I found a plastic water pitcher and arranged the roses carefully, stem by stem, then set them next to the cake dish on the dining table.

I expected Douglas to leave, but instead, he sat on the couch as if he intended to stay awhile. I sat too, far away from him. I should've offered him a slice of cake, but I didn't.

"I have dinner reservations. If you don't have plans, I wouldn't mind the company."

My eyes grew large as if he'd threatened my life. I imagined a fancy restaurant with fancy people in fancy clothes in a fancy part of town and looked down at myself. I was wearing torn sweat pants and a white thermal shirt with chocolate stains. When I saw my big toe sticking out of my left sock, I curled my toes under and shriveled up inside.

"You have time to get ready."

He thought I was pitiful. Keeping my eyes on my twiddling thumbs, I vehemently shook my head.

"It's your birthday. Why spend it alone?" His logic sounded too much like Vangie.

I peeked up at him and smiled.

He chuckled. "Where I come from, a smile means yes."

I wondered where he came from and why he was here.

I eased out of the dining chair and left the room. In our bedroom, I put on the dress Vangie had bought me, the beautiful peach chiffon one from the Cayman Islands. It was cool out for a sleeveless dress, but the day was special enough, I guessed. I threw off my holey socks and put on the summer sandals Vangie had left behind. They were made of leather, black, and strapped across my toes and around my ankles. The heel was much too high for me to walk in with confidence. I wore them anyway.

No ponytail tonight, either. I stood before the fractured mirror like Vangie, grooming my hair carefully. The only way to tame it was with loads of hair lotion, transforming me into a cave woman. I hated it and brushed it back into a ponytail.

My face burned when I reentered to the living room and Douglas stood and stared.

"You look just like your sister."

I didn't return his smile because I didn't believe him.

We drove past Wayne State University and the Old Opera House and pulled into the parking lot of a Victorian mansion. He told me it had been renovated and converted into a restaurant. Whatever it was before, it was enchanting now. I felt like a pauper who didn't belong in such a fancy place. Goose bumps popped up, covering my skin.

"Are you cold?" Douglas said, wrapping me in his warm suit jacket that smelled of him. As we passed under beautiful chandeliers and across the shiny hardwood floor, Douglas placed his hand on the small of my back. I stiffened on contact, disliking yet liking the feel of it. The quaint parlors, filled with lovely antique furniture, distracted my mind from Douglas's touch. I thought of West and his love for furniture. This place was a furniture connoisseur's paradise.

My thoughts returned to Douglas's hand as he helped me into my seat. The cozy tearoom was packed with talkative people. I wondered what we would talk about over dinner, seeing I had nothing to say.

Douglas reached over and gently caressed my elbow. "You don't have to be nervous when you're with me."

Instantly my nerves stopped buzzing and my goose bumps ironed out.

He helped me with my dinner napkin and told me which glass was for water and which was for wine. I detested alcohol, how it made people crave it like soda and drink it like water. When the waiter poured Douglas a glass, the smell brought back sad memories.

"Did you find anything you like on the menu?"

The waiter waited patiently for my reply that never came.

Douglas ordered for us both, restarting my heart.

After the waiter left, I caught him staring at me again and turned my eyes to the bay window, pretending to admire the beautifully landscaped courtyard lit by antique street lamps.

"This is one of your sister's favorite restaurants. She's not easy to please, but you know that about her, don't you?" He chuckled. "She says I'm boring. You don't think I'm boring, do you?"

I twisted my mouth to one side and rolled my eyes about.

How would I know?

While we waited for dinner, Douglas talked for the both of us, never letting my silence stand in the way. I smiled at his stories about growing up in Lansing, being the son of a preacher and the middle child between eight brothers.

When dinner was finally served, I admired my pretty porcelain plate, reluctant to disturb the arrangement of baby carrots with leafy stems, gravy drizzled over mashed potatoes, and sprigs of parsley sprinkled over the steak, all the while wondering how the cook came up with his dishes and which culinary school he had attended.

I looked up and caught Douglas staring at me. Again!

"You have the same mole in the exact same place as Vangie, the same smile, the same eyes... I had to see it to believe it."

Good thing my mother didn't hear you say that.

"Have you talked to her today?"

Suppressing my tears as best I could, I shook my head. Our birthday was practically over and Vangie hadn't even called me.

His cell phone rang.

"It's for you." He tried to hand me his phone.

I stared at it as if it would attack me.

"You might want to take this. It sounds important."

My chest suddenly felt hollow and my brain forgot to tell my lungs to breathe. I was so sure it was Dr. Adler calling to report bad news that I couldn't lift a finger. My mother had finally killed herself.

Douglas placed the phone to my ear.

"Happy birthday!" Vangie sang.

Douglas's "gotcha" smile gave away their secret. Vangie had planned the whole enchanting night just for me. I laughed and cried at the same time. Her voice was the air I breathed.

"How could I forget my own birthday?" she said, reading my thoughts again.

I pressed the phone closer to my ear, my heart filled with love I couldn't express in front of Douglas.

"I tried calling you all day, Ang. Why the heck is the phone disconnected? Are there any other bills you haven't paid I should know about?"

I envisioned her arms folded across her chest and the toe of some expensive shoe tapping the floor as she waited for my response, which she wouldn't get.

"You have to be more responsible, Angie. Really. What if something happens?"

Heat rushed my face, turning it strawberry red. If I could say something, I'd have nothing to say.

Bye! I hope she read my mind.

I handed Douglas his phone back, wanting to avoid the subject of unopened mail and overdue bills.

"She's right, you know," Douglas said when he hung up. "Anything could happen. I'll take you to get it turned back on first thing Monday."

I twisted my mouth and lowered my eyes.

When dessert arrived I looked up and smiled. The fudge brownie and ice cream were pure joy in my mouth—scrumptious, sweet, nutty, creamy, chocolate joy. It was difficult to listen to Douglas talk and distinguish the flavors flooding my mouth at the same time, as difficult as chewing and rubbing my head and stomach while walking. Douglas stopped talking in time for me to enjoy the burst of flavors in my very last bite. I couldn't keep my eyes from rolling back in my head.

"It's that good, huh?" He laughed at me.

I tucked in my smile and lowered my eyes again. I was ready to leave.

At home, he followed me inside, although I could've walked on my own. Entering the rundown apartment was like slipping my feet into a pair of comfortable tennis shoes after wearing heels I couldn't wait to take off. I stood at the apartment door with one hand on the doorknob, not knowing how to thank him for a delicious meal and this happy ending to a miserable day except to shake his hand.

He pulled me into his cuddly chest and gave me a bear hug. "She'll be back," he said as if he was consoling himself about Vangie and not me.

I shut the door in his face.

Thirteen

The sweet smell of fresh roses welcomed Vangie when she walked into her dorm room after class. She found the breathtaking floral arrangement on her desk with two notes attached. The second note, written on a yellow sticky and pasted to the handcrafted glass vase, was from Clarissa. "Guess who?" The note closed with a smiley face.

The small greeting card Vangie pulled from the envelope read, "Meet me tonight. Aquatic center. West door. 9:00." It was signed Wade F.

Vangie removed a long stemmed rose from the vase and inhaled its sweetness, grinning beside herself. She had outsmarted Wade Fitzgerald, after all.

With Clarissa out and about somewhere, Vangie had the dorm suite to herself and plenty of time to get ready for Wade. Unsure of what Wade had in mind at the aquatic center, but certain of her intentions, Vangie covered her eye-catching bikini with a peach colored mini trench coat. In Detroit, she had borne cold that turned bone to ice. In California, she could tolerate any cold night skimpily clothed. She slid her feet into platform heels and perfumed her wrists, neck, and the divide of her breasts—a valuable lesson she had learned from her mother. "If you can't look good for a man, smell good for him," Annette had preached.

Concluding that her hair would get wet and then dry into a mess of matted coils, Vangie brushed it up to the top of her head and fastened it into a tight ball.

She crossed campus eagerly. Luckily for her feet, she was accustomed to long walks in high heels. When she reached the aquatic center, she could hear a steady sloshing of water before she turned the corner. She found Wade, a lone fish, swimming from one end of the Olympic-sized pool to the other.

She watched quietly in the shadows until Wade surfaced from the water, his close-cut black hair glistening in the floodlights. He swiped water from his face and rested his elbows on the pool's edge.

"Are you getting in? It's nice and warm, " he said.

Vangie stepped into the floodlights. "Am I invited?"

"Do you always answer with a counter question?"

"Yes... I mean, no. And yes, I'm getting in." Vangie removed her trench coat to reveal a black string bikini with a sheer tie-top. Wade's piercing gaze traveled up her legs and lingered curiously around her tattoo before his eyes met hers boldly. Now her heart was rattling and her stomach rolling. She quickly dropped into five feet of water with a splash; the heated water lapped at her breasts.

"Glad you could join me." He flashed her a dazzling white smile, yet another something beautiful about him. Shying away, Vangie took the opportunity to admire the open-air stadium with its trio of Olympic-sized pools.

"So, this is where I can find you?"

"Why? Have you been looking for me?"

"What if I have?"

"You found me."

"You drew me a map."

"By the way, you're welcome."

"I should thank you?" Vangie hiked a brow.

"For the roses. It's not something I do for just any girl."

"Thank you," she breathed and lost her train of thought. She waded, nervously. "Do you always invite chicks on a pool date?"

"I have a three day invitational in Texas this week and Wisconsin next week."

"Oh. So you squeezed me into your schedule?"

Wade laughed, to her relief. She was playing hard to get out of a need to prove she was worthy of him. She needed to chill out. If she could...

"To be honest, I broke a cardinal rule. I couldn't wait that long to see you again." His piercing eyes held hers for a moment before he dove underwater and came up within kissing distance. Her heart jumped and her mouth moistened expectantly. "Can you swim?" he said.

"Yes." She caught her breath.

Wade took off toward the deep end with speed and precision, never giving her the pleasure of a kiss. Vangie quickly followed. She wasn't a champion swimmer, by a long shot, but she could hold her own. Public pools, overrun with snotty nosed kids, had been a convenient babysitter for Annette when she had more important things to do than keep her kids entertained. For hours, she and Angie had splashed about in the sun, guarding each other's lives. In time, they had become decent swimmers.

Wade had kicked off the back wall and passed her going the other way, breast-stroking his way for a second lap.

Out to impress, Vangie pushed past her exhaustion to reach the far edge of a pool that had no end. Her arms fought the water; her head swung left to right as she exhaled more air than she took in. For a terrifying instant, she dipped below the waterline and caught a gulp of chlorinated water that burned her esophagus and came out her nose. Gasping, she pumped her feet, searching for a bottom she couldn't find. Death yanked at her ankles, determined to pull her under.

"It doesn't surprise me you almost drowned." Wade wrapped a strong arm around her waist and pulled her to safety. "Your fundamentals are all wrong. Next time, relax and tread; never panic." He offered her a hand up the steps.

Vangie pushed aside her hair, which was hanging like a wet mop over her eyes, and climbed the steps without his help, nearly slipping backward and back into the pool. She found her footing on the wet surface and faced Wade with a scowl.

"There won't be a next time!"

"No?" The bridge of his nose crinkled slightly and his mouth twitched as if he was itching to laugh. "That's too bad. You look beautiful soaking wet." He walked gracefully toward the benches and returned with a towel. "You should dry off before you catch pneumonia."

"You do it for me. You tried to kill me!"

"You're mad? I asked you if you could swim." His voice rose to a falsetto.

Vangie, chilled to the bone, wrapped her arms tightly around herself. "Are you going to dry me off or not?"

His smile was wry, but willing. "Come here…"

Drawn to him like a honey bee to the sweetest nectar, Vangie stepped forward.

"Turn around."

She didn't hesitate to do as he instructed. He dried her hair first, gently massaging her scalp. The sensation of his warm breath tickling the nape of her neck melted her anger.

Once her hair was sufficiently dry, Wade retrieved another dry towel and warmed her shoulders. She closed her eyes, enjoying the feel of his practiced hands skimming her glistening body wherever he found a bead of water. When he skimmed her inner thighs, slowly and effectually, her deepest regions caught fire and found a pulse.

"Face me," he said.

She met his gaze.

With the towel now wrapped around his hand like a glove, Wade dried the pert mound of her breasts in delicate, languid strokes. He had her emotions scattered like thundery clouds. Frustration, excitement, and desire rumbled inside of her.

"Are you dry enough?" His eyes burned into hers.

"You missed a spot." Holding his intense gaze, Vangie guided Wade's hand back to the crease of her breasts.

Abandoning his self-control, Wade tossed aside the towel and pulled her into to him by the strings of her bikini, his moist mouth meeting hers. His tongue reached down deep and stirred something delicious between her thighs.

Widening her lips, Vangie chased after his tongue impatiently. Wade's tongue chased back as their kiss deepened, moving quickly to rough and reckless.

"What next?" His voice was a hot whisper against her lips.

"Your call," she breathed.

Vangie found herself back in the pool, against her will.

"If you don't face your fear, you'll never swim confidently."

"How do you know?"

"I almost drowned once. Hop on."

Vangie straddled Wade's broad back, wrapping her legs around his waist and her arms around his neck. He trudged toward deeper waters.

"You're choking me," he said.

"Sorry..." Vangie's voice was childlike. She had never been this terrified in a public pool without a lifeguard on duty. Good thing Wade was a strong enough swimmer to withstand her weight. When they reached eleven feet, the spot that had nearly claimed her life, Vangie leaped from Wade's back and seized the pool's ledge.

"You'll never learn that way," Wade said, shaking his head like an instructor who had lost faith in his pupil. He dove under water and came up between her legs.

She squealed to be put down as she teetered on his shoulders.

"Sorry to have to do this..." He tossed her back into eleven feet of water. "Relax and tread! And don't panic!" he yelled above the water sloshing in her ears. If she'd had solid ground beneath her feet, Vangie would have dug in her heels out of anger. She fought her way back to the edge, determined to live just to spite him.

"Again." Wade sent her flying a second time.

And so it went, him tossing and her flying. After the fourth flight, Vangie altered her course, swimming confidently in the opposite direction. From the other end of the pool, Wade sounded off a whistle that echoed around the arena.

"Gold medal status!" he yelled. Within minutes, he had wrapped his arms around her waist. When he kissed her softly, her eyes were slow to open, her heart slow to revive.

The floodlights shut off and left them in virtual darkness.

"Time's up," Wade said to Vangie's disappointment.

Her first unofficial date with Wade ended under the arched entrance of Toyon Hall and not as Vangie had expected.

"Can I call you?" he said.

Vangie didn't hesitate to punch her new 650 area code number into Wade's cell phone, the one she'd bought to cover her tracks when she'd arrived in San Jose. She kept her 313 area code number exclusively for family and past affiliates.

Wade gave her another sweet, lingering kiss. "I'll see you around," he said before strolling off gracefully.

Vangie believed him this time.

Fourteen

He was back, knocking on our door again.

"I thought you'd like a ride to the hospital," Douglas said, smiling at me.

I didn't let the grime settle under my bare feet before I dashed off to change. I reached our room and pivoted back, my face on fire when I opened the front door I had accidentally slammed in his face.

"I'm still here."

I stepped back, keeping my eyes on my feet. Once he was inside, I took off again. For reasons unknown to me, I wanted to dress better, smell nicer, and look prettier around Douglas. I tore apart our room in search of something clean and nice to wear. I decided on jeans worn with Vangie's beige cable sweater and my comfortable boots, ignoring the worn flat soles. I hadn't touched the pretty bottle of perfume Vangie had bought me until this minute.

Douglas escorted me out of Cambridge with his hand on my back. This time, I didn't mind.

Mr. Reese was sitting on the front steps smoking a cigarette. I kept my eyes away from his. When we pulled away from the curb, I sneaked a peek at him. His menacing eyes caught me. I smiled, feeling safe and protected inside the warm interior of Douglas's nice car.

Running my hands across the soft leather seats, I stared through the side window, enjoying the cool air blowing softly against my face through the vents. Since West and Miss Coffee had left for Ohio, I hadn't had a whiff of fresh air or felt the sun against my skin.

"It's a beautiful day," Douglas said.

I smiled and nodded. Blossoming in ripe orange, grapefruit red, lemon yellow, and avocado-colored fall foliage, the day was delicious.

Douglas opened the center compartment filled with pieces of peppermint candy. "Help yourself."

I unwrapped one and popped it into my mouth, giving it something to do other than smile.

The velvety voice of Luther Vandross came through the radio, stealing my joy. He was singing about a house not being a home when no one was there. I missed Vangie. I missed my mother. I missed the home we once had, however broken it might have been.

A feel-good rap song lured me out of a cold, dark cave. I peeked at Douglas and smiled. He had changed the station for me.

"I like this jam, don't you?" He bobbed his head to the bass beat.

I laughed out loud and slapped my hand over my mouth. He had a way of bringing me joy with a touch, a word, a smile, and now a song, just when I needed it most.

By the time we arrived at the hospital I was happy again, until Douglas led me straight to Dr. Adler's office.

"Is this the moody one?" Dr. Adler asked.

"The quiet one," Douglas answered.

With my heart thudding in my ears and too busy being terrified my mother had really done it this time, I could barely comprehend the conversation. Why else would Douglas have brought me to see the doctor instead of her?

I sat next to Douglas, staring at a photograph of an entrancing island, wishing I was there and not here.

"Ang. I want you to hear this." Douglas placed his hand over mine to stop me from twiddling my thumbs. I was prepared to collapse should my worst fears come true again.

"Your mother is improving. I'm not promising immediate discharge, but she's less of a threat to herself with the medication adjustments."

Dr. Adler's announcement slowly sunk in. I pressed my hand to my mouth as tears rolled down my face. My heart felt light enough to fly away.

"You can thank Mr. Phillips. His visits have seemed to help."

"Call me Douglas, doc."

"Douglas here…" Dr. Adler rocked back in his oversized leather chair. "I understand your mother wasn't happy with the accommodations. Douglas is responsible for her room change, a nicer view on the fourth floor, she tells me. Her disposition has improved."

"Now do you feel better?" Douglas asked as we left the doctor's office.

I nodded. I had never been so happy.

In the activity room, I sat and visited with my mother. Around Douglas her mood took an upswing.

"I ain't always this bad looking," she said, fingering through her uncombed hair.

I took it as my cue to remove the hairbrush, comb, and hair lotion from my tote bag to pull her hair together.

My mother had lost her full smile to sadness, but her ashen lips stretched a bit and her eyes batted at Douglas.

Turning red, he said, "I'll give y'all some time." When Douglas left, he took my mother's good mood with him.

"You like the movies, don't you? Sure you do. There're some good ones out this week. Let's catch one," Douglas said during our ride back to Cambridge.

Concluding that Vangie had put him up to babysitting me again, I rejected the idea that he was asking me out on a real date. Still, I couldn't stop my smile from taking over my face. I wanted to do anything but go home alone.

We decided on a *Harry Potter* movie at a Megaplex. Each time Douglas's hand brushed across mine in the popcorn bag, I melted like butter inside. I wanted the warm, tingly feeling to last forever, this day with Douglas to never end.

After the movie, we went out to dinner again, this time for burgers and fries. It was the highlight of my day, listening to Douglas talk in his gentle voice that never seemed to tire of my silence. I hung on to his every word, my throat aching to speak my mind, my heart yearning to break my vow of silence. I opened my mouth, but nothing but air came out.

I stuffed my mouth with more French fries.

Fifteen

"This is Vangie, again. Can you please call me back?" Vangie said, after listening to another voice message from Thomas Jones promising to return calls promptly.

Alone in her dorm room, she sat upright on her bed, twisting her hair around her finger. She hadn't heard from Thomas Jones since her last call to him weeks ago. Thus far, the only movement in her savings account were her quarterly tuition, housing fees, books, and other fees, all of which were eating away at the balance.

Clarissa barged into the room without knocking, a bad habit of hers. "You're not going to class?"

Vangie slid her Detroit phone under the pillow. "I don't know."

"Are you sick?"

"I think I'm going to be."

"I'll check on you after Econ."

"You don't have to, Clarissa." Vangie just wanted to be left alone.

"That's what friends do for friends." Clarissa closed the door.

Feeling sick to her stomach, Vangie scooted off the bed. Within the next hour, she had showered, dressed, and walked briskly across campus. Low clouds that hadn't let up for days blocked the sun. Despite the chill, Vangie was sweating, her mind projecting the worst case scenario. An onslaught of what-ifs assailed her mind:

What if Jacob was wrong?
What if the company she'd invested in didn't bounce back?
What if Thomas Jones had run off with her money!

She caught the shuttle off campus and found a 7-Eleven where she bought the latest *Wall Street Journal,* the most reliable source for the stock market, according to Thomas Jones. She was so anxious for answers that she bumped into someone on her way out the door and realized, too late, she hadn't apologized. She thought of Angie and her mother, of the bills she had to pay and the years of tuition and housing that she couldn't possibly cover without declaring poverty status by her junior year, if not sooner.

Without peeking at the stock indexes, Vangie rolled up the paper and stuck it inside her backpack. With one hand wrapped anxiously around her Detroit phone in the front pocket of her sweater, she headed back to the shuttle stop, praying Thomas Jones would call with good news, or any news at all.

Bikers and skateboarders whizzed past Vangie as she walked along the bustling cobblestone pathways, lost in thought.

Clarissa shoved a cup in her hand when Vangie entered their dorm room. "Drink this," she ordered.

Vangie sniffed and frowned. "What is it?"

"It'll kill the flu in seconds."

And kill me too.

"I don't have the flu, Clarissa. I feel fine." Vangie dropped down onto the couch.

"Drink it!"

Luckily, Clarissa was in a hurry to leave and she didn't have to endure a taste of the remedy Clarissa had concocted. Once Clarissa was out of her hair, Vangie wanted to climb back into bed and sleep for days like her mother, but she refused to sink to such depths. Deciding to catch her next class, she left the dorm shortly after Clarissa.

Whatever the lecture, Vangie hadn't retained it. Her French class ended with her still going over her bank balance in her mind and weighing her limited options.

After class, she walked across campus, dreading every step. The building might as well have been a welfare office in Vangie's mind. Its marquee didn't help to loosen the tightness in her chest or reduce the nausea in her stomach. "Undergraduate Assistance and Financial Aid" it read in humongous block letters for all to see. Throwing the hood of her sweater over her head, Vangie walked briskly into the building.

At five o'clock in the morning, Vangie's Detroit phone vibrated beneath her pillow. She answered swiftly. It was Thomas Jones.

"I received your messages, young lady," he said in his slow, grandfatherly way, too slow for Vangie's brittle nerves.

She wanted to scream, "Why didn't you call me back!" With Clarissa a wall away, she refrained from speaking above a whisper. "Can you hold on, Mr. Jones?" Vangie hurried out of bed and into the hallway, finding privacy in the communal bathroom where she locked herself in a stall.

"Yes, I called you," she said.

"Have you been tracking your stock?"

"Isn't that your job?"

"And also yours, young lady. You should know that your stock had moderate gains."

"How moderate?" Vangie's heart thumped.

"Nothing to get excited over—less than point one percent. Growth is growth, but the key to successful investing is diversity. Putting all your eggs in one basket isn't how you get rich. If you give me permission to diversify…"

"Thank you, Mr. Jones. I'll be in touch."

In her room, Vangie dug in the trash for the *Wall Street Journal* she had tossed out the previous day. Checking the stock indexes, she found that Thomas Jones was telling the truth. She wasn't anywhere near rich, but she hadn't lost her shirt either.

To spend time with Wade and forget about her money problems, Vangie agreed to go to a campus Halloween party. Clarissa dressed as a sexy Cleopatra; dressing up as anyone or anything for Halloween didn't appeal to Vangie. In place of a rented costume, she wore a jet-black minidress that tailed sharply in the back, with black stiletto shoe boots, black nail polish, and ruby red lipstick— her version of a sultry witch, if anything.

It seemed half the student population had showed up at Tresidder Memorial Union. Not knowing how to act in these college settings and unable to find a chair, Vangie stood around in the multi-purpose room that was too small to accommodate the crowd. The dance requests kept coming, which she politely declined, preferring to save her first and last dance for Wade.

As the hours crawled by, the room and Vangie began to swelter. Wade had done it again, left her waiting and wondering. She felt stupid, like those girls back home chasing after boys who took the little they had and left them as poor as they'd found them. Frustrated, she headed for the dorm without Clarissa, who had latched on to a football player and disappeared.

"I'm going to marry you," Todd said, blocking her exit. His voice had lost its perfect modulation, slipping into a drunken slur. Wearing a Zorro mask and cape with jeans and combat boots, he lowered himself on one knee and placed one hand over his heart.

"I confess this to thee with the purest of hearts!"

"'Better too soon than a minute too late,'" Wade said, catching them both by surprise.

Todd wobbled to his feet. "As good luck would have it, coz, I was about to steal your girl."

"'The robbed who smiles steals something from the thief,'" Wade quoted with a sly grin.

"'Boldness, be my friend!'" Todd shouted back. They laughed like boys sharing a private joke. "The lady doth protest too much, me thinks." Todd swept his cape and took a dramatic bow before exiting. He was a theatre and performing arts major at Stanford, according to Clarissa, and a tried and true thespian.

With Todd out of the way, Vangie was left in the line of Wade's penetrating gaze. He looked hot and sexy in a black-screened tee, black jeans, and black Lacoste tennis shoes. When he stepped closer, her head whirled. They stood rapt in a staring contest.

Wade licked his Cupid's bow lips. "You look…" He pressed his lips together, keeping her in suspense.

Vangie smirked to maintain her composure. "I look what?"

"I was going to say you look beautiful, but you've had your share of compliments tonight. I don't like being superfluous."

"And I don't like waiting all night."

He smiled. "I'm sorry. I'm here now, if you still want me."

"I still want you," Vangie breathed.

With a finger behind his ear, Wade leaned closer. "Say that again. I didn't hear you?"

She fought her smile. "You heard me."

He laughed and grabbed her hand. "Let's go."

She felt a need to resist. "Go where?"

"To dinner. I know a great sushi bar."

Wade took the scenic route down the main thoroughfare, coasting under the parade of palm trees. Vangie had pictured him driving a *whip*, something sporty, foreign and high speed. Conversely, he drove a Range Rover Sport.

"Is this your first car?" she asked, curiously.

He sifted air though his greeted teeth and shook his head. "I totaled my first."

"What kind?"

"A Mustang GT. V-8. Black on black. Unparalleled. My mom sleeps better knowing I drive an army tank. What do you drive?"

"I don't," she admitted with shame. His question brought back humiliating memories of the only car they had owned—Russell's dirty, rusty piece of metal not fit for the road. After her first whiff of new leather in Gun's smoky-windowed Benz, she had vowed never to own a car less luxurious, if and when she could ever afford one.

"I forgot. Frosh aren't allowed cars on campus." He glanced at her and smiled.

Vangie smiled back. Wade had given her the perfect excuse for being carless.

The sushi bar was closed. Wade found a steakhouse open that catered to a swanky night crowd. They sat at a table for two at the edge of the boutique restaurant, the clamor of incessant chatter filling the silence between them while Wade devoured his pan-roasted beef tenderloin, and Vangie, determined to develop a cultured palate, enjoyed ragout burgundy snails with fennel panna cotta and parsley puree.

"What's your major?" Wade said.

She smacked her lips. "I told you."

"Stanford is saturated with general studies majors. What's your ultimate goal?"

"Law school," Vangie answered swiftly. It was a prestigious career she believed the rich found respectable. "You're studying to be an ophthalmologist, right?" Vangie said to keep Wade engaged in a conversation.

"Who told you? The town crier?"

Vangie couldn't help but laugh. She couldn't think of a better way to describe Clarissa.

"If I know Clarissa, she's told you everything about me. I want to know about you."

"What did Clarissa tell you?" she volleyed.

"Ninety-nine percent of what Clarissa tells me, I don't listen to," he said with finality.

"So, Clarissa's your cousin?" she pressed on.

"From what I've been told. Her mother was married to my uncle, once upon a time." He sipped his ice water, keeping a steady gaze on her. "Are we talking about Clarissa or you?"

"What about me?"

"I'm asking."

"I like vintage wine," she said, wearing a cunning smile. "I had my first glass when I was twelve."

Wade slanted his head and smirked. "Twelve?"

"My father didn't have a problem with my age, so why should you?" It was a lie, of course. She had, in fact, first tasted vintage wine at seventeen, the "father" in her life being Antonio Moretti. At twelve years old she had tried to poison herself to death with a bottle of cheap whiskey.

"I embarrassed you the other night," Wade said matter-of-factly.

Her face turned red. "I don't get embarrassed."

"I must know you better than you know yourself. Did you hate me."

Vangie fought another smile. "No."

I should've.

"Blame your roomie. Clarissa has a bad habit of setting me up with any girl she thinks is my equal. You could say I've had my share of gold diggers."

Oh…

She swallowed. "Am I your equal?" Her voice quivered slightly.

Wade studied her pensively. "So far, you're only the second to meet the mark."

Vangie would've become lost in his piercing eyes if her mind wasn't playing back Wade's last comment.

If I'm the second, who's the first?

"Not to offend you, but I haven't dated a frosh since I was a nerdy freshman," he continued.

"Should I feel lucky?" She couldn't stop smiling.

Wade leaned back in his chair, putting his eyes at a safe distance from hers. "If I'm lucky, you'll come to the house." His gaze turned steamy, sending a rash of heat through her body.

G iven the way Wade fussed over the grounds, Vangie wondered if the Fitzgerald family owned the four-story luxury building looking down on the marina, chimneys crowning the rooftop of every sand-colored, Italian-style building.

"Time for new management." He picked a wadded piece of paper off the travertine floor in the luxuriously furnished lobby and tossed it in the trashcan as they entered the elevator.

On the fourth floor, they walked down a short, private corridor, entering a unit with double doors.

"I'll be right back," Wade said. He disappeared in a hurry down a hallway.

Filled with anxiety that, until meeting Wade, only her mother could provoke in her, Vangie vacillated between sitting and standing. Her legs carried her across the marble floors to the brown crushed velvet sectional. She wondered which game Wade was playing tonight. Or had the game ended on their first date, when she'd given in to his kiss as if she hadn't a spine in her body?

"Sorry to keep you waiting." He picked up a small remote control from the coffee table and aimed it at the wireless IPod speaker system. New Age music played softly as he proceeded to the kitchen.

Vangie took in the spacious living room with a quick, indifferent eye. It had a sleek, modern, European feel—glass, mahogany, and stainless steel, a wall of windows and soft track lighting. A dream residence for a poor college student like her.

"For you. Reconciliation for our blind date. No ID required," Wade said, catching her chewing on her gel nail. He handed her a Champaign flute filled with bubbly white liquid.

Vangie sipped. "Doesn't taste like vintage wine." She raised her eyes to him and smiled sheepishly.

"Only a three-hundred-dollar bottle of Bollinger," he said, as though she had mocked his attempt to make up for their night at Cappellini's. "It is, or was, Todd's. He keeps it on reserve for special nights." Wade's bold gaze suggested that tonight was "special." He sat next to her, close enough to make her stomach dip from his slightest touch.

"Thank you," she breathed. "Speaking of Todd, when did I become your girl?"

"My what?" His voice shrieked.

She laughed. "The girl Todd plans to steal from you."

"Oh. That." He snapped open bottled water and chugged. "Todd has a never-ending love of rivalry. He swears I stole his girl back in the stone ages. I do have my boundaries. She got at me first."

"You didn't deny it."

"I can accuse you of the same."

"I've never been anyone's girl," Vangie said frankly. She had been Antonio's mistress, Douglas's fantasy, and Jacob's on-call play toy. Now all she wanted was to be Wade's girl.

"Never?" Wade's eyes cast doubt. "Are you a virgin?"

In her frozen state, the music thumped in the background as if its sole purpose for playing was to fill awkward moments of silence.

"Do you want to find out?" It was her only comeback.

Wade's laugh sounded nervous. "You're pretty ballsy for a frosh. What's your rush?"

"I'm not in a rush. Are you scared?"

"That's real funny." Fire flickered in his eyes. "But okay. Let's find out."

Vangie's alter ego jumped into the driver's seat. The edges of her mouth curled, her brazen stare warning him to be careful who he invited into his bed. She had entertained men old enough to be his uncle.

She sashayed into the hallway. There were two doors on each end, and what appeared to be a study and a bathroom in the middle.

"Take a left," Wade said from behind her.

Vangie entered a room the size of a master suite. Focused on one objective—snaring Wade Fitzgerald IV—she saw only the king-sized, low post bed that sat between two windows dressed in white shutters. Vangie prowled to his bed and struck a seductive pose on the black suede comforter thrown carelessly over black-and-white-striped sheets.

The battleground was set.

"Are you getting in?" she said.

"I'm on the blocks, ready to dive."

Vangie laughed when Wade stripped down to his boxer shorts and dived onto the bed. Lying next to her, face to face, he lifted his chiseled chin and stared down his nose at her. "Who'd you say was scared?" With one hand palming her butt, he thrust her forward so she felt the length of him.

"You," Vangie muttered, shrinking behind her alter ego. She was defenseless to Wade's confident gaze.

"We'll see." His eyes held hers intensely, his lips a whisper from hers, resisting but taunting her with his self-satisfied grin as he slid his hand under her dress and the side of her panties. His touch was electrifying—his finger exploratory, pushing and probing gently for effect.

Wade's eyes smiled, as if to say, "Can you hang, frosh?" Vangie honestly worried she couldn't. Before Wade, her reaction to any form of intercourse had always been rehearsed—an act put on for someone else's pleasure and never her own. This was no act. She couldn't hold back the ocean waves, which peaked at her core and exploded against the inner walls between her thighs. Sounds new and foreign to her ears lurched from her throat.

Wade peeled off her dress. His tongue, having unobstructed access to her breasts, teased and tormented them, one by one. Before she could regain control of her body and mind, Wade had trapped her beneath his muscular frame, spreading her legs wide with his strong knees. Quick with protection, he slipped it on and drove into her. Blinding waves of ecstasy coursed through her body instantaneously. Overcome with emotion, his name slid off her tongue like wet ice.

Wade's eyes glazed over. "Say it again," he breathed.

Vangie repeated his name in a pleading groan. He kissed her with intense concentration, holding her on the edge of insanity as he shifted from slow and steady to fast and furious. She could feel him building toward a powerful release, reaching deeper and deeper inside of her, somewhere untouched, unguarded, and undamaged. Every muscle in her body clinched and quacked around him. She held on to him tightly, giving into Wade's power over her with sweet surrender.

For some time, they basked in each other's warmth, their breaths keeping time with their pounding hearts as Vangie gazed into Wade's eyes and he grinned down at her.

"What's my name?" he said

Vangie fought her own smile. "I forgot."

"You'll never forget."

"I already have."

"You can let go of me now."

Her arms and legs dropped uselessly on the bed.

They laughed together.

"I'm dripping with sweat." Wade headed for the bathroom.

Vangie twirled across the bed like a child rolling down a grassy hill. When had she felt so young and so innocent? She landed on her stomach and floated on a bed of black and white clouds. She couldn't believe Wade had won the battle—missionary style!

Having retrieved the bottle of Bollinger from the living room, along with her flute and a bottle of water for himself, Wade returned to bed. He poured a generous amount of champagne, handed her the flute, and gave her a sweet peck on the lips.

"Congratulations."

"Did I win something?" She grinned beside herself.

Wade's beautiful smile was telling. She had won the grandest prize of all.

Him.

"Let's say you are a viable candidate. You'd have to pass my litmus test first." Wade sat up in bed and turned on the lamp light.

Vangie made a lazy attempt to sit up. "How long is this test?"

"I'll make it easy for you. Tell me everything there is to know about you that I don't already know."

She swallowed Champaign. "That wasn't a question," she said coolly.

"Litmus tests aren't infallible." Wade gave her a self-indulgent grin; and he seemed to be enjoying this test he was putting her through. "This is a timed test. The clock is ticking," he teased.

He didn't have to remind her. She heard the ticking of her own heartbeat. There wasn't another man in the world with whom she wished to share her deepest, darkest secrets as she had shared with her twin. If only she could lay her cards on the table. Be it truth or lie, she would lose Wade before she had him, the only man she desired above her own ambitions.

Vangie finished her Champaign, set the glass aside, and fluffed out the pillow behind her back, stalling for time as the wheels of her inventive mind churned.

Here goes nothing...

The story had been depicted countless times in the movies, on television, and in novels. The heroine was always rich and beautiful, living luxuriously on a limitless trust fund. Her life consisted of impulsive shopping sprees and private schooling, with nannies and servants on hand to substitute for her busy, traveling parents.

Wade looked engrossed in her imaginary life story. She hadn't told him the story of the rich, beautiful heroine she'd had in mind. Instead, she'd painted a picture of a life she hoped Wade would find acceptable for his "girl."

Until a few years ago, the Vangie of her story had known little about her biological father, a Tom Blanchard, who had amassed his wealth from Canadian oil. Tom had met her mother while on business in Birmingham, a small Michigan town. Vangie was twelve years old when she first met Tom Blanchard, who since had been trying to make up for his absence in her life.

The story had taken on a life of its own, as if she were speaking in the third person, breathing life into a fictional character.

"Our lives aren't parallel, but we do have a few shared experiences. How old were you when your mother died?" His voice was full of compassion as if he understood the agony of losing a mother.

Vangie hugged her knees. "Twelve." Though the mother she knew and loved had died figuratively in her mind when she was around that age, she couldn't conjure up enough frustration and anger toward her mother not to feel awful for writing Annette's death certificate. She held her breath and choked back tears, fearing she might have to write her mother's obituary next.

Wade laid a comforting arm around her shoulders. "Where'd you live?" he asked softly.

"With my grandmother, until she died."

"That's rough. No brothers or sisters?"

Vangie shook her head slowly, disintegrating inside.

"Look at me."

She hugged her knees tighter. "Why?"

"So I can see your eyes," Wade said tenderly.

Precisely why she didn't want to face him. There were tears there she didn't want him to see. How could she kill off her own twin? Her own mother? On the other hand, how could she keep up pretenses without erasing her past?

Wade lifted her chin with his finger and turned her face his way.

Doing her best to lighten the moment, Vangie smiled thinly. "What do you see?"

He gently wiped a teardrop away. "A beautiful pair of globular organs."

Wade continued to stare into her eyes, reminding her of all she wanted to forget about herself. Fearing he might see through her façade, she almost tore her gaze from his.

"What more should I know about you?" she said.

"I'd hate to bore you. I'm a classic geek. By the third grade, I decided to become a doctor and never veered off course."

She laughed, loosening the knot in her stomach. "Stop lying."

"Ask Todd. He'll tell you."

"Did I tell you I've declared a new major?"

"What is it?"

She smiled coyly. "You."

"I'm a hard study, I've been told."

"I graduated at the top of my high school class," she said.

Wade brushed his thumb over the small, delicate mole just above her right cheekbone. "That's a dangerous combo, intelligence and beauty…and you are beautiful." Eyes holding hers warmly, he leaned in and kissed her voraciously.

He came out of his greedy kiss slowly, as if he didn't want to stop. "I like you."

"I like you too." She sounded oddly young and inexperienced to her own ears.

"You're staying over, right?" he asked tentatively.

Smiling, Vangie snuggled under Wade for the night.

The next day she found Wade gone and Todd sitting on the bed, his eyes poring over her nude body like the morning sun.

"Money trumps good looks, I always say."

Vangie registered anger in his modulated tone. She sat up, pulling the sheet up with her. "I have money."

"That's right. Daddy's rich."

No comment.

"What's his name again?"

Vangie froze, hoping Todd couldn't read between the worry lines on her forehead.

He snapped his fingers. "Tom Blanchard? Canadian. Fortune 500." He smiled as if expecting her praise for his sharp memory. Honestly, she wished Todd's memory hadn't served him so well.

He continued to gawk at her. "'She is beautiful, and therefore to be wooed; she is a woman, therefore to be won...'" he quoted.

Vangie didn't know what to say and so opted not to say anything. There had never been a competition between Todd and Wade. Wade had her at first sight.

"I accept my defeat, honorably." Before Todd left the room, he turned back and said, "Who's Angie?"

Vangie blinked and took a calming breath. "Why?" she asked casually.

"You called out her name in your sleep. Must've been some nightmare."

When Todd left the room, Vangie speculated about the dream she had no recollection of and wondered how long Todd had watched her sleep.

Seventeen

C hristmas called me to take hold of its peace, joy, and good-will, but it was too quick, slipping from my hands like a kite carried off by a gust of wind. As fast as the wind blew, I ran, determined to catch it. Swiftly, the wind was at my back, shoving me violently toward the edge of earth. I pushed against it, but the force was stronger than my will to resist. I was plunged into darkness, falling, whirling, and twirling endlessly, lost in space.

My eyes popped open. It was only a dream. I sighed out of relief.

Happy that the joy of Christmas hadn't forsaken me, I hustled out of bed and over to the window. I had hoped for a white Christmas this year, but from the look of it, I might have to settle for gray clouds and light snow showers. I blew on my hands and hurried into the living room to turn up the heat.

Sir Duke scampered ahead of me, making me laugh. Deja couldn't stop West from giving him to me as an early Christmas gift. Having Sir Duke and Douglas to keep me company had made the holidays bearable. I'd been so lonely that waking up on Christmas to an empty house would've killed me, sure enough.

The Christmas tree's pine scent had taken over the living room, its freshness opening my lungs. I stopped to admire the colorful, blinking lights that Douglas and I had strung on it last night. If not for Douglas, we wouldn't have a tree. He surprised me with the tallest, fullest Douglas fir he could find.

I moved away from the tree to where Douglas was sleeping on the couch. Out of the many nights we had spent together, he had never once tried anything, saying a polite goodnight each time before leaving. Last night, after we decorated the tree, I had lured him to stay longer with a large slice of my pecan pie and a bowl of vanilla ice cream, which had a way of coating the stomach and drowsing the brain like warm milk. He had nodded off on the couch. It was manipulative of me.

I know.

I watched him a long while, tempted to lean over and kiss his honey-brown lips. Terrified I just might, I dashed off before he caught me stalking him.

I showered and dressed in a pullover sweater paired with my old jeans and new red Christmas footies I bought at the dollar store and headed to the kitchen. After preheating the oven, I started with the basic recipe, sifting together flour, baking powder, sugar, and baking soda into a large plastic bowl. After adding chunks of butter and buttermilk, I relished its cool, damp doughiness between my fingers and the palms of my hands, kneading, rolling, and gently patting as I prepared it for a hot oven where it would rise into something sweet and flaky. I was light on my feet, my trained hands unhurried.

My recipe wasn't complete without cheddar cheese. Sliding the baking pan into the oven, I dreamed of one day having an oven that heated above 250 degrees and didn't have a broken handle, a stovetop with four working burners and chef's knives that sliced into meat like butter. I didn't have to wish for new pots and pans. Douglas had bought me a beautiful stainless steel set. He had bought me many nice, new things and had taught me things I'd never dreamed I could do.

When Douglas opened his eyes, breakfast was ready. I greeted him with a smile, twiddling my fingers behind my back as I stood over him. If only I could say good morning and ask him if he slept well, if he was warm enough or too cold. At times, I'd come close to saying something funny or thought provoking as I'd always done with Vangie, but words wouldn't come.

His smile was warm and welcoming. "I must've fallen asleep last night." He scratched his head as he sat up, looking confused. "Have you seen my car keys, Angie?" He stood and patted the front pocket of his jeans.

I rushed to my antique desk and opened the middle drawer where I'd hidden his keys last night. Sullenly, I handed them over.

"Thank you."

Relieved he wasn't mad at me, I smiled.

"Something's smelling good."

I dashed to the kitchen, grabbed a plate, piled it with food, and presented it to him.

"Eggs, bacon, *and* biscuits. I'll take it!" Douglas chuckled. "Mind if I clean up first?"

I turned red and nodded. After placing the plate in the microwave, I handed Douglas a set of Vangie's plush hotel towels from her hope chest and one of the spare toothbrushes we kept for the times when my mother's guests borrowed ours.

"You're sweet, Angie." He pinched my nose like I was a cute kid, not the beautiful, desirable young woman I longed to be in his eyes.

While Douglas cleaned up, I waited quietly by the bathroom door, listening to the shower run. The door suddenly flew open before I could dash away.

"Good morning. Again," he said with a laugh on his lips. He looked refreshed and smelled of Irish Spring. Bare chested, he held the towel around his waist with one hand and a dead rat by its tail with the other.

I didn't know if I was more shocked by the rat or seeing Douglas half naked. I hated rats. They squeezed their way through everything—holes in the wall, cracks, and pipes. The roaches too. Vangie and I had learned to live with them, much like our unwanted houseguests.

"I found this hiding behind the toilet. You gotta trash bag?"

I dashed off to find a trash bag.

We sat across from each other at the dining table. Douglas sat in one of the coordinating chairs that went with the fancy wood table Vangie had surprised our mother with. I sat in the metal one that replaced a nice one after it lost a leg and arm during a party. I couldn't wait for him to taste my buttermilk biscuits.

"The plate with the most food must have my name on it." He smiled broadly.

My eyes followed the fork from his plate to his honey-brown lips each time he took a bite.

He caught me staring at him.

"I can't believe you made these. You're a pretty good cook. The best I've ever met." He stuffed his mouth with another biscuit.

I smiled, wanting to believe him.

"Your twin's coming home next week. Are you excited?"

I nodded.

Douglas hadn't stopped talking about Vangie after she'd called to say she might be home for Christmas. I remembered his disappointment when Vangie had never showed up on Thanksgiving Day. I'd thought he might cry. He'd hung around the apartment like one of my mother's guests hoping for a good time. I did my best to show him one, cooking a small turkey dinner for the two of us. It made me wonder about his life outside of babysitting me.

Where does he live?

Does he have friends?

Does he have a girlfriend?

I thought of Vangie. He had never used the word *love*. In fact, he'd done the opposite, calling their friendship "purely platonic" and referring to Vangie as his "mentee," but his eyes couldn't lie. Whatever love Douglas had for Vangie, I prayed that the love I'd poured into his breakfast—a kiss of salt added to light and fluffy eggs, a hug of extra butter melted into my buttermilk biscuits, a caress of oil fried into crispy bacon—would find its way into Douglas's heart for me.

"That was delicious, Angie. Thank you." Taking a final gulp of coffee, Douglas stood. "Do you need anything else from the store before I go?"

Oh!

I hurried off and returned promptly with my latest grocery list.

"More eggs, milk, bread, and peanut butter? Are you feeding a small army I don't know about?" He chuckled.

I dropped my head, wanting to turn to dust on the floor and blow away. The refrigerator and cabinets looked like I'd robbed a grocery store. I wasn't a glutton. Cooking just gave me a sense of accomplishment, food a sense of comfort and security—the acidity of citrus, the freshness of bread, the sweetness of chocolate, the sharpness of cheese, the creaminess of butter, the loveliness of a frosted cake, the tenderness of marinated meat... I could go on.

What I couldn't eat alone, I shared with West and Deja; times hadn't been easy with Miss Coffee gone. I had shared meals with Deja and West more times than a few and had given West money when he had none.

I peeked up at Douglas and grinned guiltily.

He laughed, deep and throaty, like I was the funniest person alive, and wrapped me in his cuddly arms. "I'll be back." He kissed the top of my head and I tingled down to my toes. Without thinking, I threw my arms around his neck and laid my head on his puffy chest, wanting to fall to my knees and beg him to stay. Instead, I dropped my arms to my sides and took a quick step back, keeping my eyes on my feet.

Douglas placed a finger under my chin and drew my stubborn eyes upward. I stared into his kind eyes and thought I might love him.

He pulled me into his arms. "Angie. Angie," he breathed. When he kissed me, every red blood cell in my body drained of oxygen. My lips parted magically and found delight in his tongue. Warm sensations traveled from my taste buds downward, bringing an itch between my legs.

I tried not to tremble as he undressed me, and even when he lowered me onto the couch like I was delicate piece of crystal. The couch rocked from left to right when he fit his broad body on top of mine. He kissed me again and I became the fruit of the earth, mushy and moist inside.

The way Douglas found my itch and knew just how to scratch it was magical too. The more he scratched, the more I itched. I knew we were having sex, but it wasn't the kind of sex that made people hate more than love, the kind that killed off happiness and drove away joy.

This kind of sex was kind and gentle.

I wanted to go on itching and scratching with Douglas forever, but he froze as if a cramp had caught him by the leg then collapsed on top of me. I found his eyes that he'd hidden from mine throughout our magical experience and saw a look I'd never seen before—half happy, half terrified. I didn't know which to believe, but it felt as though we had committed a cardinal sin.

Douglas jumped up and put on his pants. I did the same.

"I'm sorry, Angie. That should never have happened." He zipped up quickly. "I didn't hurt you, did I? I'd never hurt you. Never."

I shook my head, wanting to tell him that he had brought me Christmas joy in a rainbow of bright, beautiful colors, but the door slammed behind Douglas before I could say anything.

I ran to my room, threw myself on our bed, and cried.

Eighteen

With three days left before winter break, Vangie was looking forward to spending every minute possible with Wade. His school and work schedule, not to mention his swim meets, made their days together few and too far between.

It was early evening, the moon lightly sketched against the gray sky. During the drive to Wade's place, he stared broodingly ahead. His mind was likely on his organic chemistry final tomorrow. Vangie's mind was on him. A girl could learn a lot from majoring in the guy she found herself falling head over heels in love with, mostly those idiosyncrasies she would learn either to love or to hate. There was little about Wade Fitzgerald that she didn't love: his sexy, playful edge that peeked out from behind his noble face; his charming, disarming qualities; how beautiful he made her feel, not outwardly, but inwardly.

"What's wrong?" Wade said, catching her studying him.

She smiled coyly. "Everything's perfect."

As soon as they walked into Wade's condo, Todd emerged from the kitchen.

"Just in time for blue agave! One hundred percent authentic, bro." Todd held up a bottle of tequila. He was shoeless, shirtless, and wearing knee-length plaid shorts, his face glistening as if he had worked up a good sweat.

"Did you finish strong?" Wade asked, smiling at his best friend.

"Like a scholar."

"Take a shot for me. I'm in a crunch." Wade never broke stride.

Vangie followed Wade, hating the feel of Todd's jade eyes, which watched her clandestinely whenever she came around. When Wade turned the corner into the hallway, Todd grabbed her by the hand and pulled her close.

"Let's make a baby," he said. Of course, Wade likely didn't hear Todd's disgusting remark.

Vangie yanked her hand away from Todd's and bumped into Todd's workout partner in the hallway, a junior named Becca who had slunk out of Todd's bedroom in a tank-top and panties, her long brown hair mussed, her cream-colored skin flushed with an after-sex glow.

"Hey, Vangie." Becca sauntered brazenly toward the bathroom.

"Hi." Quickly entering Wade's room, Vangie shut the door behind her.

"Do you need anything?" Wade asked. He had already powered up his laptop.

"A shower." Vangie found her travel bag, which Wade had haphazardly dropped on the floor along with her backpack.

When Todd barged into the room while she was undressing, Wade jerked his head in her direction as if worried Todd had seen her naked.

Too late.

"Bro! What happened to the two-knock rule?" Wade barked.

"Forgive my negligence, coz." Todd bowed out of the room, his eyes never leaving her breasts. Two rapid knocks later and Todd was back.

Vangie, by this time, had made it to the bathroom where she listened in on Wade and Todd's conversation behind the locked door.

"You can't let me go this one alone. This may be my last hurrah," Todd whined.

"Did you forget about Saturday night? At the club? I'll be there in full support of the celebration. But tonight, bro, I can't afford the hangover."

"A little TQ improves performance, haven't you heard?" Wade laughed.

By the time Vangie finished showering, Todd had left the room and had taken Wade with him, undermining her plan to spend every minute alone with Wade before Christmas break.

Wearing a babydoll sundress in rainbow pastels, she ambled down the hallway toward the choppy rhythm of reggae. The other three had gathered around the bar and were gulping back shots of tequila with salt and lime on the count of three. Avoiding the bar and Todd altogether, Vangie sat down on the sectional and watched from a distance.

Wade soon sauntered over. "Welcome to the party," he said, deadpan. He slouched down so his head rested on her shoulder and turned his eyes up. "What's that you're wearing? Love potion?" He nibbled on her neck, making her laugh and shiver. She ached for Wade in private places and was beginning to hate Todd.

"Your ticket to admission," Todd said, interrupting their good time. He handed her a shot glass of tequila and sat too close for her comfort. Becca, who now wore Daisy Dukes and a camisole, found a seat next to Todd, drawing her knees up so she sat in a squat.

Some party.

They sat around listening to Todd brag about his career plans. Having completed his degree requirements, he was certain he'd be accepted to Juilliard's graduate historical performance program in New York.

Vangie couldn't be happier to help send Todd off to the Big Apple.

"What say you about the future?" Todd stared at her, looking more interested in her body than he was in her future.

Smiling frostily, Vangie raised the shot glass to her lips. Todd couldn't bait her that easily, only to slip in one of his snide sonnets.

"Her future will be bright, if I have anything to do with it." Wade emphasized his point by giving her a juicy kiss.

Vangie had to bite her lip not to laugh in Todd's red face.

"What's a party without a dance?" Todd leaped up and grabbed Becca's hand, pulling her onto the open floor. At the press of a button, a rap song replaced reggae on the hi-tech system and the base sound of a throwback rap song pulsed from tiny speakers.

"You mind, my friend?" Todd asked Wade as he grabbed Vangie's hand.

"It's your night, bro. She's all yours." Wade lifted his shot glass.

Vangie stared at Wade. *Are you crazy or drunk?*

Before Vangie could object, Todd had forced her off the sectional.

"Show me how low you can go, Vangie," he said, bent back in some kind of weird limbo, thrusting his pelvis forward this way and that.

"Todd, are you trying to invoke a girl-on-girl dirty dance off?" Rebecca looked intrigued with the idea.

"If the spirits moves you." Todd grinned.

Becca started pumping her pelvis like a video vixen.

"Yeah, baby! Pop it!" Todd egged her on.

Wade laughed. "My girl doesn't get low, bro!"

Vangie's instinct was to knee Todd between his spread legs, but something came over her—maybe the tequila or her alter ego. She turned away from Todd and Becca and walked seductively over to Wade. Standing before him, her back arched, legs spread, and hands on her hips, she descended toward the floor in a hypnotic grind, balancing on the balls of her bare feet. When she couldn't go any lower, she wound back up in the same hypnotic motion. Turning her butt to Wade, Vangie jiggled it, slapped it, and dropped it.

When she faced Wade again, he was entranced; his sex-crazed eyes locked with hers. Vangie straddled his lap and proceeded to ride him wildly.

"I hate to kill a good party, but um…this is too good to resist." Wade cupped her butt so she sat in his large hands, her legs wrapped around his waistline, her arms around his neck.

Ignoring Todd's mocking applause, she giggled girlishly as Wade carried her away.

"Give the lady a stripper pole. She's good!" Todd called after them.

They stumbled backward and dropped onto Wade's bed, their tongues entangled as they fought to undress one another. In the throes of passion, Vangie glimpsed Todd's jade-colored eyes; or maybe she had only imagined Todd standing in the hallway, watching them clandestinely.

"You're driving me crazy," Wade said.

"You drive me crazier." Simply gazing into Wade's eyes made Vangie lose control. Wade leaned back on the bed and pulled her atop of him. Their night together had only just begun, while the party in the next room was over.

Good riddance, Todd Bryant.

"Are you going to tell me your plans for Christmas or make me ask you again?"

Vangie blinked, realizing she had forgotten one of her chief rules—never have sex with the lights on. She had no way of hiding her angst with the ceiling light so bright and revealing.

"What're your plans?"

"I hate that, Van." He climbed into his boxer shorts.

"What?"

"When you counter-question me. It's a bad habit and, frankly, evasive."

Clearly, counter questions didn't work as well on His Highness as they'd worked on Angie. "I'll leave when you leave," she said, trying another tactic. It was the talk of the campus: *When are you leaving? What are you doing for Christmas?* In contrast to most students, Vangie wasn't excited about the prospect of going home for Christmas.

"To where, Canada or Michigan?" Wade pressed.

Vangie hopped out of bed. "Does it matter?" She swiped up her panties from the floor and took off toward the bathroom.

"It'd be nice to know where my girl will be for the next three weeks." Wade sounded offended. "I might want to surprise her for Christmas."

She closed the door, practically in his face. "Surprise me how?" she called out.

"Hence the word surprise! What's your address?"

Before leaving the bathroom, Vangie took a deep breath to slow her heartbeat and opened the door to Wade's dazzling smile.

"I couldn't wait to give it to you," he said.

Vangie stared at him and then at the velvet jewelry box he had placed in her hand.

"Are you going to open it or just stare at?"

Heart arrested, Vangie lifted the lid to the box and felt a tug at her heartstrings. Antonio had gifted her diamonds and pearls, Jacob had shown her the world, and Douglas had given her the latest and greatest laptop computer... And yet, Wade's gift—a platinum diamond double heart-shaped pendant necklace—meant more to her than all the others combined. She wished she could appreciate his generosity.

"Thank you." She gave him an obligatory kiss on the cheek and crossed the room. Sitting on her knees, Vangie stuffed the gift inside her travel bag and searched frantically for a hair tie to evade Wade's pestering staring.

"Is it too soon for a gift exchange?" He sounded crushed and her heart felt his pain.

"I love it. It's beautiful."

"I'm not feeling the love."

Vangie sat back on her heels and sighed. "I hate Christmas, okay Wade."

Wade stared at her as if she was the devil incarnate. "Why would anyone hate Christmas?"

"Don't you have to study?" Vangie said exasperatedly. She pulled a tank top over her head, walked over to the bed, and slumped back against the headboard.

"I want to hear your reason for hating Christmas." He sat on the bed and gawked at her.

"I don't have one."

"There's a reason for everything."

"Generally, I hate it."

"I think I know why..."

"I'm meeting my father in Costa Rica over the break," Vangie blurted out before Wade could assume her mother had died on Christmas day or something. She fastened her hair into a ponytail, unable to meet his eyes.

"Is he sending his Learjet?" he mocked.

No comment.

It wasn't her phantom father who had invited her to Costa Rica during the holidays; it was Ronnie Livingston, who hadn't stopped calling since she left Florida.

Wade watched her for a few very uncomfortable seconds. "What exactly does your dad do that he can afford to send his jet on a whim?"

"What about your dad?"

"My dad?" Wade smiled fondly. "He's a remarkable man and a great father. I can't tell you more."

"You sound proud."

Wade smirked. "Why do I get the feeling you're hiding something from me? You dodged my question for a reason."

"I didn't dodge it."

"More proof!" Wade said, pointing a finger. "Your eyes shifted again."

Vangie chuckled nervously. "I thought you knew me better than I know myself."

Wade meditated on her. "Sometimes...but sometimes you're like a complicated theorem I haven't solved."

"Well, if you knew me, you'd know I don't talk much."

My twin does all the talking.

"In that case, we'll get along," Wade said.

Gasping melodramatically, Vangie took a mock swing at Wade. He blocked her fists with each failed punch

"You call that a jab?" He wrestled her, tickling her until she couldn't catch her breath from laughing.

"Wade! Stop!" He caught her before she tumbled to the floor and pulled her back onto the bed. Her ponytail dangled over the side of the bed as she lay on her back staring up at Wade.

"I'm sorry. Did you hit your head?" He stroked her hair and kissed her on the forehead.

Vangie got lost in Wade's piercing eyes. They fell into a deep kiss. Wade left her lips behind and slithered toward her opened legs, stopping to trace the lines and angles of her twin tattoo with his finger.

"The suspense of killing me. What does it symbolize?"

Heart already thumping, Vangie stared down at Wade and smiled covertly. "It's an ancient Chinese secret."

He raised up on his knees and hovered over her on all fours. "Let me in on the secret?"

She almost made the big mistake of shifting her eyes again. "Why do you want to know so bad?"

"I want to know everything about you. Is that a problem?"

"It stands for twins. Forever," Vangie blurted out.

Wade held a neutral expression. "You have a twin?"

"Had."

Don't cry. Don't cry. Don't cry.

"What happened to her?"

Vangie couldn't bring herself to speak another blatant lie. She couldn't speak, at all.

"Did she die at birth?"

Vangie went along with his presumption, nodding and fighting back tears.

A pause. A long stare.

"That's something I should've known about you." He pecked her lips. "Thanks for telling me." Wade suddenly sat up just in time for Vangie to wipe away a tear. "You're a bad influence. I need to get up."

She knew what that meant: back to the books. Thankfully.

At 1:00 A.M., Vangie decided she had studied long enough.

While Wade sat in an armchair sipping an energy drink, his head buried in an intimidating textbook, she closed her eyes and dosed off.

"Get up! Let's go!" Annette whispers.

Her eyes blink open, trying to adjust to the pitch-black motel room. She sits up and rubs her eyes awake with small fists. She can hear the large trash bag rustling as Annette stuffs it with their few possessions. Immediately grasping the situation, she shakes Angie awake.

Quiet as church mice, she and Angie crawl around in the dark gathering their clothes from the floor. There is no time for bathing, combing hair, or brushing teeth. They'd be lucky if they could leave with their jackets. Annette is already yanking on her arm before she can find her second shoe. She puts up a quiet fight, rearing to kick and scream. Those shoes are the nicest pair she owns. If she leaves one behind, she won't get another pair to replace it. Maybe ever.

Annette yanks her again, so close she can smell yesterday's alcohol on her mother's breath. "You want to put me in jail?" Annette barks.

She shakes her head, her cheeks bloated as she fights back her sobs.

A bang on the door stills them all. "Management! Open up!" The door-knob jiggles and turns. Annette has jammed a chair underneath it.

With her right foot still shoeless, Annette ushers her through the sliding glass door and into the night. The bright lights of the motel fade behind them as Annette's high heel boots clack briskly against the pavement. They run a good distance before Annette stops. By now, her foot is soaked with snow.

"Here," Angie says with a big smile, holding up her missing shoe.

"You happy now?" Annette twists the shoe onto her half frozen foot.

"Nooooo!" It is the only word in her vocabulary that could adequately express just how unhappy she is. Tears rain down her face.

"You're a little sourpuss, girl. Ain't never happy about nothing." Annette laughs and turns to Angie, her ally. "Are you happy, baby?" she asks Angie.

Angie nods, eager to please their mother.

Annette washes the tears and snot from her face with a heavy hand. "Crying over a two-dollar pair of shoes like they glass slippers. Grab your sister's hand."

Holding hands, she and Angie follow Annette like baby ducks. Having nowhere to go or any place to sleep for the night, they walk until the tips of her fingers and toes burn from numbness. She wants to cry but knows better. White icicles and strings of colorful lights hang from rooftops, doors, and windows, making the dark night less frightening. Despite her fear, she can feel merriment in the air and somehow knows the night is special.

When Annette comes upon a dark and eerie gas station, she leads them behind the building and finds a way to unlock the bathroom door. "Lay down, don't move, and don't make a sound," Annette orders.

She and Angie do as they are told, curling atop the bloated trash bags.

Annette cleans herself up and makes herself over in the mirror until she is as beautiful as a porcelain doll with rosy cheeks and maroon lips.

"Don't be acting all scared over nothing, okay, babies. I won't be but a minute." Annette pulls a steak knife from her purse and hands it to her. "You know what to do if somebody walk up in here."

She nods.

Annette gives them each a kiss and covers them with the blankets she has stolen from the motel room. The door shuts behind her and the light magically clicks off.

"I'm scared," Angie cries.

She's scared too but tries to be brave for Angie. "You can't be scared," she warns her twin.

Angie cries herself to sleep. She stares into darkness, her eyes afraid to close as she holds firmly to the knife, waiting and watching.

Daylight awakens them when the door opens. "I told you I had twins. They beautiful, ain't they? Sleep like little koala bears," Annette says.

"What you plan on doing with 'em?" the man says.

Annette shoves him like he is her long-lost brother. "Where I go my babies go or I ain't going!"

The man bends over, rests his fat hands on his fat knees, and stares down at them with eyes that look like shiny red marbles. "Know who I am?" he asks with a crooked smile.

Angie shakes her head slowly.
She frowns.
"Santa Claus!" he bellows.
Annette cackles. "Merry Christmas, babies!"

Vangie sat up abruptly. When her eyes cleared, she found Wade standing over her with knitted brows.

"Did you have a bad dream? You were crying in your sleep."

Vangie pulled herself out of a daze and wiped the tears from her face.

"I don't remember." She gathered her scattered notes, deciding to keep her eyes open and go the distance with Wade. Wade joined her in bed, where they studied together.

Nineteen

Boasting 2100 square feet of total living space, the luxury beachfront villa, furnished in warm and rich tropical hues, had an unobstructed ocean view and everything a girl could want at her fingertips. Vangie left her suite and joined Ronnie Livingston at the kitchen island that glimmered in granite. He wore swim trunks. No shoes. No shirt. His unruly hair wet from a shower.

"I ordered your favorite drink," he said.

"Thanks. What's it called again?" Vangie laughed at her forgetfulness.

"What is what called?" Ronnie ran his hand through his wet curls, musing. It didn't escape Vangie that he was more focused on her swimsuit—a nude colored, strapless string bikini worn with sheer white beach shorts—than on her question.

"The drink, Ronnie?"

"Right. Horchata." He handed her the ice cold glass when she sat next to him.

Vangie took a healthy sip of Costa Rica's traditional drink. Its milky sweetness—ground almonds, cinnamon, and ground rice—soothed her anxious stomach.

While they ate a traditional breakfast of beans and rice, fried scrambled eggs, tortilla's and plantains, Ronnie stole peeks at her and kept grinning.

Face flushed, Vangie said, "What?"

"I thought you were shitting me when you said you'd come."

"Why would I lie?" she said with a straight face.

"Your parting gesture left an indelible impression on me." Ronnie held up his middle finger and put on a slow grin.

She laughed. "It didn't stop you from blowing up my phone and text box."

"I'm a high stakes gambler. I place my bet on the least likely odds."

"What odds?"

Ronnie gaped at her. "That four is magic."

Left without a comeback, Vangie sipped more Horchata.

Ronnie gulped his breakfast beer. "I would've been pissed off too if I got pimped."

Vangie's mouth fell open.

"Bad choice of words?"

"I didn't get *pimped*."

"How could I forget. You cock blocked me at first base."

She smirked. "How'd Lisa turn out?"

Ronnie's cheeks reddened, but his eyes sparked. "She wasn't magic."

"Whatever." Vangie rolled her eyes.

"How'd you get mixed up with Jacob, anyway. Or is that a dumb ass question?"

"What do you mean by mixed up? Is there something else I should know about Jacob besides his nasty little play parties?"

"Too amoral for you?"

"Not for you, obviously," she shot back.

Another slow grin. "Perspective is everything."

Vangie swallowed her reply with a gulp of Horchata, contemplating whether or not to continue this conversation with Ronnie that was heading in the wrong direction. Before now, she was actually enjoying his company.

"So, how'd you get mixed up with Jacob?" she said, despite her reluctance to say anything.

"We met at a cup series in Daytona Beach. Jacob's a pretty cool dude."

Vangie's face soured along with the Horchata on her stomach. She turned her cold eyes away from Ronnie's and cut into a plantain.While a silent game of soccer aired on the TV and Coldplay's *Viva la Vida* played through the speakers, Vangie ate in silence.

She didn't bother to excuse herself. She left Ronnie and her half-eaten plate in the kitchen and walked out of the suite. Standing on the terrace, she took in the island of Jaco beach, alive with wildlife and a rich green forest. The translucent blue waters bounded by a stretch of crystal black sand held her spellbound. Last night's rain had cooled off the air, bringing in a cooler breeze. The island was beautiful, and she couldn't say she wasn't happier to be here than at home.

She hadn't planned to accept Ronnie's invitation initially, but the idea of spending three weeks at home didn't sit well on her stomach. She couldn't think of a better way to avoid going home for Christmas than to spend it with Ronnie, who celebrated Hanukkah. Mainly, this trip kept up her pretenses, impressing upon Wade that she was worldly and had sufficient means to travel as she pleased, and after her stock paid off she wouldn't have to worry about this kind of deception.

The palm trees rustled just as Wade crossed her mind and Ronnie cleared his throat.

"I take that back. Jacob is a real jackass. Pimping you wasn't cool."

Vangie turned to face Ronnie's regretful eyes.

"So *we're* cool?"

She smiled.

"I was thinking ATVs today. We can cover the terrain, check out the rainforest. Whatever you want to do. What were you thinking?"

"A massage" She needed a day off to chill. They had hardly stopped to sleep since they landed in Costa Rica two nights ago. Vangie got the feeling Ronnie would rather conquer the jungles of Central America than spend time alone with her in their suite. His carnal energy was tangible.

"I'm all in. I'll schedule a couples massage on the beach."

Vangie didn't object. She suspected he would try to sleep with her tonight, again, after her day of pampering at the spa or if he thought she had too much to drink to mind.

"Ride with me today. You might have fun," Ronnie said as he followed her back into the suite, his hands massaging her shoulders.

She turned her head slightly to the side, looking at him from the corners of her eyes. "Haven't you heard? Black girls don't surf."

"That's bullshit. I'll take you to Barbados next. Black girls are bad asses in the pocket."

Next? Vangie mused.

"You ever been there?"

Vangie shook her head.

"You're totally going to love it," Ronnie said.

After a chill day, Vangie and Ronnie's night was wild. Having consumed too many Guaros, fermented sugarcane and a potent dose of alcohol, Vangie partied in the Moroccan-themed world-class nightclub with a crowd of vacationers as if there was no tomorrow. Ronnie had practically overdosed on the drink.

When they returned to the suite, she poured Ronnie into bed and was subsequently pulled into bed with him.

"Sleep with me tonight," Ronnie slurred, keeping her bound in his arms. Vangie had agreed to this trip under the condition that it would be strictly platonic—he kept to his side of the suite and she kept to hers. But her will power was lost to Guaros and Ronnie's persistence. Tonight she would sleep with him—free of charge.

Within minutes, Vangie heard Ronnie's soft snoring. She closed her eyes and could think of nothing but home.

I thought I'd never see Douglas again, but he returned on Christmas day, bringing my mother home and bearing gifts. He looked like a cuddly bear in his red sweater worn with jeans; I itched to be scratched again. We kept our distance, however. I wasn't sure why and worried that I'd done something wrong that day.

"You look nice, Angie." He sounded very professional.

I thanked him with a sideways smile.

"We rode here in style," my mother said, a glint of happiness brightening her sad eyes. She was wearing her favorite red dress I had brought to the hospital and her silver pumps, a look she once rocked. Now her bold switch was a listless glide.

I gave her a long hug, peeping over her shoulder at Douglas. He stood by the door as if he planned to leave at any minute. When he took off his coat, my heart sang a Christmas carol.

"Smells like dinner is ready." He handed me a bottle of chilled wine and smiled. "Your sister should like that one," he said with a proud smile.

My only thought was to hide the bottle before my mother got to it.

Moments later, there was a knock. Douglas beat me to the front door. It wasn't Vangie. It was West and Deja, who I had invited over for the holiday. Deja's round belly entered first. She walked like she was ten months pregnant, although West told me she was only four. From behind, she looked like a teenager dressed-up in peasant clothes, but the gray strands of hair snaking through her French braids gave away her age. She was ten years older than West, at least.

"Where've you been, Angie? We miss you hanging around," Deja said sweetly.

I believed her as much as I believed in Santa Claus. Still, I was happy to have a house full of company for dinner.

My mother's eyes brightened too. The bigger the party the merrier for Annette Cooper.

"Merry Christmas everybody," West said, wringing his beanie in his hands. His eyes stayed on the disturbed side lately, probably because he had to take a grunt job working for old man Brown and his son. Deja was working too, at a thrift store where I bought my Christmas dress for six dollars and twenty-five cents. Between their small paychecks, West and Deja struggled to pay Mr. Reese his full rent without Miss Coffee's Social Security check to help.

While Douglas shook West's hand, I dashed to the kitchen and busied my mouth, tasting my dishes one after the other. With my stomach in my throat, nothing tasted right.

Deja, of all people, walked in, standing around and rubbing her growing belly. I couldn't turn without bumping into her. "When's your twin coming home, Angie?" She sounded as sweet as a lemon disguised as a peach.

I shrugged and turned my back to Deja, burying my face and tears in the refrigerator.

What if Vangie doesn't come home?

Vangie had a way of entering a room. It could be her expensive dress that outlined her perfect curves, her hair that softly framed her face, or her high-heeled leather boots that accented her graceful glide. It didn't matter; she snatched the attention for herself.

Douglas couldn't take his eyes off her. I knew because I had hardly taken my eyes off him.

No one's eyes but mine could see the frost icing Vangie's observant eyes. In one sweep, she surveyed the room, taking in our houseguests, the Christmas tree, and our mother. She was thinking, "Why the hell are all these people in our house, Angie? And who the hell bought that stupid tree!" Maybe Douglas could read minds too. I'd never seen him look so humble.

"This is a surprise," Vangie said, poker-faced.

"I'm here playing Santa Claus." Douglas went to kiss her cheek, but she turned away from him and toward me.

The joy of seeing Vangie after months without her had paralyzed me. Tears blinded my eyes while a thousand unspoken words clogged my throat. Once Vangie and I got our arms around each other, we didn't let go.

"Come with me to the room," Vangie whispered in my ear. She wheeled her luggage through the living room, stopping briefly to give our mother a hug and kiss and ignoring our houseguests.

I almost tripped over my own feet trying to keep up.

"There they go," I heard my mother mumble.

Vangie slammed the bedroom door behind us. She didn't have to ask the questions darkening her eyes. I had read her mind.

"It's Christmas, " I said, tugging at the hem of my red spandex dress. My loose-hanging coils were held back with a white headband, my Christmas tree earrings dangling, and my lips lustrous and red.

No excuse could justify my drastic makeover, especially not Christmas. Vangie and I hated Christmas. Well, Vangie hated it and I went along with her. Sometimes, wishing for a present under a tree was like wishing for something to eat. There were times we had awakened on Christmas morning in a strange place with strange people and times when my mother cried over the years gone by and the years to come. There were other times when a happy drunk was given a place to sleep and food to eat for days or weeks thereafter.

Vangie took a good, long look at me and said, "We could be twins."

Our hushed giggles broke free. "I've missed you so much, I could cry," I said.

Vangie folded me into her arms again. We sat on our bed and talked in hushed tones. I grew dizzy and hot as the words rushed out faster than I could assemble them, cramming months of conversation into minutes. Vangie listened quietly and answered patiently.

"I almost forgot," Vangie interjected. "I have something for you…"

"What?"

Vangie pulled a bag from her suitcase. "It's not a Christmas gift," she warned.

Inside the bag, I found a burgundy hoodie with "Stanford University" written across the chest in white letters. Regret and happiness gathered in my eyes.

"I'll wear it until the letters fall off."

Vangie laughed. "I believe you, Ang. Oh! One more thing." She opened her purse and took out a cell phone. "This is for you too."

It may as well have been a dead rat. I hated cell phones and had no use for them. They opened up lines of communication I wanted to avoid. My frown made my thoughts clear.

"I don't want to hear it. You need one. Take it. For me, Ang. Please." Vangie slapped the cell phone into the palm of my hand and squeezed.

I threw the phone inside the nightstand drawer and said, "Mom's home. Did you see her?"

"I saw her, Ang." Weariness washed over her face.

"Dr. Adler approved a day pass. She's getting better." I tried to sound excited, but my voice lost steam.

When Vangie's neck and face turned Christmas red, my shoulders wilted. "It was an accident," I muttered.

"Almost overdosing on pills is not an *accident*."

The truth was hard to swallow with a lump in my throat. The better view hadn't helped our mother in the long run, and neither had the visits from Douglas. She had fooled everybody, including Dr. Adler, faking taking her medicine while stockpiling enough pills to take a lethal dose.

"Do not start crying, Angie."

My tears started anyway.

"I can't deal with this shit. I just can't…" Vangie jumped to her feet.

I dried my eyes quickly, afraid Vangie would leave and never come back.

She sat back down and sighed heavily. "Mom is not getting better, Ang. She may never."

"Don't say that!"

"If it makes you feel any better, I have an appointment with the doctor tomorrow, which, by the way, screwed up my Costa Rica trip."

I threw my arms around Vangie's neck. "I love you."

Our hushed conversation fell silent when we heard a knock on the door.

"Angie! Something's burning!" Deja shouted.

Oh, no! My ham!

"Who the hell is that?" Vangie demanded, her face contorted with questions I hadn't begun to answer yet.

I ran out of the room without another word.

We settled into Christmas dinner like strangers.

My mother was hypnotized by the tree lights, lost in another world. Douglas was vying for Vangie's attention, ignoring me in the process. Deja was picking Vangie's brain about college life, and West was fascinated by our TV features. Vangie, based on the annoyed look on her face, was quietly wishing they would all leave or she would be the first to go.

I observed everyone while running to and from the kitchen, hoping to make this Christmas better than all the rest. Everyone loved my food: the ham with citrus and spice marinade, my broccoli casserole, my macaroni and cheese, my garlic mashed potatoes and gravy, and my golden buttermilk biscuits. For dessert, I baked a pecan pie.

It wasn't long before Deja decided she was tired and needed her rest. She packed up two plates to go and waddled home, pulling West along with her.

Once they'd left, my mother got into a party mood after getting her hands on that bottle of wine I had hidden in the refrigerator. The cheery, soulful lyrics of Otis Redding's "Merry Christmas Baby" played through our battered old CD player, one of her favorite songs.

Again, Douglas had found a way to make me happy. He led my mother to the center of the living room and started two-stepping to the merry beat, reminding me of the days when she had been happiest. A Christmas tree couldn't light up a room brighter than Annette Cooper in those days.

Standing at the edge of the kitchen, I pressed a hand over my mouth to keep from laughing out loud in front of Vangie.

Douglas danced my way and grabbed both my hands. "You two-step, don't you, Ang? Sure you do!" He held me hostage as I frantically tried to pull away.

My mother laughed like it hurt her to. "Show him what you can do, Angie baby."

To make my mother happy, I shuffled my feet and rocked my hips, synchronizing my steps with Douglas's.

"Hey, hey, hey. That's what I'm talking about." He twirled me around.

I shuffled, rocked, and swayed.

"What the hell's going on!" Vangie screamed. The music had stopped and the merriment in the room turned grim. Vangie crossed her arms and tapped her toe, expecting answers.

"We're just having a little fun," Douglas said.

"Well, I'm not having any fucking *fun*. Who invited you over here, anyway, Douglas? I know I didn't." Her eyes shot my way.

I started collecting the dirty dishes.

Douglas chuckled nervously.

My mother walked listlessly back to the couch where she fastened her lips around another cigarette and narrowed her eyes at Vangie behind a veil of smoke. "Better keep that man away or Vangie's gonna run him away," she said and added a humph.

I froze right where I stood on the edge of the kitchen. I knew my mother and I knew Vangie. They could stand their ground like enemies at war.

"Take my mother back to the hospital, Douglas. She needs help," was all Vangie had to say before she slammed our bedroom door. Only I had seen the tears behind her hurt eyes. Only I understood her pain.

Christmas was over.

Twenty

Days after Christmas, Vangie sat on the living room floor with her legs crossed Indian style. I sat on the couch while she wasted her time polishing my toenails. As she polished, she shared her secret about Wade Fitzgerald the Fourth. He was from California, beautiful, and studying to become an eye doctor, from what I gathered. I knew what love looked like on account of my mother. Vangie was in love; I saw it in the blush of her cheeks and the beam in her eyes, desperate love that troubled the face beneath a radiant surface. I'd never known her to date a dude, let alone to love one. I thought only of myself, worried she would leave me for him and never come back home.

"Has Douglas been taking care of you?" Vangie said in her next breath, sending my heart into spasms. She stared up at me.

I twisted my mouth and shrugged. "He's nice."

"How nice, Ang?"

"He takes me to see Mom; I think that's nice of him; and he's been teaching me how to drive around the parking lot."

"What else has he taught you?"

"How to play dominos, you mean?"

Her eyes darkened. "You know what I mean, Angie. Did he put his hands on you?" She asked this carefully, as if I was a mental patient.

"That's gross! Who would want to touch me?"

For a long while Vangie didn't blink. "He better not have," she said, ending the subject of me and Douglas.

New Year's day, I stood over the stove stirring a pot of cheesy grits while sautéing prawns in garlic and butter. For dessert I had baked Vangie an orange crunch cake. I was doing everything in my power to make her happy, suspecting that the walls of Cambridge were starting to close in on her and the peeling paint in our apartment had gotten under her skin.

"Nothing will ever change in this city," she said somberly, staring out of the window.

"Things are already changing, Van. West called it gentrification," I said to cheer her up.

Vangie waltzed into the kitchen with a laugh on her lips. "What does West know about anything, Angie?"

"He knows that big companies are converting crummy old buildings like ours into luxury apartment complexes, gentrifying whole neighborhoods around the country."

Vangie didn't look convinced, so I talked on, describing the wonderful possibilities of a better life, right here at home, in grand detail. While I prepared our bowls of cheesy grits, piling on shrimp and garnishing it with crispy bacon bits, Vangie sliced the garlic bread and then poured herself a glass of wine. I grabbed a soda can from the refrigerator.

"Maybe they'll convert Cambridge into luxury apartments and fire Mr. Reese," I added, not so much because it contributed to the argument but because it sounded like the best idea imaginable.

We sat in the living room, eating in front of the TV.

"In case you didn't know, Ang, gentrification helps the rich and displaces the poor. If Cambridge is renovated, the rent will go up and we'll be evicted. If shopping centers are built on the Eastside, the middle-class will take over and put poor people out in the street, but I doubt that will ever happen," Vangie stated simply.

To maintain hope, I said, "Well, West plans to persuade one of the big banks to lend him enough money to start his own furniture business." I omitted the part about my working for West.

"Be smarter, Angie. What bank in this country would loan West a dime to open a lemonade stand?" She always had a way of making me question my own logic.

"Having money isn't everything," I said indignantly, holding fast to my hopes and dreams. "Other things are important too."

Vangie stopped eating to stare at me. "Like what?"

"Like happiness, the kind you can bottle up and use it whenever you're sad or lonely."

"You sound as crazy as Mom sometimes."

"Metaphorically, I meant," I quickly said, struck by the real possibility that our mom might be crazy and may never recover from it.

"Look around you," Vangie said. "Do you see happiness anywhere?"

She waited for an answer she wouldn't get out of me.

"Nobody's *happy*. You know what they are? Miserable, like animals locked in a cage. If they had the money to get out of the hood, some of them wouldn't know how to set themselves free. It's their mentality." Vangie tapped her temple. "Rich white people never apologize for having money. They believe the world is their oyster and that they're entitled to wealth. So, why shouldn't I feel entitled?" she said flippantly.

Evidently, my argument had only strengthened Vangie's conviction that it was better to be white and rich than black and poor any day of the week. It also occurred to me that Vangie was growing by leaps and bounds and I was confined to a small space, going nowhere. Secretly I wanted Vangie to beg me to go to California with her, to remind me of our dream, to help me set myself free.

Vangie walked to the kitchen and returned with a slice of orange crunch cake, inhaling a fork full as she sat down on the couch next to me. "You're the best cook in the world, Ang," she said.

I had lost my appetite.

The next morning I woke to find Vangie gone—the only trace of her visit was a crisp new envelope filled with enough one hundred dollar bills to last me for months. The note read: "Be smarter with money, Angie. It doesn't grow on trees! Love, Van."

Twenty-One

Spring break had arrived, and so had Wade's acceptance letters to several top medical schools around the country. For the Fitzgeralds, this was cause to celebrate. They'd planned a big family celebration in Los Angeles during spring break, and Vangie was the special guest they couldn't wait to meet.

Perched on a cul-de-sac overlooking Encino Valley, the white-columned, two-story house had a tulip-red double door and a sweeping red brick porch.

One benefit of having been with rich men was having seen it all, and so she didn't bat an eye when she walked into the sprawl-ing home of the Fitzgerald family. It helped that the property was beneath her high expectations. She imagined that the neighbor-hood had the lifeblood of old money, yet Frances Fitzgerald had worked hard to conceal her wealth in overstuffed, earth tone sofas and simple, traditional wood furnishing. The home was modestly decorated, the only extravagances being Persian rugs and original artwork.

"Contrary to popular belief, we're modest people," Wade said, carrying her luggage inside.

"It's nice."

"That's a good word for it."

"Aren't you going to show me around?"

"Later. We gotta go."

They had arrived an hour behind schedule and wouldn't have time to unpack before heading to the celebration.

After a quick shower together, they rushed around, pulling clothes from their luggage. Wade zipped her dress, and Vangie, who had become something of an expert working with power neckties, helped Wade with his.

Wade's brooding look had returned, the one he had worn the entire three-and-a-half-hour drive from San Jose, it seemed. For some reason he wasn't looking forward to this gathering in his honor. Vangie wasn't either, though the special occasion had given her an excuse to spend a day shopping, body waxing, and manicuring with Clarissa as if she had a father with money.

He sped down Wilshire Boulevard, clearly taking the glamour of Beverly Hills for granted. The famed city had always brought images of movie stars and elaborate mansions to Vangie's mind. Starry-eyed, she took in the ambiance, its manicured streets, designer stores, luxury car dealerships and posh hotels, the palms of her hands itching.

When Wade parked in front of a tall building made of mirrored windows, two eager valets rushed up and opened the doors for them. Wade hopped out first, took Vangie's hand and rushed her into the lobby and through an atrium of tropical foliage and waterfall sculptures.

When they stepped through the elevator's majestic doors, Vangie squeezed Wade's clammy hand and he squeezed hers back.

"You're nervous." He sounded so sure of himself.

"I'm not," Vangie lied.

He gave her one of his I-know-you-better-than-you-know-yourself smiles. "If I love you, my family will love you. You're perfect."

His words gave her pause. "Do you love me?" she breathed.

He squeezed her hand tighter. "Do you have to ask?"

Cheeks burning, she adjusted Wade's tie once more. He wore a black suit with a white-collared shirt, yellow silk tie, and soft leather dress shoes. She had worn a gold-embellished black Prada dress that accentuated her legs, arms, and bare shoulders. Her contrasting stiletto pumps made a bold statement in platinum and copper. With her hair in a side-swept updo that left glamorous tendrils around her face, she hoped to make a good impression on Wade's family.

The elevator came to a stop on the twenty-eighth floor. They stepped into an elegant lobby with antique light fixtures that gave it a warm glow. Across the walkway, sectioned off by sea animals swimming in an enormous tank, a number of patrons, mostly middle-aged or older white men, were enjoying drinks around a full bar.

They approached the hostess seated behind a glass desk. "Welcome to the Captain's Club. First time dining with us?" she said with a smile.

Wade's jawline tightened. He adjusted his tie and bent slightly at the waist. "The Founder's Room," he said to tip her off.

Muttering an apology, she rushed around the desk to escort them.

"Right this way." She led them down a short, private hallway and into another elevator that required a code. They stopped one floor up and entered a quiet foyer with rich oriental carpeting and a towering Italian Renaissance painting spotlighted on the dark mahogany walls.

"They're expecting you." The hostess left them quickly as if eager to return to her post downstairs.

Two ornate mahogany double doors leading from the small foyer swung back and the booming voice of a lean, gray-haired man filled the foyer.

"The man of the hour!" He gripped Wade by both shoulders and pulled him into a bear hug. In the same breath he whispered something in Wade's ear. Wade chuckled and glanced Vangie's way. The man then turned to introduce himself as Wade Fitzgerald II, his smile revealing teeth too perfect not to be capped.

"Granddad, this is my girl," Wade said proudly.

"Your *girl?*" Wade's grandfather echoed with a covert grin, his soft, manicured hand lingering around hers after shaking it.

Wade frowned. "I hope that won't become the theme of the night."

Ignoring him, Wade's grandfather focused his full attention on her. "Beautiful."

Vangie tried to ignore the butterflies in her stomach as kissed the back of her hand, looking up at her with naughty brown eyes. Clarissa had given her the rundown on Wade II. He never remarried after Wade's grandmother, the first Clarissa Fitzgerald, died from early-onset heart disease, and needed to quit chasing after chicks young enough to be his daughter, according to Clarissa.

"What is your name, lovely lady?"

"Vangie Cooper." Her voice caught ever so slightly.

"Cooper! " he boomed. "A name to remember!"

"I like any girl who can make my brother late to his own party." A woman strutted through the mahogany double doors. She exceeded Vangie's height in heels and had a figure that made her little black dress look like it cost a million bucks.

"Kimmy," she said, shoving her right hand at Vangie while sipping from a crystal wine flute with her left.

Wade's sister.

Kimberly Fitzgerald was six years older than Wade and "rough around the edges," as Clarissa had put it, which didn't accurately describe Kimmy in Vangie's opinion. Handsomely pretty was a better description. Her jawline was chiseled like Wade's, her skin the same shade of brown, her hair closely cropped in a sleek pixie cut. She wore no jewelry, not even diamond studs.

Vangie managed a refined smile as she returned Kimmy's firm handshake.

Kimmy stared at her with the same piercing brown eyes as her brother's, then turned to Wade. "You have a real hankering for pretty faces, don't you, brother?"

Wade's eyes seemed to warn her to lay off whatever she was drinking.

She laughed, apparently finding his nervousness amusing. "The love runs deep."

Wade the second clapped his hands. "Are we going to celebrate or aren't we? Let's get this party started," he said.

They followed him into a private dining room with Vangie clinging tightly to Wade's hand.

"You look like you could use a little bubbly," Kimmy said. She entwined her arm with Vangie's, leading her away from Wade and straight to the small bar in a corner of the room where a white-haired bartender promptly handed them each a glass of Cristal.

Vangie swallowed a gulp of the costly champagne, thankful for a breather. Her eyes panned the intimate room. In its center sat a round table formally set for eight. On one side of the room, floor-to-ceiling windows gave the illusion of a room floating in city lights. Vangie turned to the mahogany-paneled wall. On it hung gold-framed portraits of several distinguished-looking elderly white men and one silver-haired black man. The nameplate read: "Wade Dermot Fitzgerald, Jr." Apparently, the Fitzgerald name held more "constitutional rights and unrestricted access" to the Captain's Club than Wade had let on.

"Mom. Dad. This is my girl," Wade said, walking up with his parents.

Frances Fitzgerald gave her a brief but friendly hug, which was rather awkward, given Frances's petite stature. "Welcome to the family," she said in a warm, cheerful voice.

"Thank you," Vangie managed to say. In a blink of an eye, she appraised Wade's mother. She was superbly dressed by anyone's standard, wearing a conservative gray raw silk skirt suit with frills around the collar set off by her caramel-colored skin and brownish hair, which she had brushed into a do-it-yourself ponytail. Unlike Kimmy, she wore jewelry—cultured pearls—though they were modest. She seemed the sort of woman who would rather sit in the back of the auditorium while her husband ruled the stage.

Speaking of...

Wade's father, in contrast, looked the part of the brilliant neurosurgeon. His wire-framed eyeglasses sat near the tip of his broad nose as if he didn't need them to see, but rather, to observe. Like Wade, he was tall with the same piercing eyes as his son and daughter.

"Wade has spoken highly of you." He scrutinized her from behind his glasses while shaking her hand.

Vangie simply smiled, mostly from relief. She had finally met the Fitzgeralds. The next challenge would be making it through dinner without calling attention to herself.

Dinner began with an appetizer, roasted butternut squash and shallot soup, followed by a spinach and shrimp salad with chili dressing. By the time the two-inch strip sirloin was served, Vangie was on the edge of her seat. Sitting next to Wade and too close to Kimmy, she took small bites, listening quietly to the Fitzgerald family's report of professional achievements. Kimmy's prosecution of a cop killer as the Los Angeles assistant deputy district attorney, Wade's father's successful surgery on an infant with a malignant brain tumor—described in painstaking detail—and Wade's grandfather's recent commercial real estate deal dominated the conversation. Frances had little to report about her work as a curator for the Los Angeles County Museum of Art.

Wade made it clear he would make his big announcement during dessert and no sooner.

"Poor Vangie. We're boring her to death," Frances said.

Now all eyes had turned to her, including Wade's.

Feeling as though she was shrinking while the room grew, Vangie reached for her water and took a quick sip to moisten her dry throat, reminding herself she was not out of her league. She had dined at one of the top ten private clubs in the country with a billionaire. She knew about lucrative commercial real estate investments from Jacob, had made it a point to study classical music, and knew enough about paintings and artists to get by, thanks to Jacob.

"Are we boring you?" Wade asked, looking concerned.

Vangie smiled thinly and shook her head.

"You're welcome to join in," Wade's grandfather encouraged. Hearing about the achievements of his descendants seemed to be a source of pride for him. He dug for every detail, and Kimmy, particularly, was eager to feed his ego.

"Yes, Vangie. Please. Join in," Kimmy said. "Roundtable is mandatory in this family. Tell us about one of Fortune 500's wealthiest Canadians." Vangie couldn't tell whether Kimmy was being sincere or sarcastic, but she was primed for questioning. She had mapped out the details of her upbringing: the town in

Ontario where her father had lived, the street name, the Oakville mansion where she had spent her summers, her private school education, and her world travels, though she regretted the day she had invented a white Canadian father.

"And his name is Cooper?" Wade II asked, his mouth turned down and his eyebrows folded in as if he were recalling every Fortune 500 periodical that had crossed his desk.

"Leave Vangie out of our roundtable, Granddad. She's not one to boast," Wade said.

"Touchy," Kimmy said into her crystal flute.

"There's nothing wrong with immodesty. I'm from the old school of thought: if you have it, flaunt it." Wade's grandfather smiled at Vangie with his mischievous eyes.

"I, for one, am eager for dessert." Wade's father folded his napkin neatly and placed it squarely in the center of his empty plate as he looked across the table at Wade. "Can't wait to hear the big news, son."

Roundtable was interrupted when the double doors swung back and a husky man wearing a suit and tie entered. His Afro was neatly coiffed, his thin mustache perfectly arching his full lips that angled as though the room reeked. Something about his cocoa complexion and puffy cheeks looked vaguely familiar to Vangie.

The woman holding his hand dripped of sex appeal—long, fluffy strawberry tresses, sun-kissed white skin, and plump breasts pushing through her silk blouse. They quickly took the two empty seats between Wade II and Wade III.

Frances Fitzgerald hurried to greet the woman with a hug while Kimmy took a sip of champagne, hiding her frown.

"Hi Uncle Gerald. Aunt Carrie," Wade said.

Hearing the name, Vangie put two and two together. The man was Gerald Fitzgerald, Clarissa's father.

By now she knew Clarissa's ranking in the Fitzgerald family. Clarissa was nowhere near the top tier and had been written off along with her two younger sisters when her father divorced Clarissa's mother. Whatever father/daughter relationship Clarissa had had with Gerald Fitzgerald ended in middle school. When Gerald remarried and produced a second set of kids, Clarissa's ranking in the Fitzgerald family had dropped considerably. Clarissa was fortunate to have gotten a premium education afforded by her father. Otherwise, Clarissa maintained her privileged lifestyle paid for by her mother's third husband. Vangie wondered how Clarissa would have handled this dinner party, had she been invited.

"I didn't think you'd make it," Wade's father said, observing the man from behind his spectacles.

"We wouldn't think of missing the celebration," Carrie said with a smile.

"We're not too late for dinner, are we?" Gerald said.

"Dinner ended an hour ago," Wade's grandfather said.

Whatever reeked in the room agitated the man's upper lip. It twitched. "Some of us do have full calendars."

"And some of us have our priorities out of order," Wade's grandfather retorted.

"We have righted our priorities, haven't we? We are here, and frankly, I am starved." Gerald snapped his dinner napkin open and laid it on his lap.

The servers quickly arrived with dinner for them both.

Once the latecomers had eaten dinner and everyone else had finished their dessert plates of salted caramel chocolate mousse crowned with rose petals, Wade's grandfather stood and raised his champagne glass.

"We've gathered for this very important occasion...to celebrate my grandson's acceptance to medical school!"

"Hear, hear!" Kimmy said, standing and initiating a wave around the table. All the Fitzgeralds stood and applauded Wade for his achievement.

Filled with as much pride as Wade's family, Vangie wanted to stand and applaud Wade too, but his hand was crushing hers and she couldn't move.

"Don't hate me for this," he whispered into her ear and stood.

Vangie's mind went into a frenzy, speculating over Wade's announcement. She knew he could choose any of the three top medical schools: Johns Hopkins in Baltimore, Washington University in St. Louis, and his father's choice, the University of California San Francisco, a one-hour drive or less from Stanford. She also knew his father was an alumnus board member and had pulled the necessary strings to guarantee his son's acceptance to San Francisco University's School of Medicine. Vangie was rooting for the last.

Wade gestured for everyone to sit. "Enough with the public display of affection," he said. When the room sat, he bowed his head, closed his eyes, and pinched the bridge of his nose.

"Take your time, son. This is an emotional moment for all of us," Wade's father said.

Now Wade was looking at the ceiling, rolling his tongue from one cheek to the other as if his mouth was extremely dry.

Vangie wanted to reach for his hand and give it a comforting squeeze for moral support. Instead, she sat stiffly, her own mouth feeling like cotton.

Wade cleared his throat. "There is a time in every man's education when he arrives at the conviction that envy is ignorance, that imitation is suicide, that he must take himself for better, for worse, as his portion..."

"Ralph Waldo Emerson!" interjected Wade's grandfather. "One of my all-time favorites."

"That's right, Granddad." Wade cleared his throat again. "Before I make my announcement, I want you to know, Dad, how much I admire and respect you. You are the epitome of a medical professional, a man who embodies the very essence of integrity and honor, and one history should hale as one of the greats." Wade took a breath and turned to Frances. "Mom. You know that I love you." He paused and took another breath as Frances blinked away tears and dabbed her eyes with a napkin.

"Kimmy. You're the best."

Kimmy looked annoyed. "Where're you going with this, Wade?" she muttered.

Wade pressed on. "Granddad, thanks for everything. You didn't have to do this for me."

"Indeed!" Wade II said incredulously.

Wade cleared his throat again. "Let me encapsulate this speech... Dad, if there ever was a person I wished to emulate, it is you, but I have my own roads to pave. That said, I've chosen to attend Johns Hopkins in the fall."

Vangie barely registered the gasps and sighs of the table because of the explosions going off in her head.

Wade's grandfather fired up a cigar and raised his glass in another toast. "To my only grandson! A true blue-blood. May he blaze new trails like his old granddad and carry on my name and legacy."

Kimmy gave Wade a sisterly hug, quietly congratulating him on his brave decision to defy his father's wishes. "That took guts," Kimmy whispered. "I don't care what anyone else thinks."

Vangie, on the other hand, hated Wade for being so stupid!

"I'm disappointed in your decision, son. But I respect you for it," Wade's father said.

As if torn between her husband's wishes and her son's, Frances Fitzgerald gave Wade a hug and kiss, then consolingly patted her husband's cheeks.

Like Gerald and Carrie Fitzgerald, Vangie hadn't moved from her seat or said a word. She noticed Wade taking peeks at her from the corner of his eye.

Their drive back to Encino was somber.

Wade had barely spoken since they left the Captain's Club, and Vangie didn't have anything to say. Her heart burned and her unshed tears blurred the taillights ahead.

"I know. I should've told you. Do you hate me?" Wade said, breaking the silence.

No comment.

Another mile passed on the busy highway before Wade spoke again. "Want to know what my granddad said about you?"

I really don't care, she wanted to say, but the smile in Wade's voice prompted her to look at him. "What?" she said flatly.

"He said if I don't marry you, he will. I take his advice to heart. He's a wise old man." Wade's smile widened.

Vangie couldn't even fake smile. A promise of marriage wasn't good enough. On top of losing Wade, she may have to drop out of school.

"Hey…" Wade reached over and stroked the back of her neck. "I love you."

Aside from loving her twin and mother, she had never loved anyone so deeply. Her love for Wade took her breath away and filled her with intense happiness while, at times, immobilizing her with fear. When she thought her feelings for him couldn't go deeper, she found herself drowning in misery when he wasn't around and sinking in his arms when he was. She knew what this kind of love could do. As much as it brought happiness, it could also inflict pain. Her mother had loved too hard and had lost her mind as a result. She was terrified of loving Wade so much out of fear of losing him and her mind because of it.

If she spoke her heart, she would embarrass herself with tears.

Wade made up to Vangie, taking her to the star-packed Cecconi's on Melrose Avenue, giving her a scenic tour of Hollywood, and escorting her up and down the famed, rich streets of Rodeo Drive where Vangie filled her shopping bags with designer wear. But she got as much pleasure, if not more, out of grilling hot dogs and steaks in the Fitzgerald's' backyard and horsing around in the pool with Wade.

On Thursday, Frances Fitzgerald left work early and surprised them in the middle of the afternoon. Luckily, they had wrapped up their hot pool sex by then and Vangie was back to timing Wade's laps across the pool.

On their very last day of spring break, Wade drove her to Malibu—a city whose name alone had a Southern California ring. Beachfront homes, many occupied by movie stars she supposed, sat off a stretch of highway within one hundred feet of the shoreline, while others nestled in the bushy hills above.

When they hit the white sand, the beach was alive and jumping—football, volleyball, and jet skiing, not to mention catered Mexican food, a full bar, and beer by the barrel.

In a mass of mostly white bodies, Clarissa was easy to spot in her red string bikini and sporty white baseball cap. She accosted them, kicking up sand along the way.

"I thought you'd never get here!" she shrilled.

"I think I'll catch this game. You mind?" Wade was ready to run off toward the group of rowdy guys chanting his name from the volleyball station.

Vangie shook her head but felt completely out of place.

"You can't speak?" Clarissa said before he could leave.

"What's up, Clarissa?" Wade said, jogging backward.

"You'd think we weren't related." Clarissa rolled her doll eyes and then looked over Vangie's coral-colored one piece that draped around her neck and plunged to her navel, covering enough of her breasts not to be pornographic. She hid her eyes beneath a big, floppy hat and behind dark sunglasses.

"Gucci?"

"Prada," Vangie said.

You're *perf...*" Clarissa took Vangie by the hand. "Come on. I want you to meet my BFFs from high school. They're all Yale, Princeton, and Harvard snobs. You'll love them." Clarissa led Vangie to a large beach umbrella where her three friends shaded themselves from the sun. One slim and blonde, one a plump, freckle-faced redhead, and one chocolate and chic, they welcomed Vangie into their circle, offering her their wine.

Vangie was glad to see Wade when he walked up an hour later. He had shed his T-shirt and wore only his swim trunks, flaunting rippling muscles and glistening skin.

"Hi, Wade," the girls sang out, and then they laughed.

Looking plum red, Wade lifted his chin in a cool hello. "How's it going? You ready, Van. I'm starving." He didn't look up for socializing.

"Bye, Wade!" They sang as she and Wade walked off.

After making their rounds at the taco bar, they took off toward the water. Wade had that lustful look in his eyes, as if he couldn't wait to seduce her in a dark, remote cave. He couldn't keep his hands off of her.

Vangie ran and he chased.

When the sand grew too hot for her feet, Wade carried her on his back to the frothy shoreline. Swept away by the crash of cool waves, the heat of the noonday sun, and the deliciousness of Wade's kiss, Vangie felt that love alone could sustain her.

Twenty-Two

This morning I found Mr. Reese sitting on our couch as if he lived here.

"You know what this is?" He slapped an envelope against the palm of his hand. "It's from the Department of Welfare. You can go to jail for cheating the government out of money that ain't yours." He flung the envelop at me. I snatched it up from the floor, tore it open, and read the letter inside, my eyes rushing down the page.

Welfare had found out that Vangie and I were over the age of eighteen and that our mother lived in a psychiatric hospital. Our monthly checks, subsidized rent, and food stamps had been cut off months ago. Mr. Reese had obviously stolen the notification from our mailbox.

Until this month I had gotten by without the help of welfare, using the money Vangie left me, even paying Mr. Reese his full rent on time. Then the money disappeared. It was gone—every last penny—and I didn't have to wonder who would be so evil, mean, and vicious.

I stood there, shivering and terrified that Mr. Reese would get to me before the police came to arrest me, but Mr. Reese left after giving me a warning.

"I've been nice enough to let you stay here rent free. It's time you be nice to me."

The chilly San Jose winds howled at the window and splattered droplets of rain, sending rivulets trickling down the smooth glass. Vangie watched the rain, too anxious to sleep. Angie had been weighing heavy on her heart. Some days she could hear her twin calling for her in the whisper of the wind, feel Angie's loneliness in the shadow of the trees. Those were the times that guilt strangled her.

In the dark she fumbled for her handbag and crept quietly out of Wade's bedroom.

Sitting on the sectional in the living room, Vangie powered on her Detroit cell phone to find another text message from Ronnie Livingston. He had asked her to accompany him to the Virginia Sprint Cup Series, another all-expenses-paid trip. Vangie ignored Ronnie's text message and called home. A recorded voice announced that the phone had been disconnected again. She dialed Angie's cell phone. It went straight to voicemail.

Instinctively, Vangie dialed Douglas, but she hung up before the phone could ring. Cursing under her breath, she powered off her phone and placed it back in the hidden pocket of her handbag.

When she returned to bed, she curled under Wade and forced her eyes to close.

Twenty-Three

Thomas Jones called on a rainy Monday, Vangie's heaviest class day. She had no time to return his call, nor was she eager to. At last report, her stock had dropped to thirty cents a share. She was no closer to independent wealth and financial security than she was to the moon.

After leaving her last class of the morning, she crossed the campus toward the Black Community Services Center. Her umbrella fought wind and rain as her riding boots sloshed through puddles of water. She should never have let Clarissa, who spent more time socializing than studying, talk her into attending a Society of Young Black Professionals meeting on a gloomy day like today.

Vangie reached the small log cabin, known as "the Black House," by shuttle. Students of every nationality packed every corner of the small community room, many of them enjoying the punch and cookies spread out on a table. Clarissa, no surprise, was the seminar facilitator, her guest speaker a law professor named Jonathan D. Moore.

Feeling soggy and miserable, Vangie found an empty seat near the exit. Clarissa smiled across the room and waved to her, looking primed to be the next Attorney General in her chic black business suit. She was introducing Jonathan D. Moore to the crowd when Vangie's cell phone vibrated. Not knowing whether it was her California or Detroit line, she ignored it.

In the middle of a rousing speech that had the room exploding in applause, Vangie's cell phone vibrated again. She peeked at the number. It was Thomas Jones again. She had missed five of his consecutive calls. She hadn't received that many calls from him in months. She left the room quickly and quietly, leaving her coat and backpack behind.

Standing at the entryway out of the rain, she returned the call, pressing the phone to her ear. The phone rang only once before Thomas Jones answered.

"Good afternoon."

"It's me, Mr. Jones."

"Well, hello there, young lady. Sounds like it's coming down like cats and dogs out your way. We've had a pretty hard winter back here, nothing but snow and cold. It's finally warming up."

Vangie sighed deeply. She hadn't called for a weather report.

"Have you been keeping up with your stock lately?" he asked next.

"No…" She had been too afraid to.

"Well, I'm calling with good news for you."

Vangie's heart leaped into her throat. She was standing in the rain now, having wandered off the porch without realizing it. No umbrella. No coat. She walked quickly down a pathway lined with bushy trees.

"What's the news?" Her voice quivered.

"Well…" He took a long, deep breath.

Vangie stopped walking and tapped her toe in an agony of impatience.

"You know that green technology company you gambled on?" he said finally.

"Yes!"

"The damnedest thing happened. Are you ready for this?"

A second of prolonged suspense ticked by.

"What, Mr. Jones?"

"It bounced back overnight."

Vangie kept calm, afraid to let her hopes skyrocket.

"Bounced back? How much of a bounce?" She quickly found the shelter of a low hanging tree.

"Well…" Thomas Jones began again before launching into a long-winded report about a company merger. "Thanks to a practical business deal," he said finally, "your stock ballooned to thirty-seven dollars and fifty cents a share. Do you know what that adds up to, young lady?"

"No…" She couldn't add up two plus two right now.

"Looks to me like your forty thousand shares are now worth one-point-five million dollars, there about." His voice rang like wedding bells.

"Did you say one point…*five*…*million*?" she whispered.

"I'm scratching my head too. Either you're smarter than the average bear in this business or you're in on an insider trading deal."

Vangie swallowed hard. "What do I owe you, Mr. Jones?"

"Not a single dime. I get my money up front. You never know in this business."

Vangie knew his words to be true, but somehow, she felt she owed him something for his grandfatherly advice. He talked on, something about selling while she was ahead and an impending market crash. Vangie couldn't hear much above the whooshing of adrenaline in her head.

After hanging up, she walked back to the Black House on unstable legs, her hair a mop beneath her Twill beret, her belted sweater and leggings drenched. She meant to ease into the room, collect her coat and backpack, and ease out. The seminar had ended, but many students lingered, most eating while others chatted. A few had cornered the guest speaker. Clarissa was buzzing about, doing her duties as president. Vangie grabbed her belongings from her chair and was halfway through the door when she heard, "Vangie Cooper!"

She froze. Taking a deep breath to tame the emotions exploding inside her, she turned slowly to face Clarissa.

"You missed the entire meeting!" Clarissa accused her.

"Sorry. I had to take a call."

"Who from? Wade?" Clarissa rolled her eyes as Wade's name rolled off her tongue in a singsong lilt.

Vangie couldn't maintain her composure. Aside from being one-point-five million dollars richer, only Wade could make her smile senselessly.

"You're not leaving, are you?" Clarissa narrowed her eyes.

Vangie eased toward the exit. "I really have to go."

"But you haven't met everybody," Clarissa whined.

"I'll stay for the next meeting. I promise." Vangie hurried off.

Her heart refused to stay in her chest as she walked aimlessly through the campus, the world spinning so fast around her she felt lightheaded. The rain had slowed to a light sprinkle. Turning off the main path, she came upon a lovely garden, its flowers made more fragrant by the rain. She had a compulsion to pick every flower and spread peace and love around campus.

Whoever said money can't buy happiness lied.

A million and a half dollars could buy a lifetime of happiness. Her mind ran away with ideas. Eager to share her excitement with someone, Vangie thought of calling Jacob to thank him for suggesting the stock, though she never would. She thought of Wade and her heart arrested. If she called him, what would she say? *Guess what? I'm finally rich!* She couldn't tell Wade. She couldn't tell anyone, except Angie.

She sat on one of the benches nearby and called home. The mechanical voice of the recording answered again, reminding her that the phone at home was still disconnected. Hoping, by some miracle Angie had remembered to charge her cell phone, Vangie dialed the number. No luck. She hung up and resolved to fly home to check on Angie and her mother.

It wasn't easy for Vangie to convince Wade to leave his books behind, to skip a day of his internship and to pack a suitcase, especially on short notice. To pry him away from his studies, Vangie used his final year as the reigning swimming champion for an excuse to get away. Since she couldn't tell Wade about her newfound wealth, she would show him.

They had crossed the San Francisco Golden State Bridge in a chauffeured SUV, taking in its garland of white lights and the setting sun casting a golden glow over the Bayfront.

More questions filled Wade's eyes when they took a road through the hilly streets of Union Square bounded by dense luxury condos, elegant hotels, boutiques, and five-star restaurants. She had selected the district specifically for its affluence.

The driver parked before a brick building and opened the door for them. On the outside, the French restaurant looked unassuming. Inside, the dimly lit, fine dining establishment was a statement of romantic elegance. Soft music played in the background while patrons dined quietly.

After they had dined on delicious French cuisine, they were driven to an exclusive boutique hotel situated in downtown San Francisco.

Strolling through the lobby with all of its modern ultra-chic elegance, Wade looked as though he belonged and expected no less than five-star accommodations. Together, they were young, rich and beautiful, the perfect couple, Vangie thought, strutting beside him with her arm clasped around his. She had instructed Wade to wear his best suit, and he had, a tailored charcoal pinstriped one and an open-collar white dress shirt. Vangie wore a classic crème colored dress, crème colored spiked heeled pumps, a faux fur shrug, and the heart-shaped pendant necklace Wade had gifted her. She had spent three days preparing for this night. Hopefully, she had stolen Wade's breath away as he had stolen hers away.

At the check-in desk, Vangie proudly handed the gracious reservationist her recently acquired credit card and fake ID, keeping up a façade of nobility. They were checked in promptly, no questions asked.

Inside the deluxe circular suite with a panoramic view of San Francisco, and done up in heavenly blue and white, they made it as far as the living room where Wade thrust Vangie against the twill sofa so that she sat on its back. She shuddered as he brushed his hands up her thighs, then shrugged off his suit jacket and fumbled to unbuckle and unzip his pants.

"I've waited all night for this." He voice was raspy and urgent. He took her face into his hands and fused his mouth with hers. Every pulsating muscle inside of Vangie wanted to give in to Wade with reckless abandon, but the combination of power and money gave her control over her body that her alter ego couldn't match. There would be plenty of time over the weekend to satisfy her appetite for Wade. Beside, having sex on the back of a couch wasn't on tonight's program.

She pulled out of their wet kiss and pressed a hand to Wade's pounding chest. "You'll have to wait longer."

Wade frowned. "Wait for what?"

"After my next surprise."

"Not to sound ungrateful, babe, but can it wait?"

"No."

"What is it?"

"You'll see."

Wade sighed and zipped his pants. "I love your apathy. My balls are blue."

Smiling from ear-to-ear, Vangie guided Wade outside by the hand. On the private rooftop embellished with cushy patio furnishings and elaborate tropical plants, an array of candles flickered around a Jacuzzi bath. Next to the sauna was a bottle of Bollinger, two Champaign flutes, chocolate-dipped strawberries, and two plush bath towels. Everything was perfectly arranged per her specifications.

Wade took in the romantic setting with a look of awe. "Ah, man." He scratched the side of his head. "When did you have time to make this happen?"

"I had the driver call ahead when we left the restaurant." Vangie sounded like this was routine. She had learned from the best.

"I'm feeling outdone."

"Why?"

"What does a freshman know about wining and dining an upperclassman?" He grinned, admirably.

"So, you like it?"

He pulled her close. "I love it. All of this for taking the championship?"

Vangie wrapped her arms around Wade's neck and gazed up at him. "You deserve it."

"Is that the only reason we're here tonight?" Wade's pensive look gave Vangie pause.

"Not the only reason…" she murmured. It crossed Vangie's mind to be completely up front with Wade, but fear flashed through her at lightning speed. She couldn't lose him now, not when the deck was stacked in her favor.

"So I'm right."

Her eyes fluttered. "Right about what?"

"This is a final farewell, more or less," he said.

Vangie hastily pulled away from Wade and walked toward the spectacular show of lights near the bay. Now that he had broached the subject, her heartache had returned and reality had set in. Wade would soon graduate from Stanford. A month later he would begin the long and arduous road toward becoming a physician.

Where will that leave me?

"Van. This isn't goodbye." He spoke from behind her, his voice, as always, self-assured.

Vangie faced Wade with a show of tears in her eyes. "What makes you so sure? What if it is...goodbye?"

He laughed as though she was being melodramatic. "I'm not getting locked up for six years. I'm going to medical school."

"Whatever, Wade."

"Van. I promise. I'll see you every chance I can." Wade tried to embrace her. Vangie nudged him away and crossed her arms tightly at her chest to keep from shoving the shit out of him.

"If you wanted to *see me* every chance you could, you'd be going to UCSF not stupid ass, dumb ass John Hopkins!"

Wade unfolded her arms, wrapped her in his, and stared down at her intently. "I'm not going anywhere, babe. I'm in this relationship one hundred percent. Are you? You're the wild card."

Vangie contemplated Wade's question in light of her bank account balance, feeling rich enough and free enough to do as she pleased when she pleased and without compromise for the first time in her life. She felt on top of the world, where she intended to stay.

"You didn't answer my question," Wade said.

"I'm all in." Dismissing the sinking feeling in the pit of her stomach over inevitably losing Wade to a long distance relationship, Vangie left her clothes behind, stepped into the steaming hot Jacuzzi and sunk into bubbles. "Are you getting in or not?" she said, smiling seductively.

Wade came close to tripping as he came out of his pants.

Twenty-Four

At 1:00 A.M. Pacific Standard Time, Vangie woke, cold, clammy, and shaken. Her throat ached to hoarseness. Her skull pounded. Her skin burned. No nightmare accompanied these feelings, only an urgent impulse to get home.

At 3:00 A.M, the heavy door of our apartment creaked open and shut quietly. I dropped to the floor like a war victim and crawled quietly from my mother's bed into the closet, hiding behind coats and clothes that smelled of mustiness. I could hear the distinct sound of Mr. Reese's jingling keys. His menacing voice wafted through the apartment, his footsteps treading softly from room to room.

"I know you in here somewhere," he said.

I had forgotten about Sir Duke. He scratched at the closet door and purred. I threw my hands over my mouth, my breath the whisper of butterfly wings.

It happened quickly, before I could find something to grab hold of. I groped for dresses, coats, anything to keep from being dragged from the closet by my ankles. Mr. Reese was too strong and mean. I gave up my groping, forced to hold my sweat pants up as my butt swept up the dusty floor. I was flung onto the bed with the force of two men. My head struck the headboard so hard the room turned black momentarily. Then I was yanked again, this time backward, and then flipped upright by Mr. Reese's cold, calloused hands.

"You keep quiet about this and I might let you stay another month rent free," he said, unbuttoning his pants while crushing my chest with his elbow. "Let's see if you're anything like the poor little rich girl. Ain't no nine-to-five putting them fine clothes on her back and them diamonds in her ears. She knows how to keep a roof over her head. If you're smart, you will too."

Spit sprayed my face through his gritted teeth. I screamed and cried silently, trying to fight my way out of imprisonment. It was no use. Vangie couldn't hear my silent cries. Douglas couldn't save me. West and Deja couldn't either. My limbs went limp, and I imagined myself invisible. It was a game I played back when Russell's fearsome eyes would find me alone, outside of Vangie's guard. In that hiding place, my heart could rest and my spirit was free to roam.

The creaks and squeaks of the rickety bed reverberated in my mind. If only the bed would collapse and Mr. Reese would go flying off me…

"I'll be damned." Mr. Reese's yellow eyes seemed to have witnessed a wonder.

That was when I heard my own voice ripping apart the snail in my throat. I was screaming beyond the walls of Cambridge, awakening the night.

Mr. Reese smothered my mouth with the palm of his sweaty hand to mute me again. Before his shock wore off, I kneed him between the legs, scratched him across the face, and dashed for the door like a frightened cat. I could feel my heart racing and my legs pumping. I flew up the stairs, two steps at a time, toward the roof where I found the dark corner beneath the split stairwell and curled into a tight ball on the cold cement surface and cried.

Since Christmas, Douglas hadn't come by—not on Saturday or any other day. I waited day after day, listening for his footsteps and peeking through the door. I had dismissed my mother's accusation as crazy talk, but sure enough, Vangie had run Douglas off and I would never see him again.

When daylight came, I returned to our apartment and grabbed my backpack. It didn't hold much, a few changes of underwear, my toothbrush, sweatpants, jeans, socks, one or two T-shirts, and a thermal shirt. The remaining space was stuffed with remnants of food—Top Ramen noodles, soda, half a jar of peanut butter, some crackers.

I didn't shower; I was too scared. I changed out of my ripped sweats and ripped T-shirt and into jeans, a thermal shirt, thick socks, boots, a beanie, and the Stanford hoodie Vangie had given me. In the bottom of my tote bag, I found nineteen cents and stuffed it into the front pocket of my jeans. Sir Duke jumped into my arms. I squeezed him tightly, dousing his fur with my tears.

As I was about to leave the apartment, I noticed our family photo. The frame was faded and dusty, a crack in the glass standing like a stick figure among us. It was the only family portrait we had ever taken. Vangie and I were toddlers and our mother was in her early twenties, her face more beautiful than an angel's, her smile brighter than the sun. I looked closer, overcome with tears by what I saw for the first time. It had been there all along —our mother's sadness in a rainbow of hope, Vangie's resolute independence, and my eyes lost in the clouds—a snapshot of what the future held for each of us.

Our heavy door snapped shut behind me when I left home.

Vangie caught a taxi directly to Cambridge Heights, the longest and slowest route imaginable, seemingly. "Can you go any faster? It's an emergency."

The driver picked up speed.

At Cambridge she threw him forty dollars and rushed upstairs on nimble feet. Her heart grew heavier with each step, her mind warier, her gut tauter.

She found a sheet of white paper taped to their apartment door: "Five-Day Notice to Vacate: Non-Payment of Rent. Authorized by Albert James Reese."

With trembling hands, Vangie groped through the small carry-on she'd packed for her house key. It didn't fit the lock. She tried again. "Angie!" she screamed, pounding on the door. "Angie! Open the door!" When no one answered, she hurried next door and pounded on Miss Coffee's door. By now doors were opening and heads were peeking out down the hallway.

"You not gone get no answer," Bonifa said. "West and Deja got evicted. They tryna get rid of all the old tenants so they can raise the rent."

Vangie was relieved to see the odd, but familiar, blue contact lenses on Bonifa that contrasted starkly with her dark brown skin and bleach-blonde weave.

"Have you seen my twin?" Vangie asked, rushing toward Bonifa, who tightened the belt on her drab robe and stiffened. Vangie read the disinclination to help Annette's "stuck-up" daughter in Bonifa's blue eyes.

"Hold up," Bonifa said before Vangie hurried off. "I should mind my own business...but yeah, there is something you ought to know..."

"Tell me," Vangie said desperately.

"I heard screaming last night, coming from y'all's place. Talk to Albert. He's been in and out of there a lot lately."

Vangie took off toward the basement where she would find Albert James Reese with the rest of the rodents. She had a good mind to wake him out of his sound sleep with a knife at his throat. Her heels clicked softly down the last flight of stairs that led to Mr. Reese's hideout. At the door, she could hear muffled voices from what sounded like a TV and the faint squeaking of a bed. From the sound of it, Mr. Reese had coerced some poor tenant into keeping a roof over her head by keeping him company. It took a second before the thought registered. Her fist lit into the door loud enough to startle the rats. When it didn't open, Vangie yanked at the knob, and pounded harder.

The door finally creaked open and Mr. Reese's dog-yellow eyes peeked out. "Is there something I can do for you?"

Vangie charged inside, sending Mr. Reese stumbling. Unable to catch his balance, he fell backward, cracking his back against the overturned coffee table.

"That better not be my sister in your bed! I'll kill you!"

Mr. Reese glared at her like an attack dog. When he tried to stand, Vangie lodged the heel of her boot into his chest and grabbed the first weapon she could get her hands on.

"You move and you'll be sorry," she said, raising the hammer to strike a deadly blow.

"It ain't her."

"Angie!" Vangie called out

"I said it ain't her. Got-damn-it!"

The eyes peeked over the sheet first. In the dark room, dimly lit by the thirteen-inch TV, Vangie's view was distorted. She peered closer. The hair was too short, the skin too dark, and if she wasn't mistaken, the two front teeth were long gone. Vangie sighed with relief. It wasn't Angie who had fallen victim to Mr. Reese.

The woman emerged fully, her hefty breasts spread like flat tires over her protruding abdomen. She adjusted her wig. "I'll be leaving now, Albert." She slid out of bed and into a smock of a dress, grabbed her house slippers, and tiptoed away.

"Got-damn-it!" Mr. Reese groaned.

"Where's my twin?"

"Hell if I know."

"When did she leave?"

"The notice said five days to vacate. Maybe she left five days ago. I ain't paid to keep tabs on tenants."

"Where's the key?"

"I can't give you nothing if you don't let me up from here."

Vangie eased her boot from his patch of gray chest hair, keeping a tight grip on the hammer.

Mr. Reese uncurled himself from the floor and snatched a pack of cigarettes off the bed. Next to the bed was a ragged couch littered with empty beer cans and cigarette butts where Mr. Reese sat in his nasty underwear enjoying a few puffs.

The foul odors in the windowless room assailed Vangie's nostrils. Unable to bear the dungeon another second, she held out her hand. "The key, Mr. Reese." Vangie raised the hammer higher. "I won't ask you again."

"Legally, I ain't gotta give you shit. Your apartment and everything in it is the property of CCB Enterprise until I get my rent. You enter it unauthorized, I can have you arrested for trespassing and tack on assault with a deadly weapon."

Vangie weighed her options. Much as she wanted to kick in his brown teeth for good measure, she wouldn't benefit from an assault charge.

"I'll let myself in." She grabbed a ring of keys hanging on the wall and left the basement in a hurry. If Mr. Reese tried to stop her, she would follow through with her threat.

Two cops accompanied by an anguished Mrs. Reese accosted Vangie before she could find the right key to open the apartment door.

"That's her right there! She tried to kill my husband with a hammer!" Mrs. Reese cried, pointing to the hammer in Vangie's hand. Mr. Reese, who had obviously dragged his poor wife out of bed to be his credible witness, stood by complacently while his wife, a haggard woman with dark rings under her eyes and the stench of liquor on her breath, pleaded his case.

"What's the problem here?" said one of the two black officers. Both cops stood with their arms crossed over their puffed chests in their Detroit blues and caps, well-known, imposing figures in these parts, there to enforce the law without any trouble.

Vangie looked on. Wearing her best black leather boots, tights, and black cashmere minidress, she wasn't worried about being mistaken for an armed and dangerous criminal.

"You plan on doing some damage with that hammer?" The other officer, tagged Brooks, said. With a chocolate baby face, he didn't look a day over twenty-one or long from the academy.

Vangie compliantly handed the officer the hammer.

"I have a legal right to enter this apartment. The notice states five days as of today to pay or vacate. Unless an injunction has been filed and he has a court order to evict me, I live here." Silently, she thanked Annette for her legal know-how when it came to evading evictions.

The officer tagged Powell took a closer look at the notice. "I see your point." He turned to Mr. Reese. "Let her in."

"I want her arrested for assault with a deadly weapon," Mr. Reese said.

"Step back." Officer Powell held up a stiff hand. "That goes for all of you," he said to the neighbors who had seen fit to gather in her honor.

"What happened to your face? Did she do that?" Brook's asked Mr. Reese, making note of the cat scratches that started from Mr. Reese's left ear and cut halfway across his cheek.

"I didn't touch him," Vangie said.

Mr. Reese mumbled something and then said, "What about my rent!"

"All I have is cash," Vangie said to the officer, ignoring Mr. Reese.

"Can you get a money order tomorrow?" Brooks said.

She nodded.

"Man, give her the key," Brooks said.

Resignedly, Mr. Reese handed her the apartment key and snatched his ring of keys from her hand.

Vangie rushed inside the apartment. Nothing was out of place, not a stitch of clothing or a pair of shoes. Both beds were neatly made, neater than usual. She checked the bathroom, closets, anywhere she thought Angie might hide. In the living room, she checked the desk drawer, flipping it upside down. The envelope of money she had Angie tape to the bottom was missing. Vangie collapsed on the sofa. Tears stung her eyes and an inexplicable chill took over her bones.

"Does this belong to you?" Officer Powell held up her travel bag.

Vangie nodded.

He set her the bag on the coffee table. "Anything else you need from us before we go?"

"Can you help me find my twin?" Her voice cracked and her tears broke.

Officer Powell sat beside Vangie and proceeded with a series of questions. What was her twin's name? When was the last time she had seen or talked to Angie? Could she be with a relative or friend? Did she anticipate foul play? Was Angie mentally or physically impaired?

Vangie answered to the best of her ability, excluding Angie's mutism.

"Contact us in twenty-four hours. If she doesn't show up by then, file a missing person's report." Officer Powell stood as if his work was done. "Let's go, Brooks."

Brook's brown eyes were on full alert and his hand at his holster at all times as he inspected the apartment. "You live here? For real?" His voice reflected total disbelief.

Vangie said nothing.

Before Officer Brooks left, he handed her his business card. "Hit me up if you need me."

Vangie spent the rest of the night listening for Angie and keeping her cell phone close, just in case Angie called. Her mind was her worst enemy, punishing her with terrifying thoughts and merciless guilt.

When the sun cast a faint light over the city, Vangie was up and showered quickly. She dressed for the cool, spring weather in a knit sweater, boots, and the jeans Wade loved so much on her.

Sitting on the broken-down couch in the wholly depressing apartment, she made her second call of the day, this time using her California line.

Wade answered on the first ring. "Where're you?" he barked.

"In Canada." She hated lying, but what choice did she have at this point?

"Try not to leave without telling me next time. I was looking everywhere for you." She visualized Wade's brows knitted and eyes afire.

"I'll try."

"Is everything okay?" His voice was calmer, soothing even.

Vangie leaned her head back on the sofa and closed her eyes, fighting back an onslaught of tears. "I had to take care of some business for my father."

"What kind of business?"

"Property business."

Wade's silence unsettled her. She feared he saw right through her deception.

"When're you coming back?"

"Soon."

"Have you made provisions with your instructors?"

Vangie sighed silently and rolled her eyes. She hadn't considered "making provisions with her instructors," nor had she had the time. Wade had it easy—too damn easy—and could never understand her problems if she could bring herself to confide in him. Drug houses, slumlords, evictions, and welfare didn't exist in the heavenly hills of Encino Valley. Add to it pimps, hoes and winos, and it was more than she could bear. It crossed Vangie's mind to spare them both the agony of him one day discovering that her life and his in no way paralleled.

She heard a knock at the door and sprang up. "I'll call you back."

"You forgot something," Wade said.

She hadn't forgotten, no more than she could forget to breathe. "I love you."

"Say it again. We lost connection."

She managed a chuckle. "You heard me."

"I love you too," Wade said with a smile in his voice.

She felt as if he had held her in his arms and told her not to worry. Everything would be fine.

Vangie opened the front door.

"I got here as fast as I could," Douglas said, rushing into the apartment wearing his lab coat over a dress shirt and jeans. "I cleared my calendar for the rest of the day. Where should we start?"

"There's only one place I can think of," Vangie said.

Twenty-Five

Vangie recoiled at the sight of Walter Ruggers Mental Health Center, which seemed to assault all her senses each time she walked through its automatic doors.

"Just the person I need to see," Dr. Adler said, stopping them in the corridor. Do you have a minute to stop by my office? I'd like to discuss your mother's transition."

Transition?

The low, dull throbbing in her head felt like a migraine coming on. To lose her twin and her mother in one day would surely destroy her. Vangie rejected the idea.

"Transition has an ominous ring, Doctor."

"Ah! The verbose one."

"Maybe you can help us, Doc," Douglas said. "We're looking for her twin. The...uh...quiet one."

"Yes," said the doctor, nodding.

"Has she been here in the past day or so?"

At Dr. Adler's blank expression, Vangie felt the blood drain from her face. Tears stung her eyes again. She was at a dead end.

"Can't say I have, which brings me back to my original line of thought. Your mother's transition..."

"Where is my mother?" Vangie said.

"I believe it's snack time. Try outdoors."

Finding her heartbeat, Vangie left Douglas with the doctor and headed to the lawn outback. She found Annette sitting alone, smoking a cigarette and staring at the two-story brick wall while other patients picnicked on the lush grass, played board games, or ate lunch at the picnic tables. For a moment, she stood back and watched Annette, wondering how her mother would react to seeing her after months of her absence.

"If you gonna visit me, speak," she heard her mother say.

Not sure whether Annette was talking to her or the tree, Vangie slowly emerged into her mother's view.

"You gonna just stand there or give me a hug?" Annette said.

Vangie wrapped her arms around her mother, wanting to break down and sob.

"Grab a chair and sit down," Annette said.

Vangie pulled up a lawn chair.

"How's school?"

"What school, Mom?" she said, testing her mother's lucidity.

"You're smart enough to get into college, now you wanna play dumb. I keep up with my girls, if I don't do nothing else right."

How Vangie wished that was true. Still, she smiled, catching the twinkle in her mother's dark eyes that mirrored her own. Gone was the hopelessness that had occupied them for as long as she could remember. Annette's hair spilled over her shoulders in beautiful dark coils, her maroon-painted lips bringing color to her face. Vangie's lungs filled with a breath of fresh air to see her mother looking alive again.

"I made the Dean's List."

"That don't surprise me."

"And I met someone."

"How old is he, Vangie?" Annette had taken on an overprotective air Vangie rarely saw in her mother.

"He's twenty-three, Mom."

"He gotta a name?"

"Yes. He has one."

Her mother laughed and shook her head. "You still hiding men in the closet like I don't know what you've been up to. Girl! Tell me the boy's name."

"Wade." Vangie's heart lightened at the mention of Wade and the edges of her lips curled upward.

"If he makes you happy, baby, I'm happy for you. We all deserve happiness." Her mother's voice trailed off. Vangie stopped breathing, waiting for the sadness to take over her mother's face again and resentment to consume her eyes.

"Will I ever meet this boy?"

"Yes, Mom," she lied.

"Hump." Annette inhaled smoke, saying nothing more.

"Have they been treating you okay?" Vangie said, eagerly switching subjects.

"On Wednesdays they serve ice cream and cake." Her mother blew a perfect ring of smoke. "They treat us like some damn kids up in here." Annette was sounding more like her old self again. "I ain't seen your sister in a while either. I guess she forgot about me too." Her mother turned her somber gaze back to the sky and inhaled more smoke.

A heaviness fell upon Vangie's chest. Her tears were rising again. If she cried, her mother would suspect something was wrong. Moreover, telling her mother about Angie's disappearance would be futile and would only compound her own guilt. She swallowed her tears, stood, and gave her mother a brief hug.

"I love you, Mom."

"I love you too. Don't nobody love you more."

Vangie choked back tears. "I'll talk to the doctor about getting you out of here."

"Sounds like another story that ain't got no end to me."

Vangie kissed her mother's cheek and hurried toward Dr. Adler's office.

After leaving the hospital, Vangie and Douglas ate at a Hamburger Hut a block from the University of Michigan. Seeing the students roving the area with their backpacks reminded Vangie of the "provisions" she had yet to make with her instructors.

"So, have you forgiven me or are you still not talking to me?" Douglas said.

Vangie pushed around the fries on her plate with her plastic fork. She wasn't hungry and wasn't listening to Douglas's plea for forgiveness.

"God is my witness, Vangie, it began innocently," Douglas went on.

She knew of Douglas's innocent beginnings all too well—the knight in shining armor coming to save her from the pits of poverty. Angie, on the other hand, had been blinded by Douglas's friendly smile and gentle ways. When she'd learned of the gifts he'd showered on her twin and his unauthorized visits, she'd known something was up between the two of them. She couldn't get the truth out of Angie, so she had pried it out of Douglas when she paid him an unexpected visit during Christmas break. Her silence since, apparently, had gone on too long for him. He talked as if he had agonized with guilt for the past three months. He should feel guilty. She asked him to watch over Angie, not to take advantage of her.

"I know you won't believe this, but I love Angie," he said.

Her slap to his face was fast and furious. "You don't love my twin! You used her in place of me!"

Douglas nursed his cheek. "That's simply not true, Vangie. What happened shouldn't have happened, you're right. May God forgive me."

"God may. I never will."

"Believe me when I say I'd give my life to find Angie."

"So would I!" Tears burned her eyes. "Take me home."

When Douglas wheeled his car in front of Cambridge and parked, Vangie hopped out. "Bye, Douglas." She meant it for good.

Vangie regretted the day she'd ever welcomed Douglas into her private world, but she regretted even more forbidding Douglas from seeing Angie again. If Douglas had been around, Angie would still be too.

The next morning, Officer Brooks arrived at Cambridge wearing jeans, a bomber jacket, and Timberland boots. He had done more than help her file a missing person's report; he had offered to take her to dinner and a movie. Vangie had declined his invitation, but they had exchanged private numbers in case he heard about Angie or saw anyone who looked like her. Out of desperation, she called the officer last night for his help.

"Have you had breakfast?" Brooks said as he started the engine of his souped-up pick-up truck.

"Can we find my twin, Officer Brooks?"

The officer's dimples sunk into his baby face. "You keep calling me Officer. I told you to call me Ontrell."

"Ontrell, can we please find my twin?"

"We'll find her," he said with conviction.

At a complete loss, Vangie put her faith in the officer. He had already checked the county morgue and there had been no Jane Does that matched Angie's description.

Their first stop was the nearest emergency shelter. The Eastside

Mission housed the homeless and offered other services for the poor. Once Officer Brook's flashed his badge, the receptionist escorted them deeper into the dank building. Vangie glanced through every open doorway, hoping to find Angie.

They stopped at the office of Develia Montgomary, a heavyset black woman who sat crammed between a wooden desk and the wall.

"Are you the social worker?" Brooks said.

"Who wants to know?"

Brooks showed his badge again. "Got a minute?"

"I never have a minute. Have a seat," she said.

Vangie sat on pins and needles as Officer Brooks probed and Develia answered.

"All I can tell you is our beds are at full capacity. It shouldn't surprise you that we have a real homeless problem in this city. They're in and out of here like a revolving door. Some work the program. Some can't deal with the rules and responsibility, but rules are rules. If they can't deal with them in here, they can't deal with them out there." Mary pointed to the wall. "I get anywhere from one to twenty a day. Intake starts at seven in the morning and cuts off at ten. If not, they'd be lining up at my door all day."

"I'm interested in one client...her twin. Angie Cooper's the name."

Mary Montgomery looked at Vangie like she couldn't place her face. "If your twin came through my door, I'd have her in one of these files." She picked up the stack of files and plopped them back down on her desk. "An interview would've been conducted and she would've been assigned a bed by now, and given a voucher for clothes and shoes..."

"She has clothes and shoes," Vangie interjected with an air of indignation.

"All of our clients have clothes, honey, usually the ones on

196 | Sheryl Mallory-Johnson

their backs." Mary pursed her lips.

"You said you conduct an interview. What kind of interview?" Brooks said

"An intake interview, one on one."

"She's not here. Let's go." Vangie jumped from her seat and left the social worker's office and the building in a hurry. She needed air, but even outside she couldn't breathe without choking back tears.

"I'm leading this investigation, not you," Brooks said, slamming the door of his truck. "What was that about?"

"Angie wouldn't go to a shelter."

"What makes you so sure?"

Vangie stared at him, despondent. "She's shy."

"Too shy for what? To do an intake interview?"

No comment.

The officer watched her like a squinty-eyed bloodhound. "You see this?" He touched the tip of his puggish brown nose. "It sniffs out a lie. You're holding out. Do you want to find your twin or don't you?"

He left her few options. "Yes."

"All right, then. Let's go somewhere where we can eat and talk. The more you tell me, the faster we'll find her." He cranked up the engine.

Breakfast was McDonald's—a cup of coffee and a hash browns for Vangie and a big breakfast with hotcakes and a large coffee for Officer Brooks.

"So, what's up with your twin," he said between bites.

Vangie nibbled at her hash browns before responding. "She doesn't talk."

"What do you mean?"

"Just what I said.

"To nobody?"

"To nobody but me."

Officer Brooks took a moment to ponder what he had heard. "Let me get this straight. You're telling me she doesn't talk to *nobody* but you? For real?"

Vangie refused to repeat herself.

"That's a trip! Did she ever?"

"Does it matter."

"For the purpose of this investigation, it does."

"Are you a detective, Ontrell?"

"Give me a minute and I will be. Was she born that way?"

Vangie shook her head.

"When did she stop talking?"

She sipped her coffee and turned away from Brook's baby face and probing eyes.

"I'mma ask you again. When did your twin stop talking?" His arms crossed over his muscular chest, Brooks stared at her as if she had just become a prime suspect.

"I don't remember."

"You're saying she stopped talking out of the clear blue sky?"

A stare. A nod. That was all he was going to get out of Vangie on the subject.

"What about school?"

"What about it?"

"Can she read and write?"

"I didn't say that she was deaf and dumb."

"I'm just trying to gather the facts. What about class?"

"We had the same classes, and I talked for us. She did her own work and took her own exams, if that's what you mean."

"Where's your mother?"

"You ask too many questions, Ontrell."

"I wouldn't be a cop if I didn't. Where is she?"

"Who?"

"Your mother?"

"We're wasting time."

His dimples sunk into his cheeks again. "I feel you. Where you're from, I'm from... My mother's got issues too. You feel me?" He took her hand in his. "Let's do this. You tell me where you think your twin would go and I'll take you to her."

Vangie shut her teary eyes. She had no idea where Angie would go alone, mute and lost without her.

They cruised block after block, walked park after park, even scoured the human rubble on Skid Row without any luck.

When the sun set, Vangie closed herself inside their apartment and cried until her eyes swelled. She and Brooks would search for Angie again the next day. In the meantime, her mother would transition from the hospital to home, as Dr. Adler had later explained, which meant she would have to postpone her return to school.

While racking her brain for answers and combing every corner of their apartment for a clue, Vangie found one thing out of place. Angie had left her cell phone at home.

Twenty-Six

They called this the original Kansas City, home of the industrial era, the KC Livestock Exchange and Stockyard. Late nights, if I listened closely, I could sometimes hear the ghosts of cattle crying down by the old slaughterhouses. But I'd rather imagine West Bottoms as an enchanting place, the place it was long before it became a wasteland of empty buildings and shelter for our kind. Now new businesses, vintage stores and restaurants were moving in and our kind were being pushed out.

We didn't have the benefit of a toilet, water or electricity, and the little night light we did have came from a street lamp throwing a yellow shadow our way. We warmed ourselves with sleeping bags, layers of clothing and body heat, claiming our small piece of dry land, while others fought over what remained of the narrow corridor in an abandoned building where goods were once exchanged and ranchers, who traveled here from around the country by railroad, sat down for a Kansas City steak, which I have never tasted.

All around us camps had been set up. Some camps consisted of squatters who had hung around West Bottoms for years. Those in camps like ours, however, would eventually pack up and move on.

"A little somethin'-somethin' to warm you up." Mo handed me the bottle. The sour liquid was lost to my memory as I swallowed faster than I could taste. I used to hate alcohol, how it made people drink it like soda and crave it like water. I understood its magic now: If I drank enough, I could forget everybody and everything I had ever loved.

"Dang! Somebody's thirsty. Save some for me, Angie," Mo said.

I handed her the bottle wearing a contrite smile.

She laughed. "Yeah, your ass is sorry, but I love you, girl."

I loved Mo too. Born Monisha Brown, she was beautiful inside and out, with onyx skin rich with bands of gold, deep-set brown eyes full of wisdom, and a heart of gold. If not for Mo, I might have died on the streets long ago. Mo had lived on the streets since age thirteen. She knew I would've eaten anything edible to satisfy my hunger, even out of a trashcan. With her last dime she bought me a combo meal. We became instant best friends and Mo became my new guardian angel.

Mo passed the empty bottle to Dunk, who shoved it into a bloated trash bag for recycling. Dunk was the mastermind of our small group of misfits. Back in high school he had been one of the best basketball players in the nation. He never made it through college or to the NBA. After serving time in Iraq during the Gulf War, Dunk got addicted to the same crack pipe that killed Mo's mother. He had given up the pipe, but the war had stayed with him.

In many ways we had become family, Mo, Dunk, Mental, and me.

When Mo snuggled under Dunk for the night, I set out to find Mental, walking through bodies in sleeping bags, under newspapers or, if they were lucky, in tents. Outside, I sloshed through mud and debris, and found Mental sitting curbside, rocking his head to whatever music was playing on his battered IPod. His eyes, brown and deep-set like Mo's, smiled as I ambled up. I couldn't help but smile back. Mental rarely submitted to a smile, but he couldn't fool me. Inside, he wanted to save the world, though outwardly he acted as if he could take on the world and would fight anyone who dared him not to. A thug at heart, he kept his jawline stiff, his chin raised, wore his jeans sagging and his baseball cap over his French braids that snaked down his neck. Mental was the cutest, nicest boy I'd ever met.

I sat beside him and stared at the sky. We didn't talk and didn't have to. We understood each other, Mental and me. This life was hard and no place for an eighteen-year-old like Mental with big dreams of becoming a rap mogul.

We eventually left the curb and walked through the old stock-yard, over where the colorful lights of the Kansas City skyline reproduced itself in the Missouri River. The night was still young by our clock, the Missouri sky a slice of mud pie without a sprinkle of stars. As we walked, Mental spit his rhymes, waving his hands like an orchestra director. Within the ruthlessness of his lyrics there was always a silver lining that gave me hope for brighter days.

"You hear that, Angie! My shit is dope! Haters can't touch my flow!"

I half expected Mental to beat his chest and howl at the moon. He was excitable and passionate about everything. He lifted me off the ground and spun me around and around. I laughed into the wind. When he placed me back on my feet, he held me close enough for our body parts to touch in intimate places, turning my face all shades of red.

"You're pretty cool, Angie. And fine too, when you comb that nappy head." He snatched off my beanie, allowing me time to duck out of his arms. Before I could get away, he grabbed me again and held me even closer, staring at me as if I was a beautiful sunset. I wasn't a sunset. I wasn't anything worth admiring.

"Why do you always shrivel up when I look at you?"

I shrugged, sinking my neck deeper into my shoulders.

Mental laughed. "Say something and I'll let you go."

Words I couldn't speak inundated my brain until I thought my head would explode. The more I struggled to get away, the harder Mental laughed. I was on the verge of tears when his lips met mine like soft, warm bread. My back bent in his effort to shove his tongue deeper into my mouth. I stumbled backward, landing against a fence, where he grinded me into cold metal while covering my mouth with his.

"I love you, baby." He kissed my neck and stopped to suck. I thought he might extract a vein he sucked so hard. Numbed by life and liquor, I found the courage to shove him.

You're Mo's little brother and my little brother too! My eyes scolded him.

Mental's face twisted into a new rage. "I can't touch you? I'm too dirty for you? My pockets ain't fat enough? My breath *stank*? Is that what's up?"

I grabbed his hand and placed it over my heart, telling him that I loved him.

He shoved me as hard as I had shoved him and left me alone, fighting back tears. The rain returned, dripping lightly before becoming a downpour. I ran for cover.

When I returned to camp, Mo and Dunk were planning our survival strategy.

"Did you find Mental?" Mo asked me. When it came to her little brother, Mo was a mother bear that couldn't rest without her cub nearby.

Avoiding Mo's wise eyes, I nodded and tucked myself into my sleeping bag, swiping away my tears before they could fall again. While Dunk and Mo talked, I listened, feeling like a third wheel destined to break off.

Dunk said we would catch out once we earned enough money to get by and get to our next stop, wherever that may be. For some people, hopping freights was a way of life, and for others it was an adventure; but for us it was a cheap way to get to our ultimate destination. Mo and Dunk were in search of a warmer climate, Mental searching for fortune and fame, and I had my own reason for traveling west.

When Mental walked in, I shut my eyes. Sleep didn't come easy. I'd learned to sleep like a giraffe, minutes at a time, and to fight like a hyena when I had to. Behind me, I could hear Mental breathing hard and smell the smoke from his cigarette. I kept my back to him, keeping an eye on Man and Missy until their mother, Mercedes, who walked the streets nights to feed them and her drug habit, showed back up.

Mental's kiss stayed on my mind. It wasn't magical like Douglas's kiss had been, and hadn't brought an itch between my legs, but it reminded me that I hadn't been kissed or touched in that way since Douglas. A feeling of self-pity stung me, but I felt sorrier for Mental than I felt for myself.

Well into the night, Mercedes hobbled in, one high heel boot on her foot, the other in her hand and her nose dripping with blood. I didn't have to wonder what had happened to her. Anything was possible. That was the street, one big fight, for your next meal, a safe place to rest, food, for your life.

"Thanks for watching my kids, Angie," Mercedes said, waving a tired hand my way. She climbed into the sleeping bag with Missy.

When daybreak crept through the broken windows, stealing our sleep, we gathered everything we owned and could carry. Most camps had already packed up, leaving dirty diapers, soiled clothes, broken dope pipes, and other trash behind. Sleeping in could mean missing out on shelter or a meal.

To avoid Mental, I happily followed Dunk while Mo and Mental went in the opposite direction. Outside of West Bottoms, Kansas City, Missouri bustled with Friday morning traffic. We stopped at a 7-Eleven, where Dunk took advantage of rush hour traffic, offering to clean car windows for change in return. In the meantime, I went inside to use the bathroom. It cost a quarter, a quarter I didn't have. I stood by until a lady came out and then hurried in before the door slammed shut.

Standing over the sink, I splashed my face with water, dried it with toilet paper, and brushed my teeth with soap, rinsing and spitting out the aftertaste. That was when I noticed my purple neck. I leaned closer to the mirror.

How could Mental possibly love me?

My hair hadn't been combed in so long it had begun to dread. I wore an oversized army jacket over my hoodie and grimy jeans, and I had on grubby tennis shoes taken from a "free" box someone had set out.

I double knotted the string of my hoodie to hide my hickey, and left the bathroom.

Cinnamon rolls cost two for one dollar, and coffee cost 50 cents. Between Dunk and me, we collected enough change cleaning windows to buy breakfast without touching our small savings. So far, we had saved enough for a two week stay in a cheap motel, once we got to our final destination.

We traveled by foot into the heart of Kansas City. Dunk attracted attention every step of the way. At six feet, five inches tall, with wooly dreadlocks, skin the color of a ripe eggplant, and his raincoat draping his lean body like a cape, Dunk might look intimidating to some people but in my eyes he was a gentle giant. I felt protected walking in his shadow.

Next, we stopped at the Central Library. While Dunk found the computer section, I pulled interesting books from the neatly stacked bookshelves and rediscovered the children's library all over again, a place full of imagination where the doorways, walls and ceilings read like the open page of a fairytale.

I was lost for time when the librarian found me and told me I had to leave. By then Dunk had found a hustle on *Craigslist*: "pulling weeds for pay." We each had our hustles. Dunk was handy with his hands and could build, paint, or repair anything. I loved helping him more than using my handicap to panhandle. Mo usually found a temporary job conducting surveys or soliciting for signatures, and Mental could hustle up dollars standing on a corner *free-styling*.

Day-by-day we got by.

We made it to a two-story house on Jarboe that looked in need of serious restoration and worth our walk. Before we could get halfway up the rickety wood stairs that wound up a steep hill, two Hispanic guys buried in the weeds, stood, shared a beer, and then went back to pulling weeds. The job had been filled. The light in Dunk's eyes went out, but he wasn't big on complaining about life. He took it in stride. So did I.

Turned out it wasn't a good day for panhandling either, now that the rain was coming down steadily. It gave people an excuse to hide under their umbrellas and ignore my "I'm Mute" cardboard sign and Dunk's "Injured Vet. Will Work" sign.

We gave up panhandling and caught the bus to East Troost Avenue, entering a part of town that reminded me of Eastside Detroit. Luckily, Mo and Mental had gotten to the church first and saved our place in line. We made it to the front of the line before the food ran out. After we were served mashed potatoes, ham, string beans, and two slices of white bread, we grabbed the first seats under the tents that became available. I chewed and swallowed without the benefit of tasting a single distinguishable spice other than salt. Mental sat across from me, giving me his mean mug.

"Eat!" Mo popped Mental on the back of his neck.

He swatted at her. "Get off me, Mo."

"Boy, what's your problem? You've been acting stupid all damn day."

"I got your boy. You're talking to grown man right here."

Dunk laughed. "Man, you're buggin'."

"He's about to get his little ass kicked," Mo said.

"Fuck this!" Mental pushed his plate away, jumped out of his seat, and stormed off, tugging at his sagging jeans.

"Where do you think you're going!" Mo called after him.

"He ain't going nowhere," Dunk said. He wasn't worried about Mental, and neither was I. Mental had never wandered too far, just far enough to give Mo a good scare.

After we filled up on free food, we were given a bottle of Gatorade and a pack of cheese crackers to go. We found Mental sitting on the curb smoking a cigarette, and then headed back to camp.

That night I dreamed of the sunniest skies, the whitest sand, and the bluest ocean before the cruel hand of life bolted me awake.

Twenty-Seven

D unk! Wake up! Mental ain't here," I heard Mo cry out. I sat up and looked around to see what the commotion was about. Sure enough, Mental's sleeping bag hadn't been touched last night and the day had already dawned.

"Damn, Mo. Calm down," Dunk said with one eye open.

"Don't damn me, dude. Anything could've happened to my baby brother. Are you crazy!"

Dunk sat straight up. "Yeah, I am crazy. A certified crazy motherfuckah."

Now Mo looked as if a canary had flown into her mouth.

Dunk wasn't crazy, per se. The Army had given him an honorable discharge because of his night terrors. Some nights when he couldn't sleep, Dunk would walk the streets until his legs gave out.

"Have you seen those Neo-Nazi meth-head motherfuckah's around here?" Mo went on.

"I seen 'em."

"And what about the bangers packing AKs?"

"I know all about AKs. Blasted a few .50 cals too. Tossed a few 79s, lit up an entire village, killing babies and they mommas and shit."

"I'm just saying, Dunk." Mo's tone had softened. "And what about the poe-poe?"

"What about 'em, Mo?"

"You're a black man. Figure it out." When Mo smiled, the sky lit up; when she didn't, lightning was sure to strike. She looked ready to hurt anyone who may have hurt Mental as she shoved her size 10 feet into her scruffy boots. When she stuffed herself into her winter coat, the last button popped off and flew across the room. She flipped the matted, furry hood over her short Afro and marched off.

Dunk jumped out of his sleeping bag. I jumped out of mine too.

"Hold up, little sis, in case that little nigga shows up." Dunk strapped on his pack and his gun and hurried to catch up to Mo.

I sat until I couldn't sit any longer. My hunger was eating me alive. I hated hunger; it was mean, and trying to dismiss it only made it more spiteful. I paced the campsite, chewing on my nail. If something happened to Mental, I'd blame myself.

I saw Mo and Dunk through the broken window and dashed outside to meet them halfway. Mo's frigid face and Dunk's tense walk told me that something was wrong.

"We couldn't find him," Mo said. When her tears welled, mine welled too. Mo rarely showed weakness.

I'm the weakest of the bunch.

Dunk told us both to stop crying and came up with a new strategy. As soon as we found Mental, we would leave Missouri, he said. He had a bad vibe about this city. So did I.

He directed me to find a boxcar at the rail yard while he and Mo searched for Mental. I rushed back to camp and packed up.

The freight yard was easy to find. Just follow the tracks. Once I arrived, I staked out behind a bunch of trees. Two freight trains sat idling on the tracks. If I wasn't careful, I could catch out in the wrong direction—going eastbound instead westbound for instance. I eyed the one I was certain faced westbound, mentally gauging the time it would take me to sprint across the dirt field without getting caught. There were no yard bulls in sight, but that could change in a matter of seconds. Bulls were always on patrol, looking to catch hoppers like us. If I got caught, I could get ticketed for trespassing or go straight to jail.

I can't get caught.

As fast as humanly possible, I sprinted down the embankment and across the yard, my feet plowing into mud, my blood pumping in my ears, the rain spraying my face. By the time I hid between freight cars, my heart was a beat away from stopping. I balanced on the knuckle to catch my breath, and then I ran again, crouching low. I passed up open boxcars and flat ones until I came to a closed car that looked perfect for riding. Before hopping aboard, I spray painted XOXO on the door, leaving a trail for Mo and them to follow.

The sizeable boxcar was dirty and dank. Generally, freights carry everything from chemicals to scrap metal. Whatever this one carried smelled toxic. I shut the door and was overtaken by darkness. Using my flashlight, I peered around the crates to make certain I wasn't in the company of veteran hobos. Once I felt safe, I sat by the door and waited for Mo and them to show up. Raindrops drumming against steel pacified me. When sleep came, I welcomed it.

Twenty-Eight

The engine roared first and then the horn blew. My eyes popped open. The train was moving. Thinking fast, I grabbed my stuff and scrambled for the door. It was difficult enough to hop a freight train on the fly—to dismount a fast moving one was deadly. I opened the car door and was practically thrown from the train by heavy winds and harsh rain. I slammed the door shut and rethought my strategy. I could run alongside the train as I dismounted and take the risk of being crushed by steel...

I did nothing but listen to the sound of speed increasing. For two years, time had been an endless stream as I drifted through life without a sense of direction. Now time was my worst enemy. Twenty hours could pass before the train stopped again. If I didn't jump, I would never catch up with Mo and them.

I withered to the floor, praying the train would stop at a signal soon, stop to let another train pass, or stop to refuel.

The sound of the squealing wheels sent me scrambling for the door again. I opened it against light winds and frost bitten air this time. Most freight trains travel through the back woods where only wild animals roam. In broad daylight, the wooded and lush parts of country were at times so breathtaking I felt lucky to be part of nature. In total blackness, however, I could hardly hold my pee out of fear of what awaited me on the other side of midnight.

I swayed back and forth, and as in double Dutch, I played a guessing game: when to jump. More terrified of coming face to face with a yard bull than I was of jumping, I counted to three in my mind and took a leap of faith.

First came the crack, and then came the throbbing pain that shot through my leg when I hit gravel. Unable to break my fall, I tumbled and landed in a bed of wispy weeds. I didn't move, listening to the train rumble by until the only sounds were crickets and wild animals.

I eventually sat up, groped for my flashlight, and then examined my ankle. By the look and feel of it, swollen and tender to the touch, I had sprained it, sure enough. If I couldn't walk, I couldn't catch out, which meant I might never catch back up to Mo and them. I laid flat on my back, wanting to shout to the black sky: *How many more worst days of my life do I have left, God?* My chest went into spasms as hot tears rolled down my temples and clogged my ears.

When all my tears had drained, I found the courage to live another day and crawled on all fours out of the weeds and back to the tracks, where I set up camp on gravel. Unable to hold my bladder for another second, I did my usual in the dark, and then buried myself deep inside of my sleeping bag. I could take the bite of winter's end more than the thought of rattlesnakes. I listened for rustling and rattling, my eyes zipping from left to right and my heart skipping a beat at every mysterious noise. I tried to dream up delicious recipes not to think about the hopper whose dismembered body was found spread across the Mississippi plains. Still, dreadful thoughts kept my heart pounding in my ears.

As soon as dawn painted a silver sky around the yellow slice of moon, I was up with the birds, hobbling alongside the tracks.

Guarded by trees stilted twenty-feet high, and standing like soldiers on both sides of the tracks, I walked and walked. Aside from the squirrels and jackrabbits playing hide and seek around me, the morning was eerily quiet.

I didn't know how far or how long I had walked when the tracks split in two, zigzagging around a forest of trees. When it came to freight trains, Dunk held all the knowledge and had the greatest love. He taught me that most freight trains ran approximately one mile in length and could wipe out eighteen football fields before coming to a stop. Since I didn't know the length of a football field, I couldn't possibly know the distance between here and the freight yard. I didn't even have a compass to know my approximate location. I looked to the towering trees for guidance. Whichever way the lime-green leaves blew, I would go.

I went left.

I had walked a few more miles when the forest finally opened up. The tracks had disappeared around a snow-crusted mountain in the far distance. From what I could see, there wasn't a freight yard in sight. I was too thirsty and hungry to cry, but I knew it wouldn't be long now before I died of dehydration.

In the middle of picturesque pastures surrounded by Rocky Mountains sat a mansion-sized house with a stable, a barn, and beautiful horses roaming free. Drawn to a pond, sparkling with clear blue water, I hurled myself over a white picket fence with the momentum of a tortoise and dragged myself across the land.

"Trespassing on private property will get you in a heap of trouble!" The man had come out of nowhere, charging at me with a shotgun in his hand. Too terrified to blink, I didn't look past his angry gray eyes and show of gray hair curving around his mouth and sprouting from under his cowboy hat.

He yanked me by my jacket sleeve. "Let's go!"

Kicking, scratching, and snarling, I fought like a hyena to break free.

"I've tamed cattle stronger than a frail thing like you," he said.

Out of breath and strength, I went completely limp. He carried me like a suitcase across his land and shoved me into the passenger's seat of a pick-up truck

"Don't you move!" He pumped his shotgun again, threatening to shoot me. Before I found the courage to jump out of the car, he climbed into the driver's seat.

"Where're you coming from girl?" he said, speeding down a winding road to nowhere.

I said nothing. I kept my head bowed.

He groaned and grunted in response to my silence.

Hearing but not listening to country music on the radio, I pressed my shoulder against the door, holding on to the handle while discreetly looking for a weapon or something to hit him with. His truck was spotless and smelled of old leather, cigar smoke, and cedar. Catching me eyeing his shotgun, he placed it in the backseat, leaving me defenseless.

We turned off the one-lane road that widened to four lanes. More pick-up trucks and cars appeared, along with signs of city life. When I saw "Welcome to Colorado Springs" displayed on a billboard, I clutched the door handle, ready to leap to freedom or to death. I didn't care which one. I was only a state away from Missouri. If I caught back out today, I could catch up to Mo and them in no time.

"This truck has the horsepower of a fine thoroughbred. Jump and you'll be road kill." He grabbed my arm before I could jump.

Terror, by now, had turned my stomach upside down. My eyes stayed as big as an owl's as the man blew through one light after another, never letting go of me. Soon my life would end, more tragically than I had ever imagined it would. I was sure of it.

He entered the highway and drove for miles before exiting. In a neighborhood with houses that sat far apart, he drove down a road flanked by boulders and piney trees, and then through automatic gates with a "Private Property" sign. I glanced over my shoulder to see the gate cage me in.

He parked at the bottom of the hill and between a pink Cadillac out of the 1950s and a gray Volkswagen Beetle in front of a brick two-story house with turquoise shutters. A cherry tree sprouting the pink buds of spring arched the driveway and marigolds peeked their tiny heads from behind brick planters.

I didn't know where I was and didn't plan to find out. If I was going to die anyway, I'd die with a bullet in my back. I jumped out of the car and whimpered like a puppy when I landed on my injured ankle.

The man helped me from the ground and ushered me up the front steps of the strange house. A bell jingled and the wood door swung back before he could knock. The lady standing in the doorway had apple-red hair and grape-green eyes. Her black dress hugged her tiny waistline and flared around her narrow hips. She wore pearls around her neck and low-heeled pumps, as if she had just come back from sunrise service.

"Top of the morning, Jim! I see you caught yourself another one," she said with a smile.

All sorts of terrifying thoughts crossed my mind.

He pushed me through the door. "Caught her dead to rights coming from those blasted tracks! A good scrub will do her some good. She smells like something my cattle wouldn't eat. Test her for drugs too. She's stronger than an ox and mean as a buzzard. I can't tell you where she's from. Couldn't get a peep out of her. At least she didn't try to do what my wife, may she rest in peace, wouldn't do. It's downright ungodly, I tell ya! Downright ungodly!" He gripped my arm tighter. "I catch you on my property again I'll skin you alive!"

"Jim!" the woman said as if to warn him.

Jim grunted and folded his arms across his chest.

The woman handed me a brochure from the oak desk that sat in the middle of the entryway. "Welcome to Roxanne's House for Women, Roxy's for short." She paused to smile. "Our beds are for girls with no home or family, recovering addicts and those ones with treatable mental problems. I'm the house manager. Our sweet little program director, Susan, assigns the beds, depending on if yah meet our criteria and all. Fill this out if yah can." She handed me a form attached to a clipboard. "There's hot coffee and warm donuts, if yah please." She winked at me and my heart beat lighter.

I decided to stay for the free coffee and donuts. I needed the sugar boost to get my strength back. Besides, that Jim man was blocking the door like an immovable object. I followed the woman through a living room warmed by carroty colored walls, floral paintings, and a burning brick fireplace.

She sat me in the dinning room. There were twelve seats in all around the country style table. My eyes went straight for the spread of donuts, their sweet aroma making my head spin and my stomach cramp from hunger pangs. The scent of savory coffee excited my senses.

"There's plenty more where that came from. I pick them up hot and fresh every Sunday morning from Sammy's Bakery. Donation, yah know. Help yah-self," she said as though catching me drooling. "What's yah name, by the way?" She watched me curiously, and then said, "Where're my manners? It says Florence Kilgore on my birth certificate, but you can call me Floe."

She didn't shake my hand, and instead rested hers on her

narrow hips. I understood why. My hands were grimy.

"In case you're interested," she continued, "we place on a first-come first-serve basis, so I advise yah to get that form filled out as quickly as yah can."

As soon as Floe left the room, I stuffed my mouth with four donuts and followed up with two cups of coffee. Flakes of sugar peppered the wood table. I dotted every single crumb and licked my finger clean. The sugar and caffeine shot to my brain, giving me a nice high. I looked around leisurely. This was another brightly painted room, mint green. A picture of Jesus Christ with open arms hung on the wall between two small wooden crucifixes. A placard on another wall read "Keep Praying," and another one read "A Clean Home Is A Godly Home." Another one read "In God We Trust." There were Godly signs everywhere.

Feeling guilty for planning to eat and run, I picked up the form and looked it over. I had always avoided places like this, where people might ask questions I couldn't answer and dig for secrets I couldn't tell. When asked my name, I accidently wrote Angie Cooper, scribbled it out, and then wrote Angie Brown instead, borrowing Mo's last name. In the past, I'd used Angie Coffee, Angie Frank, Angie Davis, and other last names.

I answered the other questions honestly: D.O.B., last permanent address, ethnicity/race, education, monthly income, housing status.

When I came to "reason for homelessness," I didn't know which one to choose—stranded/transient, insufficient income, substance abuse, or high-risk neighborhood. My reason for being without a home was lost to me by this point.

I checked "all of the above."

The next question read: How long have you been homeless?

I wrote two years, though the wind seemed to have carried me across seven seas where I had drifted endlessly.

Floe returned and looked over the form I had partially filled out. "Detroit? Don't think we've had anybody come through here from those parts. I'm from Massachusetts myself."

I twisted my mouth and lowered my eyes.

"I see yah tried the cherry fritter. That one's my favorite," she whispered behind her hand as if someone might overhear her. "Follow me. Susan is ready for yah."

To keep clear of Jim, I followed Floe down a long hallway where pictures of happy faced women hung on the magenta painted walls. At the end of the hallway, she directed me to sit and wait, and then disappeared behind a door. A few minutes later, Floe returned with a thin lady who had pasty white skin and boy-short brown hair. She wore a long skirt, cotton button up, and flat soled boots and looked to be in her thirties.

"Hi Angie. Susan." She shook my hand. "Let's talk in my office."

Taking tentative steps, I entered Susan's teal, gray, and orange office, which contrasted with her plain looks. To go with the cool colors, there was a purple couch, where I sat; Susan sat across from me in an psychedelic print chair, her big, brown eyes never leaving mine. To avoid them, I dropped my eyes to the coffee table cluttered with swinging pendulum balls, candles, and other objects while I twiddled my thumbs.

"I'll tell you a little about myself. I'm the program director for both houses. I've been with Roxy's for six years and love it here. My cat's name is Snickers and my poodle's name is Peanut..."

Tear filled my eyes.

"Do you have any pets, Angie?" She looked deep into my eyes as if she could read my mind.

I closed my teary eyes and shook my head, imagining the feel of Sir Duke in my arms and his soft fur tickling my chin. I told myself he was better off dead. I couldn't even take care of myself.

"Tell me a little about yourself. What brings you to Roxy's?"

This was the moment when the snail in my throat choked me. I stiffened and bunched my mouth.

"It's okay. Take your time. You came to us on the perfect day. The whole house is in the mountains for a retreat, and Sunday is my day off, typically." Susan smiled as though it was my choice to be here.

I took all the time in the world before Susan interrupted my silence.

"I have a friend. He injured the frontal lobe of his brain in a car accident and lost his voice. Can you talk, Angie?"

I zipped my lips and tugged at my right earlobe, explaining in my cryptic sign language that I didn't talk but I could hear.

"Do you sign?" Susan bent her fingers and hands into shapes I had never learned to interpret.

I shook my head.

"It's okay. You can read and write, which is awesome! Write your answers for me, whatever you want to say."

I frowned at the notepad she tried to hand me and shrunk back. I had nothing to say.

"It's okay. Do you have family, Angie?"

I bit the inside of my lip to keep from crying and tasted blood.

"I understand," Susan said compassionately. "Are you in contact with your family, Angie?"

I shook my head.

"It's okay. One of our girls graduated to the next phase of the program and a bed has opened up. If you follow the rules and work our program, you're welcome to stay. You should know that Roxy's is a safe, Christian environment."

I didn't know how to tell Susan I didn't want to stay, but I didn't know how to leave without being arrested for trespassing.

"I'll just need to go over our policies and procedures with you."

Susan explained the rules at Roxy's, such as no drugs, no weapons, and no stealing allowed. When she asked for identification to prove my name was Angie Brown, I didn't have any way of proving it.

After I signed papers stating I understood the rules, Susan turned me back over to Floe, who took me on a tour of the house. Our first stop was the community room painted an invigorating ocean blue.

"As you can see, the girls love to read, and we have plenty of Christian books for yah. There's a nice big TV over there, lots of wholesome DVDs, and this pinball machine here donated by one of the church members…" Floe patted the glass top. "The girls fought over it so much we had to restrict their time. Let's see. What else?" She looked around. "We have plenty of places for yah to sit, tables for yah to write or do artwork or what have you. Some of our girls go back to school, get their GEDs or enroll in college, whichever you please." She looked around again as if she had left something out. "In the cabinet you'll find art supplies, and behind that door there…" She pointed. "Is our computer lab."

The tour continued, but my thoughts stayed on the computer lab. If the computers had Internet, I could contact Dunk on his free email account and catch back out tonight.

After glimpsing two counseling rooms and a reading/prayer room, Floe took me upstairs. "I see you're pampering your foot," she said. "We've had a few girls come through injured. Takes cojones to hop trains. I'll see what I can do for yah."

I thanked her with a small smile.

Upstairs, down a long hallway, were six bedrooms and two bathrooms. It didn't look like those shelters Mo hated, the places that stuffed our kind into one big room, had one big bathroom and no stall doors, and showers with no privacy.

Floe unlocked the door to "my room." There were two of everything: beds, chest of drawers, and end tables, all made of plain pine wood. The walls were painted soft yellow, and white blinds covered both windows.

"You'll room with Ashley for the time being. She's been with us for a while and knows the ropes. I think the two of yah will get along just fine." Floe opened the closet. "Place your things in here."

Holding firmly to my stuff, I shook my head. My pack and bag were all I had to my name. I couldn't survive the night without them.

"It'll be here when yah get back. I promise yah."

Putting my life in Floe's hands, I placed my stuff inside the closet and followed her back down the hallway, wondering where she was leading me next. She stopped at a linen closet and gave me a bath towel, a washcloth, a bag of toiletries, and rubber flip-flops, which I had to sign for.

"I'm not sure what size yah are up top, but see if any of these fits yah." She unlocked one of three drawers inside the closet and whispered behind her hand, "We're all women. We understand what a woman needs to feel good about herself."

I grabbed a size 32B bra and a three pack of new underwear, in basic white, and tucked them under my arm.

From another drawer, she handed me two pair of socks. "We advise yah to write your initials on everything. Things are known to show up in the wrong drawers, if yah know what I mean."

Next, she opened a walk-in closet and insisted I pick out something to wear from the neatly stacked, gently used clothes that filled the shelves like a store. The residents were issued three outfits, two casual wear and one professional outfit for job-hunting purposes.

I grabbed a pair of size three blue jeans, a pair of black sweat pants, a black sweater, and a pink, gray, and white flannel button-up shirt before Floe could change her mind.

The bathroom was decorated in blues and pinks and smelled of bubblegum. A sign hanging on the wall warned me to wear shower shoes. Standing in the blue tub, I turned the shower on full blast, smiling sadly as hot water beat against my skin and poured over my face. I couldn't remember the last time I'd held a bar of soap or washed my hair. Grime gathered around my feet and washed down the drain. I scrubbed until the suds were snow white.

Flo had given me ten minutes to shower and dress—the house rule. I dried off quickly and brushed my teeth with real toothpaste. The bra fit perfectly, the jeans and plaid shirt a bit loosely. Deodorant was a treat I had learned to live without. I used it anyway, and then stuffed my old clothes into the plastic bag Floe had given me. I had lost my hair tie fighting Jim, and did my best to tame my hair, braiding it Apache-style.

Floe smiled when I stepped out of the bathroom. "Yah look like a new penny."

I gave her a sideways smile. I didn't feel like a new penny. I felt like the same old me.

"I'll take those if yah please." Floe had to pry the plastic bag from my hands. "Just putting them in the wash for a good cleaning, that's all."

My eyes pleaded for her to return them in one piece.

After Floe iced my ankle, she placed me in the community room and told me to stay off of it and rest.

Left alone, I limped over to the computer room and stomped my good foot when I found the door locked. I checked each window. They were securely screened in. The only exit led back to the main area of the house. Feeling like a trapped bird whose wings had been clipped, I grabbed an interesting book from the shelf and sat in a rocking chair in the corner, lulling myself to sleep.

"Sorry to wake you, Angie," I heard.

My eyes flipped open. Susan was standing over me.

"The girls are back from their retreat. We're holding a debriefing in the community room shortly. You'll get to meet everyone."

I blinked to gain focus, feeling lost and confused. The stained glass Jesus clock on the wall read 11:30. I had slept for too long and had gotten too comfortable here.

When I heard a choir of voices flooding the house, I thought to run, but the appetizing aroma of basil, thyme, cumin, oregano, and other distinguishable spices wafting through the house called for me to stay for lunch.

Twenty-Nine

They filed into the community room one by one. I counted eleven in all. Most of them looked my age, plus or minus a few years. A few looked old enough to be the others' mother, one their grandmother even. They came in all shapes and sizes, styles and dress, and various shades of white. Being the only black person in the room, I couldn't hide.

"Prayer time, girls!" Floe said, ringing a bell like the Good Fairy.

The girls cheered and jeered; several of them complained of being tired and hungry.

"The faster yah huddle, the faster y'all get to eat," Floe said.

Ceaseless chatter floated around the room as they all gathered. It took the tall mother with long black and silver hair to step in. Her husky voice had the power to quiet the room and inspire everyone to form a circle and hold hands, including Floe and Susan.

"Angie! Join us if yah please!" Floe said.

I solidified into a popsicle and stayed hidden behind my book.

"It's okay, Angie," Susan said, coaxing me out of my shell.

I limped across the room, never taking my eyes off of my feet. Floe squeezed my right hand and Susan squeezed my left, welcoming me to the circle.

Floe delivered a passionate prayer. The girls said amen and thanked Jesus; a few of them looked entranced, as they swayed with their eyes on the ceiling.

Susan then opened a Bible and read an inspirational passage. Taking Floe's cue, they all sang "Jesus Loves Me" in perfect harmony. When they finally took their seats, I was left standing.

"This is Angie, everyone. Let's welcome her to Roxy's," Susan said.

They each said hello in their own way: "Hi Angie... Hey Angie... Welcome Angie... How do, Angie... What's up, Ang... Hola, Angie..."

I threw up a hand, my eyes wandering involuntarily as the room orbited around me.

A hippie looking girl with a headband around her fluffy blonde hair was nice enough to bring me a chair. I dropped into it, wedging myself between the grandmother with skin as wrinkled as sundried tomatoes and a girl with a buzz cut and tattoo sleeves.

"Let's pray for Angie," Susan said.

"Jesus, we thank you for bringing Angie to us. May your holy blood wash away her sins. Amen." Their voices resounded.

"Who gets to sleep with the new girl?" said the girl with the buzz cut.

Laughs circulated around the room.

"Girls. We sleep in our own beds." Floe's skin was reddish-pink.

"It's okay. Angie is rooming with Ashley," Susan interjected.

"That'll be cool." The girl who spoke watched me with fidgety hazel eyes. She wore rings, one in her nose and one through her left brow, and her long black hair was as unkempt as mine.

"Everyone should know that Angie doesn't talk but she can hear perfectly."

They responded to Susan's announcement by staring at me like I was a freak of nature. Arms folded tightly over my chest, I dropped my eyes to my lap and slid down an inch in my chair.

For the rest of the meeting, while they each debriefed about their retreat experience, I repeatedly chanted in my mind, "*As soon as I get out of here, I can catch up to Mo and them... As soon as I get out of here, I can catch up to Mo and them... As soon as I get..."*

The debriefing ended and Susan dismissed us for lunch. Before I could leave, several of the girls introduced themselves, shaking my hand, patting me on the back and squeezing my shoulder as if to offer their condolences for my handicap. The others ignored me. A few of them mean mugged me.

"We're all screwed up the day we're born, man," said the girl with the tattoos. Her name was Chris. I met Verna too, the Native-American woman with the husky voice. She called herself the "lead resident." Ashley, my roommate, introduced herself, and Summer, the hippie girl, too.

At lunch I sat between Ashley and Summer. During grace, I thanked God for a meal, a shower, clean clothes, and these nice, strange people. I prayed for Mental, prayed to get back to Missouri, and prayed for my mother and Vangie the hardest. My eyes were wet with tears when I opened them to a mound of noodles heavily garnished in pasta sauce and meatballs. My stomach growled and my mouth watered. I wanted to slurp up noodles, crunch on crispy salad with creamy dressing, and sip lemonade and ice water like the others. I stared at my plate, reluctant to alter its perfection. I might never see another meal like this in my lifetime, served on plates made of porcelain and not of paper and with real silverware not plastic, and drinks served from sweating glass pitchers and over ice cubes.

I picked up my fork slowly, twirled it with noodles, and took a bite; the delicious flavors brought my taste buds back to life. The food comforted me while the girls talked about their jobs, boyfriends, husbands, kids, living in the streets, God and whatnot. I was the last one to finish eating, and I didn't move until Floe came and got me.

Free time followed lunch. Some girls left the house, and the others did whatever they wanted to do. I did nothing but stand by the computer lab, looking desperately stupid.

Verna eventually came along and unlocked the door for me. There were six computers, three on each side of the room. I sat in the first chair I could get to. After an eternity of waiting for the sluggish computer to power up, I was asked for a username and password.

Fifteen minutes later I was still staring at the computer screen, waiting for something miraculous to happen. Forced to face my fear, I peeked my head out the door. Summer sat at the art table. I felt most comfortable approaching her.

She raised her pale green eyes when I limped up. "Hi, Angie," she said with a delicate smile.

I pointed to the computer room.

"What about it?"

When I reached for her pen, she got the message and ripped a page from her journal and handed it to me.

Having no other way to communicate, I had perfected my print and penmanship like a speaking person would perfect their speech. I wrote out "user name" and "password." She turned up her nose and handed the note right back to me.

"You have to get your own," she mouthed as if I was deaf not mute, and then hunched over her journal and went back to writing.

Get it from where?

Feeling even dumber, I walked back to the computer room and stared at the screen, again.

When Susan walked in, I displayed the innocent eyes of a frightened deer.

"I need to see you, Angie." Her mousy voice sounded unusually cold. I followed her upstairs and into my temporary room with disinclination.

"For safety precautions we search everyone's property. Spray paint is a contraband. I have to confiscate it," she said, referring to the contents of my backpack, which now sat like a pile of garbage on the bed. I shoved the filth back inside my pack, my tears percolating as Susan dictated more house rules.

"Between wake up and lights out, bedroom doors must stay open when occupied. No one, other than your roommate, is allowed in your room or on these premises, boy or girl." Her eyes dropped to my purple neck.

Hugging my pack, I glowered at Susan, my thoughts mean and distrustful. She didn't have to worry about me and boys. I wasn't the girlfriend type anyway.

"You can visit with the other girls in the community room, the backyard, or in other areas of the house anytime during free time. This is your room key." The single key in her hand dangled from a ring. "If you lose it, report it right away, and always lock your door when you leave. Roxy's is not responsible for stolen property."

I took the key I would never use from Susan.

"It's okay, Angie. We're glad you're with us." Her soft, mousy voice had returned. "If you have any questions, I'm always here to help."

Not long after Susan walked out, Ashley waltzed in, amusement dancing in her hazel eyes. "Random search and seizures are routine. You'll wise up." She shut the door, locked it, kicked off her flip-flops, stepped on the bed, reached over the window sill and came up with a pack of cigarettes. Then she jumped down, raised the window, and lit up. Sheer sophistication washed over her face when she inhaled. Bending forward, she blew a stream of smoke through the open window. A cool breeze blew it back into the room. Ashley fanned her hand, sprayed body freshener, and then repeated her ritual: inhaling, blowing, fanning and spraying.

"You look like a smoker. Want one?" She held out her pack of cigarettes.

I shook my head, though I could sure use one. I wondered what had given me away. Smoking was a habit I could easily break and one I couldn't afford to keep.

"If you're worried you'll get busted, Susan already clocked out. If you don't believe me, see for yourself." Ashley watched the window. "At 4:30 on the nose, she jumps in her buggy and boogies up the hill. There she goes..."

I didn't look and didn't care to. Struck by a terrifying thought, I leaped for the closet door and yanked it back. It was gone. *Gone!* I rushed out of the room and hopped down the stairs on one foot. I couldn't find Floe anywhere. Coming out of the hallway, I collided with a woman who was tall and sturdy enough to knock me off of my feet.

"You must be the new girl." She helped my off of the floor. "Deloris is the name. I'm the resident monitor, or as the girls call me, Night Mother. If I'm not on duty, you can count on Ava taking my place. We don't run through the house and you girls are not permitted in the office area after hours. How can I help you?"

I stared at Deloris in a state of confusion. She wore a black turtleneck shirt, black pants, and her silver hair was closely cut to her head.

"Oh!" she said as though a light bulb went off in her brain. She walked to the desk, her heavy feet in black nurses' shoes, and returned with a pen and paper.

"My stuff is missing?" I wrote.

She read my note. "Nothing in this house is missing unless it has been stolen, and I don't think anyone has stolen your stuff. What *stuff* can I help you find?"

"Sleeping bag. Clothes," I wrote.

"If it's anywhere, it's in the laundry."

I followed her to the laundry room. While she searched the dryers, I searched the shelves of neatly folded clothes. The moment I laid eyes on my Stanford hoodie, I snatched it up and hugged it. Tears rolled down my cheeks as I pressed my nose into the soft burgundy cotton and inhaled. It had lost its letters and now spelled "S-anf-rd Un-vers--y." I didn't care. If I had lost my hoodie, I would've lost a piece of myself.

"Is this the sleeping bag you're after?" Deloris said.

I nodded, removing it from her outstretched hand. Nothing had changed. It was still navy blue with a checkered interior, still washed out and still ripped on the outer layer. I thanked Deloris with a genuine smile.

"Floe caters to you girls more than she should, if you ask me. This might be a charity house, but you're not a charity case. You are able-bodied from what I can tell." She looked me up and down and shooed me away. "Go! Bible study has started."

I left my jeans, my army jacket and my new clothes behind. My pack, bag, and hoodie were all I needed to survive the night. Thankfully, no one was guarding the front door. I flew through it. Once I stepped onto the porch, I didn't take another step. It wasn't anything the security guard had said or done that immobilized me. It was his crooked smile, which sent a chill up and down my spine. He sat tilted back on two legs of a metal chair, chewing gum. When he nodded hello, I eased back into the house and shut the door, fighting back angry tears.

Deciding to ditch Bible study altogether, I hid out in my room. Ashley had the same idea. She offered me another smoke. This time I accepted. While she sat on her bed with a cigarette dangling between her lips and polishing her nails, I paced the room, puffing and blowing, and gathering my nerve to ask Ashley for the computer code. At the thought of opening up the lines of communication between us, my vocal cords swelled.

"Computer code?" I finally wrote on the palm of her hand.

She stared at me as though I had suddenly appeared before her eyes, and then she told me a "techie" named Phil assigned the usernames and passwords and I would eventually be assigned my own once I'd lived here a month or so and proven my trustworthiness to communicate with the outside world.

"It's a dumb policy. Just use mine." Ashley wrote her username and password on the inside of my forearm. I wanted to hug her. I didn't.

We heard keys jingling outside the door. Miraculously, Ashley stubbed out her cigarette, flicked it behind the bed, jumped to her feet, put on her flip-flops, and grabbed her Bible before Deloris flew into the room.

"Get!" she said, pointing down the hallway.

Ashley got away. I didn't.

Bible study was mandatory, I learned through Deloris's harsh lecture. Girls who ditched lost free time and were given extra chores, and of course smoking was a major violation of house rules. Because I was new to the program, Deloris excused me with a warning. Next time I'd be kicked out, she said.

Verna led Bible study, and did her best to explain why God allowed times of war and sickness, pain and death. I listened and did my best to understand. When Bible study was over, I still didn't get why life was so kind to some and so cruel to others.

Dinner was chicken potpie. Before I took one bite, I excused myself from the table, awkwardly explaining to Verna with hand gestures that I had to use the bathroom.

I left the dining room and took a detour down the hallway, which led me straight to the computer lab. My knees jittered as I waited for the computer to power up.

"OMG! Dunk! I'm in Colorado Springs! I fell asleep and the train took off on me. I hurt my ankle jumping. They locked me in a shelter for trespassing! Did you find Mental? Is he okay? If you get this message, please, please, please reply!"

XoXo

Thirty

The birds perched in the cherry tree outside the bedroom window awakened me with a beautiful ballad. I stretched and yawned on a mattress of feathers, beneath the warm yellow and blue comforter. In the background, a cowbell rang and someone yelled, "Rise and shine!"

From that moment forward, I was put through a rigorous indoctrination of "shelter life." After a ten minute shower, I put on the clothes I had worn yesterday and met up with Ashley for breakfast: oatmeal, a banana, and a glass of orange juice.

A community meeting followed. Every morning we were to report on our plans for the day in group, as well as our progress toward independence. The group was led by Jamie, the case manager. She was stocky and had freckled skinned, wore jeans and a Boulder University sweatshirt, and her crinkly hair was in a high ponytail. She could've easily passed for one of us girls.

Since I didn't have anything to report and anywhere to be, Jamie took me under her wing. Based on my file she had somehow gotten hold of, I needed to visit the health clinic for "a full body servicing to get me up and running," she said.

Before I could check for Dunk's email reply, Jamie put me into a sixteen passenger van with six other girls. I took in another cool, gray day and inhaled the clean air like a long drink from a spring of water.

We made frequent stops, dropping off girls here and there. I logged every turn, street name, and highway to memory. Besides Jamie, who sat in the driver's seat, I was the only passenger left when we arrived at Mahoney Family Health Clinic. The building looked new and modern and sat in a remote business park. Everyone, from the janitor to the receptionist to the X-ray technician, treated me kindly, as if I was the first client to walk through the automatic glass doors.

My full body servicing started with a kind old man named Dr. Frankford. He had white hair and shaky hands. As it turned out, I had a grade two sprained ankle with a partially torn ligament. The doctor guaranteed I didn't need surgery, but he told me to put as little weight on it as possible for the next six weeks.

I left the doctor's office in an ugly shoe brace, wrestling with crutches, and bumping into walls. Along with losing my wings, I had practically lost a leg. My hope to catch up to Mo and them died with my will to live.

A nurse then took my blood, examined me for TB, and screened me for drugs. The dentist was my last stop and the very last door at the end of the brightly lit hallway. Similar to Dr. Frankford's office, this one also had oak cabinets and white countertops. A dentist chair took the place of a doctor's table, and alien gadgets jutted from the walls.

I stood by the door, biting the inside of my lip until I tasted blood, while Jamie and the dentist talked about me as if I was invisible. The dentist wore a lab coat over his jeans and dress shirt like Douglas and hiking boots like Jamie. His locks were clasped off of his broad forehead, the lean, loose twists of dark brown hair neatly draping his shoulders. I wondered how many dentists in Colorado Springs looked as young as him. I imagined he must not have come across many bony, homeless, matted-headed black girls in Colorado either. At the first sight of me, his brows shot up before they folded downward as though a thousand questions crossed his mind about me.

"Hey Angie. I'm Doctor Laurence…" In the middle of shaking my hand, his eyes dropped to my foot. He scratched his head. "Let me give you a hand."

"I'll help!" Jamie bound forward.

"I think I can handle her," the dentist said.

"Awesome!"

For reasons unknown to me, I stopped breathing all together when he cradled me in his arms and lowered me into his dentist chair.

"You're trembling. Are you nervous?" He was staring down at me. When reflected off of the light, his eyes brought to my mind golden-yellow almonds; his complexion reminded me of a perfectly baked pecan pie.

I nodded.

"If you're nervous, I'm nervous." He looked at Jamie. "Do you mind giving her some privacy."

Jamie blinked. "Sure. Angie, will you be okay if I step out?"

Feeling hot and red faced, I twisted my mouth and nodded, terrified the dentist might ask me a question I couldn't answer on my own.

A look of relief washed over the dentist's face when Jamie left. "I feel more comfortable, if you don't." He smiled down at me with teeth as white as the walls. "We won't do anything too invasive. X-rays and an examination and you'll be good to go." He rubbed his hands over his jeans as if to wipe sweat from them. "I'm without a hygienist, so I'll be doubling as your X-ray man today, if that's okay." He sounded embarrassed by this.

Once he finished my X-rays, he probed and poked at my gums with a sharp metal instrument while I squirmed and squinted.

"I'm not hurting you, am I?"

I shook my head and looked off, focusing my attention on the fluorescent lights and not on his golden-yellow eyes.

"I thought I'd lost my touch. A little wider if you can. You're doing great, Angie. Perfect. All done. See? Painless."

The doctor removed his mask and gloves. "Do you see this?" He held up a model of fake teeth. "Your upper and your lower jaw are properly aligned, and you have an ideal bite. You're what we call a golden patient."

I crinkled my nose. I didn't believe him.

He laughed. "That's news that usually gets me a pretty smile, but I wouldn't be in good mood either if I was in your shoes. Or shoe. How'd you get hurt?"

I was spared the embarrassment of silence when Jamie walked back into the room.

"Perfect timing," Doctor Laurence said to Jamie. "Can I speak with you in private?"

They left the room and left me staring at the ceiling, wishing to be anywhere but here.

Dr. Laurence returned and stood over me. "The bad news, Angie, is that you have two cavities that require fillings and you're past due for a thorough cleaning. The good news is I get to see you again." He seemed to expect me to laugh, or at the very least return his smile.

When all was said and done, I hobbled out of dentist office without a spoken word.

After receiving Dunk's email, I didn't mind losing my wings, a leg, or being caged in at Roxy's. Mental was alive, and Mo and them were coming for me as soon as Mental completed three weeks of community service work for stealing five cartons of cigarettes. Mo was acting crazy, Dunk said, scared Mental would renege and get thrown in jail for twelve months for a misdemeanor. Dunk wasn't worried, so I wasn't worried either.

Each of us girls had to put in four hours of work five days a week around the house in return for our room and board. I had been assigned to kitchen and gardening duty until I got back on both feet.

I woke up this morning excited to get started. Skipping breakfast, I hobbled through the swinging doors of the peach-walled kitchen. Everything else was made of stainless steel: the countertops, the refrigerator and the vintage stove, which had eight burners and four small ovens.

Betina, another grandmother type, was in charge of the cooking. Rumor had it that most of the girls would take bathroom duty over kitchen duty any day of the week so they didn't have to work under Betina. The last person to hold the morning shift was Melissa, which ended in a small fire. I wondered if Betina had gotten trapped in it. Sadly, half of her face had melted away and transformed into unidentifiable flesh while the other half showed her lost beauty. Knowing how it felt to be a freak of nature, I didn't shy away from her annoyed black eyes in spite of my shock.

She wagged a finger at my bad foot. "I'll not be responsible. Leave my kitchen!" she said in her Portuguese accent.

"Top of the morning, Betina," Floe said, coming through the swinging doors. "You've met our newest girl, Angie, haven't yah?" Floe wrapped her arm around my waist and held me in place. "She's here to help out mornings. Just a few hours a day. You'll treat her Christianly, won't yah, Betina?" Floe was smiling, but her voice wasn't.

Betina made a hacking sound and threw up her hands. "Come with me!"

I followed her around the spacious kitchen as she pointed things out.

"The community cupboard. The honors cupboard. Pots and pans. Glasses. Cups. Dishes. Fridge. They'll eat us out of house and home if we let 'em. I put in for locks, but getting things done takes an act of God in this place. Knives. They are to stay locked away. Stove." She stood in front of it. "Don't touch!"

She walked me behind the kitchen and into the walk-in pantry. "Stay!" she said, and then left me turning questions in my mind.

What do I do?

I started unpacking and reorganizing. There were four industrial shelves and stacks of boxes loaded with non-perishables. I sorted through them and took my time rearranging and alphabetizing each item by its function. The pantry was a comforting place for me to hide out and I was in no hurry to leave my cozy corner. Every fifteen minutes or so, Betina would walk in, look at the mess I'd made, throw up her hands, and walk back out.

The second half of my work day I maintained raised beds of herbs and vegetables set among sweet smelling fruit trees. Roxy's backyard was a serene place where loneliness was far from my thoughts and silence was safe. The smell of cucumbers, squash, shallots, garlic, snow peas, carrots, and leafy greens were candy to my nostrils. I picked off bugs and their eggs from leaves, and I dirtied my hands with enriched soil, planting a fresh crop of dill, oregano, and rosemary for spring.

I earned ten dollars for each day I worked and ended my first week at Roxy's feeling happy. On a good day of panhandling, fifty dollars wasn't easy to come by. The only drawback was having to sign over half of it to Jamie, who would put it in a savings account

I may never see. I hid the rest of my money in my right shoe and slept with it under my pillow.

Week two closed and I couldn't sleep. Ashley couldn't sleep either. Going along with her plan, I pulled my hoodie over my gently used pajamas and quietly followed her through the bedroom window. Cigarettes kept her from craving meth and candy kept her from craving cigarettes. We sat on sloped shingles eating goo-gobs of candy and staring at a cluster of stars floating above the Rocky Mountains. There was something about the great outdoors that made me feel as if I could do anything without the pressure of doing anything at all. I think Ashley felt it too. We were alike in that away, though Ashley had been lucky enough to have freight hopped across the country and back. And just like me, she had been run off from home by a creep and gotten busted for trespassing on Jim's property and sentenced to time at Roxy's.

"He can have you charged with criminal trespassing, you know. He's filthy rich." Ashley dug into her bag of candy and then carefully unwrapped the foil from a mini peanut butter cup, which she popped into her mouth.

"You want to hear something so freaking funny! I offered to blow that old douchebag if he let me go, and he told me it was an abomination and I'd burn in hell. Who turns down a blowjob?" She laughed and dug for more candy. "The douche is closing both houses, by the way."

I stopped sucking the sweet off of a Sour Patch to digest the news. Since I hadn't planned to make myself at home here, I gave it little consideration and thought only of those girls who had nowhere else to go.

"That's just what I've heard, but who freaking knows," Ashley continued. "Jim Mahoney is capable of anything since his wife died. I mean, like, I can't blame him for being a douche. When my mom overdosed I kind of lost it too. But hey, I was thirteen and living in a house full of meth sluts, not a rich, cantankerous old fart. By the way, nothing is confidential. Susan'll swear on the Bible that it is, but these walls have big ears, you know."

I nodded, having more than a casual understanding of her warning. I already knew, through rumor, that Summer was a cutter, that Chris was gay but pretended to be straight so as not to be burned at the stake, and that Verna's husband had broken half of the bones in her body the last time he tracked her down.

I also knew, from everything that I had read and heard about Roxy's, that Jim owned Roxy's House I and II, the Mahoney Family Health Clinic, and half the town. His wife, Mary Mahoney, had opened both houses to keep their daughter Roxanne's memory alive. At age eighteen, Roxanne had died of an OxyContin over-dose, and Mrs. Mahoney believed she could save girls like us by giving us a Christian foundation and life skills, even if she couldn't save her own daughter, I imagined.

"So, what's your story, Angie? We all have one or we wouldn't be here; that's what they'll tell you. It's a head game. Don't fall for that crap."

I shrugged and stared off into the enchanting night.

"I forgot. You don't talk. No wonder you're so easy to talk to."

We finished the entire bag of candy and climbed back through the window.

Thirty-One

Susan and Jamie were full of bright ideas about my future, and had concocted a list of steps they felt I needed to take to overcome homelessness. After attending more group meetings than I could keep up with, getting educational guidance and learning a few life skills, they had scheduled me to meet with a psychologist!

I sat in the purple counseling room, wondering if it was Dr. Slater's mothering ways, plumpness, blushing cheeks, soft black eyes, or her storyteller's voice that made me want to open up to her and share my secret. She had brownish-gray hair, which she had gathered into a loose bun at the crown of her head, and her eyeglasses hung from a chain that draped her neck and fell over her navy blue blouse worn with a black pants suit. She wasn't the grandmother type, but she looked close enough to it.

Two hours sailed by while we played card games that held my interest and tested my intelligence. We also played a board game that told her things about me that only Vangie would've known. She didn't pressure me into talking, which only deepened my fondness toward her.

We would meet again, same time next week, she said. I wouldn't be here.

Typically, when I entered the kitchen, I found Betina fussing over the day's lunch before she served oatmeal for breakfast. Today I found her sitting at the kitchen table with her feet resting on a chair while she read the Bible.

I limped past her and toward the pantry. Now that it was organized, there wasn't anything left for me to do other than bust suds, sign for deliveries, or sort through new boxes of donations. Otherwise, I read the books I smuggled in from the community room.

After kitchen duty, I would cut stems, strip leaves, and gather herbs that collided into appetizing fragrances. With spring in the air, I would get to plant cabbage, asparagus, and arugula seeds. Besides what Betina and a few of the other girls on garden duty had taught me, I already knew what a garden needed to thrive.

Lots of love.

I looked forward to gardening duty more than kitchen duty.

"I have a project for you," Betina said.

I stopped and faced her.

"Sit!" she ordered.

I sat at the kitchen table.

"Chop!" She pointed at the bowl filled with onions, bell peppers, celery, and mushrooms. "Peel!" she said, pointing to the bowl of russet potatoes.

I happily peeled and chopped, and with perfect precision.

Sirens woke us up at the crack of dawn instead of a cowbell today. We all gathered in the hallway as Summer, stretched out beneath a bloodied white sheet, was wheeled out of Roxy's by a band of paramedics. They couldn't revive her, though they tried until their foreheads were covered with sweat. The slits to her wrists were too deep and she had lost enough blood to shut down the bathroom.

None of us could talk, seemingly. Maybe we all saw ourselves on that gurney, sleeping for all eternity. I saw my own mother, and my knees and hands trembled as tears rained down my face.

Susan called an emergency meeting before breakfast to deal with the crisis. With the help of Doloris and Floe, who sat at pivotal points around the circle and watched us like mother hens, she facilitated group, encouraging us to share our feelings about Summer's suicide.

I was excused from speaking, of course.

"I pray God forgives us," Summer's roommate, Arabelle said, finding another reason to pick at her red pimples.

"Jesus always forgives. Jesus loves yah." Floe patted Arabelle's pudgy thigh.

"What if God is just a figment of our imagination?" Chris said.

"A figment of our imagination?" Deloris's feathers looked ruffled. "Of course there's a God!"

"There's a God, Chris, there's a God," said a choir of voices, as if we all needed the validation.

"Have you seen him?" Chris turned to Verna. "Have you?" She panned the room. "Have any you?"

"We don't have to see God; we feel Him, right here." Verna laid her hand over her heart.

Chris leaned on her knees, panning the room again with doubting eyes. "Okay, so like, if there is a God up there somewhere, why doesn't He eradicate all the evil shit in the world? Why are our lives so fucked up? Why is Summer a mutilated corpse?"

"Why is the sky blue, Chris? Who freaking knows? It's too early for Jeopardy. Can we adjourn, please. I'm starving." That was Ashley.

"It's okay to question God at times such as this, Chris," Susan said, and I thought of all the unanswered questions I had about God.

"Yeah, Chris. And everybody don't feel God's love, everybody ain't Christian, and everybody ain't in His good graces," Melissa said and glanced at me. I didn't know her and didn't want to know her or her roommate Emily. Rumor had it they called me "a dirty nigger," and said I didn't belong at Roxy's House.

"So, like, why not?" Chris countered. "Summer was fed the same religious crap we've all had crammed down our throats, making us feel ashamed of being born, and God stood by in the big blue sky and watched her kill herself. Like, come on! He could've stopped her. He's God, right?" Chris was on a roll.

"This is blasphemous!" Deloris said to Susan. "Have we any limitations in this house?"

Wearing a saintly smile, Susan nodded. "It's okay. We want to share our feelings without reprimand or judgment. Summer touched all of our lives." She faced Arabelle. "Did something happen last night, Arabelle, something you feel needs God's forgiveness, something you'd like to share with the group?" Susan concentrated on Arabelle's every movement and expression. We all looked eager to find out why Summer took her own life. A lump sat in my throat.

Arabelle sobbed, blaming herself for letting Summer leave the room last night. As it turned out, she was too busy reading Summer's diary to notice Summer's absence. Hours later Verna had found Summer on the bathroom floor and called 911.

"She left it out in the open," Arabelle said, pushing her eye-glasses up the bridge of her nose and sniffling. "I thought she wanted me to read it."

We prayed for Arabella, read from the book of John, sang a hymn, and adjourned.

The rest of day slugged by. I refused to shower in the upstairs bathroom once it had been sanitized. I refused to shower at all today.

Thirty-Two

Friday morning rolled around. Ashley slept past the cowbell. I was too busy rocking and cradling my jaw with the palm of my hand to wake her. Something was drilling a nail straight through my molar and down into a raw nerve. My brain felt the initial shock and sent a jolt of pain throughout my entire body. I couldn't lift my head. Any slight movement triggered another shockwave. The cowbell rang again, hurting my brain.

Verna got Ashley out of bed and Jamie got me to the dentist.

"It looks like your tooth has abscessed," Dr. Laurence said, as he removed his white mask. "This may scare you, but you need a root canal or you'll run the risk of losing that tooth and your pretty smile." He laughed at my tears in a sympathetic way and patted my shoulder. "Candis, can you hand Angie a tissue, please."

Candis was Doctor Laurence's new dental hygenist. I cannot say I liked her. She was pretty and had a pony tail that swung across her back every time she turned her head. For reasons unknown to me, she made me feel dirty and ugly. My hair was in its usual state of mess and my overall appearance hadn't improved since my last visit to the dentist office.

Candis handed me a tissue. "You can trust Laurence. He's as gentle as they come."

"You'll come through it alive," Doctor Laurence said with his perfect smile. "We'll get you started on antibiotics and give you something to take away the pain. Candis, confer with Jamie about scheduling."

During the ride back to Roxy's House, I imagined Doctor Laurence on a white horse, escorting me away from Roxy's House in a beautiful carriage. If I should ever love again, I could easily love him. In my brief flight of fantasy, I knew I would lose him too, like I had lost everybody else in my life I had loved.

That night, I stole a pair of scissors and chopped off my hair. I chopped and chopped until it was as short and curly as a boy's.

The next week I was back in the counseling room, but this time the purple walls were closing in on me.

"I'm confident you have selective mutism," Dr. Slater said, which didn't surprise me. School psychiatrists and doctors had deemed me selectively mute since the 6th grade, like an official seal stamped on my forehead. But there had never been anything wrong with my ability to speak or to hear; what had gone wrong had gone wrong years ago, though neither Vangie nor I would ever forget the day my voice was silenced.

"I'm sure verbal communication invokes a high level of anxiety for you. Am I right?"

I bobbed my head.

"Sometimes talking is terrifying, and silence feels safe. When our brain takes this kind of protective stance, it will disable speech outside of places of comfort and familiarity. To speak about our fears makes them tangible, and certainly more frightening. Am I right?"

I bobbed again.

"With younger patients, I reintroduce speech and language through non-verbal tasks to help them regain their confidence. But you're not a child, are you, Angie?"

I shook my head, wondering if I would ever grow up.

"No, you are not," Dr. Slater said without a shadow of doubt in her tone. "You have above average intelligence, from what I can tell, and a determination to *win*." She chuckled as if reflecting on something funny. "Both Susan and Jamie said you're making good progress in the program, which speaks to your motivation to better yourself."

She brought forth an old-fashioned tape recorder, with a microphone attached, from her desk.

"I know this will push you outside of your comfort zone, but I think you're ready."

I shrunk back against the couch cushion and massaged my throat with my hand. My feet shuffled forward and backward as if they would take off running on their own.

"Sometimes we view our personal strengths as weaknesses. You are not weak, Angie. You are strong, and you have traveled many miles to get here and you have survived! Give yourself credit."

Before I left, Dr. Slater told me to think of the one person I was most comfortable talking to, to find a quiet place, and to record myself talking to this person before our next meeting.

It took me two days before I got up the guts to follow Dr. Slater's instructions. During my free time, I looked for the perfect place to hide. With over an acre of land to explore in the backyard, I wandered around until I found a low hanging tree, where I sat with my back against its bark and my feet pressed up against the chain link fence that looked out into the mountains and the wilderness.

I pulled the recorder from my pack and brought the microphone close to my lips. There was so much I wanted to say, but even alone I couldn't free my voice and got choked up. I turned off the recorder and stuffed it back into my pack, saving it for another day.

I didn't try again until Sunday afternoon, after attending mandatory sunrise service at Hope Revival Christian Center and following lunch, when the other girls were taking advantage of their own free time. If my anxiety climbed too high, Dr. Slater told me to focus on breathing slowly and deeply. If that didn't work, she said to think of something funny. I closed my eyes, feeling the kiss of spring warm against my face.

"Wanna see my house?"

Vangie's voice reverberated in my mind as crisply as the rustling trees, and in my mind's eye, I could see the mischievous look in her dark, mysterious eyes. It was a game we had played. We called it "pretend" when we were little. We would pretend we had a nice house, pretend we had a nice car, or pretend we were rich. Sometimes, we would dress in our nicest clothes—which weren't very nice—walk far away from home and find the nicest place to eat. Some days, we had enough money to order sodas. Usually, we didn't so we would eat free bread with butter, giggling and whispering over our water glasses, pretending we could buy whatever we wanted from the menu. If we ate a crumb, it was because a nice waiter or nice couple felt sorry enough to feed us. Otherwise, we were politely put out.

I laughed out loud as I imagined Vangie sitting across from me, her toes touching mine as she leaned on her knees, and laughed with me.

"I miss you so much I could die." The words flew out of my mouth as free as a kite before my tears buried me.

Thirty-Three

Week four came and went. I was losing hope that Mo and them were coming for me. Hope was hard to hold on to when there was little left, and I was running on empty, an emptiness that all the food in the world couldn't satisfy. Hopelessness woke me up each morning and troubled me throughout the day.

Tonight it aroused something inside of me and got me out of bed. The quiet house was a good indicator that the other girls were sleeping or pretending to sleep. I had ditched my crutches altogether by now and could move around quickly and less clumsily. At the end of the hallway, a light glowed beneath the door of Verna's room. I hurried by and limped downstairs, one step at a time.

I had become familiar enough with the kitchen to feel my way around in the dark, but I appreciated the light streaming in from the back porch. I preheated two ovens at 425 degrees and quietly gathered flour, baking soda, baking powder, and salt. In the refrigerator, I found cheese and butter, no buttermilk. Accustomed to making my own at home, I combined fresh lemon juice with plain milk and set it aside, then doused the countertop with flour, spreading it thinly with my hand. Once the milk curdled and soured, I combined it with the dry ingredients, cut it with butter, and folded in cheese.

Whisked away by the joy of cooking, I forgot I was without a home or kitchen of my own, forgot to feel scared and alone, forgot to feel hopeless, and thought nothing of the past or the future.

Using a glass, I cut out twenty-four biscuits in perfect rounds and laid them out evenly on two greased cookie sheets. I was sliding the last pan into the heated oven when the kitchen doors swung open.

"Well, well. Looks like I caught myself a mouse."

Without looking back, I knew it was Otis, the security guard; his drowsy drawl alerted me. I closed the oven door and faced his blinding flashlight. In the dark, his lanky frame, stretching over six feet, and his slouched shoulders formed a silhouette against the wall.

"You got permission to be in here?"

I shook my head slowly.

Otis stared at me as if I was a mouse and he didn't know how to kill me. He then placed his hand on the Taser gun attached to his holster and strolled up to me.

My heart hummed quietly as I stared into his hooded green eyes set perfectly between his bushy brows and above his lean nose. His hair was extra moussed today and slicked back into a ponytail.

He moved me aside, opened the oven door, and peeked inside. When he stood, he stared down at me, chewing his gum. "That batty old cook won't like you dirtying up her clean kitchen." He paused to chew. "I could wake up Miss Deloris, but she won't like it either." Another chew. "Or you can fix me a plate of biscuits and pour me a glass of milk and we can keep this between you and me." He ambled over to the table, sat down, and clasped his hands behind his head. "I like mine with strawberry jam, if you got some, and butter. Lots of it," he demanded.

While my biscuits baked, I contemplated whether or not I could trust Otis. I doubted he knew my name or wanted to know it. I knew him, however, or of him. Everybody did. He had slept with practically every girl in both houses, everybody but Maddy, and only because she was too old. It was an exaggerated story, but I didn't put it past Otis. Ashley would've slept with Otis too, if he wasn't such a creep.

Ignoring Otis altogether, I peeked inside one of the ovens. With ten minutes of baking time still remaining, the dough had a small hump. I stood around biting my nails and watching the digital clock jump from one minute to the next.

"Angie," Otis sang in a slow tune. "I'm getting *real* hungry." He beat the table like a drum, bobbing his head to an imaginary song.

The sweet, buttery aroma began to float from the oven and circulate around the room. My biscuits were golden, plump, and ready. Using a spatula, I transferred four of them from the baking pan to a porcelain plate, poked holes in each with a fork, and spread on lots of butter for Otis.

Still in shock that he knew my name, I took baby steps toward him, stopped at the opposite end of the table, and slid the plate and then the jelly jar his way.

"Want to bet you can't slide that glass of milk without spilling it," he said with a challenging smile in his eyes.

Taking his bet on, I slid the glass of milk too, without spilling one drop.

Otis laughed as slow as he talked and chewed. "Impressive. You must've been a bartender." He dosed a biscuit in strawberry jam and took a hefty bite out of it. Milk stained his thin mustache after he gulped. He wiped it off with the back of his hand.

"My grandma bakes good biscuits, 'cept hers don't have cheese in 'em," Otis grumbled, chewing a mouthful.

I decided Otis wasn't such a creep after all. Sitting there hunched over his plate and watching his cell phone like a TV, he resembled a teenaged boy more than he did a fearsome twenty-something-year-old packing a Taser.

I caught myself smiling when he asked for seconds before finishing his first, and I hurried off before he could notice. I was back in a flash with a new plate. Noticing my close proximity to him, I took a giant step back.

Otis stared up at me, the shadow of light from the back porch making his green eyes glow. "Somebody told you I bite or something? Who was it? Emily? Yeah, I bet it was her." He grinned. "I don't bite 'less you like it." He bit into another biscuit. "They said you can't talk. That true?"

I swept my eyes across the ceiling, wondering if he expected me to answer him.

"I bet you're faking to get out of those group talks?" He licked jelly from his fingers, making me tingle inside. "That's smart."

Milk splattered across the peach walls when Otis sprang to his feet and toppled the glass. Deloris had come flying into the kitchen like a bat.

The kitchen suddenly turned bright. "What on God's green earth...?" Deloris's short silver hair stood on her head like a rooster's feathers, her sleepy eyes spreading wide at the sight of the kitchen, which I hadn't had the chance to clean up. She wore her favorite black pants, black turtle neck, and her black nurse shoes.

I was speechless, of course, and Otis couldn't talk with his mouth full of food, or at least what he said was not decipherable. Verna barged through the door next, followed by Ashley and several of the girls who stared at the both of us as if we had slept together.

"Angie, you come with me. *You*, stay right where you are," Deloris barked at Otis.

"Yes, ma'am." Otis stood at attention.

"The rest of you, back to your rooms. We are not running a circus."

"Back to your rooms, everybody," Verna said, rounding up the girls.

In the state of emergency, Susan was called in. She had arrived to Roxy's wearing what looked like a nightshirt over her jeans and a pair of furry boots. She dealt with me while Deloris dealt with Otis. I had violated a major rule and endangered the other residents, and I would likely be discharged from the program. Adding to my list of infractions was my email to Dunk. Residents were prohibited from sharing their user names and email passwords. Ashley lost free time and her old email account had been deactivated. My fate would be decided at the morning's collaborative meeting, Susan concluded.

Before the cowbell rang and Ashley could talk me out of it, I was hobbling up the hill toward the automatic gate. I walked right through it without stopping or being stopped. A taste of freedom showered me like the early morning dew, but instead of sweetness it left a sour taste in my mouth.

At some level in my thinking, needing an excuse to set out on my own again and face the unknown, I had expected to get busted, to get kicked out and to be set free. Whether I died catching out didn't matter anymore. No one would miss me. I'd be buried in a pinewood box anyway, covered with mounds of dirt to mark the end of Angie Cooper.

I trekked down the middle of the street, following the double lines like a yellow brick road. The blue morning was peaceful, the neighborhood sound asleep. At my current pace, it might take a while to get out of the neighborhood on foot. I didn't mind. I had no place to be and no one expecting me to arrive.

I rounded the first block and was halfway up the second when a car's wide headlights, shaped like cat eyes, inched toward me. I veered to the left side of the road to let it pass. It swerved to the right and stopped inches from me.

"It's a mighty cold world out there on your own." Floe was leaned over in her seat, talking to me through the open passenger's window. Her curly hair looked like a red halo on her head. "If it suits your fancy, I'll drop yah off at your destination. No strings attached."

I shook my head and started to walk away.

"I think old Betsy here'll get yah there quicker than that bum foot." Floe patted and rubbed the dashboard of her pink Cadillac as if the car had a mind of its own.

I gave in to my stubbornness, opened the door, and slid into the long front seat, keeping my head covered with my hood. My bag and pack I stuffed under the dashboard for safe keeping.

Floe made a six-point turn, maneuvering her batmobile in the opposite direction. It backfired and clunked as we took off down the quiet street.

"Point and I'll drive," she said.

I pointed until we came to Highway 25.

"The only freight yard I know of is forty minutes down the way, out in Pueblo, if that's where you're planning on hanging your hat."

I nodded.

"I don't mind taking yah, if yah don't mind stopping by Sammy's Bakery first. We have a collaborative meeting this morning, yah know, and I'm in charge of the donuts." Floe, leaning forward as though she couldn't see past her headlights, kept her eyes on the road and a firm hold on the steering wheel.

We entered the highway sluggishly, left behind by fast moving cars. The heat from the vents, Floe's rosy fragrance, and the guitar strumming softly to a woman's angelic voice on the radio as she sang a gospel song caused my stiff back to curve into the leather seat and a heaviness to tug at my eyelids. I wanted to sleep and never wake up.

"Yah girls think I don't remember being young and impressionable," Floe said, jolting my eyes back open. "Oh, I remember. Life back then was nothing but dirt roads, thorns, and broken glass, and I didn't think I'd get from that side of road to this side in one piece. But the good Lord has a way of showing us what only His eyes can see. Yes, He does." She hummed along with the song, her head and the car swaying.

"I may not have left home for the reasons some of yah girls did," she continued. "But I didn't leave in the best way or the smartest either. Oh, I could've stayed and finished college, but Daddy made it easy for me to leave without a plan. He wasn't a nice man, yah know." She swung her eyes my way and back to the road. "So, I ran off and married Clyde Fenton. God forgive me for saying this, but he wasn't worth a hill of beans. Our marriage lasted, oh, for just about as long as I could take the beatings and put-downs. Divorce isn't the Lord's way, but sometimes it's best…"

We ran over a curb and I realized we had arrived to the Sammy's Bakery.

"I can use a hand," Floe said, killing the engine and headlights.

Not wanting to be impolite, I stepped out of the car and into the early nineteenth century. The square city block was constructed of Hansel and Gretal-style boutiques, restaurants, and other businesses, but with a modern twist. From what I could see, all the stores were closed except for Sammy's Bakery, whose bright lights, pink and white interior, and bakery themed wall art greeted us when a lady unlocked the door. I guessed her to be thirty-something; her pale eyes looked wired, as if she had just gotten started for the day and was up to her elbows in flour. Her red hair stuck out of the sides of her head in two pigtails, and a crucifix tattoo stained the right side of her neck.

"Hey there, Aunt Floe. You're early today," she said, drawing back the door.

"I brought one of our girls to help me with my selection. Anything new? Hot and fresh, if yah please." Floe waltzed through the glass door. She wore a trench coat, and much like her flare dresses it swayed from side-to-side as she crossed the tiled floor in low-heeled pumps.

A few feet from the door, I slid into a bistro seat. The collective scent of freshly baked bread, donuts, and pastries awakened the beast in me. My stomach growled ferociously and I regretted not packing up what was left of my buttermilk biscuits to go. Then I remembered the money I had earned that was tucked inside my shoe. I wiggled my toes to make sure I wasn't dreaming.

"Hi. I'm Sammy," the lady said, and she gave me a polite curtsy, holding out the hem of her white apron as if she was wearing a prom dress.

Flo slapped her own forehead. "Where are my manners? Angie, Sammy. Sammy, Angie. Angie hails from Detroit."

"Do you have a sweet tooth, Angie?"

I nodded slowly.

Childlike, Sammy bounced across the bakery in jeans and pink tennis shoes. From behind the glass case displaying all things delicious, she reached inside and pulled out a donut.

"Chocolate chip cookie dough. New on the menu. Fresh from the oven. Have a taste." She held out the donut.

Floe watched me like a mother waiting for her child to take its first step.

I limped over to the counter, removed my hands from the pocket of my hoodie, and gave the donut a try. My eyes would've rolled around in my head if I hadn't held them in place. Packed with sweet delight, the donut melted on my tongue and stayed on my mind.

"What do you think?" Sammy said, leaning on the countertop.

I nodded my approval. Chewing a mouthful, I pressed my lips together so as not to smile, but they curved at the edges anyway.

Sammy gave me two thumbs up.

"Angie's a good cook. Makes the best buttermilk biscuits west of the Mississippi, I've been told." Floe gave me a sideways glance and winked. "Hey, Sammy. Don't mean to be a bother, but aren't yah in the market for a donut girl?"

"Pastry chef, you mean? I haven't advertised for it, Aunt Floe, but I guess I am. Why?"

"Isn't that just the way Christ works? Angie is a great baker and you need a pastry chef. 'For those who love Jesus all things work together for good.' It says it in the Good Book, yah know."

Sammy looked as if a bee had stung her. I stood there catching fire, realizing I had been deceived by a conniving old lady. Ashley was right. Nothing at Roxy's was confidential.

A cop knocked on the front door and peered through the window. A short line had formed outside. Sammy took a step forward and then a step back, obviously unsure of what do: see to her customers or obey the Good Book.

"When can you start, Angie?" Sammy called over her shoulder as she bounced toward the door.

I spit the last of my donut into the napkin not to gag.

"I'll let yah know, Sammy," Floe answered for me. "We have a little red tape to untangle back at the house." Floe turned to me. "What do yah say we get three or four of those cookie doughs before they sell out?" She whispered to me behind her hand.

The morning had gone from blue to gray with specks of yellow, the sun slowly opening its eyes after days of uninterrupted sleep.

"I didn't finish telling yah about Clyde…" Floe started the engine of her bat-mobile and another gospel song played. The man sang, "He Will Carry Me" in an upbeat style.

"I shouldn't blame Clyde for the divorce. He wasn't much of a man to begin with. We never had kids, the two of us, so when I packed up and left, I didn't have much to carry. Just me and old Betsy, who carried me across the country and everywhere I hung my hat." She rubbed the dash again as we took off on the highway at forty miles an hour. "This'll date yah, but Elvis Presley had a pink Cadillac, which were all the rage back in my day, and Clyde was a big fan of Elvis. I think he thought he was Elvis." She chuckled. "Betsy is all I have left of my time with Clyde. Sometimes leaving can be fruitful and sometimes staying is worth our while." She swung her eyes my way again. "I didn't stay, but I let the Lord lead the way and left when He saw fit!"

The sign directing us to Pueblo was left behind when Floe got off the highway headed toward Roxy's House. "I just need to drop off these donuts and you'll be on her way."

The realization that there were strings attached to everything Floe said hit me. She had a way of making me feel as if my choices were my own.

"Oh, I married again," she continued. "Mr. Dan Dunlevy. The nicest man yah ever want to meet, sweeter than apple pie he is…"

I couldn't say for certain that I had chosen to return to Roxy's House, but when we drove through the automatic gates, I knew this was home—for a short while anyway.

Part Three

Thirty-Four

Six years of waiting, hoping, and speculating was worse than plodding through wet snow in the dead of a Michigan winter for Vangie, her time served a prison sentence replete with guilt and remorse. Two months earlier, she and Angie had turned twenty-five, a birthday that had gone uncelebrated. Some nights, Angie appeared in her dreams—alive, well, and full of chatter. In the mornings following those gentle dreams, Vangie awakened with a smile. On other nights, her nightmares reflected her fears—too many frightening possibilities and not enough leads.

Initially, her trips home had been frequent, propelled by her sudden urges to scour the streets of Detroit for Angie. Now, her visits home were few and far between and for a single purpose—to care for her mother and manage the property she had purchased. Otherwise, Vangie supported Annette from afar, sending her love in an envelope stuffed with a check and keeping a decent roof over her mother's head.

Ten minutes after 1:00 P.M., Vangie left LAX's self-park in her white Benz and drove to Beverly Hills where she retrieved her personal mail, kept private at a Beverly Hills Mailbox. She hopped back into her car and tossed the mail onto the passenger's seat. Her bills were mounting. Why bother looking at them?

Fifteen minutes later, she drove up the last leg of her street, having finally acclimated to the area's narrow, steep, hilly roads.

Her Benz was a source of pride, reflecting the status of the neighborhood. The road stopped at the foot of her vintage house in Hollywood Hills. She zoomed into the private driveway of the fully furnished one-bedroom cottage tucked neatly on a hillside.

Some days she missed her high-end turnkey Studio City apartment, her first home upon her move to Los Angeles after graduation. With the balance in her savings account uncomfortably low by her standards and no cash coming in, she had packed up and moved the moment her lease was up, avoiding another astronomical monthly payment.

When Vangie stepped out of the car, the Belgian Malinois on the other side of the wooden fence wasn't barking and snarling, which meant the dog and its owner, a retired or burned-out actor, were out on their afternoon walk. Vangie could do without the barking dog, but she had taken a liking to the cat posing elegantly on the wooden fence between the two properties. Its lush black fur reminded her of Angie's favorite cat, Sir Duke. It leaped from the gate, walking toward her with poise and grace before welcoming her home with a furry leg rub. She appreciated the show of affection from the perceptive animal. It was the only homecoming she would get. The cat followed her home.

Inside the cottage, Vangie walked to her feng shui bedroom with cream-colored walls and bamboo furniture, located her home safe deposit box—hidden in the bedroom wardrobe closet where she locked away her mail—then unpacked, undressed, put on a pair of shorts and a tank-top, and fastened her hair into a ponytail. Things had begun to rot during her three day absence. The kitchen trash smelled rotten and the fruit basket was attracting gnats. She swatted them frantically, cursing aloud and tossing the rotted fruit in the trash bag before carrying it outdoors.

Starting in the great room, which combined the luxury kitchen with Mexican terra-cotta and blue tile, the dining area, and the living room, Vangie washed the few dishes left behind in the sink, vacuumed the hardwood floors and Persian rugs, and fluffed the white pillows on the shabby-chic sofa, the cat staying on her heels every step of the way.

Not wanting to kill the cat, she avoided feeding it the leftovers in her refrigerator. Instead, she fed it a small amount of canned tuna on a saucer. While the cat nibbled, Vangie swung back the French doors off the sundeck that opened onto the hills of Hollywood. The weather was perfect; nature's hand had brushed the sky in heavenly shades of indigo and a balmy breeze blew her way from the Pacific Ocean. She was more lost in the view than in admiration of it. However successful she appeared to others, she had accomplished little since graduating from Stanford, other than keeping up pretenses. She had taken Thomas Jones's grandfatherly advice, selling her stock long before Wall Street bottomed out. The money that remained was slowly drying up and she couldn't find a well deep enough to draw from.

Old Gold Eyes finished his tuna, and Vangie felt like she'd lost a friend when he scurried outdoors. The pain was always there, a hollow in her heart that couldn't be filled. She missed her twin so much that she felt only half alive.

Gathering energy, Vangie retrieved her cell phone from the charger and dialed Wade in New Haven, Connecticut.

"Wade Fitzgerald." She opened her mouth, primed to speak. "Please leave a message. I'll call you back." Vangie grunted, hating that stupid delay, and hung up.

Within minutes she received a text message from Wade. "In the middle of something. Call you later."

Some time that night or early the next morning, Wade would return her call. Until then, her heart would race each time her phone rang. She hated that too.

She kept the phone close, curling up on the living room sofa under a chenille throw.

Startled by a noise outside, Vangie jumped up from the couch, walked tentatively to the kitchen, and found a butcher knife. She might be living in Hollywood Hills, but she didn't come from these parts and she didn't leave anything to chance.

She peered through the tinted French door that led to the deck, unable to see past her own reflection. It was probably her furry little friend.

When Vangie flicked on the patio light, she found Ronnie sitting at the breakfast bar, smoke drifting above his head. She unlocked the door and stepped onto the redwood deck.

"Did I scare you?" he asked, glancing over her shoulder. Ronnie turned his melancholy gaze back to the hills and took another hit of his joint.

"To death. I must've missed your call," Vangie said sarcastically, fanning away the flying embers.

He stood and shook out the legs of his skinny jeans. "I got the tickets. First class. We leave Christmas Eve."

"Tickets to where, Ron?"

"Bora Bora."

"Can we take this inside? I'm freezing."

"Gladly." Ronnie took a final inhale, snuffed out the embers with his fingertips, and jammed the last of his joint into the pocket of his jeans. He had tamed his unruly ash-blonde curls over the years, and taken on a rugged, sexy look, but he was still the same old Ronnie. He hadn't curbed his penchant for fast cars, drinking, and gambling.

"Nice weapon of choice," he said, staring at the knife in her hand. "I have something more high powered you can borrow next time." He eased through the French door as if she might actually cut him.

Vangie returned the knife to the kitchen drawer.

Ronnie attacked the refrigerator to cure his munchies. "I see rations are low again."

"I wasn't expecting company."

Ronnie moseyed to the great room with a slice of three day-old pepperoni pizza and sat in one of the two rustic chairs near the fireplace.

Vangie sat on the sofa, one leg crossed over the other, watching Ronnie chow down as if it were lunchtime as opposed to midnight.

"It's an incredible island, Van. It has everything you love: jet skiing, snorkeling, mountain climbing...

"I can't go, Ron," Vangie said quietly.

He stopped chewing. "What the fuck? Why not?"

"My bar exam, for one. Graduation. Work."

"The dickhead, right? For some reason I forgot you two are an item." Ronnie's remark reeked of sarcasm.

Vangie narrowed her eyes. "Jealousy isn't part of the deal, Ron."

"What *is* the deal? Because, frankly, I don't know anymore. One minute we're on and the next minute we're off." Ronnie tossed his half-eaten pizza on the coffee table and wiped his hands on his jeans.

"You have your life, and I have mine. It's always been the deal."

"The perfect arrangement, wouldn't you say?"

"Until the two conflict, ostensibly."

Their conversation fell to dead silence.

Vangie sighed. Her friendship with Ronnie was one of mutual understanding, she had thought. She did not ask for Ronnie's gifts, nor would she, a hard lesson she had learned from Jacob Stein.

Negotiate with a man and you get more than you bargained for.
Keep things clear and all parties involved understand the terms.
Ronnie knew and understood hers. As long as they remained
friends, she had her life—which included Wade—and he had
his, including an unspecified number of Hollywood groupies at
Ronnie's disposal. After all, he was Ronnie Livingston, son of Zeke
Livingston, a man with enough power and money in Hollywood
to buy an Oscar.

A year ago, the cottage had been home to Jackie Palmer, a
reality show beauty queen turned Hollywood star. With a Golden
Globe Award added to her credits for a film directed and produced
by Zeke Livingston, Jackie Palmer had outgrown the place and
needed something bigger to house her ego. The timing was perfect
for Vangie and convenient for Ronnie. Now he knew where to find
her, at least until the next Zeke Livingston protégée needed free
room and board. Though Ronnie insisted, Vangie refused to accept
free rent. Instead, she had negotiated what might be considered a
nominal fee with Ronnie, given the premium location.

"I admit I'm jealous. My bad for calling the dick a dickhead.
Can that be the end of it?" Ronnie said.

"Yeah, right, Ron."

It wouldn't be the end. She knew this, as did Ronnie. He wanted
more of what she couldn't give him. It wasn't enough that she'd
given him her time when Wade's wasn't available. The NASCAR
Sprint Cup, Hollywood premieres, club hopping, runs to Vegas,
and impromptu getaways would never be enough. Since Jacob's
"play party," Ronnie had remained on a quest for another chance
to make love to her. Opportunity had yet to knock twice.

Ronnie had moved from the chair and sat next to her, taking
her hands in his. "I need this trip, Van. I'd do it for you. Don't flake
out on me."

Vangie sighed, wearily. These spur-of-the-moment getaways were also Ronnie's way to dry out under a tropical sun. She was part of his great escape. She, too, had troubles to forget, especially at this time of year. The previous year they had spent the Christmas holiday in Tahiti. The year before they had made a quick run for the border, spending the dark days under the Puerto Vallarta sun.

Sometimes she viewed herself as one of Ronnie's forbidden fruits, like drinking, gambling, and fast cars—an addiction dangerous to his wellbeing and hers. She couldn't deny she was just as addicted to Ronnie. Their friendship had become mutual codependence.

"I'll think about it."

"Sweet deal." He kissed her forehead. "I'll call you later."

When Ronnie left, Vangie checked her cell phone, worried she may have missed Wade's call. She would likely hear from Ronnie before she heard from Wade.

Thirty-Five

The melodious ring of Vangie's cell phone sent her running from the shower. Heart pounding, she wrapped herself in a bath towel and hurried out of the room. Listening for the direction of the ringing, she sprinted into the great room, found her bag on the dining table, dug out her phone, and quickly redialed her missed call. Her heart came back to life when Wade answered.

"Hi, baby." She dropped into one of the teakwood dinette chairs.

"You sound out of breath. Did I catch you in the middle of something?" Wade said.

"I was in the shower."

"Are you indecent?"

"Yes."

"Wet?"

Vangie giggled. "Dripping."

Wade released an agonized sigh. "Say no more. I'm turning blue out here." Wade sighed again. "I miss you more than I can express."

"I wish you were here." Vangie's eyes glazed with tears.

"Better there than here."

"Another long day?"

"You can't imagine my days, Van. I performed my third extra capsular cataract extraction, and successfully, if the old dude's eyes don't bleed out post-surgery."

She chuckled. "Anything else interesting happen?" she said to keep him near.

She listened attentively to Wade, never tiring of hearing the perils and pitfalls of his final year of residency at Yale. She was prouder of his achievements than her own. In a sense, his life had become hers, while her life remained her own. She cherished every stolen moment they spent together during their fleeting breaks: rainy weekends in Wade's New Haven condo, romantic getaways during his rare visits home, and their FaceTime nights.

She could hear the preoccupation in Wade's voice already. It wouldn't be long before their conversation came to an abrupt close. A patient needed attention, surgical rounds, the outpatient clinic, and so on.

"Listen, babe, I gotta go," Wade said as she predicted. "I just called to tell you I'll be home."

Vangie's sat straight up. "You will! When?"

"For Christmas."

Her mouth dropped open. "But that's...next week."

"Is that a problem?"

"What happened to Haiti?"

"The mission was cancelled. I thought I told you."

Wade was saying something about unforeseen circumstances and civil unrest in Haiti. Vangie only caught a fraction of what he had said, half listening. She and Wade had never celebrated Christmas together—deliberately on her part and inadvertently on his. Wade's medical missions at that time of year, helping those who otherwise had no access to healthcare, had given her the perfect excuse to escape the wholly depressing holidays.

"I'll be in Bora Bora." She'd instantly made up her mind to call Ronnie and take him up on his offer.

"Bora Bora!" Wade practically shouted.

"You sound surprised."

His laugh was strained. "Nothing surprises me about you, Vangie. You'll just have to cancel your trip."

"I can't cancel it."

"I'm not giving you an option."

"My father's looking forward to seeing me." She moved about the room, unable to sit or stand in one place.

"Tell him I said, if he wants to see you, he'll have to go through me first this time."

"Are you serious?" She laughed as if he couldn't be.

"I couldn't be more serious."

"But we agreed, Wade." Her pitch rose to a whine.

"Agreed to what?"

"We agreed we wouldn't celebrate Christmas."

"When?"

She needed air. She walked outside in her bath towel before she realized it. "You don't understand, Wade," she said pleadingly.

"How can I understand when you've kept me in the dark for so long. Why don't you enlighten me."

"I don't want to talk about it," she snapped.

Wade sighed. "You can't expect me to agree to your terms under those conditions. Be fair, babe."

Blood rushed to Vangie's face. There was only one way out of this—fight her way out. "What about last Christmas, Wade, and the Christmas before that, and all the other holidays when you weren't thinking about me and didn't give a shit where I went or what I did?" Back inside, she sat down to catch her breath.

"If I can offer a rebuttal, you're all I think about. And for the record, you were always free to tag along on my mission trip. In fact, I begged you to go with me," he said, countering her argument rationally.

What could she say? It was true. He had always invited and she had always declined, finding one excuse after another. Now she had run out of excuses.

"Maybe I didn't want to *tag* along," she said with unadulterated sass.

"Van. You and I are spending Christmas together. Call your father or I will." His words held a brusque finality she hadn't heard before.

"I'll call him," she acquiesced quickly.

"Was that so hard?" His voice smiled. "I have to go, babe. I'll see you soon. Okay. I love you."

After Vangie hung up, she sat in a daze for a long while, wondering what was so important about *this* Christmas.

An hour later Vangie arrived at Loyola Law School on the southern edge of downtown Los Angeles. She parked on Albany Street, close to the William M. Rains Library, and walked into the building. Many of the other students at Loyola Law School likely appreciated the architectural design of the campus with its box-shaped buildings in an array of bright colors. Vangie didn't have an opinion one way or another. In two and a half years, she hadn't gained much of an affinity for the campus or the legal field.

She would like to believe her love for Wade and his drive for achievement put her on this trajectory. That might make some sense of her life. He liked that she was "goal oriented" and "paving her own way," in spite of her alleged father's wealth.

Because Clarissa had talked her into law school and Wade had insisted on it, her life had taken unexpected twists and turns, her close friendship with Clarissa being one of them. In some ways,

Clarissa had become the twin she'd lost, the main reason she was spending a day holed up in a library.

Clarissa sent a text message, directing her to the basement. Descending the stairs, Vangie regretted wearing a mini sweater dress, boots, and a neck scarf. The building's temperamental thermostat had decided on hot and sticky today. As she reached the last step, she yanked the scarf from around her neck, wishing for a cold drink of some kind.

She found Clarissa slumped in an overstuffed chair in a corner, her eyes glued to her laptop, her tousled hair and drowsy eyes showing clear signs of insomnia.

Vangie set her backpack down and took a seat in the chair opposite Clarissa. A round coffee table stacked with Clarissa's copiously documented notebooks, sectioned and tagged by subject, separated them.

"Face it. I'm not cut out for law." Her weary doll eyes grew wet with tears.

Telling Clarissa not to worry was a wasted effort. After failing the bar exam on her first attempt, Clarissa had grieved for months before she found the nerve to reapply. Clarissa would retake the exam in February. Vangie would take it for the first time in six months, post-commencement. These study sessions gave her a needed edge and something to do besides mourn her own loss.

"I'm sure you'll pass," Vangie said for what seemed the thousandth time.

"Coming from someone who got accepted to Yale Law School, my confidence after ranking lowest on the totem pole is restored. Thanks, Van." Clarissa rolled her eyes.

"Be smarter, Clarissa. You'll pass." It was a kneejerk reaction whenever Clarissa sounded too much like Angie.

Clarissa frowned. "What does that mean, anyway? Be smarter than whom? A halfwit? A dunce? This is as smart as I'm going to get. I wasn't fortunate enough to get the Fitzgerald genius gene. Be honest, Vangie. You hate being stuck here with me. Say it."

Vangie sighed. Clarissa's problem wasn't her test-taking ability or her intellect but her anxiety level. Passing the bar exam for Clarissa meant life or death. She had her lifelong passion for law on the line, the Fitzgerald legacy to compete with, and a prospective job as a public defender awaiting her. It was a less glamorous job than Clarissa had hoped for, but the best she could land her first year out of law school. If she didn't pass the exam this round, Clarissa would remain a clerk, assisting the real attorneys representing the indigent.

"It means you're as smart as anyone at this school and I'm not stuck at Loyola. I love it here." Vangie's voice dropped with her eyes. As she dug into her backpack for her own laptop and copious notes, she could feel Clarissa gaping at her, mouth likely hanging open.

"You're saying you'd rather be at LLS than at Yale with Wade? You really do think I'm stupid. Oh my God!"

Vangie chuckled. "I don't think you're stupid, Clarissa, and one fifty isn't considered low ranking, FYI." What else could she say? She certainly hated being in a long distance relationship, but the farther she was from Wade, the easier it was to keep up pretenses. She thought of mentioning Wade's homecoming and changed her mind.

Clarissa shrugged. "One fifty is average. Not to mention it gives me a high chance of failing again."

"Is that supported by empirical evidence?"

"By Professor Dunham, the top-tiered professor of criminal law, summa cum laude, Yale alum, bar exam tutor. He should know. He's God."

They snickered and were shushed by a nearby student.

Vangie powered up her laptop. "Where should we start?"

"Criminal procedures," said Clarissa as if she couldn't imagine studying any subject of lesser importance.

Sweating in the hot, humid room, they sat for hours, studying intently.

Saturating their brains with the principles of law called for cocktails. They left the library as sluggishly as a pair of bears emerging from hibernation.

After hours of confinement in a hushed atmosphere, the bustling ambiance of the Gourmet Market downtown was music to Vangie's ears. She and Clarissa chattered as incessantly as the other patrons.

Their conversation moved from rehashing torts to revisiting Clarissa's grievances. "I know you don't want to hear this again..."

Vangie asked anyway. "Hear what?"

"I finally called him."

"And?" Clarissa wasn't looking for a reply, just a sounding board—a role that Vangie played well.

"Did I call to ask him for money or ask him to walk me down the aisle or invite him to any of my commencements only to receive a check and congratulations card in the mail, not signed, but stamped with his and his plastic wife's signatures? Stamped, girl!" Clarissa took another gulp and slammed down her drink, looking as if she might cry but couldn't bring forth the tears. "No! I called to check in on my dear old dad after months without a call."

Vangie would've offered a word or two of understanding, but the Moulin Rouge was talking; and had she so much as cleared her throat when it came to the subject of Gerald Fitzgerald, particularly when Clarissa had more vodka than she could handle, Clarissa would take her to court. Besides, this was Clarissa's monologue and Vangie knew to treat it as such.

"Do you know his first utterance to me?"

Vangie slipped in an utterance of her own. "What?"

"'What is it that you need, Clarissa?' As if I need shit from him."

"What'd you say?"

"*Click!*"

"You hung up in his face again?"

"Nothing ventured, nothing gained, right?" Clarissa stared off. "The more I think about it, being a Fitzgerald has really fucked up my life."

Vangie swallowed her rebuttal. Becoming a Fitzgerald was what she lived for. Her love for Wade and reverence for the Fitzgerald family and Clarissa's change of heart about the family she believed had disowned her and her two younger sisters had been the cause of much disagreement over the years.

Clarissa raised her glass. "Here's to dear old dads and their invaluable contributions to our lives!" She gulped back her drink in a dramatic gesture. "Speaking of dads, how's yours? Still overseas evading taxes?"

Vangie finished off her glass of wine before responding. "Apparently so."

"How can you stand being excommunicated?"

Vangie laughed. "Excommunicated, Clarissa?"

"Call it hyperbole or whatever, but it's a disgrace the way these rich men neglect their offspring, start whole new families, and forget about us."

Vangie buttered a dinner roll, not because she was hungry—she was stuffed—but because she needed to busy her nervous hands. "The difference between you and me, Clarissa, is that I have low expectations of my father."

"Father, dad, baby daddy... Whatever you call him equals expectations. You must expect something from him."

Vangie shook her head. "He's never been a big part of my life. Why should I expect more than he already provides?" The story, by now, had grown on her like tartness on the tongue.

Clarissa harrumphed. "For one, it's your birthright, and I can tell you from firsthand experience that money doesn't compensate for love or time."

Their cheerful, energetic waitress returned to clear their plates. "Have you tried our macaroons, girlfriends?"

"I'll take lemon."

"Make that eight. Four apiece," Clarissa said.

"You got it." The waitress walked away, balancing empty plates.

While they waited for their macaroons, Clarissa began a new monologue. "I read somewhere that people like us, born with money, are ruled by it. Look at our lives, buying handbags worth a small fortune and exclusive designer shoes and clothes. Most people in this economy are homeless or losing their home. Shouldn't we feel guilty, pay homage to their struggles in some way? I don't know. Feed them?"

There was much Vangie could have said in response to Clarissa's rant. What Clarissa and Wade and other bleeding-heart silver-spooners grossly underestimated was the power of poverty. She had witnessed its destruction, lived with its shame, and suffered its wrath. There was nothing like starvation to drive a person or deprivation to defeat them. Poverty would drive anyone to kill, lie, cheat, and steal, and shame them into doing things they never thought they would or could do. Once it had a person, they would never be free of its disgrace. Poverty was the root of evil. Money was freedom.

Their macaroons arrived, nice and fresh and just in time to end the discussion.

"You've been clerking for the PDO for too long, Clarissa." Vangie placed her half of the bill, along with a generous tip, inside the billfold and handed it to Clarissa, who did the same.

Clarissa leaned over the table, her bloodshot doll eyes wet with tears again. She was back to her library voice. "Do you realize that our generation is responsible for changing the course of history? We elected the first African American president in this country's history. Twice! That has to mean something. If our generation has that kind of power, what more can we do to advance justice?"

It's the Moulin Rouge talking.

"There's your answer to eradicating poverty right there," Vangie said, proudly shouldering her designer hobo bag and standing to leave.

"We paid homage to the poor at the ballot box, you're saying?" Clarissa said with a frown.

Vangie welcomed the subject change. They would debate it until they said good night.

By midnight, Vangie lay in her feng shui room snuggled under the covers. Fatigue had descended on her, but her mind refused to rest. It played and replayed conversations as Annette had replayed her favorite songs. She wished she could quiet the internal dialogue, but the questions kept coming and her mind kept trying to outmaneuver them.

Years of deception hadn't been easy. If she wasn't dodging Clarissa's questions, Wade was interrogating her about her inaccessible father, her visits "home," and the impromptu getaways. Vangie closed her eyes and sighed. What a fine web she had woven to trap herself.

Giving up her fight for sleep, she walked to the kitchen where she found her macaroons. She had never had a passion for sweets. She ordered the macaroons for Angie, who loved sweet delicacies more than anything. She carried the box back to her room as if it contained a sparrow with a broken wing. Back in bed, she propped her pillow against the bamboo headboard and bit into the sweet, creamy cookie in memory of her lost twin.

Thirty-Six

The Law Offices of Fenton and Stanton occupied the fifth floor of a corporate building approximately twenty miles north of Los Angeles. Vangie clerked from fifteen to twenty hours a week during the school year, but this week Fenton and Stanton would get four hours out of her, max.

Snowed under with pre-trial motions, research, and whatever else was thrown at her, she walked briskly through the modern minimalist designed lobby, past the depressing ten foot Christmas tree, and down the wide hallways, eager to get through her short workday.

"I expected to see you ten minutes ago, Vangie," Danica said as she stepped out of her office. Her blonde bangs hung just short of her weary green eyes and she wore a tightly wound smile.

"Am I late?" Vangie said, certain she wasn't.

"Later than usual. I need a motion to suppress by noon. Do you have the time?"

Vangie smiled cheekily. "That's all the time that I have today, but yes, I have the time."

"It is your last day, isn't it? What I wouldn't pay to have time off for Christmas." Danica handed her the legal file and stepped back into her executive office suite, closing the door behind her. Vangie trudged toward her own office, which had been reduced to a cubicle. The new junior associate confiscated her previous office, which had a lovely view of San Fernando Valley. The stock market crash, prompted by the new great recession, had sent white-collar criminals scrabbling for legal defense, and Vangie felt unfortunate to be part of the feeding frenzy.

By 11:00, neglecting all of her other assignments, she had drafted Danica's motion to suppress evidence.

"I love your efficiency and your writing is impeccable." Danica's eyes gleamed as they ran over the motion. "I'm on my way to a hearing. Would you like to ride along?"

This wasn't a question, and Vangie didn't take it as one. A top associate in the growing firm, Danica had taken a liking to her. According to the office buzz, the partners planned to offer her a junior associate position, should she pass the bar, working under Danica's tutelage. Vangie hadn't given the opportunity serious consideration, however.

"I'm not dressed for court," Vangie said in an attempt to politely deny Danica's request. She had worn pants and a sleeveless blouse too seductive for court, no blazer and open toe sandals.

Danica swatted the air. "These days, you're presentable. I'll fill you in on the way." Danica, never one for overdressing, wore a basic black skirt suit and basic black pumps.

They drove to court in Danica's hybrid Prius and stopped for lunch along the way. The case, Danica explained, involved a real estate scam. The client, a property investment company, had taken advantage of homeowners on the verge foreclosure, speciously promising to prevent foreclosures by taking title to properties for personal gain. The case was open and shut, but Danica had found a loophole that might clear her client of all wrongdoing. That was the legal business of white-collar crimes—exploiting ambiguity.

During her drive home, while depressing Christmas carols flooded her radio, reminding her that Christmas was just days away,

Vangie noted that festive Christmas lights had made their way around the city. The only bright light was Wade's homecoming.

How would she possibly get through her darkest days of the year without crumbling to pieces in front of him?

"I need your advice." Ronnie walked into the house as if his dad owned the place and sat in his usual seat by the fireplace, his desperate look enhanced by his five-o'clock shadow.

He was the last person Vangie needed to see the day before Wade arrived. She took her usual seat on the couch wearing the short slip dress she had just rolled out of bed in.

"What's up, Ron? Something must be or you wouldn't be here."

"I got busted for another DUI," he said too casually.

"What does that make, your third or your fourth?"

He frowned. "That's a cheap shot. Only my third."

"Only?" Vangie leaned forward, elbows on her knees, genuinely concerned for her friend. "Here's what you're facing—a revoked driver's license and a possible felony conviction. Is that what you came to hear?"

Transforming into the business-savvy corporate executive, Ronnie crossed his legs and stroked his stubble pensively. "I have legal advisors, Van, a team of cutthroat sharks. If I wanted your professional advice, I'd pay for it."

Vangie knew this to be the case and part of Ronnie's problem. Money could buy a rich man's way out of anything, including a six-month jail sentence and community service. For a nominal fee and a slap on the hand, Ronnie would be back on the road in no time.

"Here's my advice, pro bono. Another DUI and you're going straight to jail."

"That's it? What happened to one of your hard kicks in the ass. I like it rough." Ronnie's lips bent into a closed mouth smile, but his eyes showed his inner turmoil. Vangie didn't know the real source of Ronnie's pain any more than he knew hers. What more could she say to someone headed for self-destruction when she was on the same trajectory.

"I *should* kick your ass, Ronnie. Another DUI?" She shook her head, walked to the kitchen and poured herself a generous glass of wine from the built-in wine cooler.

"What's up with Bora Bora? Are we on?"

Vangie retook her seat and sipped her wine, unable to meet Ronnie's eyes. "Wade's coming home," she mumbled.

In the midst of the silence hanging between them, she could feel Ronnie's cold stare.

"It's not like I haven't heard that lie before. To be honest, I don't think this guy gives a fuck about you, Van. He's a selfish dick."

Vangie went white before turning red. "That's a pretty messed up thing to say."

"I'm pretty messed up right now."

"That explains it. Go home, Ron. You're high."

"High as shit. I think I *will* go."

"Why don't you." Vangie walked him to the front door, feeling guilty for putting Ronnie back on the road in his condition, but her fear of Wade finding Ronnie at her house again fought against her better judgment. She had run out of excuses for why the property owner's son was always stopping in unannounced.

"I'll call and check on you in the morning," Vangie said to satisfy her guilt.

"Right." Ronnie stood in the doorway, staring into the night as if he'd forgotten something. "There's a problem."

"What problem?"

"My car got impounded. A friend dropped me off," he explained.

Vangie glowered. "How presumptuous of you."

"Notoriously." He put on his slow grin.

"You can't stay, Ron. Not tonight. I'm serious."

"No sweat." Ronnie walked into the night toward the dark hilly street.

The ironic possibility that Ronnie might be struck down by a drunk driver dawned on Vangie and accelerated her heartbeat. "Ron! Where're you going?"

"To the boulevard! I'll catch a ride from there. Have a nice night!"

Vangie cursed under her breath. "Wait!"

Ronnie turned back, his blue eyes flashing in the night.

She drew back the door. "On the couch, Ron. I mean it this time."

"You got it." Ronnie eased his way inside.

Wade's flight landed at noon. His penchant for timeliness hadn't changed over the years. It was 10:30 by her cell phone clock and she was already running late. Vangie leaped out of bed but paused abruptly.

Ronnie!

He had climbed into her bed last night and fallen asleep. He could sleep like her mother in a "spell." Vangie left Ronnie sleeping and rushed into the bathroom.

Showered, face lightly made-up, hair falling over her shoulders in soft curls, she wiggled into black leather shorts. After slithering into a form-fitting sweater that dipped dramatically off one shoulder, she zipped up her toe-out shoe boots and dabbed on orange blossom extract perfume that would leave her smelling delectable the entire day.

In the kitchen, she filled a cup with water, returned to her bedroom, stood over Ronnie, raised the cup high, and poured a stream.

Ronnie jackknifed. "Son of a bitch!" He swiped water from his face with both hands. "Was that called for?"

Vangie laughed. "Lock up when you leave and be gone before I get back." She grabbed her cell phone from the nightstand.

"Leave in what, my Converses?" Sitting on the side of the bed, Ronnie jammed his feet into his tennis shoes.

Vangie huffed. "Driving you to Hermosa Beach will make me late picking up Wade."

"Certainly wouldn't want the erudite prick wasting a second of his valuable time."

"Whatever, Ron. Let's go."

"Drop me off at the studio, if that's more convenient for you." He shrugged on his blazer and trailed her outside.

Paramount should have been fifteen minutes away, tops. It took Vangie thirty to weave her way through Boulevard traffic. She zoomed down back streets, up Sunset Boulevard and Melrose Place, and through the wrought iron gates of Paramount Pictures.

It was every tourist's dream to traverse the studio of the stars, witness movies in the making, or experience Hollywood's rich history dating back to the 1900s, but Vangie wasn't there to sightsee. She had seen enough of Hollywood, including its cast of characters. She drove as far as security allowed and let Ronnie out where he could hitch a ride on a tour cart or walk to Zeke's office.

Ronnie stepped halfway out of the car and paused. "Promise me something," he said, looking unsettled.

"I don't make promises," Vangie reminded him. After Angie's disappearance, she stopped making promises she couldn't keep.

"Assure me, then."

"Assure you of what?"

"If he doesn't marry you…"

"What? You will?" She pursed her lips.

"I will." Conviction filled Ronnie's voice and eyes.

Vangie's heart stilled when Ronnie kissed her lips tenderly. In a fleeting moment, she wondered, *could I marry Ronnie Livingston?*

"Have a merry Christmas," he said.

"Yeah, right. Bye, Ronnie."

"Bora Bora. It's still not too late."

"As tempting as it sounds, have fun without me."

Ronnie ambled away, his hands in his jean pockets and wearing a devilish grin, which meant that some Hollywood groupie was about to get her lucky ticket.

Vangie sped off before she could change her mind. Ronnie was right, whether he said it outright or not. Her dream of marrying Wade was the foolish fantasy of a disillusioned teenager. Six years and she was no closer to becoming Mrs. Wade Fitzgerald the Fourth than she had been the day they first met.

Thirty-Seven

Vangie didn't have to open her eyes the next morning to remember her incredible night with Wade. The distinct scent of his spicy cologne lingered on her pillow and the sheets, making her smile wistfully in her light sleep.

Wade was gone, a note left in his place, resting on his empty pillow. "Meet me on deck." W.F." She chuckled, remembering the first note he had sent her, summoning her for a date in the pool. Didn't he know by now he didn't need to identify himself? She knew his garbled handwriting like she knew her own. He'd had a doctor's handwriting long before medical school.

Vangie read the note again, this time sitting up, her brow creased. *What's he up to?* She forced herself out of bed to face the dreadful holiday.

In the bathroom, she washed her face thoroughly with a facial serum and brushed her teeth. Her hair was a tangled mess after last night, leaving her "unput," as Annette would say. She could use a touch of mascara and a lip tint too. She decided on a natural, just-rolled-out-of-bed, crazy-hair-day look. She just didn't care.

Wearing her Asian print summer robe over a matching silk chemise, she ambled out of the room. Before entering the great room, she stopped and peered around the corner. Wade had the fireplace burning and Christmas carols playing on a wireless speaker. She took a calming breath to slow her downward spiral. She could feel it starting already.

She found Wade standing in the kitchen wearing a floral print apron over jeans. Having matured into a twenty-eight year-old man, he had a noble air about him, even wearing a woman's apron. He mesmerized her with his smile, looking so beautiful Vangie wanted to snap a picture of him and post it online for all to see. Too bad she avoided social-networking like a pandemic.

"You're up," Wade said as if she'd slept for days.

"What time is it?"

"Late."

Vangie checked the microwave clock. "Not late enough." It was only 10:00. Her plan had been to sleep the day away.

"Do you have to wear that thing?" She pointed to Wade's Santa hat.

"This, you mean?" Wade adjusted the God-awful hat. "You like it?"

"I hate it."

He laughed. "That doesn't surprise me."

"What is all this?" she said, peeking inside each of the petite chafing dishes spread out on the kitchen counter: poached eggs, Canadian bacon, breakfast potatoes, and sweet smelling buttery biscuits. The smell permeated the air and stirred memories in her mind like a sad love song.

"It's Christmas," Wade said, pulling her into his arms and pecking her on the lips. His eyes alone filled her with desire; his touch was more powerful than any aphrodisiac. But nothing could excite her today.

"There's Starbucks too. Check the microwave," he said.

Vangie, reminded of the last Christmas she and Angie had spent together, blinked back tears, not sure if she could get through the day without falling apart. She opened the microwave, grabbed her nice, hot mocha grande, and headed for the outdoors, eager to escape the too-familiar aroma and all the Christmas crap.

When she stepped onto the sundeck, she came close to choking on the hot coffee. The breakfast bar was draped in white linen and set formally for two with Versace butterfly garden dinnerware, lovely crystal champagne flutes, and a breathtaking arrangement of red roses embellished with a bright red bow. Everything was too exquisite not to have been catered.

"What do you think?" Wade asked, sneaking up on her. He wrapped his arms around her waist from behind and squeezed.

"I think you're trying to make me hate you."

"On the contrary." He pulled out the barstool and directed her to take a seat. "Breakfast for my girl coming up." He kissed her cheek, swiveled her toward the hills, and left her discombobulated.

It was warm for this hour of morning and unlike any December twenty-fifth she had known before moving to California. Her mind ventured back to Angie and a shiver trembled her bones. She hoped her twin was keeping warm, wherever she might be…assuming she was alive. The thought darkened Vangie's mood again and brought tears to her eyes. She was half a person again, and only Angie could make her whole.

When Wade returned, he served her like a queen. She wished she could feel appreciative, but instead, she felt like Ebenezer Scrooge.

"I didn't think I could go wrong with bacon and eggs," Wade said midway through breakfast.

"I'm sorry. I'm not very hungry." Vangie poured herself a third mimosa.

"Then lay off of the champagne. It'll go straight to your head."

With any luck… Vangie swallowed another gulp.

"Van, get in the spirit. Christmas is a big deal for my family."

"Forgive me for *spoiling* a Fitzgerald Christmas. Some of us didn't have it like that."

"I'm not trying to be insensitive, but personally, I enjoy family traditions. Take this hat, for instance. Do you know this is a Fitzgerald tradition?"

"How would I know?"

"I'm telling you. You'll see, tonight."

Great!

He squeezed her hand, grinning like a five-year-old.

"About tonight…" She moved her hand away. "I'm not going." Her tone was brusque.

Wade gaped at her, his mouth slightly parted.

She lowered her eyes and went for another round of champagne to swallow the lump in her throat. Wade, looking genuinely agitated, beat her to the bottle.

"Are you really serious?" The disappointment in Wade's eyes made her turn away. She watched the sun settle in for the day, her thoughts far off and bleak.

"Okay. Don't go. But you'll miss out on the special occasion," he said.

Vangie forced herself to look at him. "What's so special about a Christmas party?"

"A Christmas party with one appendage. It's also an engagement party."

Wade's announcement hung in the air like sweet cherries on a vine Vangie wanted so badly to taste, but the possibility of this engagement party being hers was too much of a stretch. Kimmy had a better chance of getting married than she had of marrying Wade. And who knew? Maybe Wade Fitzgerald II finally decided to take a second wife.

"So, who's engaged?" Vangie asked casually.

A weary smile played around his lips."I had hoped to be."

If Vangie could breathe, she had forgotten how to.

"This isn't how I planned to propose, but..." Wade reached behind the vase of roses and presented her with a Tiffany box. Inside Vangie found an elegant ring with one brilliant diamond encircled by a double row of bead-set diamonds on a diamond-encrusted platinum band.

Wade took hold of her left hand and slid the ring on to her finger. "Vangie Cooper, I ask for your hand in marriage," he said ceremoniously. "I love you, babe."

Shedding the tears that longed to fall, Vangie's voice snagged when she tried to speak. Choked up, she sat on Wade's lap and wrapped her arms around his neck. She didn't need to tell him what he already knew. Instead, she kissed him deeply.

Thirty-Eight

I ts façade a sand color with cream trimming, the Mediterranean mansion of Wade Fitzgerald II spanned a corner lot in the prestigious and coveted Beverly Hills neighborhood. An array of white lights twinkled in the tall cypress trees and peppered the immaculately trimmed hedges lining the flagstone driveway.

Wade zipped up the elongated driveway in Vangie's Benz and parked.

His grandfather greeted them in the showy foyer shortly after they entered the mansion. He was dashing, as always, in a double-breasted dark suit and power tie. He held out his arms and drew Vangie into them. "Always a pleasure." He kissed her on the cheek, prolonging the moment before stepping back to gape at her. "You, young man, are fortunate to take this beautiful bride. If I were twenty years younger…"

Wade laughed. "Twenty, Granddad?" They exchanged the look of two men with great respect and admiration for one another.

"Fair enough. Forty years younger." He clapped his hands. "Let's go. The brood is restless."

Vangie took a calming breath before they followed Wade's grandfather through the maze of brightly lit rooms with cathedral ceilings and marble floors etched in gold. She was clinging tightly to Wade's hand. No matter which way she turned, she was reminded of Christmas and all of its glitz.

They entered the intimate music room where a formally dressed pianist played peaceful carols on the grand piano. It was cocktail hour. The Fitzgerald family and guests mingled, sitting or standing around in their festive cocktail dresses and tailored suits. True to Wade's word, all the Fitzgerald men wore Santa hats.

"Our couple has arrived!" Wade's grandfather announced.

The room erupted in applause.

"Merry Christmas, Vangie!" Frances Fitzgerald hurried over to give Vangie a warm hug.

From Wade's father she received a quick embrace. "It's about time you two were married."

"We can safely say dinner is served!" said Wade's grandfather.

The guests moved gracefully toward the formal dining room.

Wade caught Vangie by the hand and pulled her into his arms. "You look so good I had to get you alone for a second."

"How good?" Vangie said, caught up in Wade's sizzling gaze that brought her momentary happiness.

Wade did that lip-licking maneuver that made her stomach dip. "I don't know if I should tell you."

"If you're smart..."

"You tell me how good you look." He spun her around so she was staring at her own reflection in a gold trimmed wall mirror. She had chosen to wear an emerald green cocktail dress made of satin, the strapless bodice glistening in a cluster of jewels, crystal-embellished platform pumps, and her hair in a flawless updo. Her face she had highlighted with shimmery powder and soft, smoky eye shadow.

"How do you look?" Wade said.

"Beautiful," Vangie replied, her eyes set squarely on him. He stood beside her in a slim-cut tailored black suit, a white dress shirt, and red silk tie with laceless soft leather dress shoes.

"More beautiful than I could dream up." Wade drank her up with his piercing eyes.

"We're alone. Now what?" Vangie wrapped her arms around Wade's neck, grinning up at him.

He leaned down, his kiss all consuming, taking her like a midsummer storm.

"Put your penis away, Wade. We have guests." Kimmy, dressed in a stylish black pantsuit trimmed in rhinestones about the collar and sleeves, was standing in the wide doorway, her arms folded across her chest, a champagne flute dangling between her fingers.

Wade laughed, but color rose to his cheeks. "Did I tell you Kimmy flunked out of charm school?"

"I'll gladly reenroll if you take a course in manners. You've completely abandoned yours."

"When did you become the officiator of this event? I thought Mom was in charge."

"Mom hatched the idea; this little chick carried it out. I don't have to tell you the role your granddad played."

"Financier!" Wade and Kimmy said in unison, finding their timing funny.

It was a heart-wrenching reminder of her twin that brought back Vangie's grief and blues like an arrow aimed straight at her heart. Today, more than any other, Vangie yearned for her twin, the only person in this world with whom she wished to share the happiest/saddest day of her life.

"You know, Van, as a matter of tradition, the bride's side of the family finances the wedding..."

Wade cleared his throat and gave Kimmy a tight-faced scowl.

"Let me finish, Wade Dermot." Kimmy moved toward Vangie, entwining their arms as they crossed the marble corridor toward the formal dining room. "Before Wade rudely interrupted, I was going to say that we understand your situation and wouldn't want to worry you about the financial obligation."

"Thanks, Kimmy. I talked to my father. He's sorry he couldn't be here…"

"I didn't think he would be, " Wade cut in, looking fed up with her Daddy tales.

"Well, it *was* short notice," Vangie retorted. "He's covering the wedding expenses, so don't worry."

"I'm not worried. Tell him thanks but no thank you. It's taken care of."

"He won't have it any other way and neither will I." Vangie cut a sharp eye at Wade.

He inhaled sharply and glared at Kimmy.

"I didn't mean to start a family dispute. I thought I was being helpful." Kimmy shrugged.

Vangie hoped she had dispelled the questions anyone might have about her fake father, even if it meant paying for her own wedding.

She and Wade entered the room hand in hand, receiving another round of applause as flashes from professional cameras blinded them. Vangie hadn't taken a breath before they were whisked across the room and positioned in front of an abundantly ornamented Christmas tree towering next to the two-story wood-framed windows.

"Grin and bear it," Wade said from the side of his mouth.

Vangie mustered a glowing smile, but she didn't know how much longer she could bear this night.

Finally they took their assigned seats at the exact center of an elongated U-shaped banquet table that accommodated forty people or more. Kimmy had poured her heart into this affair, giving exquisite attention to every detail: heavenly red roses festooned the center of each table along with elegant candelabras, dinnerware stenciled in platinum, teacups filled with confections, and glassware of different shapes for each drink served. Each red cloth napkin had been shaped into a rose with a beautifully wrapped party favor at its center.

And this was only the engagement party. Vangie didn't want to imagine a Fitzgerald wedding. It would wipe out her savings account. The strands of the silken web she had woven tightened around her throat.

Just as the waiters brought out the first course, Clarissa made her grand entrance. She looked Clarissa-classic in a strapless red satin cocktail dress with a dramatic black sash. Escorting her was her boyfriend of nine months, Ross Lewis, a public defense attorney where Clarissa clerked. Ross was eye-catching in his three-piece pinstripe suit, diamond stud earrings, and fashion-forward eyeglasses.

Kimmy looked at her brother, who looked directly at Vangie, cautioning her to stay out of it.

"She's my best friend. What do you expect me to do?" Vangie hurried over to Clarissa. Being excluded from the engagement party was the *coup de grâce* for Clarissa. "Those pretentious bitches!" Clarissa had yelped when Vangie shared the news of her engagement party.

"I wasn't expecting you or your guest," Kimmy said, marching up as if Clarissa's arrival constituted an emergency. She gave Ross a disapproving once-over. He had a distinctive look, a cross between a used-car salesman, a thug, and a cutthroat attorney.

"The seats were preassigned. Had I known that you were on the guest list..."

"Clarissa is my maid of honor, Kimmy. Please seat her and her guest." Vangie left Kimmy no room for negotiation.

Kimmy looked clearly offended that she had usurped her authority. "I'll see what I can do to fit them in."

"Hold up!" Clarissa's eyes flashed red. "My name is Clarissa Fitzgerald, named after *my* grandmother. This house belongs to *my* grandfather and you'll see if you can fit *me* in?"

"Must you be so demonstrative, Clarissa?" Kimmy huffed.

"I know when I'm not welcome. Let's go, Ross!" Clarissa was pulling Ross toward the exit when Wade intervened.

"Seat them at the head table with Vangie and me. There's room, Kimmy," he said.

"Indeed there is!" said Wade's grandfather as he walked up. "My house is your house. Is that understood?" He gripped Clarissa by the shoulders and kissed her forehead with an affectionate smack.

Clarissa turned to Kimmy and smirked. "Thank you, Granddaddy."

"Oh, grow up, Clarissa." Kimmy marched off.

"And who are you?" Wade's grandfather asked of Ross, looking him over thoroughly.

"My boyfriend," Clarissa said proudly. "Ross, this is my granddad."

Ross pumped the grandfather's hand as though extremely honored to meet the patriarch of the Fitzgerald family, who Clarissa billed as Rockefeller in everyone's mind.

"If you ever need an attorney, you're looking at the best." Ross handed Wade's grandfather his business card, which he placed in his lapel pocket without a glance before returning to the table.

"I can't take you anywhere." Clarissa dragged Ross off by the hand.

"You don't know what you've spurred," Wade said to Vangie. "When the fireworks start, remember, I'm on your side."

Vangie rolled her eyes. She was one foot closer to the door and seconds from fleeing.

Thirty-Nine

The fireworks had sparked by the third course. As a nonessential member of the family, the Fitzgeralds paid Clarissa little mind, with one exception. Gerald Fitzgerald kept a perturbed eye on his daughter.

Clarissa refused to look at her father, using Vangie as her eyes.

"What's he doing now?" Clarissa mumbled, her mouth stuffed with poached pears and baby arugula salad.

"Standing and buttoning his suit jacket," Vangie reported.

Clarissa's eyes broadened. "Is he coming this way?"

"Don't look now."

Gerald Fitzgerald stood behind Clarissa and cleared his throat. "Clarissa," he said in a formal tone. "May I have a word?"

"Hell, no!" Clarissa said. She kept her back to her father, chewing her salad slowly, a childlike defiance in her eyes.

Wade's mouth was pinched, his piercing eyes demanding that Vangie intervene or he would.

"It won't hurt you to talk to him, Clarissa," Vangie said quietly.

"If he wants to talk to me, he can pick up the phone and call me."

"This is ridiculous! You will have a word with me and you will speak to Carrie and your siblings out of decency." Gerald Fitzgerald's voice was low and stern.

Clarissa stood and faced him audaciously. "It's always about them!" Clarissa shouted, causing every head to turn toward the head table. "What about me? What about *my* siblings? When did you last speak to us 'out of decency'?"

"I am your father!" Gerald Fitzgerald yelled, squaring his shoulders. "Respect me in my father's house!"

"You're not a fucking father. You're deadbeat dad whose only value is your money!"

Gerald Fitzgerald's slap to Clarissa's face sounded like a firecracker going off, sending a shockwave through the room. Silence ensued before the room rustled.

Carrie Fitzgerald ushered her three little ones out of the room. The other three Fitzgerald men pulled Gerald aside while Kimmy jumped from her seat and took command.

"In honor of the prenuptials, the show must go on."

As heads and eyes lowered around the table and mouths whispered of the shame and disgrace of it all, the servers swarmed in, offering more wine and bubbly.

Tears ran down Clarissa's reddened cheek like water from a faucet.

Before Vangie could console her friend, Clarissa said, "I knew I shouldn't have come."

Realizing that Clarissa had set her mind on fulfilling her own prophecy, Vangie recoiled. She was of no use to anyone anyway. Left alone after Clarissa stormed off with Ross behind her, Vangie kept her poise in the face of onlookers.

"We're causing pandemonium today, aren't we?" someone whispered.

Vangie turned her head to the right and found Kimmy's face inches from her own.

"If I didn't know better, Vangie, I'd think you were conspiring to sabotage this engagement party."

Vangie could've laughed, but she came close to tears. "And the night is only half over. Merry Christmas!" She raised her wine glass to Kimmy and took a needed gulp. "I'd like a refill, please," she said to the server standing by. "Don't stop. Keep pouring."

Kimmy threw up her hands and walked off.

When Wade returned, his face was plum red.

Not in the mood to be scolded by his speechless condemnation, Vangie stood. "I need to use the restroom..."

"I told you I'm on your side." Wade held her tightly by the hand to keep her from running off.

Vangie sighed and retook her seat. As much as she expected the worst of this day, she had hoped for the best. It had always been that way. Even as a kid, she had hoped for the best, but the worst had always showed up.

By the fourth and final course, Vangie's head was buzzing sweetly, Christmas past was a fog and Christmas present tasted as sweet as the pumpkin cheesecake iced with fresh strawberries and cream. She didn't want her high to end. She looked over at Wade, who seemed at ease now. They had survived the fireworks and could enjoy what remained of their prenuptial celebration.

"How do you feel?" Wade asked, as though his emotions rested on hers.

Vangie looked into his eyes and felt the happiness that her mother had spent her life in search of, that all-encompassing word that Angie had honestly believed she could bottle up and use whenever she was sad or lonely.

"Happy." Her face grew warm with thoughts, past and present.

"The real celebration is the after-party," he whispered.

The tickling sensation of Wade's lips to her ear electrified every nerve in Vangie's body. She couldn't help herself. She slid her hand between his thighs.

He hardened instantly and groaned softly. "I'm calling this party off," he said under his breath.

Vangie giggled. "How much longer?"

"One or two more formalities and it's you and me gettin' it, all night."

Lost in Wade's eyes, she forgot they weren't alone. When they came out of their tender kiss, the guests clapped and cheered.

"Time to toast our bride-and groom-to-be!" Kimmy announced.

Servers flew forward to refill glasses as the room stood.

"Dad," Kimmy said, prompting Wade III to raise his glass to his son as the first toaster.

"I'd like to propose a toast," someone else said. The mysterious male voice came from the back of the room. When Todd Bryant emerged, Vangie wanted to puke.

What's he doing here?

The last she had heard about the jade-eyed creep was that he was touring Europe in a stage production of *Othello*. He had risen to stardom on Broadway since graduating from Julliard and was now trying to make inroads into the Hollywood scene.

"Todd's here, everyone!" Kimmy seemed happier to see Todd than she had been to see her first cousin.

Wade, too, was beaming, as if Todd were the guest of honor.

Vangie summoned another refill of wine after throwing back a full glass.

"You may do the honors, Todd," Wade's father said.

Eccentrically dressed, Todd wore a black suit jacket, white shirt with a candy-striped tie, black slim-cut pants, and black-and-white patent leather high-top tennis shoes. He stepped into the center of the U-shaped table and saluted Vangie and Wade with his champagne flute. The room followed suit.

"To you, coz, and your superlative bride-to-be. 'If music be the food of love, play on.'"

"To food and love!" the room echoed as everyone raised glasses and sipped.

Wade came to his feet and pointed at his friend in an over-the-top display of affection. "You got me, man!" he said, smiling broadly. They were still playing that "got you" game she didn't get.

"Everyone knows my bro, my childhood chum, two-time Tony Award nominee!" Wade said, beaming.

The guests applauded. Todd tipped his black fedora, pivoting right to left in acknowledgment of his admirers.

"I couldn't wish for a better friend," Wade said of Todd.

"Nor I," Todd said, bending at the waist.

"To friendship!" the guests roared.

"And childhood chums!" said Wade's granddad.

The room sipped.

"May I toast the groom-to-be?" said another mysterious voice. As though hiding in the wings waiting for her cue, Cameron Calloway boldly took center stage, joining arms with Todd.

Vangie didn't know whether she should be angry at the sight of Wade's "First" or laugh at the fashion model's fashion faux pas—a fuchsia pink gown at a Christmas cocktail party in the dead of winter.

Really?

She knew all about Cameron, thanks to Clarissa and Google, and no thanks to Wade. She had memorized Cameron's biography cover to cover and scrolled through the portfolio of glamour shots highlighting her dramatic almond eyes and exquisitely carved features, and some highlighting her lengthy cinnamon-colored legs that put her at five eleven. Vangie had taken note of the relevant details: Full Name: Cameron T. Calloway. Profession: Fashion model. Agency: Elite, Los Angeles. Travels: Paris, Milan, Madrid, New York.

In the strictest confidence and fear of being permanently disowned by Wade, Clarissa had disclosed the details of Wade and Cameron's relationship from start to finish. They had met at an exclusive private high school. Cameron's father was a well-respected businessman and local politician, her mother a college dean. According to the source, Wade and Cameron had entered Stanford together. By their sophomore year, her modeling career and a hot male model known only as Marco had become more important to Cameron than a degree or Wade. She had dropped out of college in passionate pursuit of both.

Clarissa insisted that Wade would've married Cameron if the circumstances had been different, but that was hearsay.

Vangie looked to Wade for answers only to find that blood had drained from his face until he looked like a vampire. She wanted to laugh, but her emotions were dueling.

Kimmy intervened before Cameron violated the rules of etiquette by speaking out of turn. "Wade, it's your turn to toast your future bride."

The urgent look in Kimmy's eyes seemed to snap Wade out of his trance. He cleared his throat and loosened his tie.

As he helped Vangie to her feet, the room tilted, throwing her off balance. She giggled.

"I love you and only you. Don't ever forget it." Wade gave her a quick peck on the lips.

"Hear, hear!" Kimmy said.

"To Wade and Vangie!" chanted the guests.

"Post-dinner cocktails and gift exchange in the music room!" Kimmy announced. "Also, please place all donations for the

Fitzgerald Foundation's After-Christmas Giveaway in the large red boxes. Thank you, everyone!"

Vangie's head was spinning as bodies shuffled out of the room.

"I'll meet you in the music room?" Wade pecked her on the lips again and hurried off.

An arm slipped around her waist and spun her around.

"If you ask me, you're the fairest of them all," Todd said.

"I didn't ask you, did I?" She meant to bite Todd's head off, but her words poured out like sweet molasses. She glanced over her shoulder, and the image of Wade gripping Cameron by the arm and pulling her through the side exit flashed through her mind. She dismissed it.

"We would've made a pretty pair, you and I." Todd wrapped both arms around her waist, his face close-up and too personal.

"Let go of me, Todd." He didn't take her command seriously, probably because she couldn't stop giggling.

"I like this position. Perpendicular. I hear you're amazing in modified missionary."

"Well, *you* will never find out." She pointed her finger at Todd's nose, struggling against his embrace.

He clucked his tongue. "Too bad. It's been my fantasy since first we met."

"Forget dreaming about me. I love Wade." Vangie looked back again. She and Todd had been left behind with the event staff. "I need to go find him."

"I wouldn't do that if I were you." Todd tightened his restraint.

"What is it about this night that's making everybody lose their fucking manners?" Kimmy demanded, barreling into the room. "Where's Wade?"

"I don't know, but his bride-to-be is faded."

Kimmy threw up her arms again. "Just what I need!"

"I'm not drunk!" Vangie slurred. "He won't let go of me."

"If I let you go, can you try not to fall." As though she would fall flat on her face without his help, Todd released her carefully.

"You're a really good actor, Todd," Vangie said. Unfortunately, her slight sounded like a compliment.

"Why, thank you." Todd tipped his fedora again. "I'll go find my boy." He rushed away.

"I hope you have the sense to properly thank your guests before they leave." Kimmy's face was one red hot chili pepper.

Vangie giggled, again. "Can I pee first?" She needed to go like a racehorse.

"Can you find your way back to the music room or do you need a guide?"

Vangie took off her heels to steady herself. The room was spinning again. "I'll find it."

Carrying her shoes, she roamed aimlessly down the endless passages, pushing open door after door.

Finally! A bathroom.

She was leaning on the sink bowl, feeling dizzy and nauseated, when she heard voices on the other side of the wall. The arguing drew her out of the bathroom and toward the library. She thought she heard a woman. Or was it a man? No, it was two men and a woman. Maybe Clarissa had come back to give her dear old daddy a piece of her mind.

Tell him, Clarissa! You're a Fitzgerald too! Pretentious bitches!

Vangie didn't mean to walk in, but her natural inhibitors were compromised. The door to the library flew back without warning, landing her in Wade's arms.

"There you are," she said sappily, staring up at him.

"I was just on my way to find you." Wade closed the library door behind them.

"Kimmy's going to kill me if I don't say a *proper* goodbye to our guests. Where's the music room again?" Vangie teetered on one leg, struggling to put her shoes back on.

"Are you sure you can walk?"

She set both feet firmly on the ground. "I can walk, Wade. I'm not drunk. I'm happy! Did you know you can bottle up happiness and use it whenever you're sad or lonely?"

"That's groundbreaking. Who told you that?"

"My twin told me."

Wade laughed. "You don't have a twin, baby."

"I don't, do I?" she mused.

"You have me. I'm all you need."

"And my mother!" Her loud voice rang in her ears. "She died, you know, over and over and over again." She twirled her finger around and around, growing dizzy enough to pass out. She felt a sting in her chest and thought she might cry, but she wasn't crying. She was laughing hysterically, hot tears rolling down her face.

Wade went on to say something she couldn't comprehend, something about her being drunk out of her mind...that she needed to go home...that he would deal with Kimmy.

"I'm not drunk! I'm happy!" Somehow, she found herself crawling on the floor before she was carried away upside down.

How she had gotten home and undressed, Vangie couldn't recall. She sensed someone else in the room and strained to the see through the darkness, her vision gravely blurred.

Minutes later she felt Wade's warm, bare skin pressed up against her back, his excited hands kneading her erect nipples while he hungrily suckled her earlobe. The feeling was incredible, a slow burn that started from the base of her neck and descended rapidly, kindling the fire between her legs. Eagerly, she reached back to guide him inside of her. When he entered her from behind, she melted inside.

"Yeah, baby," he whispered. "Give it to me."

And she did, every bit of herself. Their lovemaking was frenzied, culminating in deep penetrating orgasm before Vangie slipped into what felt like a coma.

Forty

The sun was blinding, the barking dog next door maddening. Vangie tried to sit up before the room tilted and a million stars came out. She groaned and fell back onto the pillow. Her mother sometimes drank pickle juice to cure a hangover. Maybe she would try that. She needed something in her stomach. She tried sitting up again, this time successfully. There was a note on the nightstand, written by "Dr. Wade," along with a glass of melting ice, a jug of water, and a pill of some kind. The note read:

Take this and drink up. Let me know how you're feeling.

I love you.

Vangie popped the pill into her mouth without hesitation, swallowed a stream of water directly from the jug, and then dragged herself to the bathroom naked. She vaguely remembered making love last night, which felt more like a sweet dream than reality.

As her thoughts became clearer, she tried to fit together the events of the previous night, but pieces of the puzzle were missing. She took a quick shower; the hot pink and yellow tile was harder on her eyes than the sun had been.

She left the shower, grabbed a towel, and checked her cell phone. Most of her missed calls were from Clarissa; a few were from Wade. Hoping her best friend could help her piece things together, Vangie called Clarissa first. They agreed to meet for lunch.

After putting on faux leather leggings, a slouchy sweater and platform stilettos, she backed her Benz out of the driveway and wound her way carefully down the hilly streets.

They met in Burbank, home of Walt Disney, Warner Brothers, and NBC. Nothing fancy, a breakfast bar not far from the condo Clarissa shared with Ross. Apparently, everyone had brunch in mind on the day after Christmas.

She held a spot in the long line until Clarissa walked up wearing shorts, a sweatshirt, and flip-flops, her hair tucked under a cap. Not the usual classic Clarissa.

Vangie frowned. "I thought I had the hangover."

"Do I look that bad?" Clarissa lowered her cap toward her puffy, red eyes.

"You look like you haven't slept."

"I've been analyzing hypotheticals all night. Did you know that rage is a great study motivator? I'll have to get slapped in public more often." Clarissa's attempt at humor died miserably. Her laughter never reached her eyes, only a show of cloudy tears.

"I'm sorry, Clarissa," Vangie said, somehow feeling responsible.

"Forget it."

They reached the head of the line. Service was quick and easy: grab a plate and load up at the buffet.

"So, where's Wade? At the annual Fitzgerald after-Christmas charity or whatever it's called these days?"

"If I'm not on Kimmy's bad side after last night, I am now. I promised her I'd be there."

"Your benevolent efforts wouldn't make a difference with that ball buster. I couldn't earn enough brownie points kissing Kimmy's ass."

"You're probably right."

They found two vacant seats with a window view. Clarissa picked up the syrup dispenser, drowned a stack of pancakes, and slopped up a big bite. Vangie's plate held only a cheese omelet and an assortment of fruit. She didn't have an appetite and the little room in her stomach was taken over by a nagging feeling that wouldn't go away. It helped that the fog encasing her brain had dispersed. Thanks to Wade's magic pill, things were becoming a lot clearer.

"So, what happened after the most humiliating experience of my life? They all hate me, huh?"

Vangie knew how much Clarissa wanted to be loved by her family, particularly her father, and simply said, "I was hoping you could tell me what happened. I can't remember a thing."

"Are you saying that you got stupid drunk, Vangie Cooper?" Clarissa laughed.

"Stupid and drunk are synonymous in my book."

"I'll bet that pissed off Kimmy. I wish I'd been there, but I can't help you. I left early, in case you forgot."

Vangie's forehead wrinkled. "But you came back...?"

"Came back where?"

"To the party."

"To be treated like a stepchild? Hell no! I'll never speak to those bitches again. They're not my family and never have been!"

Vangie's fog had returned.

"We should catch the after-Christmas sales!" Clarissa suggested suddenly, as though needing to work-off steam

Maybe a shopping spree was just what she needed to clear her head, Vangie decided.

"I see what you've been up to all day," Wade said when Vangie got home. "You must've sobered up." He sat at the kitchen bar, his laptop powered up, papers of some sort spread around him, and a bottle of beer in his hand.

Weighed down with shopping bags, Vangie stood by, debating whether to unload a mouthful of questions or her bags.

"It looks like something's on your mind. What's up?" Wade said.

"Food." Vangie decided she didn't want to know what happened last night, like every other Christmas she wanted to forget.

"Where do you want me to put these?" Wade said, relieving her of her load.

"Anywhere." Vangie stepped out of her heels and went straight for the kitchen. "You want to eat out or in tonight?"

"In. I'm swamped." Wade put her shopping bags "anywhere" as instructed and returned to his computer.

Feeling the ache of her impending loss, Vangie stared longingly at him. In a few days her time with Wade would end. For weeks, if not months thereafter, they would have no window of opportunity to break away, Wade putting in overtime for board certification and her time spent preparing for graduation and the bar exam.

"Do you have to leave," she whined.

"I have to, babe. I'm not afforded a long break like you. This is medical school."

"Save me the lecture." She prepared a plate of cheddar cheese and cracker sandwiches, as she and Angie had done when food was low and government cheese was plentiful. "Where've you been all day?" She sliced four perfect squares. "At the after-Christmas thingy?"

"Everybody was asking about you."

Kimmy, you mean...

"You missed a great opportunity to give back," Wade talked on. "You should've seen the line, Van. It was wrapped around the block."

I didn't have to. I've stood in those lines for hours on end.

"It's disheartening, in hindsight. We travel to penurious countries to aid the needy when there are enough people in need right in our own backyard…"

A depressing thought.

"The day after Christmas and most of those kids hadn't seen a gift or a hot meal…"

"Did you do anything else today?"

Anything to move on with the conversation.

"Other than think about you?" Wade's eyes took on a mischievous glint and she knew where his mind had gone, straight to the gutter. He moved in for the kill.

She laughed and tried to dodge him. He caught her around the waist and pulled her into him.

"Don't you have work to do?" she teased.

"Work can wait. I want what's due me."

She laughed. "What're you due?"

"Our all-night celebration. Thought I forgot?"

Vangie's cheeks burned, the memory of their hot and frenzied lovemaking last night wafting through her mind like a sweet dream again.

Wade brought his mouth to hers in eager anticipation, sweeping his tongue in soft, deliberate strokes across hers, making her spasm in places she hadn't known she had muscles.

Vangie broke from their kiss. "I gave you your due last night," she taunted.

Wade laughed. "It must've been a wet dream. You were out cold when I got in last night." His tone was matter-of-fact.

Certain he was wrong and she was right, Vangie gnawed at her bottom lip. The scattered puzzle pieces had returned. She tried to assemble them, but her mind drew a total blank.

"You don't remember anything about last night, do you?" Wade spoke circumspectly, as though he didn't want her to remember something.

"Is there something I should remember?" Suspicion resounded in her tone and she didn't know why.

"There is one thing you should know," Wade murmured into the bottle as he swigged.

She followed Wade from the kitchen to the living room, watching him closely.

"I recommend you sit for this." He sat on the couch.

Vangie folded her arms tightly over her chest and tapped her foot. "What is it, Wade?"

When Wade lowered his head and pinched the bridge of his nose, Vangie knew instinctively that she hadn't imagined what she'd suspected.

"She was at the party last night. Your ex? What's that trick's name? Cameron?"

Wade raised his eyes but didn't open his mouth.

Vangie shifted her weight and tightened her arms. "Wasn't she, Wade?"

"I hope you don't think anything happened between us."

"I haven't had time to *think*, Wade."

"Think nothing of it. I haven't seen Cameron in months."

Vangie's brows arched dramatically. "Months or years?"

His gaffe, evidently, had taken him by surprise. He looked as though he might regurgitate his beer. "Months..." he admitted quietly. "Three or four. It wasn't important enough to keep count. Her visits were unannounced and unsolicited. I swear, Van."

Another gaffe.

"Visits? As in plural!" If she was beet red before she had to be molten green, now. Vangie stood by not knowing what to do with her anger and unadulterated jealously, but feel homicidal. She found herself stepping backward, shaking her head and waving her hands.

"I can't, Wade. I can't..."

Wade stood. "You can't what?"

"I can't do this! Whatever this is. Us! The whole long distance charade. Have Cameron. However the hell you want her. I'm done!" Her voice was surprisingly level given the rise in her body temperature.

Wade rushed up to her. "Van. Here's the God's honest truth. Cameron dropped in on me uninvited. The most that happened, and the most egregious, I'll admit, was that we had dinner. And I made it perfectly clear to Cameron then and last night that you're the only girl I've ever loved or ever will love. Whatever illusions she's holding on to I did not foster. I swear to you, babe. I didn't." He took a deep breath. "I planned to tell you everything..."

So did I...

"I don't know what else to tell you but I'm so sorry. You know Todd. He has a twisted sense of humor. That shit wasn't funny."

Ad nauseam. Todd crawled under her skin and gave her the creeps. But Todd and Cameron were the least of her worries.

"I still don't want to marry you, Wade," Vangie said, resolutely.

"You don't want to or you're not going to?"

"I'm not." Unable to meet Wade's pain stricken eyes, Vangie pushed past him and stormed off.

In her bedroom, she flung herself across her bed out of pure emotional and mental exhaustion. For six years she had awaited her wedding day with bated breath, and for those same six years she had feared it. It was finally over. Her fantasy of becoming Mrs. Wade Fitzgerald the Fourth was just that, an irrational notion. It was time Wade knew the sordid truth, which only skimmed the surface of the secrets she harbored.

The bedroom door creaked open and the bed dipped. Vangie could hear Wade's shallow breaths rise and fall in concert with hers.

"Van. Look at me."

How could she face him? She was the deceitful one who didn't deserve to marry him, just poor ghetto trash who had slept her way to the top.

"Babe. Please. Look at me."

Solemnly, Vangie rolled over and faced Wade. She dried her eyes, but the tears kept falling.

He lay down before her and cupped her face in the palms of his hands. "You don't know how much I love you, do you? I can't live without you, Van. Don't make me. Please." He pressed his mouth to hers passionately, keeping her face bound in his hands.

Against what Vangie knew to be true—that nothing was ever what it seemed—she trusted Wade unquestioningly.

"Christmas isn't the best day for me," she whispered.

"I'm know, babe. I know." Wade smoothed out her hair, kissing away her tears. "I have the feeling Mom and Kimmy masterminded the engagement party to get me home for Christmas. It has been a minute…" His voice rang with regret, his eyes remote as if his years of medical school and their time apart had finally dawned on him. "I promise you, Van, once I'm board certified, I'll never leave you again. Never." He embraced her fully, his chest caving into hers as if thanking her for her patience.

She should thank him. He had forced her to face the only truth that mattered in her life— she loved him, no matter her truth or his.

Staring deeply into Wade's piercing eyes and their future together, Vangie said, "I love you too."

Enough to die for...

Forty-One

Vangie had officially earned her Juris Doctor degree after finishing law school and was now focused on passing the bar exam and becoming Mrs. Wade Dermot Fitzgerald IV in the fall. She and Wade had decided they couldn't wait the extra year that Kimmy and Frances thought necessary to properly plan the nuptials. At 11:00 she would meet with Kimmy to discuss the details, a lunch date Vangie wasn't looking forward to.

Backing out of the driveway, she hit her brakes, coming to a jerking halt. Something or someone was balled up on the rattan bench on her porch. She raised her umbrella, darted through the rain across the wet pavement, and approached the figure cautiously.

"Ronnie." Vangie shook him frantically. The sight of Ronnie did not so much shock Vangie as scare her to death. First, he was supposed to be in China negotiating a new investment deal. Second, after an all-night drinking binge, Ronnie had never looked this bad. He wore a scruffy beard, his clothes were soaking wet, he reeked of alcohol, and he had slammed his head into something, leaving a bloody wound. Her heart clinched.

Ronnie opened his melancholy eyes, blinked like he didn't recognize her, and closed them again.

"Ron…" She shook him again.

"Hey, Van." He tried to sit up but plunked back down.

"How long have you been out here?"

315

He scratched his head, looking delirious.

"Let's get you inside." Vangie pulled Ronnie upright by the arm, tugging against gravity.

Inside, she dropped him onto the sofa. He curled up like a snail again and closed his eyes. Now was not the time to ask questions. She went straight to the kitchen and heated water in the microwave for instant coffee. She was sure he needed a cup or two and a sobering shower. She thought nothing of undressing him and helping him into the bathroom.

Showered, bandaged, and somewhat lucid, Ronnie sat near the burning fireplace in his boxer shorts, running his hand through his wet curls. He had given Vangie a full report of his downward spiral. Apparently, he had never made it to China as planned. He had blown much of the investment money intended for his new technology manufacturing deal on a thoroughbred named Lady Lightning. After too many hits of potent cannabis and shots of 150 proof tequila, he couldn't recollect the last seventy-two hours and didn't know how he'd wound up passed out on her porch. He remembered getting into a scuffle at a club and having a bad argument with Zeke, after which he'd been banned from the studio and cut out of his family inheritance.

"Why can't you be more like Gabriel? I was five when that became his catch-phrase of the day. It's bolted into fucking my brain." Ronnie massaged his head with both hands as if he had a migraine. "He ranks us like a German General, man. My position in the hierarchy is the gutter compared to big bro and my sister Sarah." Ronnie's internal suffering resonated in his sad eyes. "What do you see when you look at me?"

Myself... Vangie thought.

"Someone I can count on. Someone who gives more than he takes. My road dog." She smiled, fondly.

"Don't bullshit me. You see a thirty-two year-old fuck-up." A tear slid down his cheek. "I need help, Van."

An unexpected tear dropped from Vangie's eye. She wondered if she was crying for Ronnie or for herself. "Whatever you need, I got your back. Just ask."

"Do you mind if I stay here for few days to get my shit straight?"

"Stay as long as you need to." Vangie didn't have to think it over. Ronnie was as much like family to her as he was a close friend.

"Thanks, Van."

Vangie was late for lunch and it didn't sit well with Kimmy. This was a power meeting for Kimmy at one of West Hollywood's exclusive restaurants where the who's who dropped in for a bite. Kimmy, who wore a gray power pantsuit with a wide-collared white blouse, sat at an elegantly set table with a bouquets of white chrysanthemums and a sweeping view of the city.

As Vangie walked to the table, Kimmy snapped open her napkin and spread it over her lap. "It wasn't easy reserving a table here, Vangie. Fortunately, the manager understood when I told him you had an emergency. What was it?"

Vangie sat. "A friend needed my help."

"Not Clarissa, I hope."

"And if it *was* Clarissa?" Vangie said with hiked brows.

Kimmy cleared her throat. "I ordered you red salmon caviar with sour cream for an appetizer, if that doesn't offend you."

"I'm not offended."

"Good."

Over wine and caviar, they made small talk, within the scope of what Kimmy could disclose under the principles of confidentiality and rules of legal ethics, about Kimmy's latest murder trial at the

DA's office. "Common sense would've told those punks that DNA technology isn't just a nomenclature. It's material. They should've taken the plea bargain. I nailed their asses to the wall."

"I'm not surprised."

"You shouldn't be. So, how's your prep coming along? Are you losing hair yet?"

"Hair and sleep. Do you have any advice for me?"

"Every successful attorney will have advice for you, Vangie. Hindsight is twenty-twenty. My only advice is don't expect to score third highest unless you want to become homicidal and suicidal."

"I just want it to be over."

"Join the club." Kimmy finished her drink. "Did my crazy cousin ever pass?"

Vangie took a slow bite of her caviar, knowing Clarissa would kill her if she disclosed the test results to Kimmy.

"Let me guess. She failed...again."

Vangie said nothing, neither affirming nor denying Kimmy's speculation.

"If you want my advice, find a new study partner."

"She has test anxiety, Kimmy."

"We all have test anxiety."

"There are degrees."

"Don't get testy. I know Clarissa is your best friend. "

"She's also a Fitzgerald."

"And no brain surgeon either. What do you two have in common anyway? Don't answer that question. I'm short on time." Kimmy opened her leather attaché case and handed Vangie a spreadsheet. "This is the budget checklist. Amy is sorry she couldn't be here today. She's up to her ears planning another wedding. You'll never guess whose it is, a certain hip-hop mogul..."

Too busy focusing on the bottom line figure, Vangie half-heard Kimmy. She set the spreadsheet aside and nursed her glass of wine.

"You know Wade is head over heels in love with you. We all are. I am, especially. And I mean that in a familial way. You're not my type."

Kimmy smiled up as the waitress, a brunette with long legs sprouting under a black miniskirt, served their whitefish salads. Evidently, the waitress, who returned the smile, was Kimmy's type.

"So, what do you think?" Kimmy asked after the waitress had left.

"Of the budget? It's fine."

"If your dad objects, we can scale back."

"Why would he?"

"You should know not to ask me a leading question. For a billionaire, that's a drop in the bucket. Why *would* he object, Vangie?"

"That was my point, Kimmy."

Kimmy chuckled. "You'd make a great witness on cross-examination. You don't volunteer much."

"If I ever have to come before you in a court of law, I'll request a change of venue."

"If you didn't, I'd nail your ass to the wall too!"

They laughed.

"Since we're on the subject of your father, will he be walking you down the aisle?"

"It's only proper." Vangie lowered her eyes and took a small bite of salad.

"Amy will need the correct spelling of his name and his current address. Which country this time?" Kimmy raised an eyebrow and smirked.

Over the years, Tom Blanchard had moved from country to country. Even Vangie couldn't keep up with where he lived and for how long. "You can give the invitation to me. I'll get it to him."

"All that shuffling to avoid a high tax bracket. Is that the story he told you?"

Kimmy had all the makings of a killer attorney, and Vangie sensed her question was leading somewhere.

"Why do you ask?"

"I think there's more to the story."

"You must know something that I don't." Vangie nursed more wine.

"I hadn't thought about this until Granddad brought it to my attention. Why not create a network of offshore holding companies and trusts like most men in the one percent? Why defect, unless he's got something to hide? I'm thinking securities fraud or money laundering." Kimmy wiped her mouth with the cloth napkin, then stared at Vangie as if assessing her reaction.

Should she challenge Kimmy's allegation against her fake father or appear shocked by it? Silence, sometimes, was the best response.

"Well, think about it. What about other members of your family?" Kimmy pressed.

"What about them?"

"Not an aunt, uncle, cousin, or grandparent on either side, paternal or maternal?"

Vangie shook her head, disliking Kimmy's suspicious tone.

"Well, we're your family now." Kimmy reached across the table and squeezed her hand.

Outside, while they waited for the valet, Kimmy handed Vangie a sealed manila envelope. "I forgot to give this to you. If you have questions, call me. Think nothing of it. It's just a formality."

Kimmy hopped into her sporty car and zoomed away.

As she drove home, navigating the wet road, Vangie thought of staging Tom Blanchard's death, possibly his Learjet crashing. Or she could hire a male escort, a rich-looking white man to pose as her fake father.

Vangie sighed loudly. Her fabricated life was the least of her problems. How could she possibly afford a million-dollar fairytale wedding at one of the most exclusive and expensive wedding venues in Los Angeles? Even if she still had that kind of money left in her savings, she would be penniless before she said, "I do."

After a pizza dinner by the fire, Ronnie was back on the sofa where he had spent much of the day drying out. Vangie was in the kitchen, pouring herself another glass of wine before she hit the books. With so much on her mind, she had forgotten about the envelope. It was still in her car, sitting on the passenger's seat. She dashed outside on bare feet. The late night air was frosty, but the sky had finally dried.

"What's in the package?" Ronnie asked as she passed him while examining the unopened envelope.

"I'm about to find out." She hurried to her bedroom, closed the door for privacy, sat down on her bed, and slowly unsealed the envelope. "Confidential," the manila envelope read, stamped in red ink.

Vangie had to press her hand to her mouth to keep from screaming.

After a fairly innocuous paragraph about wishing to establish respective rights and responsibilities, the document went on to state, "Prospective Husband and Prospective Wife will provide full and complete disclosure to each other of all of their financial assets and liabilities, as more fully set forth in the accompanying Financial Statements…"

She read on, her eyes a pool of tears.

The prenuptial contract, which would be legally binding when signed by both parties, was five pages supplemented by an item-ized list of Wade's assets, including all prospective future financial interests as Exhibit A. Kimmy had even incorporated Exhibit B along with a sticky note instructing Vangie to disclose the nature and value of her assets and liabilities for the record.

She ran through her list of assets in her mind: the two-bedroom loft back in Detroit where she housed Annette and the row of abandoned, boarded up houses in a distressed area of the dying city, property she had purchased dirt-cheap when the market bottomed completely out. Oh, yes, and her penny stock, which hadn't yielded a cent.

That summed up her net worth.

For a moment Vangie sat frozen before leaping from the bed and hurrying into the great room, wiping furious tears away.

Ronnie watched curiously as she searched for her handbag. Finding it on the floor next to the sofa, she snatched it up and stormed back to her bedroom. Vangie couldn't power up her cell phone fast enough. She called Wade expecting answers. She got his damn voicemail. When she opened her mouth to tell him exactly what he could do with his prenuptial agreement, she was speechless.

She hung up immediately.

"Go away, Ron," she said when Ronnie entered her room. Certain her eyes were bleeding mascara, Vangie buried her face against her knees.

Ronnie sat beside her. "I'm not going away."

Vangie looked up. "I really wish you would."

"Tell me what's up? I want to help."

"You can't help me, Ron. No one can."

"Fuck-ups do have moments of lucidity. What's up?"

"You think your life is so fucked up? It can't be anymore fucked up than this." Vangie flung the contract at him.

Ronnie perused it, page after page. "Are you surprised by this?"

"You'd be surprised, too, if he put his sister up to it and never mentioned it."

"That's bullshit."

"I wish."

"Don't expect me to defend this guy. You know what I think of him."

Unable to defend Ronnie's assessment of Wade at the moment, Vangie said nothing.

"I'm going to say something you won't like."

"Then don't say it."

"Think about this rationally, Van. Prenups are protocol for rich dudes. I'm just saying…"

"Really?" Her brow shot up. "Would you make me sign a prenup?"

"Would I?" Ronnie pointed to himself as if someone else were in the room and shook his head. "I wouldn't, but I'm not your dickhead boyfriend." He leaned in and kissed her forehead. "Sleep on it. If you can't deal with his shit, call off the wedding. Personally, I don't think he deserves to marry you."

Vangie would've taken Ronnie's advice, if she could sleep. While Ronnie slept in the living room, she was up half the night reading the contract again and again and wanting to burn it. Obviously Wade's first impression of her hadn't changed. She was just another gold digger to him like every other chick Clarissa had introduced him to, not his "equal."

She hit the books. Clarissa was right. Rage was a great motivator. Her mind had never been more alert. She flew through the Multistate Bar Examination's online practice course with ease. Out of two hundred questions, she had completed more than three-fourths when she sighed aloud. Money aside, she loved Wade deeply.

Against all her emotions and instincts, Vangie found a pen and signed the prenup. Then she picked up her cell phone and called Wade.

"I signed it," she said when he answered. "I would've been less insulted if we'd talked about it first."

"You signed what?" Wade sounded sleepy. At 6:20 Eastern Standard Time, she expected him to be on his second cup of coffee by now.

"Don't act oblivious. What am I supposed to think?"

"Think about what, babe?"

"Stop playing dumb, Wade."

Wade sighed. "Van. What're you talking about? I'm half asleep."

"The prenuptial agreement." Vangie tried not to sound as hurt and angry as she felt. After all, as the daughter of a billionaire whose family purportedly had as much to lose as Wade's did, she had no logical reason to oppose a prenuptial agreement.

"What prenuptial agreement?" Wade voice's rose and she imagined he had risen with it.

"Ask Kimmy. You put her up to it."

"First, I wouldn't marry you if I thought I needed a prenup, and as for Kimmy, I'd expect that of her. She lives by conventions."

"Meaning what?"

"Meaning I love you and I'll have a talk with Kimmy."

Vangie slumped back against the headboard. "Good!"

"So you signed it?" Wade said with a smile in his voice.

"Why wouldn't I?" She stared at her signature, questioning her own intelligence. She understood contract law. She had signed away her marital rights and all future rights to the Fitzgerald fortune.

"Maybe you just want me for my body," he said

Tickled, Vangie said, "I do.

"My brain too, I hope."

"Yep."

"Now, can we get off the subject of prenups? I'd like to get married before we talk about divorcing and dividing assets."

Vangie couldn't be happier to end the subject.

When they hung up, she hurried into the great room to tell Ronnie the good news. Instead of finding Ronnie, she found his note sitting on the coffee table.

> *Hey, Van. I hope everything works out for you. I'm cool. Take care.*
>
> *Ron.*

Where had Ronnie gone and how had he gotten there in the middle of the night? Vangie cringed to think he might be behind a wheel.

Forty-Two

One day before her grueling three-day bar exam, Vangie received a beautiful bouquet of flowers with a note from Wade wishing her good luck. Clarissa had called earlier to say, "Don't freak out!" The warning came too late. Vangie was already shell-shocked.

Her day had begun as planned: sleep in late; take a long, hot bubble bath; and enjoy a ninety minute relaxing Swedish massage at Blossom Spa Hollywood. She had returned to the cottage and was sitting down to a healthy lunch on her deck with a glass of wine when she received an anonymous text message that turned her ice cold.

"Annette Cooper. Detroit, Michigan. Ring a bell?" The sending number had been blocked.

Heart hammering, Vangie responded to the text. "Who is this!"

"Call me Jane Doe."

"What do you want, whoever the hell you are?"

The person's delayed response had Vangie pacing. When a new message popped up on the screen, her stomach plummeted.

"I thought you'd never ask. Meet me Friday night."

"Or what?"

"Or else…"

Hot blood filled Vangie's eyes and ears. She wanted to smash her cell phone to pieces. How the hell had this person found out about her past? Terrified this person would contact Wade, she punched the keys on her phone, accepting Jane Doe's invitation to meet at a specified location. Barring any unforeseen circumstances, the meeting would take place on her terms. She had her own resolution in mind to eliminate this problem.

Vangie knew little of Laurel Canyon, only that it was home to many famous actors and musicians. She sped off the 405 Freeway and up Lookout Mountain Road. When her car's navigation system read six hundred feet ahead, she slowed down to twenty miles an hour, searching addresses in the dark. The street was as narrow as an alleyway, with hillside mansions concealed behind brick walls, ornate custom garage doors, and plenty of palm trees. When she made out the address she was searching for, a rush of adrenaline hit her. She stopped in the middle of the street and stared up with speculation. A soft light glowed through the lofty leaded glass windows of a two-story bungalow.

After pulling into the sloped driveway, Vangie parked and shut off the engine. All at once the stress of her pending meeting and post effects of graduation and now her bar exam became an incredible weight to bear. She rested her forehead on the steering wheel to summon her strength and courage. Once gathered, she bounded out of the car and charged up a steep flight of steps leading to the bungalow.

At the arched wooden door, however, she lost her courage. What if this person had set her up? Wade could be inside. Kimmy. Anybody. She had to be smarter about this. Before she could run off, the front door flew open.

"Lady Macbeth!" Todd said. "You never disappoint. You look beautiful, as always."

328 | Sheryl Mallory-Johnson

Vangie's head swirled as her anger climbed. "Is this some kind of joke?"

"Please, do come in." He swept his arm melodramatically.

"Whatever you have to say to me, you can say it right here, right now."

"I have a better idea. We'll talk inside. Or... " He glanced up, tapped his chin, and leveled his gaze. "I'll call my boy and the three of us can have a stimulating chat."

Vangie's pulse pumped faster. Against her better judgment, she stepped inside, looking about as though Wade was hiding behind the doors and furniture, ready to jump out.

"What can I get you to drink?"

"I don't want a drink. What do you want, Todd?"

"We'll get to that. First, dinner." Todd walked toward the dining room where a formal table, too small for the expansive living space, was set for two and lit with candles.

Vangie didn't move from where she stood by the door even after Todd uncovered their prepared meals, poured two glasses of something bubbly, and pulled out her chair with a flourish. He couldn't possibly expect her to have dinner with him? To top off the absurdity, romantic music played in the background through invisible speakers.

"I hate to eat alone," Todd said, cutting into a steak.

Under the circumstances Vangie had no choice but to hear Todd out. She sat, but she refused to eat or drink anything Todd offered her.

"Give the filet mignon a try. It's prepared impeccably." Todd chewed, gaping at her and making her skin crawl.

"I'm not here to eat, Todd. I'm here to resolve whatever problem that you think I have."

Todd wiped his mouth with a napkin, leaned back in his chair, and sipped his champagne. "What do you think of my place?" His eyes wandered around the room. The living room, furnished in royal blue leather and artsy glass tables, sat just opposite the dining area. The walls were stark white and decorated with oversized artwork. A massive photograph of the jade-eyed egotist dressed as Othello hung over the fireplace.

"I don't think anything of it."

"I think it has aesthetic appeal, myself, in a Neo-Gothic sort of way. It's a lease property. I thought I'd check out the Hollywood scene before I return to the stage." He smiled tightly. "I'm curious. Do you know the story of Lady Macbeth?"

His question hung in air, over Vangie's cold silence.

"You'd have to be unread not to—a powerful protagonist, godless, cold, and ambitious, willing to commit the most egregious acts to get to the top," Todd continued.

Vangie stiffened, twisting the leather strap of her bag. "I know the story, asshole. She did have a conscience in the end."

"Ah! Sigmund Freud's Conscious Mind." Todd tapped the side of his head with a finger. "What did Freud assert...that everything is in our awareness or something to that effect? Tell me. Are you aware that your mother is alive and living in the ghetto?"

Vangie stayed composed, watching Todd through a screen of rage. She didn't miss anything, from the curly strands of hair sprouting above his V-neck summer sweater to his manicured fingernails or the way one eyebrow curved slightly higher than the other. She watched quietly and waited patiently. It was a simple game of chess. Whatever move Todd made, she would counter it strategically.

"Annette Cooper," Todd went on. "A complex character a playwright would have a field day with. If I were directing this modern day tale of treachery, I'd recommend a name change. Annette doesn't capture your mother's spirit." He laughed.

Vangie swallowed spit to keep from hurling it at Todd. "If you know so much about my mother, why ask me about her?"

"I have a better question. Why deceive my best friend? He's crazy about you, to a fault."

"You're not Wade's *best* anything!"

Todd cut and chewed. "He'd beg to differ. If I called him and told him what I know about his blushing bride-to-be, he'd thank me for being his best friend. But 'what I have discovered, the law of friendship bids me to reveal.'" He clucked his tongue and shook his head. "I've seen gold diggers go to extreme measures to get with my boy, but you... You deserve a standing ovation."

Vangie came close to lunging over the table. "You don't know shit about me," she seethed.

"You mean, what *don't* I know about you. Alcohol is a truth serum if you overindulge."

"What is that supposed to mean, Todd?"

"It was a pleasure getting to know you," he said with a smile that chilled her to the bone.

Vangie's mind raced back in time, and her heart kept pace. "You drove me home Christmas night?"

"I did my boy a solid."

"My twin... Do you know about her too? " Her voice was barely audible.

"Angie?" Todd clucked his tongue again. "The real tragedy in this treacherous tale. Was she as beautiful as you?"

Vangie closed her wet eyes, frightened by all she may have shared with Todd in her drunken state. The men? The money? Tom Blanchard ? Russell?

"I did my homework and had an interesting discovery about Tom Blanchard. The odyssey with you never ends."

Vangie bounded to her feet and shoved her untouched plate aside. It crashed to the floor and splintered. With unsteady hands, she plopped her handbag on the table and fumbled to unsnap it. "I have money. Twenty-five thousand. Cash! Will that shut you up or do you want more?"

"I'm flattered by your show of selflessness, but I'll press my bet you have more to give. So much more."

"Well, that's all you're going to get from me. Take it or leave it!" Vangie closed her handbag. "Better yet, don't take it. I'll tell Wade. Everything! And let him know just what kind of pathetic friend you are to him."

"Throw down the gauntlet. I accept the challenge."

"Try me!"

Donning a cunning grin, Todd twirled the wine glass between his fingers. "You really should try the Bollinger. I bought it expressly for you. I heard it gets you nice and ready to fuck."

For a moment Vangie was taken aback, which gave her time to gather her senses. "Is that what you want from me? Why does that not surprise me?"

"I think it's what we both want."

In spite of her disgust, Vangie laughed. "I wouldn't let you touch me. Go fuck yourself!"

Now Todd was laughing as he rose to his feet. Caught off guard, Vangie found herself in Todd's arms, bound about the waist, his twinkling jade eyes holding her as if the moment brought him pure physical pleasure.

"Oh, I've touched you, my lady, in places I'll never forget. If memory serves, you came with a bang." He ground his pelvis against hers.

The missing puzzle piece snapped into place, knocking the wind out of her lungs. She remembered now, the fog around Christmas night dispersing in her mind. The room had been dark when she felt Wade climb into bed. Or she had thought it was

Wade. It had been Todd all along. Viscerally, Vangie recalled Todd's excited hands squeezing her breasts, him hastily penetrating her from behind, his breath at her ear. "Yeah, baby. Give it to me." His words resounded in her mind, making her physically ill.

Her tears rushed forward. When she came out of her daze, Todd's mouth was overpowering hers, his slimy tongue snaking its way between her clenched teeth, his hand cupped firmly between her legs.

"You're mine," he breathed.

Ears ringing as the romantic music rose to a crescendo in her head, it came back in a flash, the night neither she or Angie would ever forget.

Russell King wasn't frightening in size, but what his diminutive stature lacked, his quiet fierceness more than compensated for. From the day he entered their lives when she and Angie were just nine-years old, they noticed his careful eyes that followed them to bed at night and greeted them every morning—cold brown eyes lying in wait. Toward Annette, Russell's cold eyes had been deceptively warm. She had seen only his love for her and his willingness to be the father her daughters never had.

Russell had stabilized their lives and Annette couldn't have been happier. With his steady employment as an auto mechanic and Annette's part-time job at the auto plant, they were finally on their way out of the poor house.

What happened occurred one day shy of their twelfth birthday. Annette had worked the evening shift, leaving them under Russell's watchful eye. Russell had sent her to the store to buy him a six-pack of soda and the missing ingredients for Angie's homemade cake recipe. She was only gone for a few minutes, just a few minutes, it had seemed.

A few minutes was all the time it took for Russell to get his hands on Angie.

"You don't want her! It's me you want! Take me! Take me!" *Vangie*
screamed, beating Russell with all the fury in her fists.

Russell turned his fearsome eyes on her.

Angie sat crouched in the corner watching and crying.

Then Annette came home in the middle of it all.

A guttural sound jerked Vangie out her blinding reverie. When
she came to, she found Todd stumbling backward, blood soaking
the soft tan fibers of his summer sweater, filling his open mouth,
and spewing from his lips. A steak knife had been plunged deep
into his gut. Vangie stood frozen and dazed, watching Todd plead
silently for his life. He reached out for her, shock widening his eyes.
Suddenly he went limp and crashed to the floor.

Without thinking, Vangie grabbed her bag, dashed out of the
house and down the flight of stairs, and hopped into her car, driving away as fast as she dared.

Interstate 10 was nearly empty of cars. Vangie pushed ninety,
her tears flowing incessantly. She didn't know where she was going,
only that she had to vanish from Wade's life without a trace.

Forty-Three

Murder.

"The unlawful killing of a human being or a fetus with malice aforethought, punishable by death, imprisonment for life without the possibility of parole, or imprisonment for a term of twenty-five years to life."

Vangie could recite California Penal Code 187 (a) and 190 (a) in her sleep, if sleep should come. She knew the law extensively and knew she had committed the most aggravated type of homicide imaginable. If she thought long and hard about her predicament, her nerves would shatter. Afraid of falling apart, she kept tight control of her emotions and the steering wheel as she raced her Mercedes across the country.

When she'd fled Todd's house twenty-four hours ago, she didn't have an escape plan in mind. Her only motive for running was her fear of facing Wade. She had driven across country, stopping only to fill up on caffeine and fuel. Des Moines, Iowa welcomed her with a bright sign off the highway. Vangie drifted toward it in a dream state, feeling her way down the dead streets.

Like most low-end lodges, the room was void of luxury. Vangie didn't care. She was grateful for a bed...anywhere. She locked the door and chained it quickly.

Drenched in sweat, Vangie was startled awake by her own heartbeat. She sat up and looked around frantically, expecting to find uniformed officers with their guns drawn and a warrant for her arrest. She found only a dark, dreary room that took her back in time.

She hadn't changed out of her romper since the fatal night. Splatters of red stains wedged into the black knit fabric seemed to light up when she walked into the bright white bathroom. As though her clothes had caught fire, she shed them and leaped into the shower. After scrubbing her skin raw and her hair clean, she toweled off haphazardly. Though sickened by the thought, she put back on the bloodstained clothes. Hair wet and fastened into a ponytail, she checked out of the motel and barreled her Benz onto the highway. The serenity of the road was a disquieting reminder that, on a Sunday morning, most people were at church, not fugitives on the run.

She had driven quite a distance on the open highway through a road of dense trees when her cell phone rang. Her breath caught like a puff of wind in her chest. It was Wade. Again. She didn't answer. He called three times this time before the message tone chimed.

In Cedar Rapids, Iowa, Vangie filled up with gas and on coffee and found a department store open. She purchased a travel bag, toiletries, a few basic tops, panties, jeans, a hoodie sweatshirt, a white cap, and flip-flops.

Somewhere around Chicago, she destroyed both her California and Detroit cell phones, changed her clothes, trashed the bloodstained ones, and continued her flight.

Detroit was the last place Vangie wanted to seek temporary sanctuary, but here she was, back in the city that had bound her to poverty. The heat and humidity suffocated her the moment she crossed the city line.

Brush Park certainly wasn't what Vangie would call plush living, but the historic community, with clean streets and trimmed grass, suited Annette, who hadn't lived better. Annette survived the way she always had, on a meager income, her disability checks subsidized by Vangie's monthly contributions. She lived comfortably in a luxury three-bedroom, two-bath loft with a view of Downtown Detroit purchased by her daughter.

Vangie turned the key to her home away from home. The exposed brick walls, pine wood floors, and semicircular living room off a modernized kitchen were a welcome relief. She knew, if all else failed, she had Detroit to fall back on.

Her unannounced visit came as no surprise to her mother.

Seated on the tan sectional, soaking her feet in a tub of water and puffing a cigarette, Annette Cooper was still the same china-like doll figure Vangie remembered as a child, her copper skin wrinkle free and her coal black hair no better combed on days like today, when Annette wasn't entertaining a houseguest. At least she appeared lucid, a good sign that she had been taking her prescribed meds.

"Hey, Mom." Vangie tried to sound casual while on the verge of tears.

"Who drug you through the mud?" Annette said with a frown.

"I really gotta to go…" Vangie bee-lined to the bathroom to avoid more questions, but her mother knew her better than that. She wasn't herself. She locked the door behind her and dropped to her knees, crying over the commode and wondering if she'd make it through the night without confessing.

Vangie had never shared the intricacies of her life with her mother, and Annette had never seemed to care about the details. Without Angie present, they had been drawn closer, if only to fill the void that stood between them. Annette no longer speculated or questioned her about Angie's disappearance, but the blame was forever present in Annette's condemning eyes, compounding Vangie's guilt.

That night they ate lean frozen dinners, as much as Vangie could stomach without up-chucking again, and watched a variety of mindless reality TV shows that played in the background of Vangie's jumbled mind.

When Annette went to bed, Vangie lay on what felt like a bed of thorns while listening to the tune of her heartbeat. Wade barged into her thoughts, bringing an onslaught of beautiful images of the two of them together. She curled up with a pillow and sobbed into it.

Forty-Four

Vangie knew if she didn't compartmentalize her life, she would crack into a million pieces. Thinking like a bona fide criminal, she woke before her mother, showered and dressed quietly, and drove to Mexican Village in southeast Detroit. For an affordable fee, she could purchase false identification. Back in high school she had purchased her fake driver's license, but that was a far cry from a forged passport. She would take her chances over facing the death penalty or Wade.

She parked her car blocks away from the heart of the village and loitered near a colorful row of restaurants and shops on Bagley Street, trying to look inconspicuous. In the past, she had dressed to distinguish herself from such neighborhoods. Today, she had dressed in a pair of Annette's leopard print leggings, old sandals, and a sweatshirt, wearing no makeup or jewelry of any kind in order to blend in. Her money, enough to handle her business for the day, was stuffed in every concealed place she had, including her bra. She had left her expensive handbag, loaded with cash, at home.

She had lingered for less than ten minutes when a Latino man decorated with tattoos approached her. "You need something?" he said with a Latin twang.

"What if I do?"

"I can get it for you."

338

339 | The Hand She Played

"ID?"

He jerked his head to the right. They walked like strangers for two blocks, rounded a corner, and came upon an alley of narrow houses where he came to a stop. Heart hammering, Vangie kept her head on a swivel.

"Three hundred and I get you birth papers, green-card, social security, and license."

"No passport?" she asked as quietly as possible.

"You need a passport? I get you a passport."

"A valid one?"

"Me. I don't cheat nobody. Okay. You pay me half now, I get your papers."

Though leery, Vangie took the deal.

He jerked his head again. "This way."

She didn't take another step, casting a mistrustful glower. He could be an undercover cop or a thug.

"You good, Mommy," he assured her.

Her only assurance was his puppy dog eyes that appeared harmless. Out of desperation, Vangie followed him deeper into the alley. They came to a chained gate, which he unlatched then led her across the dying grass of someone's backyard where two bloodthirsty pit bulls barked and snarled. She walked stiffly, hoping they didn't break loose from their chains and maul her to death.

They entered the row house through the rear door. In the lavishly furnished living room, five kids and possibly their grandmother sat watching cartoons on a large screen TV. A baby cried in the kitchen. A woman rocked it in her arms and pushed a bottle into its mouth.

"Wait here," the man told Vangie and disappeared. She was completely ignored by those in the room, as she stood by terrified for her life and questioning her smarts.

A Latina girl, no older than sixteen, pretty and heavily made-up, entered the room minutes later.

"Hi. You can come this way," she said in perfect English.

She led Vangie to a closet-sized room where she took several passport-sized photos of Vangie, two with her hair down and one with her hair in a ponytail, this included a wardrobe change. No questions were asked before the girl sent her back to Mexican Village where she was to wait for her papers.

An hour later, Vangie was still waiting. The hot sun mingling with her fear had her perspiring profusely. To avoid suspicion, she meandered in and out of stores around the village. When a police car cruised toward her, she ducked into a liquor shop where piñatas hung from the ceiling. After purchasing bottled water, she hurried outside, slamming into a man who was whizzing by.

"Your papers. Seventeenth Street taco shop," the man whispered as he broke her fall.

When the police car turned the corner, Vangie broke into a run-walk.

On Seventeenth Street she found a taco shop, entered casually, slid into the first booth available, and picked up the paper menu.

The longer she sat the more nervous she grew. She considered ordering something, but the thought of eating on her nervous stomach made her nauseous. She didn't think she could stand the greasy spoon smell much longer when a woman placed a to-go box wrapped in a plastic bag on the table.

"Your order, señorita," she said. "One fifty, you pay," she said placidly, wiping down the table with a wet rag.

After a moment of confusion, Vangie caught on, hurried to the checkout counter, and forked over one hundred and fifty dollars for what she hoped was not an expensive taco meal.

On weak legs she made her way back to her car, taking back streets and alleyways. When it was safe, she opened the to-go box and stared at her new identity.

In Highland Park, Vangie parked her Mercedes and left it right where it sat, hoping it would be stolen, stripped down and sold, part-by-part, in no time.

From there she took a stroll through the rough neighborhood. As she had in the past, she walked with the appearance of untouchability and fearlessness.

At a Walgreens on Woodward Avenue she purchased a disposable cell phone without GPS tracking ability and caught the Metro back to Brush Park.

There wasn't a better time to vanish than now. Her mother had apparently gone out for fresh air, which gave Vangie time alone. The note she left for her mother was short and sweet:

I took care of everything. You know where to find the money. See you soon. I love you, Mom.

Van

Vangie left a good portion of her cash in the bottom of Annette's mattress, stuffed inside a hole she had cut out. How well her mother would handle thirteen thousand dollars was cause for concern. The money might be squandered during one of Annette's highs or completely forgotten during one of Annette's lows. Vangie didn't have the time to worry about it now, though.

She changed her clothes, tied her hoodie around her waist, fastened her cap over her ponytail, grabbed her travel bag, and left home for good.

Taking the Metro again, she arrived in no time at the Detroit Windsor Tunnel crossing—the quickest way to leave the country. In forty minutes or less she would be in Canada…if her new identity held up to scrutiny.

When her time came at the front of line, Vangie took a deep breath, keenly aware of every nerve in her body.

"Passport and birth certificate please."

She handed the guard her forged documents, keeping her trembling hand steady. She was now Daniela Silva, twenty-seven, and a Michigan native. The only hitch with her new identity was whether or not Daniela Silva's identity had been reported stolen. If so, this was the end of the line for her.

The officer examined her passport, and then examined her closely. "Can you remove your sunglasses please?"

Her heart revived. She removed her shades promptly.

"The reason for your trip to Canada today?"

"I'm visiting friends," Vangie said coolly.

She stiffened when he searched his computer.

"Enjoy your time," he said.

When Vangie walked off, her knees almost buckled. Once seated on the bus, a tear rolled down her cheek. She was one step closer to a new life, though nowhere near home free.

At the Windsor International Airport there was no avoiding the security camera's electronic eyes at every corner, and so Vangie didn't even try. She walked leisurely through the airport, just a college student on summer vacation.

After purchasing the first one-way ticket to Toronto she found on the departure screen, she approached another security checkpoint, hoping her heart and new identity would hold up again.

To her overwhelming astonishment, she made it past the initial checkpoint.

"Raise your arms," said the transportation security officer when Vangie passed through the metal detector.

"Is there a problem?" she piped out.

"Raise your arms please," the female officer repeated, stone faced. Vangie raised her arms slowly. After patting her down, the officer said, "Step over there. He'll let you know if there's a problem."

"He" was a TSO, male and red faced. He ordered her to an area designated for suspected criminals, she gathered. Vangie did as she was instructed, though beneath her cool were brittle nerves on the brink of a breakdown.

"I need to see inside your travel gear," he said with a discernible Canadian accent. As he confiscated the envelope she had hidden underneath her few possessions, he kept a watchful eye on her.

"You have a lot of bucks here." He thumbed through the stack of large bills inside. "What will you do with so much cash?"

"Spend it."

"Spend it, eh?" He wasn't charmed. "Spend it how?"

"Shopping."

"Where?"

"On vacation."

"You seem awful jumpy for someone vacationing." He kept his eyes glued to hers as if watching for criminal tendency.

Unless he pulls out his gun and calls for backup, stay calm, Vangie thought, talking herself out of a nervous breakdown.

She smiled in a way that softened his steely gray eyes. "I'm a nervous flyer," she said coyly.

"One of those. You should meet my ex-wife. She hates aircraft." He reassembled her bag. "Won't leave Hogtown for the life of her."

Vangie asked nicely if she was free to go. After a few more ancillary questions, the officer released her from his custody.

Hour and a half wait on pins and needles followed by a rocky one-hour flight, and Vangie landed in Toronto. The Toronto Pearson Airport had floor-to-ceiling paned windows and was filled with international travelers connecting to destinations worldwide.

Vangie had one destination in mind, a place where she could easily blend in and disappear; but getting there would depend on flight availability. She ran her eyes up and down the departure screen and found that the last flight of the night to her desired destination had departed an hour ago.

Shit! She almost cried.

The next flight out was at six-thirty tomorrow morning. Sticking to her original plan would mean an overnight stay in Toronto, which also meant finding a hotel or sleeping at the airport, neither the best laid plan.

She had to find another flight, one that departed within the hour. She picked the next flight on the departure screen, which was heading to her second most desirable destination. It departed in an hour and twenty minutes. She rushed to the ticket counter.

She couldn't have picked a worse flight. This one had two layovers, one in Montreal, the other in Los Angeles. She would be a sitting duck for three hours should she hop this flight.

"Are you okay?" The reservationist likely noticed the look of horror on her face. Vangie nodded, backed away from the counter, and hurried off.

Unable to move forward or turn back, Vangie walked the terminal aimlessly, feeling caught in an endless maze. At a contemporary cafe, she ordered a glass of wine to relax her nerves. The booths had padded white chairs and sleek white tables equipped with iPad computers for customers to browse the Internet or check their flight status. While sipping her Chardonnay, Vangie's fingers itched to find out about Todd. Had his body been discovered yet? Was his murder national news? Had her name been linked to the crime? Too afraid to find out, she avoided the devices all together.

She sat a few minutes longer before making the call she had been contemplating. Using her traceless phone, she dialed Ronnie's number and got right to the point.

"I don't have time to talk, Ron. I just need a big favor…"

"Anything you need," Ronnie said.

Ten minutes later, Vangie returned to the ticket counter. If she had to layover in Los Angeles, she would use the opportunity to her advantage, a gamble she was willing to take.

"If you want to purchase this ticket, we should hurry," the reservationist said.

Forty-Five

I almost didn't recognize you," Ronnie said, opening the car door for her.

Vangie didn't expect he would. She hardly recognized herself. "Thanks for the favor."

"Anytime."

Vangie squeezed herself into the passenger's seat of Ronnie's souped-up silver Lotus. He hopped into the car after her and maneuvered the nimble sports car out of the LAX airport terminal and toward the highway.

"Want to tell me where you've been?"

"Why? Is there a warrant out for my arrest?"

When Ronnie smiled, her lungs opened up. Hopefully that meant her name hadn't become national news.

"I was about to send out an all-points bulletin," he said. "Did you get my messages?"

"What messages?"

"All ten of them."

"I lost my phone."

"Where have you been hiding out?"

"Out of town, Ron."

At the stoplight, Ronnie gave her an uneasy stare. "And now you're going on vacation?"

"Is that problem?"

"Depends. Where to?"

"Somewhere remote."

"Are you going alone?"

"Yes."

"Would you like company?"

"No, Ron."

"Just a thought. Where to first?"

"Sepulveda."

They crawled for miles in bumper-to-bumper traffic on the 405 northbound. It hadn't escaped her that Ronnie's unruly mane, usually a shock of curls this time of morning, was brushed back off his face neatly and his jeans and T-shirt didn't look like he had just rolled out of bed. After a brief stint in rehab, Ronnie had maintained sobriety for forty days, last count, and Vangie couldn't be prouder of him.

"Sobriety looks good on you, Ron," she said, finding a reason to smile.

"I haven't fully embraced the one-day-at-a-time, keeping-it-simple aphorisms. To be honest, I'm a selfish son-of-a-bitch. I like my vices. But I'm giving it a one hundred percent go." Ronnie put on his charming slow grin, staring at her longer than necessary.

After maneuvering his way across three lanes, he exited the highway. They reached the Beverly Hills Mailbox where Vangie had twenty-four hour access to her private mail. She cleaned out her box and left a request form to close out, along with the key. No forwarding address needed.

Hearing a siren in the distance, Vangie raced over to Ronnie's car and hopped inside. "Let's go!"

He turned down the deafening music and stared at her. "I sense there's more to this espionage than you've let on. If I didn't know you better, I'd think you robbed a bank."

"Can you drive?"

"Not until you tell me what's up with you?" His melancholy eyes probed for answers. "You can tell me anything, Van."

"If there was something to tell…"

"Would it be pure conjecture for me to assume you called off the engagement with the dickhead?"

Vangie took a slow breath and closed her eyes. When she reopened them, they were dry and contemptuous. "If you're any kind of friend, you won't gloat, Ron."

"Honestly, Van, I wouldn't think of gloating at a time like this. I fucking love you, man. I always have." He squeezed her hand.

The police siren neared. Heart thumping in her ears, Vangie slid way down in her seat. "Ronnie! Drive!"

Ronnie sped off, peeling into the oncoming traffic NASCAR style. The car's wheels skidded to a stop at a light.

"That's it. I'm going with you," he said.

Vangie jerked her head up. "You're going where?"

"Wherever you're going. You obviously need me. You're having a meltdown."

What she was about to say would hurt her more than it would hurt Ronnie, but she would rather him never speak to her again than for him to become an accessory to her crime.

"I've never needed anybody in my life, Ronnie. You think I need you? You're a *drunk*. When you get yourself together, call me. Until then, get a life and stay out of mine." Though her heart was breaking, Vangie kept a stone face.

"You got it." Face varnished in bright red and eyes blue ice, Ronnie took his anger out on the accelerator, speeding down the boulevard. They rode for blocks in deafening silence. Vangie resisted her impulse to beg for Ronnie's forgiveness, and instead kept her eyes on the clock. Her flight would depart in less than two hours. With one final stop to make, she was running out of time.

All was peaceful when Ronnie raced into her driveway and came to a violent stop. The cottage house was like a dream in a fairytale life she had once lived, and for a moment, Vangie thought it had all been a dream.

She dashed out of the car and rushed into the house, thankful that Ronnie didn't follow her. Inside her wardrobe closet, she unlocked the home safe, threw any traceable documents she had into a suitcase, along with her diamonds and fifty thousand dollars in cash she kept for a rainy day. Vangie then yanked clothes off hangers and out of drawers and grabbed several pairs of decent shoes. She didn't have time for much else.

She should've left the cottage and never looked back, but her curiosity had gotten the best of her. To her regret, she had turned on the TV. Nearly asphyxiated by the lump in her throat, she listened to the newscaster's report on the "Hollywood Hills Stabbing."

"I'm standing at the murder scene at this Hollywood Hills home once owned by Todd Bryant, a two-time Tony Award nominee, set to co-star in his first Hollywood film. Authorities have interviewed Todd Bryant's housekeeper, who discovered his body just days ago..."

The camera cut to a press conference.

"We've ruled the death of Mr. Bryant a homicide," said the Los Angeles Police Chief. "We think we have a solid lead on who might be responsible for this heinous crime and are confident the assailant will be apprehended and behind bars real soon."

Vangie turned hot one minute and clammy the next. The thought of escaping to an exotic island sounded less attractive. Realistically, how far would she get? If she turned herself over to the authorities, she would save herself from the inevitable. She could plead self-defense. Any decent defense attorney would have a sound argument, if she were thinking like a defense attorney. Thinking more like a prosecutor, she knew the evidence was stacked against her, her motive for murder clear and convincing. A shrewd prosecutor would seek the death penalty, knowing a jury of her peers would never rule her not guilty.

Next came Annette's warning, entrenched in her psyche since childhood. "Don't tell nothin' you ain't willing to lay your life on the line for." Vangie would rather be selectively mute than confess to her crime.

Her head a swirl of hot vapors, Vangie darted out of the cottage only to run right into Ronnie, who shoved her back inside.

"Get out my way, Ron! I'm going to miss my flight." She barged forward.

Ronnie stiff-armed her. "You think I give a shit about your flight? I hate to say this, but you can be a real bitch, Vangie. Get my shit together? Look at you. On your bad days I've never seen you look like this."

"Like what?"

"Like pure shit, to be blunt."

"News flash, you've never seen me, Ronnie. You don't know me. Move!"

Ronnie leaned against the door and crossed his arms. "Make me. I'm not moving until you talk to me."

"Oh my God! I don't have time for your games, Ron!" Vangie shot toward the patio door and was stopped in her tracks by Ronnie, who had bound his arms around hers from behind.

"Let. Go. Of. Me!" Vangie twisted and turned and let out a wretched scream.

"I'm not letting you go." Ronnie squeezed her until she could hardly breathe. When she stopped resisting, he spun her around, gripped her by the arms, and got in her face.

"You're right. You don't need me. You never have and I can live with that. But right now, I'm all you got. Talk to me Van. Whatever's going on, I've got your back."

Vangie went limp in Ronnie's arms, unleashing a torrent of tears.

Forty-Six

Three months later...

G ood evening. I'm happy. I mean, I'm honored…"
"Good evening. I'm honored…happy…"
I took a deep breath and started over.

"Good evening. I'm honored and grateful to stand before you tonight!" I said without stumbling or stuttering.

I looked myself over in the mirror, trying to embody the woman standing before me. I couldn't recall a time in my life when I hadn't compared myself to Vangie. In that respect, I hadn't changed. Vangie was always with me, staring over my shoulder, telling me to be smarter, to dress nicer, to aim higher. I wondered if she would like my dress or think it too understated, too long, or too pale peach. The rhinestone corset was a touch of her elegance.

My lipstick, a soft shade of maroon, was a tribute to my mother. I guess I needed them both with me tonight, even if only in spirit. Personally, if I could trade in this fancy dress and these high heel sandals for a pair of jeans and tennis shoes, I would in a heartbeat. But I wouldn't trade this opportunity for all the money in the world.

I said a silent prayer for courage and left the bathroom. When I stepped into the Broadmoor hotel's corridor, I ran right into Doctor Laurence. He was standing in the crowd gathered for the

352

reception outside of the banquet hall, talking to Dr. Frankford and a few other invited guests. I wanted to walk the other way. I didn't get the chance to.

"You look like you're ready to run out of here," he said as he walked up and flashed his golden smile. "Are you nervous?"

I opened my mouth to speak, closed it and pressed my lips into a smile. With Dr. Slater's help, I had worked hard to give up my muteness, but sometimes my voice still failed me.

I nodded, gravity pulling my ear toward my shoulder as I twisted my finger around the short curls at the nape of my neck.

Dr. Laurence gently removed my fingers from my hair, held both of my hands, and gave them a warm squeeze. "You're going to knock us dead," he said, peering deeply into my eyes. "I'd tell you to imagine us naked, but.." He glanced around at the crowd. "It may scare you," he whispered.

I laughed out loud and found myself imagining Dr. Laurence naked, again. I glanced down, taking a mental snapshot of his body. His suit jacket fit his medium frame nicely, and his pants fit snug enough to show the outline of his slightly bowed legs. He was wearing his locks pulled back into a ponytail, and a new growth of sparse facial hair lay neat and trimmed around his kissable lips. I told myself to stop staring at him, but my eyes wouldn't listen.

Our relationship had always been professional, nothing more and nothing less. Every six months, like clockwork, I had sat in his dentist chair just to stare into his sunshine eyes. To him I was just another patient. I didn't want to hope or dream I could be anything more.

When Candis walked up with her husband, Doctor Laurence released my hands and took a step back. "I'm looking forward to hearing your story," he said.

"So are we, Angie," Candis said.

"Thank you." I hurried away and pushed through the banquet hall's double doors. As soon as I entered the room, I was reminded of why I was here—to deliver a speech that I hoped would help change someone's life.

I maneuvered around the banquet tables covered with red cloth and topped with lovely white chrysanthemum centerpieces, reading the tent cards along the way. Mahoney's Health Clinic. Sammy's Bakery. Hope Revival Christian Center. Silver Springs Trust and Loan. Goldwater Insurance. And there were cards for other local businesses, community members and family and friends here on behalf of people like me and to support the Mahoney Family Foundation. The chairs sat empty while the catering staff set dinner salads and filled water glasses.

I sat at one of the three tables reserved for the Mahoney Foundation and designated for a select few of us who had graduated from the program. The other tables were reserved for Jim Mahoney, his special guests, and the foundation staff. On stage, two jumbo TV screens displayed "A Night of Shooting Stars!" in bold gold letters, and a jazz band warmed up, tuning guitar strings and testing out horns.

A blonde haired lady wearing a fancy tuxedo suit walked up to me. "You must be Angie. I'm Betty. We spoke on the phone."

I stood and shook her hand.

"Let me show you the lay of the land..."

I followed Betty onto the stage. She told me where to enter the stage, where to stand for pictures, and how to exit the stage.

Back at the table, I dropped into my seat and sipped ice cold water. My knees felt weak and my throat too dry. The grand room made me feel small and insignificant. Maybe Susan had made a mistake by inviting me to speak instead of any one of the other program graduates. To be certain, I picked up a program and read

my name in black letters: "Special Guest Speaker, Angie Brown."
No mistake. I was about to speak in front of a large crowd.

Me!

The doors opened and the guests flowed in. Ashley and
Arabella arrived first. Deloris, Floe, Susan, and Susan's husband
arrived next. They all hugged and congratulated me. I didn't want
to speculate on the number of guests scheduled to be here tonight,
but Arabella brought it up.

"I heard three hundred people are coming."

"Way to help Angie keep calm," Ashley remarked.

"Well, I didn't know. Did you?"

"Ask me if I care," Ashley said. "I'm here for Angie."

"You're not the only one, Ash. Gosh."

"Thanks for coming, guys. You really didn't have to." I took
another gulp of water.

The band stopped playing and a woman took the podium,
introducing herself as a news anchorwoman of a local station and
master of ceremonies.

"Welcome to a night of shooting stars! My-oh-my, the stars
have come out tonight, haven't they!" she said.

Following the introduction and benediction we enjoyed steak
and mashed potatoes while the jazz band played. I spent much of
dinner sweating and reviewing my cue cards. The sight of Ashley's
face on the jumbo screen caught my eye. Someone had even
captured an image of me in the garden, kneeling in the dirt and
planting seeds. We laughed and cringed as the slide show of Roxy's
House in action played.

When a picture of Chris popped up, our laughter ceased. Some
of us had made it off the streets and moved on with our lives,
and some of us hadn't. After Summer had committed suicide,
Chris had been the next girl to take her life. Her death hadn't been

intentional, but overdosing usually isn't. We took up a collection to help bury Chris and held a candlelight vigil for her.

Jim Mahoney walked on stage and took the mic. He wore a tuxedo and his mean mug, but his puffed out chest couldn't hide his pride. He didn't have the heart to close Roxy's House after all. When word got out that Roxy's doors would stay open, the donations and other forms of support had poured in. Now Roxy's House III would soon open its doors to homeless teens and Ashley would be the new Jamie of the house, working as a case aide.

"An estimated six hundred thousand people in this great country experience homelessness each night," Jim began. "It's a fact. You can believe me or not believe me. Frankly, I don't care what you believe. Look around. Open your eyes. Take a stroll under the bridge or downtown. Spend a night or two in the open air, in bone chilling temperatures without the accoutrements of luxury. Just you and mother nature. I dare you…" Jim stared out at the audience. The sound of silence resonated around the room.

"I'd bet my finest thoroughbred you couldn't make it past midnight. The only difference between you and me and them is choice. You have a choice to freeze to death or the choice to sleep in a warm bed. They don't. That's what the Mahoney Foundation provides…choices. Choices for people to get jobs, get an education, and become taxpaying citizens who contribute to this great nation. That's not much for anyone to ask, is it?" He paused and seemed to reflect. "I'm not a groveling man, but I'd be remiss if I didn't ask you to pull out your pocketbooks, your wallets, your credit cards. I don't care how much you give. Give whatever the good Lord expects of you. It's your choice." Jim Mahoney left the podium.

"You're up next, Angie," Arabella said.

I hurried toward Betty, who was frantically waving me over. It didn't dawn on me that I had left my cue cards on the table until I was on the stage.

"It looks like I forgot something," Jim said, eliciting laughs.

Jim and the Foundation Board President presented me with a gigantic mock check, made out in my name, in the amount of forty thousand dollars. Every penny would help pay for my culinary training. I wanted to cry, but my nerves had gotten the best of me.

"From homeless to Culinary College," the emcee said. "This *is* a night of shooting stars! Let's welcome Angie Brown to the podium, our special guest speaker and tonight's honoree."

I heard clapping and someone shouted, "Way to go, Angie!" It sounded like Ashley, but I couldn't be sure. Time suddenly stood still. Moments later, I was standing at the podium before a microphone and had no recollection of how I got here.

The room came back into focus and I heard myself say, "Good evening. I'm honored and grateful to God to stand before you tonight!"

I didn't wait for the applause to die down. I kept talking, afraid if I stopped I might never speak again.

"The Bible says: 'For everything there is a season and a time for every matter under heaven. A time to be born, and a time to die; a time to plant, and a time to pluck up what is planted, a time to kill, and a time to heal.' I died thirteen years ago and was born again...""

Applause erupted. In the crowd I saw Dr. Laurence. His smile brought me comfort and reassurance. I continued, completely off script and off the top of my head.

"Death isn't always physical. Our minds can die before our flesh. I know that now. When my mind died, my spirit died too. People like me...those six hundred thousand people out there...

we each have a story about how we wound up on the streets. We have families too. People we loved and people we have lost. We had homes. We had hope and dreams…

"My story is long and sad…about a girl from Eastside Detroit who lost her voice when the worst thing a twelve-year-old could witness happened. But that's not the story I want to share with you tonight. This story is about the woman who found her voice and a reason to live—pouring love into food and spreading happiness one stomach at a time…"

I heard laughs and applause and loosened up.

"Because of transitional programs like Roxy's House," I continued, "And charitable organizations like the Mahoney Foundation, and small businesses like Sammy's Bakery who took a chance on me and believed in me, I have a warm bed in the apartment I call home. I don't worry about how or when I'll eat. I take showers and long baths. I watch the sun set and the sun rise without dreading what the night or a new day will bring. These mundane activities may sound small and unimportant, but for people like me, they give us a chance to live…to hope…to dream a little."

I took a deep breath to keep from crying.

"Now that I'm finally living, I know our spirits never die. They rise up and fly like the wind. Thank you!"

The applause intensified to thunder as I left the stage and the auctioneer took over.

Ashley, Arabella, and the other girls decided to stay for the after-party. I left with the early birds. I had an early train to catch in the morning and needed to pack the last of my things. I took a moment to let the night sink in, walking the grounds of the beautiful hotel surrounded by mountains and pine trees. The sky was clear and the stars shining brightly. Worried I'd screwed up, I went over my speech in my mind a million times. Halfway around the lovely lake, I heard the patter of footsteps. I looked back to see Dr. Laurence.

"Angie!" He trotted up. "You didn't tell me you were leaving."

"I'm sorry." I couldn't think of anything else to say.

"Excellent speech, by the way. The whole part about our stories. Spot on. I'll tell you my story one day."

The edges of my lips quivered in a smile. "Thanks, Dr. Laurence."

"Laurence," he said. "When're you leaving?"

"I don't have to," I said before I knew it. "I mean. I can stay longer..."

He smiled. "I meant for good. What's this I'm hearing about culinary school in Los Angeles?"

I read something in his expression, in his tone, and wasn't sure if I had heard praise or registered disappointment. He watched me with his golden-yellow eyes and I began to heat up inside.

"You're losing your grip." He caught the mock check sliding from my armpit before it fell into the lake.

I suddenly felt clumsy and awkward again. I laughed it off. "Thanks."

He smiled. "Let me help you to your car."

We walked to the parking lot and up to my dirty white 1985 Ford Mustang two-door sedan.

"Is this your new ride?"

"This is it," I said, producing the biggest smile. I don't think I've ever loved an inanimate object so much. I bought it for five hundred dollars through a charitable organization. It could use a new paint job, reupholstering, and rims for all four tires, but I didn't care. I loved it.

"A little pimping out, and you'll have some wheels," he said.

We both laughed.

With only two doors and not much backseat space, we couldn't fit the humongous check inside without risking damaging it.

Dr. Laurence had room in his car and asked if I wanted him to follow me home.

"No thank you," I said, and immediately regretted it.

What if I never see him again?

"Are you sure? Last chance."

I took a chance. "Okay."

I lived in a studio apartment that was the color green like a lodge and not very far from the bakery. It was nothing fancy, but nice and affordable with a lovely courtyard just outside my front door. My neighbors were quiet people, and there weren't many kids around.

Dr. Laurence walked me to my front door.

"I guess this is goodbye," he said. "You haven't told me when you're leaving."

"Tomorrow."

His brows shot up. "Tomorrow?"

"But I'll be back," I quickly corrected. "I'm just going home for a few days to visit."

"So, you're *not* going to Los Angeles tomorrow?" He sounded relieved.

I shook my head. "In the spring; that's when I start culinary school."

"Now I understand." Dr. Laurence nodded. "Home, huh? On the Eastside of Detroit?"

The thought of home choked me up and I almost cried.

Dr. Laurence leaned the mock check against the wall and took both my hands in his. His eyes turned warm and shiny. "I'm proud of you, Angie. And don't think I'm patronizing you. You're amazing. And, beautiful, I'll add."

I didn't shy or shrivel up. I received his complement with a smile.

"I've been meaning to tell you I like your hair short." He brought his hand to my face and my heart stopped. "It brings out your eyes and your cheekbones." He feathered the contour of my left cheek with his finger.

When he kissed me, his lips magical against mine, I closed my eyes and let myself dream a little.

"I've been wanting to do that since you first walked into my office, believe it or not."

He laughed when I crinkled my nose, and then caressed my chin, his eyes holding mine. "I'll be in touch before you officially leave. That's a promise." He kissed me again. "Have a good night, Angie."

I touched my lips as Dr. Laurence walked away, and later took his kiss to bed with me that night. I was ready to love again and let the past back in.

Forty-Seven

The first leg of my trip included a bus ride to Denver. From there I caught out for the first time as a passenger on the train and not a hopper. The feeling, as the train rumbled through the woods and lush parts of country, gave me the same sense of freedom as the old times. I thought about Mo, Dunk and Mental, wondering if they'd made it off the streets. I thought about my mother and Vangie and cried silently. How could I explain my disappearance, my shame, my fear, and my guilt that kept me on the streets? I couldn't, but I would have to try.

I slept or stared out of the window in a dream state for two days.

That's the nature of riding trains.

At 12:00 A.M. I arrived in Detroit. The station was closed and I didn't have money to spare for a motel. I walked across the street to White Castle Hamburger where I ate a burger and fries and sipped goo-gobs of coffee, waiting for the light of day.

When the sun rose slightly, I caught the Metro home. Walking, I passed the church bathed in graffiti, the barren lot, and the drug house that now sat deserted. People I didn't remember waved at me from their porches and I waved back.

I would've rejoiced in the destruction of Cambridge Apartments, knowing I didn't have to face Mr. Reese ever again, if the realization that I didn't have a home to return to hadn't hit me so hard. Cambridge was now a bed of ashes. The economy that had destroyed neighborhoods across the country, putting people out of work and on the streets, had practically wiped out my old neighborhood. My eyes burned with tears as the memories struck me like bolts of lightning. I felt completely lost again.

What if I never find them?

Lugging my suitcase, I caught the Metro to Mack Avenue on a hope and a prayer that I'd find information about my mother at Chucky's Eastside Lounge. I didn't have to wait long in front of Chucky's place before a Mercedes pulled up and parked by the front door. Chucky was six feet lengthwise and practically three feet wide. He squeezed out of his two-seater and wobbled up to me with the help of a cane. I remembered his hair black. Now it was a gray overgrown Afro.

"If you're looking for your mother, I ain't seen her for a coupla' weeks now."

Happy my mother was still alive, I asked, "Do you know where she lives?"

He blinked. "Damn. I can't tell you two apart no more. I thought you were the other one. You still a pretty little something." He unlocked the barred gate securing the double-door entrance. "You know that's a got'damn shame, don't you? Who don't know where their own momma live at?" He wobbled inside the building.

I followed him. The place smelled like dirty gym socks and stale cigarette smoke. When he turned on the lights, I saw that nothing had changed. The pool table hadn't moved from the corner, mirrors still covered the walls, and the chairs and barstools were still standing but practically on their last legs. I felt frozen in time.

"I don't know where she live at, somewhere down in Brush Park, I think. Let me text somebody who say he know, say he been over there a coupla' times, let him tell it." He pulled his cell phone from his pocket and punched the keys with pudgy fingers. "Might take 'em a minute to hit me back. What you wanna drink while you waitin'?" He poured himself a drink.

"Nothing. Thank you."

I stood around while Chucky cleaned things up. I thought I should help out, since he was helping me, so I grabbed the broom standing in the corner behind the bar counter and swept the black and white checkered floor. It gave me something to do besides worry.

I heard his cell phone vibrate. A few minutes later, Chucky tore a matchbook in half, wrote down the address, and handed it to me.

Tears of joy overcame me.

I had died and come back to life right before Annette Cooper's eyes. First shock resonated on her face; then her hand flew to her open mouth, muffling a scream, and then she yanked me inside the house and into her arms and cried.

I cried too.

"I thought you were dead in the ground!" she said.

I dropped my eyes and peeked up. "I'm so, so sorry, Mom."

She stared at me, her eyes vacillating. "Girl! What you trying to do, give me a heart attack? I thought you were Angie. Don't play with me."

For the first time our mother couldn't tell us apart. I said nothing to correct her mistake. I sat down on the couch beside her, contemplating how to tell her I wasn't Vangie without nearly giving her heart attack again.

I took in her clear black eyes, void of sadness and loneliness, and the beautiful condominium and the nice furniture I suspected Vangie paid for. A thousand apologies couldn't make up for the time I had lost and wouldn't get back. Things had changed in my absence. Or maybe nothing had changed.

My mother picked up a cup of coffee from the coffee table. "The cops been here looking for you," she said. "They tried to come up in here without a search warrant. I told 'em to go to hell and stay out of my trashcans."

For reasons unknown to me panic set into my bones and my heart pumped in my chest.

Why are the cops looking for Vangie?

My mother reached up and played in my hair. "Why'd you go and cut off all your pretty hair? What's going on with you?" She arched her brow in a covert gesture. "Something you want to tell me, Vangie?" Her callous tone hinted of something more. I couldn't be sure. I had to find out.

"I'm not, Vangie, Mom. I'm Angie." I spoke quietly.

Recognition dawned in her eyes. She slid her hand from my hair down to my cheek. "Angie, baby?"

In tears again, I nodded. "It's me, Mom."

"I knew I wasn't crazy! I know my girls!" She threw her arms around me, again.

"Why're the cops looking for Vangie?" I whispered in her ear.

My mother turned up the TV volume like the house was bugged and waved me into one of the two bedrooms, shutting the door behind her. "They said you sister killed somebody. Now I know and you know that's a damn lie." She walked to the bed and lifted the mattress. I dashed over to help. "Look at all this," she whispered, pulling handfuls of cash from a hole at the bottom of the mattress. "I'm too scared to count it." She pressed a handful of cash into my hand. "Take some of it."

I shook my head, trying to give it back. "Vangie left it for you, Mom. I don't need it."

"You rich too or something?"

I shook my head.

"Girl! Take this damn money. What am I'm supposed to do with all of it?"

I didn't argue with her. We lowered the mattress and put the bed back together.

"Ain't no telling what Vangie did. The girl can keep secrets like a dog hides a bone."

When things calmed down, I called Vangie's cell phone number programmed in my brain, a call I had avoided for six years. Closed in Vangie's room, I pressed my cell phone to my ear. "This number is not receiving calls at this time," a recording said. I dialed again and listened to the same recording, chilled to the bone.

For dinner, I turned the leftovers in the refrigerator and what-ever else I could find in the kitchen into a meal: wedge salad with homemade citrus dressing, meatloaf Parmesan, and homemade garlic bread. We ate and talked in front of the TV. I talked the most, closing the six-year gap between us. At one point my mother stared at me, her eyes glossy and wet.

"Find your sister, Angie," she said with immediacy.

I nodded, feeling the weight of her demand, and could imagine how Vangie must have felt when I disappeared. Whatever Vangie had done, I knew she needed me more than I had ever needed her, and I hoped and prayed I would find her. Getting lost was easy when a person didn't want to be found.

That night I slept in Vangie's bed and felt her presence to the depth of my soul. *No stretch of the sea or the circumference of the earth will ever come between us*, I whispered in the dark. Tears soaked the pillow as I cried myself to sleep.

A vivid dream jarred me awake in the middle of the night. The memory fading fast in my mind, I jumped out bed and turned on the light. Moving about quietly, I began my search. I didn't know what I would find, only where to look. I sat on my knees in front of the dresser, leaned over and reached my arm between the wooden frame and the wood floor. Palm turned up, I ran my hand across the bottom surface of the dresser. My hand scraped against something. I unpeeled the tape from around it to find a letter size envelope.

Forty-Eight

I had taken up running. It set well with me and cleared my mind. I ran approximately five miles, flying through Downtown Detroit, past those who lived as I had once lived. I hadn't run my usual ten miles before I headed back home, my heart pumping as fast as my legs. I knew what I had to do.

The excuse I gave my mother for leaving sooner than I had planned was work. I had a five-layer wedding cake to bake and decorate. I choked up with tears, embracing her for so long she had to pry my arms from around her neck. Truth was, I never wanted to leave her side or say goodbye. I reasoned with my guilt, telling myself she at least wouldn't be alone.

Her latest houseguest wore a tired gray suit and had kind brown eyes and graying hair. His name was Mr. Young. I had found the two of them sitting at the dining table, drinking coffee, laughing and talking like old friends when I returned from my run, and had decided then it was a good time to leave.

I caught a cab instead of the Metro. During the ride, I took in Detroit through the open window, took in the sunny sky and hot day, inhaling the fresh air, possibly for the last time.

My ride ended at the Detroit Metropolitan Airport. I approached the ticket counter at the first airline I came to and requested a one-way ticket to Los Angeles, California using a portion of the two thousand dollars my mother had sent me off with.

"Identification," the woman said.

I handed her the passport I had found sealed inside the envelope.

"Have a pleasant flight, Mrs. Cooper," she said, and handed me a boarding pass.

I floated off in a daze. Everything around me seemed to move in slow motion as I inched forward in the security line.

At the front of the line, a man requested my identification and my boarding pass. Again, I handed him Vangie's passport, and again I was free to leave.

I made it through the metal detectors and onto the airplane without a problem.

I was too nervous to relax, with this being my first flight and all. Planes didn't seem to agree with me like trains. My heart stayed in my throat the entire flight, and I couldn't stomach the thought of eating.

The pilot finally announced our arrival to Los Angeles. As I gazed out at the city's clear, sunny skies, mountains and oceanfront, I couldn't bring myself to smile. Once I landed and was home free, I would let the thought of reuniting with Vangie sink in.

I grabbed my luggage and followed the line of passengers toward the exit. I could hear a commotion ahead and see people parting like the Red Sea.

"Hands above your head!" I heard, and then saw the high-powered guns aimed directly at me. I dropped the handle of my suitcase and slowly raised my hands.

"Vangie Cooper, you're under arrest for the murder of Todd Bryant," one of the police officers said.

I placed my hands behind my back without resisting arrest, feeling the clamp of cold metal binding my wrists together. As the officers marched me through the crowd, I walked with my back straight and chin high.

Vangie is my hero, my guardian angel, and my defender who spoke the words never whispered from my lips. I owe her my life.

Epilogue

Vangie walked among the locals and travelers on Course Lafayette, a street with age-old apartments stacked above shops, taverns, and restaurants. At a boulangerie she bought fresh bread; at the food shop she bought an expensive bottle of French white. She knew enough French to get by and blend into the scene inconspicuously.

Off a side street, she entered the medieval apartment unit she now called home, temporarily. On the fourth floor, she walked into the turnkey flat with all the trappings of eccentric Europe, left her shoes by the door and walked straight to the small, box-shaped kitchen to pour herself a glass of wine. She had run out of stock and needed something to dull her senses and help her to forget.

Three months earlier she had fled the U.S. on a private jet bound for San Quintin, Mexico. For two days she smoldered in a hot house at a marijuana plantation waiting for Ronnie's guerilla grower to smuggle her to Columbia.

From Columbia she flew by private jet to France and had since stayed under the radar in the city of Lyon, known for harboring fugitives without the risk of extradition.

In a way, the solitude brought Vangie inner peace. There was nothing left to gain and nothing left to lose. Much like death, her façade of a life had been put to rest. If only she could bear the grief…

ACKNOWLEDGMENTS

I am grateful to so many people and for so many reasons I don't know where to begin. When I started this novel, I wasn't sure of its direction and feared I would never see it through. I thank God, my North Star, who gifted me this unquenchable thirst to write about our humanity. He guided my hand throughout this extraordinary journey, and for that, I am eternally grateful.

All my love, from the bottom of my heart to the top, goes to my husband, Rudolph A. Johnson III, and my children, Rudolph A. Johnson IV, and Mallory T. Johnson. There are no words in the dictionary to describe the love I hold in my heart for my nuclear family.

A standing ovation to Shawna Cook and Mary E Gilder, my pre-readers. Mary, an awarding winning author, read this book in its initial stages of development, cheered it on and proposed critical scenes that made it pop. Shawna, an avid reader, sent me back to the drawing board (smile). Because of her no-holds-barred critique, this story shaped into one I am proud to call my own.

Special thanks to my editors, Carol Thoma and Debra Britt-Hays, for cleaning up my mess.

Thank you, Michah Whitley, for schooling me on stocks and bonds.

I must also thank two very kind ladies, Miss. Francis Washington of Detroit, Michigan and Miss Eartha Keatings of Kansas City, Missouri. I value your tour guide.

Warm thanks to all the readers who have been eagerly awaiting the next installment to my growing list of novels. Keep asking and I promise to keep writing.

Last but never least, love and gratitude to my entire family and my dearest friends for their unwavering love, support and encouragement.

Coming Fall 2016

HAND FOR HAND
by
SHERYL MALLORY-JOHNSON

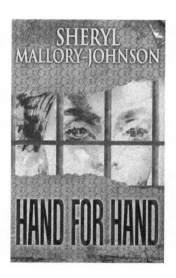

The Sequel to
THE HAND SHE PLAYED

For More Information Visit: www.sherylmallory-johnson.com
or Email: WanaSomabooks@cox.net

CPSIA information can be obtained
at www.ICGtesting.com
Printed in the USA
LVHW031125160720
660841LV00001B/49

9 780982 208540